IF YOU WANT TO STAY ALIVE, KEEP MOVING.

GATHERING PREY

"An edge-of-your-seat read." —Bookreporter.com

They call them *travelers*. They drift from city to city, always on the move. Now somebody is murdering them, one by one. When Lucas Davenport's adopted daughter, Letty, gets a phone call from a female traveler she'd befriended in San Francisco, Letty urges her father to investigate. The woman's male companion is missing—and the woman is very afraid.

Though he suspects Letty is getting played, Lucas volunteers to help. Little does he know, in the days to come, he'll embark upon an odyssey through a subculture unlike any he's ever seen, a trip that will not only put the two of them in danger—but just might change the course of his life.

"A testament to Sandford's amazing career and readers are going to love it . . . Sandford tells this story with the energy of a speeding bullet . . . This is his freshest, most thrilling story ever. He is a master of this game, and *Gathering Prey* proves he still reigns supreme."
—*The Huffington Post*

"[Sandford] is at the top of his writing game . . . Read it."
—Journalstar.com

"Engrossing . . . [an] artful combination of suspense and humor." —*Publishers Weekly*

"Sandford is back with a vengeance! . . . The ride is harrowing, unpredictable, and compulsive, right up to the jaw-dropping denouement . . . The next chapter for this popular fictional protagonist has just begun."
—Curledup.com

TITLES BY JOHN SANDFORD

GATHERING PREY

John Sandford

BERKLEY BOOKS, NEW YORK

BERKLEY

An imprint of Penguin Random House LLC
375 Hudson Street, New York, New York 10014

GATHERING PREY

A Berkley Book / published by arrangement with the author

ISBN: 978-0-425-27885-7

PUBLISHING HISTORY
G. P. Putnam's Sons hardcover edition / April 2015
Berkley premium edition / April 2016

PRINTED IN THE UNITED STATES OF AMERICA

10 9 8 7 6 5 4 3 2 1

Penguin
Random
House

For Michele

SKYE AND HENRY stood on a corner of Union Square on a fading San Francisco afternoon in early June, the occasional odor of popcorn swirling through, trying to busk up a few dollars. Skye saw the devil go by in his black '85 T-top, crooked smile, ponytail, twisty little braids in his beard. His skinny blond girlfriend sat beside him, tats running across her bare shoulders like grapevines, front teeth filed to tiny sharp points. Skye turned away, a chill running down her back.

Henry was strumming on a fifty-dollar acoustic guitar he'd bought at a pawnshop. Skye played her harmonica and kept time with a half tambourine strapped to one foot, jangling out into the evening, doing their version of "St. James Infirmary," Henry banging between chords and struggling through,

"When I die, bury me in a high-top Stetson hat . . ."

He did not sound like any kind of black blues singer from the Mississippi Delta. He sounded like a white punk from Johnson City, Texas, which he was.

SKYE WAS STOCKY with high cheekbones and green eyes. She wore an earth-colored loose knit wrap over a sixties olive-drab army shirt, corporal's stripes still on the sleeves, and gray cargo pants over combat boots. Her hair was apricot-colored and tangled, with a scraggly braid hanging down her back.

Henry was a tall apple-cheeked man/boy with a perpetually smiley face, dressed in a navy blue Mao jacket buttoned to the throat, and matching slacks, and high-topped sneakers. Their packs sat against the wall of the building behind them, big, capable nylon bags, with a peeled-pine walking stick attached to one side of hers.

"Put a ten-piece jazz band on my tailgate to raise hell as we roll along . . ."

They both smelled bad. They washed themselves every morning in public bathrooms, but that didn't eliminate the musty stink of their clothes. A laundromat cost money, which they didn't have at the moment. A cigar box on the sidewalk held five one-dollar bills and a handful of change. They'd put in two of the dollar bills themselves, to encourage contributions, to suggest that their music might be worth listening to.

They weren't the worst of the buskers on the square, but they were not nearly the best, and in terms of volume, they couldn't compete with the horn players.

As Henry wound down through the song, his shaky baritone breaking from time to time, Skye noticed the young woman leaning on a fire hydrant, watching them.

Was she with the devil? She was the kind he went for. Thin but hot. Not blond, though. The devil went for blondes.

The young woman was casually dressed in a loose multicolored blouse, jeans, and sneakers, each of those separate components suggesting money: the blouse looked as though it might be real silk, the jeans fit perfectly, and even the sneakers suggested a secret sneaker store, one that only rich people knew about.

Her dark hair had been styled by somebody with talent.

Skye thought, Maybe with the devil—but if not, maybe good for a five? Even a ten? A ten would buy dinner and a cup of coffee in the morning . . .

Henry gave up on the "St. James Infirmary," said, "Fuck this. We ain't doing no good."

"Don't have enough cash to eat. Let's give it another ten minutes. How about that Keb' Mo' thing?"

"Don't know the words yet." He looked around the square. "We should have gone up to the park. Can't fight these fuckin' horns."

THE YOUNG WOMAN who'd been leaning against the fire hydrant ambled up to them. She smiled and nodded to Henry, but spoke to Skye. "I don't give money to buskers . . . or panhandlers . . . because I'm afraid they'll spend it on dope. I got better things to do with it."

"Well, thank you very fucking much," Skye said. Her voice was harshed by smoke and a good bit of that had been weed.

"You're a traveler," the woman said, showing no offense.

"You know about us?"

"Enough to pick you out," the woman said. "My name's Letty. What's yours?"

"Skye. My friend is Henry." Skye was calculating: this woman was either with the devil, or . . . she could be worked. And Skye was hungry.

"Let's go up to the park," Henry said.

"Hang on," Skye said. Back to the young woman: "If you won't give us money, could you get us a bite?"

"There's a McDonald's a couple blocks from here," Letty said. "I'll buy you as much as you can eat."

"Them's the magic words," Henry said, suddenly enthusiastic, his pink face going even pinker.

THE TWO TRAVELERS shouldered their packs and Henry carried his guitar case and they started down Geary, walking toward Market Street, weaving through the tourists. "Where are you coming from and where are you going?" Letty asked.

Skye said, "We were in Santa Monica for the winter, then we started up here a couple weeks ago. Planning to be here for a couple of weeks, get some money, then go on up to Eugene, and maybe Seattle."

Henry said to Skye, "I could have sworn I saw Pilot go by a few minutes ago. I heard they were traveling this summer."

"We stay away from that asshole," Skye said. "He's the devil."

"Is not," Henry said. "He's cool."

"He's not cool, Henry. He's a crazy motherfucker."

"Been in movies, man," Henry said. "He said he might be able to get me a part."

Skye grabbed his shirtsleeve, turning him: "Henry. He'll kill you."

"Ah, bullshit." Henry started walking again and they could see the McDonald's sign beyond him. He looked back at the two women. "You don't know a chance when you see one, Skye. He could get me a part. I'd like to be in a movie. I'd really like that."

"Why? So you know you're alive? You're alive, Henry. Let's try to keep it that way."

Henry shut up and they got to the McDonald's.

INSIDE, THE TWO travelers loaded up on calories: Henry ordered a Double Quarter Pounder with Cheese, large fries, a chocolate shake. Letty said, "Get a couple burgers, if you want."

"You serious?" Henry asked.

"Go ahead."

They did—two sandwiches, two fries, and a shake for each of them. Letty got a fish sandwich and a Diet Coke. When they'd spread out at a table, Letty asked Skye, "So . . . you feel safe when you're on the road?"

"Yeah, I'm pretty safe," Skye said. She took a big bite of the first burger and said, "I'm usually with somebody. Which helps. When I'm alone, getting ready to move, I'll find a festival, or something like that, where there are a lot of people. You can ask around, find somebody going in your direction. Check up on him. Or her. Sometimes, when I got the money, I'll ride the dog. One time, I met this guy in San Antonio, he was a dope dealer but, you know, he was okay. He bought me a ticket on the train to Los Angeles. More than three hundred dollars. And he didn't want anything for it."

"They usually want something for it?" Letty asked.

"Oh, sometimes they think they might get something . . . but they don't," Skye said. "If they're the kind of guy who's going to push it, I can usually figure that out ahead of time and I don't go."

"Ever make a mistake?" Letty asked.

Skye grinned at her, showing her yellow teeth, and said, "You're kinda snoopy, aren't you?"

Letty smiled back and said, "I used to work at a TV news station."

Skye bobbed her head and took another bite of the sandwich. Eventually she said, "I made a couple of mistakes."

"What'd you do about it?" Letty asked.

"Nothing. What could I do?"

"I would have killed them," Letty said.

Henry was examining the side of his sandwich, and his eyes cut over to her and he said, "Easy to say, not so easy to do."

"Not *that* hard," Letty said.

SKYE AND LETTY locked eyes for a few seconds, then Skye said, "Jesus." She swallowed and said, "You're with Pilot, aren't you?"

"What?"

Henry brightened up: "Hey, really? You're with Pilot?"

"I don't know who Pilot is," Letty said. "I'm a student. At Stanford. I'm meeting friends in fifteen minutes, back at the square. We're on a last shopping trip before summer vacation."

Skye looked at her for another moment and then said, "Yeah. I can see that. You don't know Pilot? He likes college girls. Or at least, college-girl types."

"No. Who is he?"

"He's an asshole," Skye said. "Maybe the biggest asshole in California. Travels around with his disciples, he calls them. Fucks them all, men and women alike."

"Does not," Henry said. "Nothing queer about Pilot."

"You hang with him, you'll find out, little pink cheeks," Skye said. She reached out and pinched his cheek. "And I'm not talking about these cheeks, either."

"Fuck you, Skye." He didn't sound like he meant it, though.

"'BIGGEST ASSHOLE IN California' would put him in the running for the national title," Letty said. "What'd he do?"

Skye looked at her steadily for a moment, then said, "Might be a little more than a college girl would want to know."

Letty said, "I'm not the standard-issue college girl. What's he do? Besides being hot for Henry?"

"Shut up," Henry said.

"Hot for Henry—we ought to write a song," Skye said to Henry.

Henry knew the two women were teasing, and said again, "Shut up," and, "You want all them fries?"

"Yes, I do," Skye said. "So: Pilot. Pilot has these people he calls disciples, and they steal for him, the men do, and the women give him their paychecks and sometimes he sells them, the women. He peddles dope to TV people and sometimes these TV guys need to hustle a deal or hustle up some money, and Pilot's women will go over and do whatever the money-men want."

"Nasty," Letty said.

"That's not even the bad stuff," Skye said. "There are probably twenty guys in Hollywood doing that. Pilot's like one of those cult guys. He says the end of the world's coming—he calls it the Fall—and the only thing that'll be left are the outlaws. Like him and the disciples, and the dope gangs and bikers and Juggalos and the skinheads and like that. He believes that the groups need to bind themselves together with blood. By killing people. We both heard that he's killed people. That the whole gang has."

"All bullshit," Henry said.

The women ignored him and Letty asked, "Why don't you call the cops?"

"Nothing to call them about," Skye said. "We say, 'We heard he's killed someone.' They go, 'Who?' 'We don't know.' 'When?' 'We don't know that, either.' 'Who told you?' 'We don't know. Some street guy.' The cops say, 'Uh-huh, we'll get right on it,' and hang up."

Letty said, "Huh."

Skye: "He'd snatch you off the street in a minute."

Letty showed some teeth in what wasn't exactly a smile. "He'd get his throat cut."

Henry swallowed a smile and said, "Yeah, right. Pilot eat you right up . . ."

Letty stared at him until he turned his eyes away. Skye squinted at her: "Where'd you get that mean streak?"

"I grew up dirt poor out on the prairie in northern Minnesota," Letty said. "My old man dumped us and my mom was a drunk. I kept us going by trapping muskrats and coons, wandering around in the snow with a bunch of leg-hold traps and a .22. Must've killed a thousand rats with that gun. Pilot's just another rat to me."

"Bet you had to trap a lot of coons to get into Stanford," Skye said.

Letty smiled again, and said, "Well, my mom got murdered and the cop who was investigating, he and his wife adopted me. They're my real mom and dad. It was like winning the lottery."

Skye: "For real?"

"For real," Letty said.

Skye said, "Huh. How about your real pop?"

"Never really knew him," Letty said. "He's a shadow way back there."

"He never . . . messed with you, or anything?"

"No, nothing like that," Letty said.

"Sorry about your mom," Skye said.

"Yeah, thanks. She . . . couldn't deal with it. With anything."

Skye nodded. "My mom is like that. She didn't get murdered or anything—as far as I know, she's still living in her old trailer."

"What about your dad?"

"He's probably still around, too. Probably messing with my little sister, if she hasn't taken off already."

Letty didn't ask the obvious question; the *little sister* comment made it unnecessary.

SKYE FELT THAT and bent the conversation in another direction. "What's that little teeny watch you're wearing?" she asked, poking a finger at the red band around Letty's wrist.

"Ah, it's one of those athlete things. Not a watch. Tells you how many steps you've taken in a day, and how high your heart rate got, and all of that."

Skye held up a wrist. A piece of dark brown, elaborately braided leather was wrapped around it, and she said, "My bracelet doesn't tell me anything."

"Yours has more magic," Letty said.

"Wanna trade?"

Letty's eyebrows went up. "Are you serious? It isn't important to you?"

"Nah. I buy the leather in craft shops, we go in and ask if they've got any scraps, and I make these up, then we sell them, when we can."

"Even up," Letty said. She peeled the band off her wrist, and Skye did it with hers, and they traded.

"IF THIS PILOT guy is such an asshole, why does Henry like him so much?" Letty asked.

Henry: "He's a movie guy."

Skye turned on him: "You know, I don't usually think you're stupid, but you're stupid about Pilot. He tells you he was on TV and you believe him. If he's on TV, why's he driving around in a piece-of-shit Pontiac? That thing is fifteen years older than you are, Henry."

"It's a cool car, man."

"It's a piece of shit." Skye turned back to Letty. "We made the mistake of hanging round with some of the disciples for a while. If you're on the street, down in L.A., if you're around the beaches, you'll run into them."

"If you hate him so much, why'd you hang with them?" Letty asked.

"They share," Henry said.

Skye nodded. "They do. That's one thing about them. They'll feed you if you're willing to listen to Pilot talk about the Fall. You get hungry enough, you'll listen."

"I would have been curious to meet him," Letty said.

Skye said, "Not unless you're crazier than you look. I'm not kiddin' you: he is an evil motherfucker."

THEY TALKED FOR a few minutes more, then Letty checked the time on her cell phone. "I've got to go."

"Where's your home?" Skye asked.

"Still Minnesota."

"Really? Maybe I'll see you there. Henry and I are gonna hit the motorcycle rally in Sturgis, the bikers are usually good for something. Problem is, Pilot's going there, too. To Sturgis, to sell dope. That's what he told a friend of ours, anyway."

Letty took a miniature legal pad out of her shoulder bag and scribbled a phone number on the page, with her first name only. "If you make it to Minneapolis, give me a call, I'll buy you another cheeseburger," she said. She took a fifty out of her purse, folded it to the same dimensions as the note, and pushed it across the table. "Emergency money."

"Thanks. I mean really, thanks." Skye took it and asked, "Do you really think you could kill somebody?"

Letty nodded: "I have."

Skye cocked her head: "Really?"

"Really. Believe me, Skye, when it's you or them, you tend to choose *them*. And not feel bad about it."

Skye said, "If you say so. If we get there, I'll call. In fact, I might come there just to get the sandwiches."

"I'll look for you," Letty said, and she slid out of the

booth and added, "Take it easy, Henry. And if you get in the shower with the devil, don't pick up the soap."

Skye laughed and Henry nodded, his mouth too full to reply. When Letty was gone, he swallowed and said, "Man, this turned out good. That killing stuff, though, I mean, what a bunch of bullshit."

"I don't think it was," Skye said. After a moment, "You weren't looking in her eyes."

SKYE AND HENRY spent June in San Francisco, then Eugene, and the Fourth of July in Seattle. Later that month they caught a ride to Spokane and made a little money before the cops started hassling them. They got lucky at a truck stop and a trucker hauled them all the way to Billings, Montana.

IN BILLINGS THEY took a big risk—or Henry did, but if there'd been trouble, they both would have gone to jail.

The trucker dropped them off on the edge of I-90, a few blocks before he'd have to turn off to his terminal. "They wouldn't want to see me giving people a ride," he told them, and they thanked him, and he went on his way. It was nearly ten o'clock at night, and they found themselves in an industrial area on the edge of town, with some farm fields and brushy areas mixed in.

Three hundred yards away, a dark building stood under a dozen orange security lights, which illuminated a bunch of farm equipment—tractors, trailers, combines, as well as a few bulldozers and graders. They went that way, walking along the frontage road, because it seemed to be more toward the center of town.

As they were walking along, a man pulled into the parking lot of the farm-equipment dealership, got out, locked his car—the car was small and swoopy and expensive-looking. The man went to a glass door on the side of the building, unlocked it, went inside.

They continued to walk along the frontage road, moving slowly in the dark, and were fifty yards away when the man came back out of the building. He'd left a light on inside and they could see he was now wearing shorts and a T-shirt. He took off running, or jogging, away from them, along the frontage road, moving fast.

Henry said, "Take my pack."

"What?"

"Get off the road and take my pack. Get back in the weeds," he said. "Wait for me."

"What?"

He didn't say anything else, but wrenched the walking stick off her pack and ran toward the building. Skye watched him cross the parking lot, crouch by the door, and a minute later, heard the distant sound of breaking glass. Henry disappeared inside, and a minute later, crawled back out and ran toward her.

As he came up, he said breathlessly, "C'mon—we got to go. We got to go."

"What'd you get?"

"Got his billfold."

"Oh, Jesus, Henry."

They jogged until Henry got a stitch in his side, and then they walked for a while, swerving off the frontage road whenever a car came along, going down in the ditch, crouching, catching their breath, then running some more. They were a mile south when they heard sirens and saw the flashing lights of the cop cars back the way they'd come.

They kept going, another mile, and another, and then a cop car went by on the frontage road, as they lay in some weeds in the ditch. When the cop was gone, they ran some more, the best they could, nearly panicked, until after midnight, when Skye couldn't go any farther. She told Henry, and they swerved off into a farm field, dark as pitch, and eventually stumbled into a copse of trees.

They spread out their bags, broke out a flashlight, and looked in the wallet.

Eight hundred forty dollars. They couldn't believe it: more money than they'd ever had at one time.

"They'll be coming for us," Henry said. "They'll be all over us. I never thought it'd be this big."

"So we hide out," Skye said. "Maybe right here. To-morrow night, we start walking again."

"Which way?"

She pointed back the way they'd come with the trucker. "There were some diners back there, some gas stations. We find some broken-ass guy with out-of-state plates, going through. Give him fifty dollars for gas."

"And we're gone," Henry said.

———

THAT'S WHAT THEY did. They buried the stolen wallet in the field, and on the next night, found a ride that took them back through the city, and then south and east. On the fourth of August, a hot day, a trucker with an eagle feather in his hair dropped them off in Sturgis, South Dakota.

Right in the middle of the annual Sturgis Motorcycle Rally; thousands of bikers, mostly old guys with beards and full-sleeve tattoos and hefty old ladies who looked like they'd be more comfortable making Jell-O salads with little pink marshmallows.

And there were a few people like themselves.

Travelers.

They'd been there two days when Skye saw the devil, loafing through town in his black Pontiac with the gold firebird decal on the hood, the blonde still riding shotgun.

Henry saw him, too.

HENRY WAS WANDERING through the Sturgis marketplace in the gathering dusk, looking at tattoos, thinking about getting one, something small and stylish; looking at chaps, the leather jackets, the Harley accessories. Henry was a traveler, but wouldn't always be one. When his traveling days ended, he thought, maybe he'd get a Harley. Really, though, he liked the looks of another bike, might be Italian . . .

He was checking out a tall, muscular man dressed all in black leather and silver, with wraparound black shades and a harsh black goatee—Henry liked the look, but realistically, he wouldn't get a goatee like that in this life-time; he barely had blond fuzz—when a woman slipped in behind Henry and licked his ear.

He tensed and turned and there was Kristen, she of the filed teeth. She was wearing a leather bikini bottom and a strip of black duct tape across her breasts, little bumps where her nipples pushed against the tape, and black high-heeled boots. She had a silver ring through one wing of her nose, and a bead through her tongue. Her body was a riot of tattooed Wonder Woman comic art.

She said, "Well, well, well. Our Henry. Pilate's been looking for you. He talked to the producer and he thinks they have a slot for you in the miniseries. Think you could do a cowboy?"

Henry didn't know how to answer and didn't know where to look. He backed a step away, blushing, but said, "Well, shoot, I grew up in Johnson City, Texas. I guess I could do a cowboy."

"We're out scouting locations, right now. You know what that is?"

"Yup, I do." He'd once talked to a location scout in Pasadena, California.

"Well, fine. Me and Ellen are meeting up at the Con-oco at eight o'clock. Be there. You got one chance. Okay?"

"Okay. I don't know where Skye is . . ."

"We don't want Skye. Skye is a pain in the ass. She's so negative, you know what I mean? You bring Skye, Pilate will say forget it."

Henry swallowed, scratched his nose, glanced over at

the black leather guy, who winked at him. He turned back to Kristen and said, "I'll be there."

She stepped right up to him, pushing her breasts into his chest. He tried to step back again but she grabbed his package and squeezed, a little, and said, "Me'n Ellen are looking forward to it." Then she turned and ambled off, her hips swinging off the pinpoints of the boot heels.

ELLEN LOOKED LIKE either a mean schoolteacher or a mean prison guard, Henry thought, when he met them at the Conoco an hour later. He thought it was her hair: short, tightly curled, her ears sticking out like semaphore signals. He was having second thoughts about going off with them, but the idea of being in a movie: a *movie.* He'd be *somebody.*

Ellen was gassing up a Subaru station wagon when Henry wandered up, and Kristen came out of the Conoco carrying two grocery bags, heavy enough that the muscles stood out in her forearms. She'd changed into jeans in the cool of the evening, but still had the black duct tape across her breasts.

They got in the Subaru, Henry in the back, with his pack and the grocery sacks, the women in the front. Ellen started the car, and then Kristen, in the passenger seat, threw her arm around Ellen's shoulder, and the two women kissed, a long, sloppy French kiss, with Kristen's eyes cutting to Henry in the back, who looked away.

After ten seconds or so, Ellen turned away, put the car in gear, and they headed out through town, past the roaming bikers, country people in trucks, out of the built-up area, and into the hills.

"Where're we going?" Henry asked, ten minutes out. There were no lights along the road they were on. Ellen said, "Got a camp out here. The movie's set out in the wilderness. The thing is, you can't have shit like road signs and telephone wires when you're shooting a cowboy movie. You gotta get way out in the countryside."

They drove along for another few minutes, then Henry asked Kristen a question that had been bothering him a bit: "Aren't you a little . . . cold?"

"Mmm, yeah, you know. There's a shirt right behind you, in the back, toss that to me, will you?"

Henry turned in his seat, looked over the back, saw the shirt, got it, and handed it to her. She ripped the tape between her breasts and peeled it off, then turned to Ellen and said, "What do you think?"

"We get back to camp, and I'll suck them right off your body."

"You wanna help?" Kristen asked Henry.

"Uh, I don't know," he said.

"You don't know? What the fuck does that mean?"

"I think he's queer," Ellen said.

Kristen nodded. "Yeah, he looks queer."

"Not queer," Henry said, turning to look out at the night. He really wished he'd stayed with Skye.

"He's queer," Kristen said. She pulled on the shirt and buttoned it. "Maybe he could blow Raleigh."

Henry shrank away into a corner of the seat. "Why don't you guys let me out. I can walk back from here."

"Oh, fuck that. Pilate wants to talk to you about the movie. We told him you were coming, and if we don't bring you up here, he'll kick our asses."

The road had started out bad and had gotten worse, gone from gravel to rutted dirt. Ellen slowed, slowed some more, and Kristen said, "There's the rock."

An orange rock, looking like a pumpkin, sat on the edge of the road. Ellen took a right and started climbing a hill. The headlights no longer showed any road at all, although here and there, Henry could see tire tracks. They topped the hill and off to the left, and higher, he saw a sparkle of lights coming down through a stand of trees, and as they got closer, an oversized campfire.

"Here we be," Kristen said. Ellen pushed the Subaru past a circle of cars, and the group's RV, and stopped.

The two women got out, collected the grocery bags, and Henry, toting his pack, followed behind them, through some trees and between a couple of older cars, toward a campfire whose flames were reaching to head height.

He looked up and saw the entire Milky Way, right there, on top of him. He staggered a little, looking straight up as he walked. The stars looked like the lights of L.A., from up on top of the Santa Monica Mountains.

"Got him," Ellen called, as they walked into the fire-light.

Henry could see fifteen or twenty people sitting on camp chairs and stools around the fire, and then Pilate stood up and called, "Everybody say, 'Yay,' for Henry the traveler."

The people around the campfire all shouted, "Yay,"

and Pilate came over and wrapped his arm around Henry's shoulders and said, "Glad you could come. Hey, Raleigh, come over here and say, 'Hi.' Bell, come over here . . ."

Three or four men came over, and wrapped up Henry, tighter, really tight, and he tried to laugh or smile and at the same time push them off, and then Pilate said, "Take him down, gentle," and the whole mass of them collapsed on the ground, and somebody said, "Give me the tape," and Henry tried to fight them then, but his arms were pinned, and he tried to bite, but there was a hand on his forehead, pushing him back, and then somebody rolled a strip of tape over his eyes and they turned him and rolled him and in the end, he was helpless, his hands taped behind him, his feet taped at the ankles, his legs at the knees, another strip around his mouth so he couldn't scream.

He could still hear.

He flopped around on the ground, hit the back of his head on a tree root, and everybody laughed and then Pilate said, "Shred him."

Somebody had a knife or a razor, and they cut his clothes off him, until he was buck naked except for the tape, and then Pilate said, "Kristen . . ."

"I got them," she said. She clanked something together. Steel.

Henry was dragged for a while, rough, over rocks and tree roots and spiky brush, and then somebody said, "Gonna cut the tape, hold his arms."

For a few seconds, Henry thought they were going to

cut him loose, and he stopped struggling while some-body he couldn't see cut the tape around his wrists. Two or three people had hold of each arm, and he fought them, but couldn't get free, and they pushed him up against the rough bark of a pine tree and Pilate said, "Higher, get them really high."

Henry's tormentors levered his arms overhead, his back against the bark, and a woman said, "I can't reach that high," and a man said, "Give'm to me."

They nailed him to the tree. Drove big spikes through his wrists, just below the heel of his hands. Henry screamed and screamed and screamed and not much got out, because of the tape over his mouth.

Then he fainted.

He came to, what might have been a half minute later, his hands over his head, his entire body electric with pain.

A woman said, a rough excitement riding her voice, "Look at this kid. Really. Look at this—"

He fainted again.

2

LUCAS DAVENPORT KNEW he was stinking the place up, but he couldn't help himself. He'd snarled at his wife, growled at his daughter, snapped at his son, and probably would have punted the baby had she crossed his path.

Okay, he wouldn't have kicked the baby.

He was out trying to run it off without much luck.

His problems were both strategic and tactical.

The strategic difficulty derived from a case the year before, when a madman's body dump had been found down an abandoned cistern south of the Twin Cities. The killer had kidnapped a sheriff's deputy and had been beating and raping her, and was about to kill her, when Lucas arrived. The madman had been killed in the ensuing fight. The deputy had eventually left the sheriff's department and had moved to the Bureau of Criminal Apprehension, where she was working as an investigator.

Catrin Mattsson was doing all right. She was still screwed up and admitted it, but drugs and shrinks were moving her around to the place where she could live with herself. She'd become friends with his wife and daughter, and would occasionally drop around for dinner and a chat.

Lucas had taken it differently. He wasn't bothered by the fact that the killer had died in the fight. He didn't worry about the secret that he and Mattsson shared, about what exactly had happened down in that basement in the final half second of the confrontation.

He worried about the world. Everything seemed off-kilter. Everything. That was bad.

He'd once suffered through a clinical depression and had sworn he wouldn't go through that again, not without drugs, or whatever else the docs said he had to do. Even then, depression was to be feared—and he could feel it sniffing around outside his door, looking for a way in.

He'd never been a particularly cheerful guy, but he'd done all right—he had an interesting job, a great family, good friends, even made a bundle of money a few years before, on a computer simulation system.

Which had nothing to do with depression.

William Styron's book *Darkness Visible*, which he'd read while going through his own depression, had argued that *depression* is a terrible word for the affliction. Should be called something like *mindstorm*. Still, Lucas's intuition told him that mindstorms didn't just show up: they needed something to chew on.

His problem was that he'd looked a little too deeply

into the souls of a lot of bad people; done what he could to track them down. He'd been largely successful, over the years, but there was apparently a never-ending line of assholes, who would continue to show up after he was long gone. He was beginning to feel helpless.

Not only helpless, but unhelped.

The bureaucrats at the BCA didn't much like him. They didn't mind his catching criminals, as long as it wasn't too much of an inconvenience; as long as it didn't shred their overtime budget. As long as nothing required them to go on TV and sweat and do tap dances.

Lucas had always simply dismissed bureaucrats. They were the guys who were *supposed* to fix overtime budgets and do tap dances and take the blame for the cluster-fucks, because they were always sure to be there when credit was being taken.

No more. Now it was all about keeping your head down, while figuring ways to push the budget up. About not pissing anyone off. About, *Hey, people get killed from time to time, that's just the way of the world, let's not bust a budget about it . . .*

It was getting him down, because he made his living by hunting killers, and had always thought it was a righteous thing to do. Important, intelligent people were now saying, you know, *not so much.*

That was the strategic part of his problem.

TACTICALLY, A LAWYER named Park Raines was running legal rings around the BCA, and if he won out, a killer named Ben Merion was going to walk. Even more annoying, Raines was actually a pretty good guy, ethically sound, and he'd take it to the hoop right in your face and not go around whining about foul this and foul that.

Still, Lucas didn't like being on the losing side in a murder case and the prospect was churning his gut.

Park Raines's client, Ben Merion, lived in the town of Sunfish Lake, probably the richest plot of land, square foot for square foot, in Minnesota. On the last day of February, he'd hit his wife, Gloria Merion, on the head, with a carefully crafted club, and had then thrown her down the stairs in their $2.3 million lakeside home, where her head had rattled off the wooden railings—railings that fit the depressive fracture in her skull exactly perfectly.

The fall hadn't quite killed her, though it had knocked her out, so Merion put his hand over her mouth and pinched off her nose until she stopped breathing.

Lucas's group had run the investigation, and over a couple of months, he and his investigators determined that the Merion marriage was on the rocks; that Ben Merion had signed a prenup that said he'd get nothing in a divorce, but would inherit half if she predeceased him; that in case the house and ten million in stock wouldn't work for him, he'd taken out a five-million-dollar insurance policy on her three months before she was murdered—or died, as Park Raines put it. As icing on the BCA's cake, Merion had a girlfriend named Connie Sweat, or, when working at the Blue Diamond Cutter Gentleman's Club, Honey Potts, and his wife had found out about it.

Two of Lucas's investigators, Jenkins and Shrake, had further determined that Ben met Gloria while remodeling her house—he was a building contractor—and as Shrake put it, "He spent more time laying pipe than laying tile, if you catch my drift."

"So what?" Lucas said.

"Well, that staircase had a custom set of balusters. Those are like the spokes in a railing—"

"I know what balusters are," Lucas said.

"The thing is, Merion turned the balusters himself on his handy little wood lathe. If he needed to make an exact copy to whack her with, it'd take him about ten minutes."

"You guys are your own kind of geniuses," Lucas said.

"We knew that."

They had the medical examiner on their side: death, he said, had come from asphyxiation, not from the blow to the head. The blow may have been intended to kill, but when that didn't work, a second blow would be unseemly for the simple reason that a good medical examiner could determine the time difference between the first and second impact, gauged by the amount of blood released by the first whack. If the second impact came, say, three minutes after the first . . . well, falling down the stairs didn't often take three minutes. Not unless you had a lot longer staircase than the Merions had.

PARK RAINES HAD, of course, gotten his own medical expert, who said that the fall had forced the unconscious woman's face into the carpeting on the stair tread, and *that* had smothered her. He found carpet threads on her tongue.

The medical examiner pointed out that Gloria Merion's mouth may well have been open during her fall down the stairs, and she could have picked up the carpet threads that way.

Could have, might have. Beyond a reasonable doubt? Maybe not.

SO THERE'D BEEN some legitimate doubt, even in Lucas's mind . . . until Beatrice Sawyer, leader of the BCA crime scene crew, discovered three bloody hairs stuck to a baseboard . . . in the bathroom. And tiny droplets of blood, invisible to the naked eye, on the wallpaper and baseboard, but none on the floor, because the floor had been washed.

That added up to murder.

Unless, Raines argued, in the preliminary hearing, incompetent cops had tracked the damp blood in there— they *had* gone into the bathroom after tramping up and down the stairs, before the crime scene people got there.

And that insurance policy? Nothing but a legal maneuver rich people used to get around the federal estate tax, and commonly done, Park Raines said. It had been intended to benefit the children from her first marriage, not Ben Merion.

The wood-lathe business? Sure, he could have done that. Proof that he'd done it? Well, show me the proof.

And the girlfriend? Yes, Ben had once been intimate with Connie Sweat, but that ended when Ben and Gloria married. He'd visited Connie's town house a couple of times, but only to retrieve personal property that he'd left at her place, back before Ben got married.

The trial was starting in three weeks and things did not look all that good. The best trial prosecutors had begged off, worrying about their high-profile conviction stats, leaving the case to a twenty-eight-year-old hippie who'd gotten out of law school three years earlier, played saxophone in a jazz band at night, and showed more interest in the music than the law. He'd never been the lead prosecutor on a major case.

Lucas believed that he would be a good prosecutor someday, if he chose law over music, but he wasn't yet.

Running five miles, until it felt like his wheels were coming off, didn't do all that much for his physical condition, but the pain helped Lucas stop thinking about Merion.

And the combination of it all, the strategic and tactical, had the depression monster sniffing around his doorstep.

So he ran.

AS HE WAS out running, his daughter Letty was lying on the carpet in the den, nine o'clock at night, her legs, from her knees to her feet, on a couch. She was staring at the ceiling, thinking about life, or that part of life that involved a guy named Gary Bazile. Bazile was a junior in economics at Stanford who also played lacrosse; he had big white teeth and large muscles. He was calling her every night and her father had begun to notice.

Early in her freshman year, Letty, who had avoided carnal entanglements in high school—"I don't want to be the girl that the jocks practice on," she'd told a friend—had decided that Now Was the Time. Bazile had benefited greatly from the decision, but Letty's interest was beginning to wane.

In contemplating the ceiling, a telephone by her hand, she thought perhaps she'd cut Gary off a little too abruptly a few minutes earlier. "Gotta put my baby sister to bed," she'd lied. When her phone rang again, she picked it up, willing herself to be kind to him: but the screen said the call was coming from Unknown, in an unfamiliar area code, 605. California? She didn't get many solicitation calls, because she'd listed her number on the "do not call" registry.

She punched *Answer* and said, "Hello?"

"Is this Letty?" A woman's voice, rough, vaguely familiar.

"Yes, this is Letty."

"Letty, this is Skye, do you remember me? From San Francisco, me and Henry were singing on the square? You bought us dinner at McDonald's?"

"Hey, Skye," Letty said, swinging her feet down to the floor. "How are you? Where are you? In town?"

"Rapid City. Man, the devil got Henry. They cut his heart out."

"What? What? Henry?"

"They cut his heart out." Skye began to sob into the phone. "That's what Pilot's girlfriend told me, and she was laughing. She said Pilot keeps it in a Mason jar. She said they're going to get mine, next. Man, I am in some serious shit out here and they cut Henry's heart out."

"Where are you, exactly?" Letty asked.

"Rapid City . . . I got dropped off by this guy," Skye said.

"Are you safe? For right now?"

"For right now. I'm in the bus station. It's the only public phone I could find."

"Okay, slow down. Now, tell me," Letty said.

"The devil was in Sturgis—"

"When you say 'the devil'—"

"Pilot. Pilot. We told you about Pilot. Pilot was in Sturgis with his disciples. They were camping out there and they were pretending to be bikers and some of the women were turning tricks out of their RV. I told Henry to stay away, but he disappeared. We were supposed to meet, and he didn't show up. We had a backup meet, and he never showed there, either. All the bikers left, and the town was almost empty. I spent three days walking around, looking for him, and he's not there. Then I was in a grocery store and the blond bitch came in and when I went out, she came out at the same time, she said that they killed Henry and they ate part of him and Pilot put his heart in a Mason jar. He said Pilot made some guy roast Henry's dick over a fire and eat it."

"Oh, Jesus," Letty said.

"I'm calling because you said your old man was a cop, and because . . . you're the only friend I got," Skye said.

Letty was on her feet now, pacing. "Let me call and charge a bus ticket for you, to get you here, where we can figure something out. Stay in the station until you're on the bus."

"I got money for a bus, but I didn't know where to go. Then I thought about you. What about Henry? What if they killed him?"

"They're probably trying to freak you out, but I'll get you with my dad, and he can check around," Letty said. "The main thing is, to get you somewhere safe. How much money do you have?"

"Two hundred dollars. It's left over . . . We got lucky. Two hundred dollars."

"Can you buy a ticket to Minneapolis?"

"Wait a minute."

Letty heard some talk in the background, and then Skye said, "Yes, it's a hundred dollars."

"Then do it. I'll give you the money back, no problem," Letty said. "Call and tell me when you'll get here."

"It's the Jefferson Lines. I can get a ticket now. Wait a minute, let me ask this guy." She was gone for a minute, and Letty could hear some talk in the background. Skye came back to the phone and said, "The bus leaves here at midnight and arrives in Minneapolis at noon tomorrow."

"All right. All right, I'll meet you at the bus station. Stay away from Pilot and stay away from that blonde."

"I will. Oh, Jesus, what about Henry?"

"We'll work that out. I'll get my dad, and we'll work that out."

HER DAD WAS Lucas Davenport.

Lucas was a tall man, dark-haired except for a streak of white threading across his temples and over his ears, dark-complected, heavy at the shoulders. He had blue eyes, a nose that had been broken a couple of times, and a scar that reached from his hairline down over one eye, not from some back-alley fight, but from a simple fishing accident. He had another scar high on his throat, where a young girl had once shot him with a piece-of-crap street gun. So his body was well lived in, and he'd just turned fifty, and didn't like it. Some days, too many days lately, he felt old—too much bullshit, not enough progress in saving the world.

For his birthday, his wife, Weather, a surgeon, had bought him an elliptical machine: "You've been pounding the pavement for too long. Give your knees a break."

He used it from time to time, but he really liked running on the street, especially after a rain. He liked running through the odors of the night, through the air off the Mississippi, through the neon flickering off the leftover puddles of rainwater. He needed to run when he was dealing with people like Ben Merion.

By the time he reached the last corner toward home, he'd worked through his grouchiness. He turned the corner and picked up the pace, not quite to a full-out sprint, but close enough for a fifty-year-old.

And through the sweat in his eyes, saw Letty standing under the porch light, hands in her jeans pockets: looking for him.

Letty had gotten herself laid: he and Weather agreed on that, although Weather called it "becoming sexually active." Lucas was ninety percent sure that she hadn't been sexually active in high school, aside from some squeezing and rubbing, though she'd been a popular girl. Once at Stanford, she'd apparently decided to let go.

Lucas deeply hoped that the sex had been decent and that the guy had been good for her, and kind. When he was college-aged, he hadn't always been good for the women in his life, or kind, and he regretted it. He also knew that there was not much he could do about Letty's sex life, for either good or bad. Keep his mouth shut and pray, that was about it. Trust her good instincts.

He turned up the driveway and called out, "Whatcha doing?"

"Waiting for you. Something's come up," Letty said.

He stopped short of the porch, bent over, his hands on his knees, gulping air. When he'd caught his breath, he stood up: "Tell me."

WHEN SHE'D TOLD him, he said, "Have you thought about the possibility that she's nuts? Or that she's working you?"

"Of course. I don't think she's crazy—I mean, I don't think she's delusional," Letty said. "I have to admit that she talks about a guy being the devil, which doesn't sound good, but when she does it . . . you almost have to hear it. She's not talking literally: not a guy with horns and a tail. She's talking about, what? A Charlie Manson type. A Manson family guy. He calls himself Pilot."

"Pilot."

"Yeah. Pilot. She flat out says he's a killer," Letty said. "She didn't come up with that today, she said it weeks ago, when we first met in San Francisco, when there was no money in it. As far as working me goes, she tried to work me a little in San Francisco, because they weren't making any money with their singing. Then she realized she didn't have to work me, because I was going to buy them a McDonald's anyway. She's not dumb."

Lucas sat on the porch next to her and said, "Okay. First of all, you know, she *is* crazy. Somehow, someway, because all street people are. Not necessarily schizophrenic, or clinically paranoid, but almost certainly sociopathic to some extent, because they can't survive otherwise. If they're too sane, their whole worldview breaks down, and they wind up in treatment or in a hospital or dead: dope or booze."

"She's not exactly street," Letty said. "She's a traveler. They're kind of street, but they're different. A lot of street people are . . . bums. Beggars. Travelers are different. For one thing, they travel. They're usually pretty put together—they buy good outdoor gear, they stay neat, they try to stay clean. Lots of them have dogs that they take care of. They have objectives. They make plans. They know each other, they meet up."

"More like hobos," Lucas suggested.

"I don't exactly know what a hobo is. Aren't they on trains?"

"Yeah, but these travelers sound like hobos," Lucas said. "They have a certain status."

"Exactly," Letty said. "Will you come with me, when I meet her? She'll be in around noon."

"Yeah, sure. I might have to push a meeting around, nothing important," Lucas said.

"She said they had Henry's heart in a Mason jar," Letty said.

"Ah, the old heart-in-the-jar story," Lucas said.

"That Pilot made a guy eat Henry's penis . . . roast it and eat it."

"Ah, the old roasted penis story . . ."

"What if it's true?"

"It's not," Lucas said.

Lucas stood up and dusted off the seat of his running shorts. "There are certain kinds of stories that pop up around crazy people, especially street people. Apocryphal stories, urban legends. Slander: cannibals are the big crowd favorite. I've run into all kinds of stories like that—the most extreme ones you can think of, people eating babies or feeding babies to dogs, and so on. Exactly none of them have been true."

"But . . ."

Lucas held up a finger: "There are cannibals out there, but there aren't any true stories about them. Cannibals are quiet about what they do. When you hear cannibal stories, it's *always* about somebody trying to get somebody else in trouble. And usually about roasting and eating somebody's dick. Or somebody's breasts. Sexual fantasies, made up to get somebody else in trouble."

"All right. But—come with me tomorrow."

LUCAS MOVED HIS meetings around and at noon the next day, he and Letty were in Minneapolis. The Jefferson Lines shared a terminal with Greyhound off Tenth Street, a relatively cheerful place compared to most bus stations, built under a parking garage.

They could see the green-glass top of the IDS tower peeking over the surrounding buildings as Lucas parked his Mercedes SUV on the street. He and Letty walked over to the station, where they were told that the bus was running forty-five minutes late. "Hasn't even gotten to Burnsville yet. There was a big accident out on I-90. The driver's trying to make up time, though, so they won't be in Burnsville for more'n a couple minutes," said the guy behind the Jefferson Lines desk.

They decided to kill the time by walking over to the downtown shopping strip, so Letty could check out new arrivals at the Barnes & Noble and Lucas could look at suits at Harry White's.

The Harry White salesman was happy to see him, as always: "You're running late in the season this year, but I snuck a suit off the rack, put it in the back, until I could show it to you. Italian, of course. It's not quite as dark as charcoal, you couldn't call it charcoal, but it's a touch deeper than a medium gray, with a very fine almost yellow pinstripe, more beige, I'd say."

Lucas was a clotheshorse, and always had been. He spent a half hour looking at suits, had a couple of them put back for further examination on the following Saturday, spent five minutes looking at ties, another five with shoes, checked out a black leather jacket—$2,450 and soft as pudding. He spent nothing, and walked across the street to Barnes & Noble, where he found Letty checking out with a Yoga tome and a book on compact concealed-carry firearms.

"You're *not* going to start carrying a gun," Lucas said.

"Of course not, but I want to stay informed," Letty said. "We oughta go out to the range this weekend, if it doesn't rain."

"Let's do that," Lucas said. "It's been a while."

SKYE WAS THE last person off the bus. She was wearing the same outfit as in San Francisco, but smelled like soap. She and Letty shared a perfunctory hug, Letty introduced Lucas, and they waited until Skye's bag was unloaded. Lucas said, "We got you a hotel room in St. Paul. We'll drop your stuff there and grab something to eat, and figure out what we're doing."

"That's great, but I really don't think I can afford—"

"We got it," Lucas said. "For two or three days, anyway."

"Appreciate it," Skye said. She'd learned not to decline kindnesses; they might not be offered a second time.

A half an hour later, they'd checked her into a Holiday Inn on the edge of St. Paul's downtown area, and from there went to a quiet Bruegger's Bagels bakery on Grand Avenue to talk. They all got baskets of bagels and Lucas and Letty got Diet Cokes and Skye a regular Coke—the calories thing again—and as they settled down at a corner table, Lucas said, "You're worried about your friend."

"One of Pilot's disciples—one of the women he sleeps with—told me they cut out Henry's heart and put it in a Mason jar and they take it out at night and worship it."

Lucas stared at her for a moment, then asked, "Do you believe that?"

She held up her hands, palms toward Lucas, like a stop sign. "I know what you're thinking. It's all road bullshit. But I'm telling you, Mr. Davenport, this is not like that. We go back a way with Pilot, all the way back to Los Angeles, and there are stories about him. That he kills people, that they all join in, killing people. Not like some black Masses or something, that weird shit. They do it because they like it, and because it makes them feel important. I call him the devil because that's what he wants people to think about him. He loves that. He loves that whole idea of being evil to people, and have people talking about him."

Lucas leaned back and smiled, and offered, "He does sound pretty unlikable. You know his real name?"

"No. Everybody calls him Pilot. He has this tie-dyed

sleeveless T-shirt that he wears all the time, it's yellow with a big red *P* on it. The *P* is made to look like blood, and he tells people it *is* blood."

"You think it is?" Letty asked.

"Looks like regular tie-dye to me, kind of faded out." She turned back to Lucas: "Mr. Davenport, Pilot *is* full of shit. He's a liar and he's lazy and he's crazy and he sells dope, but that doesn't mean that he doesn't do some of the stuff he says he does. I know for sure that they have all these food-stamp cards, and they sell them for money at these crooked stores in L.A. They've been running that scam for a couple of years. He talks about how the Fall is coming, and how the only way to survive will be to join up with the outlaws . . . and you gotta be willing to kill in cold blood. They've got guns, and everything."

"The Fall?"

"Yeah, you know, when everything blows up and all the survivors wear camo and drive around in Jeeps."

LUCAS AND LETTY threw questions at her for fifteen minutes, and when they were done, they had character sketches of Pilot and four of his disciples, named Kristen, Linda, Bell, and Raleigh, no last names. "Raleigh plays a guitar and Pilot calls him Sledge, like a combination of Slash and Edge, and Kristen used a steel file to sharpen her teeth into points, and she's like inked from head to toe," Skye said, but she had few hard facts.

She knew that Pilot's group traveled in a caravan of old cars, including at least one RV, and she thought they'd been hassled by the South Dakota highway patrol at some point, because Henry, before he disappeared, but after he spotted Pilot at the rally, said they never stopped talking about it. "They had all kind of drugs in their cars, and they almost got busted by a South Dakota highway patrolman, but they didn't because the cop was on his way home for dinner."

"That sounds real enough," Letty said, glancing at Lucas.

In the end, Lucas said, "All right. You've got me interested. Let me take a look at the guy. I need to know Henry's full name, and it would be good if we could get the license plate numbers on Pilot's vehicles."

"It's Henry Mark Fuller and he's from Johnson City, Texas. He went to Lyndon B. Johnson High School, but I think he dropped out in eleventh grade. I don't know any license plate numbers."

Lucas wrote Henry's name in his notebook, and then said, "If you ever see any of Pilot's people, take down the license plate numbers, if you have a chance. That can get us a lot of information. If you run into friends you trust, ask them to keep an eye out."

"I will."

"If Pilot was ever in serious trouble, where would I most likely find a police report?" Lucas asked.

Skye considered that for a moment, then said, "I heard that he was originally from Louisiana, somewhere, but he claimed that he was an actor in Los Angeles for a long time. I think Los Angeles. I don't know where in Louisiana."

Letty asked, "Will you see any more travelers here?"

"I think so. The St. Paul cops are mellower than the Minneapolis cops, so people come here and hang out in Swede Hollow. I've been there a couple times."

"You can walk there from the hotel," Lucas said. He said, "Check around, but don't be too obvious about it. Don't ask about Pilot, ask about Henry. Mostly just listen."

"I can do that," Skye said. "I've been asking about Henry everywhere."

LETTY DIDN'T WANT to end the interview there, so they all drove back to the house, where Letty borrowed the SUV to take Skye to a laundromat.

"I'll drop her at the Holiday Inn after we finish with her clothes," Letty told Lucas. "Meet you back here."

LUCAS WENT ON downtown in his Porsche, made calls to friends in Los Angeles, and talked to one of his agents, Virgil Flowers, who had good connections in South Dakota, and then ran a database search on "Pilot" as a known alias.

Oddly enough, nothing came up. Lucas had been under the impression that almost any noun in the dictionary had been, at one time or another, given to the cops as a fake name.

Flowers called back with the name of a South Dakota highway patrol officer working out of Pierre, and when

Lucas called him, he said he'd put out a statewide request
for information based on Lucas's description of the caravan. Lucas especially wanted license plate numbers.
"Won't take long," the cop said, "unless whoever saw
them is off-duty and off-line. I'll call you, one way or
another."

Lucas also asked him to put out a stop-and-hold on a
Henry Mark Fuller of Johnson City, Texas.

Late in the day, he got a call from a lieutenant in the
L.A. Special Operations Bureau, who said he should call
an intelligence cop named Lewis Hall in Santa Monica.
Lucas did, and Hall said, "You're looking for a guy
named Pilate?"

"We're interested in him. Don't know where to look.
He apparently travels with a band of followers in a bunch
of beat-up old cars and an RV. Some of the women with
him may be turning tricks."

"Yeah, I know about that guy. I've seen him a couple
of times," Hall said. "Never talked to him. Somebody
would come in and say that he'd heard that Pilate had a
satanic ritual somewhere. I'm not real big on tracking
down satanic rituals, since they usually involve people
who know the governor."

"I hear you," Lucas said. "Any indication of violence?
I mean, specific reports?"

"Nothing specific. Rumors," Hall said. "I know they
used to hang out in Venice for a while. I know some
people down there I could ask."

"If you get the time, I'd appreciate it," Lucas said.
"He supposedly says he's an actor."

"What'd he do?"

"I kinda hate to tell you, because it sounds like more bullshit. We have a traveler here who says she was told that Pilot cut out her boyfriend's heart, and keeps it in a Mason jar."

Hall laughed and said, "You must have some extra time on your hands."

"You know what? If I were in your shoes, I'd have said the same thing. But this girl we have here, this traveler, she's sort of . . . convincing."

"Uh-oh. Okay, I'll see who I can round up in Venice and get back to you. Lord knows, we've got enough really weird assholes around here."

"Thanks, I know you're busy. If we hear anything at all, either up or down, I'll call you," Lucas said.

"Wait—you've got nothing more to go on? Nothing that would point me in any particular direction?"

"No. I've been doing database searches and I can't find a single person with a Pilot alias. I'm wondering if I should start checking airports."

Another couple seconds of silence from the other end, then Hall said, "Uh, the guy I'm talking about, it's not Pilot, like airplane pilot. It's Pilate, like Pontius Pilate. You know, the guy who did whatever he did, to Jesus."

"What?"

"Yeah. P-i-l-a-t-e, not Pilot."

"Ah . . . poop. Back to the databases," Lucas said.

Hall laughed again. "Good luck with that."

———

LUCAS WENT BACK to the databases and Pilate popped up immediately, and twice: once in Arkansas and once in Arizona.

The Arkansas hit was tied to a man whose real name was Rezin Carter, who had a long rap sheet that started in 1962, when Carter was twelve. Too old for Pilate, who Skye had said was probably in his early thirties.

The second was a traffic stop on I-10 in Quartzsite, Arizona, six years earlier. The driver had no license, or any other ID. He said he'd bought his car for five hundred dollars in Phoenix, and was trying to get to Los Angeles, where he had the promise of an acting job. He gave his name as Porter Pilate. The cop who'd stopped him had given him a ticket, and had the car towed to a local commercial impoundment lot that had several dozen cars inside.

At one o'clock the next morning, the night man at the impoundment lot had a pistol stuck in his face by a man wearing a cowboy bandanna as a mask. The night man was tied up and left on the floor of his hut. Keys to the impounded cars weren't available, because they were in a drop safe, and the night man didn't have the key. Nevertheless, the gunman drove away a few minutes later.

The night man couldn't see which car was taken, but an inventory the next morning indicated that the 1998 Pontiac Sunfire driven by Porter Pilate was gone, which was the only reason a routine traffic stop showed up in Lucas's database, on a warrant for armed robbery. The Sunfire was later located after it was towed in Venice, California, a week after it disappeared in Quartzsite.

Both the Arizona and California cops listed the same license tag, which tracked back to a man named Ralph Benson, a professional bowler from Scottsdale, Arizona, who said he'd left his car in the long-term parking at Sky Harbor airport.

He'd had two keys in a magnetic holder under the rear bumper. When contacted by L.A. cops, he declined to travel to Los Angeles to retrieve the car, which he said wasn't worth the trip. The car was eventually sent to a recycling yard, and that was the end of it.

Porter Pilate.

Lucas ran the full name through the database and came up with nothing except the Arizona hit.

He called the Arizona Highway Patrol and found that the cop who'd issued the ticket had retired, but they had a phone number. The cop was in his swimming pool and his wife took a phone out to him.

"I *do* remember that guy, because of the robbery that night," the cop said. "He was like an advertisement for an asshole, if you'll excuse the expression. You know, wife-beater T-shirt, smelled like sweat, black hair in half-assed cornrows."

"White guy?"

"Yeah. Dark complexion, but sort of dark reddish. No accent, sounded native-born. Had some prison ink, one of those weeping Jesuses, on his shoulder, crown of thorns with blood running down. From that, you might've thought he was a Mexican gangster, but he wasn't."

"No ID at all?"

"None. Not a single piece of paper. Gave him a ticket and he signed it. After the robbery, we went back to the ticket to see if he'd left prints, but there was nothing there but mine. Of course, we didn't have the car. When they found it in California, we asked them to process it, but it wasn't a priority. When they finally got around to it, turned out it had been wiped."

That was it. Lucas thanked the cop, said it must be nice to be in a pool, and the cop said it was 108 on his patio: "It's not so much nice, as a matter of survival."

Lucas called the South Dakota highway patrolman, gave him the new name and the details, and then the L.A. cop, who said the Arizona Pilate sounded like the Pilate he'd seen.

Lucas closed up and went home.

LETTY WAS OUT somewhere, and the housekeeper had taken Sam to Whole Foods, and the baby was asleep, and Weather said that her back had been feeling grimy, probably from the hot weather. Lucas took her up to the shower and washed her back, thoroughly enough that she wouldn't really *need* another back-washing for some time. Lucas was getting himself back together when Shrake called.

"I talked to your guy Wilfred. He said some college dropouts were making a supercomputer in a barn somewhere, but he doesn't know what for. But: they're paying fifty bucks for any computer, in any shape, as long as it has a certain kind of processor. I don't know shit about computers, but have you ever heard of something called Sandy Bridge? Or Ivy Bridge?"

"That rings a bell," Lucas said. "I think it might be some kind of Intel chip."

"Okay. Anyway, they're paying fifty bucks, cash money. As I understand it, those chips cost a few hundred bucks each. The cash-money aspect means that every asshole with legs is over at the university stealing computers. They met at a park-and-ride lot last week down in Denmark Township, and the story is, people had a thousand computers. Not all of them had the right chip, but most of them did. These guys paid out a shitload of money and left in a white Ford F-150 with no plates."

"When you say a thousand, is that a guess that means 'a lot'? Or does that mean a thousand?"

"I asked that. Wilfred actually thought it might have been more than a thousand. The buyers had a laptop with a list of every computer in the world on it, and you'd step up with your computer, and they'd tell you yes or no, and if it was yes, they'd peel a fifty off a roll and throw the computer in the back of the truck. When he said throw, that's what he meant. He said they'd just toss it in the back, didn't care what happened to the video screens."

"Will there be another meeting?"

"I'm told there will be . . . but it might not be around here. The rumor is, these guys are from Iowa and they've been buying all over the Midwest. Wilfred will keep an eye out. Supposedly, these guys need sixteen thousand, three hundred and eighty-four processors. That's the number Wilfred gave me, and he claims it's exact."

"Ah, Jesus."

"Oh. He said the buyers had guns."

"Ah, Jesus."

LETTY WAS BACK at dinnertime. Lucas told her what he'd found out about Pilate, and she asked, "What do you think now?"

"Skye has me interested. There is no doubt that hundreds of people are murdered every year, and their bodies are never found," Lucas said. "I could even tell you where a lot of them are: if you took a search team out in the desert south of Las Vegas, and searched for a mile on both sides of the highway down to San Bernardino, you'd turn up a hundred bodies without looking too hard. The most likely victims are like Skye, because nobody ever really knows where they're at, or where they might have gone to. If you had a serious, insane predator out there, a crazy guy, travelers are natural targets. If this guy Pilate is really like she says he is, he could be dangerous."

Letty said, "Good. You're interested. That's all I wanted."

Weather said, "Letty, I'm begging you. Don't hang out with Skye. Let her do her own thing. You'd stick out like a sore thumb, and the word would get around that you're affluent, and you could get in pretty deep trouble—even without Pilate."

"I'd be okay if I had a carry permit . . ." Lucas opened his mouth, maybe to scream, but she grinned and said, "Just messing with you, Dad."

AFTER DINNER, LETTY called the Holiday Inn, Skye's room, but she wasn't in. She was in at eight o'clock, and said she'd had no luck talking to other travelers in St. Paul. Letty asked about the Jesus tattoo on Pilate's shoulder and Skye said that she knew Pilate had some ink, but not the specifics. Otherwise, the description of the man in Quartzsite fit the man she knew.

When Lucas told Skye that the guy's name was Pilate, not Pilot, she said, "I don't think that's right, Mr. Davenport. He didn't tell people his name was Pilate, he said, 'The Pilot,' like a title, not like a name."

"All right. I'll keep looking under both names. You keep asking around," Lucas said. "We'll either find him, or Henry. Okay?"

"I hope," she said, but Lucas heard the doubt in her voice.

3

FOR A FATHER and daughter who had no blood relationship, Lucas and Letty not only looked alike—dark hair, blue eyes, athletic—but behaved alike, especially when it came to sleep. Both could stay up all night, neither liked to get up early. At ten-thirty, Lucas was up and had picked out a suit, was wearing the slacks and a T-shirt and was considering the dress shirt possibilities, when Letty knocked on the door to the bedroom suite.

"Yeah, come on in," Lucas called from the dressing room.

Letty came in holding her phone. "I didn't hear the phone go off, but Skye left a message. She said that early this morning she went out to Swede Hollow and met a guy who said that Henry is up in Duluth, with some other travelers," Letty said. "She said she was going to catch a bus and go there. I called back to the hotel, but they said she'd checked out. I called the bus station, and they said a bus to Duluth left a half hour ago. She doesn't have a cell phone."

"Do *not* go to Duluth," Lucas said.

"I'm not going to. I don't expect you to, either, but it was . . . I don't know. An anticlimax. I thought we might be getting somewhere yesterday, and now she's gone."

"She's a traveler," Lucas said. "I suspect she'll be back in touch." He slipped a shirt off a hanger, held it next to the suit jacket he'd be wearing, said, "Good," and put it on and started buttoning it up.

"In case you're not getting this, I'm a little concerned," Letty said.

"So am I—but I'm not freaking out," Lucas said. "I've still got some lines out on this Pilate character and we'll see what we see. When she finds Henry, she'll call back and we'll see what she has to say then."

"All right. Well, I've got things to do today. I'm hooking up with Carey and Jeff, we're going over to the U to hang out."

"Don't worry too much," Lucas said. He held up a tie: "What do you think?"

"I would never advise you on ties, any more than Mom would," Letty said. "You're better at it than we are."

"That's true," Lucas said. He looked in his tie drawer, then settled on his original choice. "I'll call if anything comes in on Henry. Or on Pilate."

———

LETTY LEFT, AND Lucas stood in front of the mirror to tie his necktie. As he did it, he mused on what he'd almost said to her. He'd almost said, "Take your phone with you." Of course she'd take her phone with her. She was never more than fifteen feet from it. She'd eventually have it epoxied to the palm of her hand.

Not necessarily a bad thing, he thought. Women had been on the verge of taking over the world—the Western world, anyway. Then some sexist pig in Silicon Valley invented the cell phone and women took a sidetrack on which all four billion of them would soon be happily talking to each other twenty-four hours a day, getting nothing else done, and Men Would Be Back.

He whistled a few bars from Lyle Lovett's "Don't Touch My Hat," and checked himself in the mirror. He looked terrific. Not that any women would notice: they'd be too busy talking to each other on their fucking cell phones.

WHEN LUCAS GOT to the office, a few minutes after eleven o'clock, he had a voice mail from the South Dakota cop: they'd been through a full shift cycle with the patrol, all officers had been queried about Pilate's caravan, and there'd been no responses. "If I hear anything, I'll call you."

He also had an e-mail note from the L.A. cop, Lewis Hall: "Call me."

The e-mail had come in at ten, eight o'clock L.A. time, so Hall had been up early. Lucas called him back.

"Listen, I talked to some of the rough trade down in Venice last night, and your boy Pilate could be a problem," Hall said. "I may even owe you. I talked to a guy who's been around the beach for twenty years, runs a massage place. He says there was a rumor that Pilate knows about the Kitty Place murder. I don't know if you heard about that . . ."

"I heard something, I don't know the details," Lucas said.

"Kitty was an entertainer . . . I don't know what you'd say, not a hooker, or anything, she'd get small parts in movies, she had lines, now and then, she had a SAG card and she was doing some stand-up work. She had an apartment down on Main Street in Santa Monica."

"What's a SAG card?"

"She was in the Screen Actors Guild. Sort of a big deal out here, getting a card. Means you're recognized as a human being. Anyway, she was putting that kind of life together. Then one day about a year ago, she turned up dead. Found her floating in the water off Marina Del Rey. She'd been slashed to pieces: tortured with a knife, raped. Pretty goddamn awful, even for L.A."

"DNA?"

"No. She'd been in the water for a while, so we never got good DNA, and we never got a whiff of who might've done it. No current boyfriend. Her former boyfriend seemed like a decent guy and he had a solid alibi, he was playing trumpet up in Vegas all through that period. I was talking to my boy Ruben last night and he mentioned that some time, some fairly long time, after the body came up, he heard that some people thought she might've been tied up with this Pilate. I talked to the homicide guys this morning, and nobody had ever mentioned Pilate to them."

"Does Ruben know where Pilate used to hang? Or who he'd hang with?" Lucas asked. "If I could get car tags, we could probably run him down. He was supposedly in Sturgis, South Dakota, at the biker rally last week, probably heading east. The trouble is, we don't have any solid ID, no solid photo, no real history, nothing we can use to get our hands on him. He claims he's been in the movies. You think he'd have a SAG card?"

"I could check. I got the impression from Ruben . . . and I'm not sure how much Ruben really knows, he tends to talk bigger than he is . . . but I got the impression that Pilate's a street guy. Moves around a lot, lives here and there, and sometimes out of his car, sells a little weed. Ruben thinks he had a girlfriend named K—like the letter K—and she might still be around. I'll try to run her down today."

"I'd appreciate anything you could get me," Lucas said.

"Not just for you, anymore. Kitty Place was a very pretty blonde, the vulnerable-looking kind, and a really nice girl. When she got all slashed up, the shit hit the media fan around here. The homicide guys want me to push it—they'd give their left nuts for a break. A good break wouldn't do me any harm, either."

"All right. Call me if you hear anything, and if I get anything, I'll call you."

"Talk to ya," Hall said.

DEL CAPSLOCK LIMPED in the door, carrying his cane. Lucas said, "Good thing you got that cane to hold you up."

"It's become a . . . shit, I was about to say 'crutch.'" He sat down and said, "I talked to Honey Potts. She's interested. I talked to Daisy Jones. She's interested, too. I told Honey that we'd fix up a letter saying that we wouldn't prosecute if she changed her story, and remembered something different, as long as she didn't perjure herself."

"Again," Lucas said.

"Yeah, again. Jenkins was doing his cynical-guy act, told her that if she really thought Merion was going to share the take with her, she was crazy. She'd only get a cut if he was acquitted, and once he was acquitted, he couldn't be tried again. Then he'd have no reason to pay her off. Jenkins asked her, does she really want to hang out with a guy who murdered his wife by beating her to death? He suggested that kind of thing tends to become a habit."

"She bought it?"

"I'm not sure, but Daisy is going to talk to her tonight, see if she'll do an interview." Daisy Jones was a longtime reporter for WCCO television, known for her confessional talks with Twin Cities celebrities who'd managed to step on their dicks.

Lucas said, "Worth a shot."

"Hey, if she says she was banging Merion after he married Gloria . . . I think we're better than fifty-fifty."

"Maybe, but it'd be nice to get one more thing," Lucas said. "Anything on Cory?"

"As a matter of fact, there is." Del stood and put two hands against the wall and stretched his bad leg, bouncing on it. He'd been shot up by elderly gunrunners the year before, and had gone through four operations, trying to get things straight. He now had so much metal in his pelvis that he carried a TSA Notification Card just to get on an airplane. Despite the lingering disability, he'd gone back to full-time in April. He sat back down again.

"I found Brett Givens working as a sign man for a real estate dealership over in Edina," he said. "He drives a pickup, goes around putting up signs, or taking them down."

Lucas knew Givens: "Better than working at the chop shop."

"Yeah. Anyway, he says Cory is definitely back, because he saw him up in Cambridge last week, at Kenyon's. He said Cory didn't see him, because he ducked out—I think he was afraid that Cory might try to talk him into something. He likes the sign job."

"Givens didn't know where Cory's living?"

"No. But he said there were random people in the bar who seemed to know Cory, like he might be a regular.

He said Cory doesn't look especially prosperous, so he might still have the safe. I thought I'd go up this afternoon, have a few beers."

"All right. Take care. Jenkins and Shrake are out of pocket. If you need backup, call me, and I'll either come up or get Jon to send somebody."

Dale Cory was believed to be in possession of a safe that contained two million dollars in diamond jewelry, at wholesale prices, taken from a jewelry store in St. Paul on the night of New Year's Day.

The store's owner had been confident in the safety of his jewelry, because the safe he kept it in was made of hardened steel, weighed as much as a Hummer, and was kept in a room made of concrete block. He hadn't counted on somebody backing a wrecker through the front wall of the store and the concrete block wall, throwing a cinch-chain around the safe, lifting it straight up, and then hauling butt.

He hadn't counted on it because the idea seemed so goddamn stupid.

The wrecker had been stolen and was found behind a supermarket eight blocks from the jewelry store, where the cops also found in the fresh snow the tread marks from an eighteen-wheeler. Where it went, they didn't know, but by the end of the week, there were rumors that tied Cory to the job. A couple of weeks later, there were also rumors that Cory couldn't get the safe open, which made him something of a laughingstock among Twin Cities lowlifes.

The jeweler was not laughing. His safe had been so

good that his insurance-loss ceiling was lower than it should have been. Much lower. He got a third of the wholesale price back from Chubb, and that was it.

He called Lucas once a week to ask about his safe.

DEL TOOK OFF, and Lucas started working through the rest of the caseload. A lot of it was more a matter of coordination than investigation, keeping the various suburban police departments up-to-date on who was doing what, and who was looking for whom. Minneapolis, St. Paul, and Bloomington could generally take care of themselves, and had their own liaisons.

Lucas's current priorities included two armed robbers, one who specialized in credit union branches, and another who scouted out, and then hit, businessmen who were taking money home on Sunday nights, after business hours, when they couldn't run it out to a bank during the day.

The credit union guy was careful, and while he claimed to be armed, he never showed a gun. Lucas thought they'd probably get him, if he didn't move out of town, and wasn't overly worried that he'd shoot someone: he seemed too careful.

The other guy, he thought, would eventually kill someone. He was almost certainly an ex-con, and didn't carry a gun. Instead, he carried a pipe. He was a big guy, dealing with businessmen who so far had all been elderly. He used the pipe for intimidation. One of the old guys had fought him, and had gotten an arm broken for his trouble. Sooner or later, Lucas thought, the thief would smack somebody in the head, and then they'd be looking for a killer . . . if the cops didn't get him first.

All of that was important; and it bored him.

So did the U.S. Secret Service. Somebody in town was passing exceptional copies of fifty- and one-hundred-dollar bills, and there was some evidence that the currency was coming in from Lebanon. The Secret Service had three agents poking around, and they generally considered the BCA to be their assistants in the matter. Sort of like secretaries, or maybe receptionists. Or maybe golden retrievers.

Lucas had been the latest designated BCA liaison, and he'd eventually handled the Secret Service information requests, which always arrived by e-mail, by referring them to his shared secretary, who was told to do the best she could. Her best sometimes involved the wastebasket.

Jenkins called: "Shrake and I hooked up for a beer, and we got to thinking."

"Uh-oh, that's not recommended."

"I know, we try to avoid it when we can. But, we'd like to stop by later and talk."

"Come ahead, I'm mostly sitting on my thumb."

LETTY CALLED HIM late in the day. She was back home, and hadn't heard from Skye. Lucas hadn't heard from Hall, in L.A., and had gotten busy with a flurry of phone calls when another credit union went down— turned out not to be the guy he was looking for—and never called Hall back.

Letty was unhappy with the lack of movement, but Lucas asked, "What should we do? We're not getting anything. I suspect that Skye and Henry have hooked up, and moved on."

"She should have called," Letty said.

Lucas shrugged, though there was nobody around to see it: "She's a traveler. Like you said, she doesn't have a cell."

SHRAKE AND JENKINS came in. Jenkins did the talking. "One of the problems with the Merion case is that we could never produce the club."

"Probably burned it," Lucas said.

"Probably not. Takes too long, and he was on a tight schedule. We know he didn't burn it in the home fireplace, because crime scene checked it, did samples, and said the last fire was a long time ago. And Merion had to drive like hell to get up to his cabin before Gloria's daughter came home and found the body. The fireplace at the cabin was gas, not wood, so he didn't burn it there."

"So . . ."

"What we're thinking is, he whacked Gloria in the bathroom, threw her down the stairs, pinched off her nose and mouth, wiped up the bathroom floor with that Foaming Bubbles stuff, jumped in his car and took off."

"Nobody saw him," Lucas said.

"Because Sunfish Lake is darker than the black hole of Calcutta, and he's up on that ridge. He looks out the window, to make sure nobody is coming down that little road, then he jumps in the car and takes off," Jenkins said. "Once he's out of the house, who's going to see him, or know who's in the car? Anyway, he goes up to the cabin, the club is in his trunk. Carefully wrapped in something, because he's no dummy. He gets up there, knowing that the daughter could, at that point, get home anytime and find the body. When that happens, he's going to have to drive back to Sunfish Lake *right now*, like a grieving husband should. So he gets to the cabin, still got the club, has to get rid of it. Can't burn it, because it would take too long. It's dark, he goes out into the woods with a shovel . . . some obscure spot, buries it. We're thinking, probably in that vacant side lot. Not the front lawn, not between the cabin and the road, but in that empty lot, or maybe in the woods across the road. Doesn't need a deep pit, the club's only two inches in diameter. Carefully rakes some leaves over it . . . and it's gone."

"Or maybe he just threw it in a ditch on the way up," Lucas said.

"He's more careful than that. Throw it in a ditch, it could be found," Jenkins said. "It's pretty distinctive and it'd have some blood on it."

"So, what you want to do is . . . ?"

"We don't think he would have gone *way* deep in the woods, because he'd want to hear the phone ring. Remember, the daughter called him on the cabin phone, and then the cops called him on his cell, and they both put him up there . . . So we're thinking, we should go up there and mark out the likely spots, and walk it inch by inch."

Lucas thought about it and said, "Say, aren't there a lot of golf courses around Cross Lake?"

"Lucas, for Christ's sakes, we're trying to help out here," Jenkins said.

"What about the computer chips?" Lucas asked Shrake.

"Those guys are long gone. We got the word out, so people are watching for them . . . but we don't think they'll pop up here again. Not for a while, anyway, and the Merion trial is coming up."

"If you motherfuckers play more than one round a day . . ."

SKYE DIDN'T CALL the next day, either, or the next.

On the morning of the fourth day, the South Dakota highway patrol guy called and asked, "I threw away the note you gave me, but you were looking for a Henry Mark Fuller, correct?"

"That's my guy. You got him?"

"A body came up in Sheridan County. The DCI's got him, you need to talk to a guy named Steve Clemmens. The word I get is that the body has been identified as Fuller."

Lucas took a few seconds to digest that, and then asked, "How long has he been dead?"

"I guess he looks like he's been down for a week or so. They'll be doing an autopsy today or tomorrow, crime scene is out there now. I heard that it was really rough, what they did to him."

Lucas got a number for Clemmens, called him, got him on his cell phone. Clemmens was in rural Butte County, north of Sturgis, up in some piney hills, looking at the crime scene. Lucas explained who he was and why he'd been looking for Fuller.

"We need to talk to that Skye, if you can find her," Clemmens said. "Doesn't look like a domestic, though, no way. This wasn't one guy cutting him up. This took at least two or three, that's why we're looking at the bikers, or a group of people. And if you can track down this Pilate . . ."

Clemmens said Fuller's body had been found by a couple of Indian kids who'd been out with .22s, shooting around the countryside. Whoever had buried Fuller had only gone down a couple of feet before they hit rock, and the body had been partly uncovered by coyotes.

"What they did was, or what it looks like, is that they nailed him to a tree, and then took their time cutting him up. We got the tree, signs of blood on the bark, no weapon, we got a few tracks, but we got nothing definitive, what might be a pair of Nike athletic shoes, and a boot mark. There was a campfire right there, and fresh, we think it's related, but no way to tell for sure. There was some partly burned trash in the fire, food wrappers, we're processing those for fingerprints, but like I said, we're not sure it's related."

"When you say he was cut up, do you mean, dismembered?"

"No. Slashed. Long cuts running all down his body. Looks like he was castrated, but we're not sure about that, because that part of the body and the stomach area was worked over pretty good by the coyotes. His hands and arms were in good enough shape to take prints . . . That's how we got the quick ID. He was arrested in Johnson City, Texas, for burglary, three years ago, fingerprinted. We got a hit in the first ten minutes. We can still see the spike holes in his wrists, below the heels of his hands."

"Pretty crude," Lucas said. "Listen, there was a woman killed out in L.A. . . ."

He told Clemmens about the Kitty Place murder. "I'm worried because both you and the L.A. guy used the word 'slashed.' I'd like to see the autopsy photos of the wounds, and have the L.A. homicide guys take a look."

"We'll get them to you," Clemmens said. "You're the guy involved in that Black Hole case last year, right? The guy who got that female cop back?"

"Yeah, that was me," Lucas said.

"Hell of a thing," Clemmens said.

LUCAS CALLED HALL in L.A., told him about the find in South Dakota. "I'm going to hook you up with the homicide guys," Hall said. "This is something."

An L.A. homicide detective named Rick Robinson called Lucas back a few minutes later and Lucas gave him the story. "They're doing the autopsy later today. We

should be able to get the raw digital photos right away—
the South Dakota guy said he'd make it a priority. If you
want to call him, I've got a number, he could send them
directly to you."

"Need to see 'em," Robinson said. "Sounds like the
same thing somebody did to Kitty Place—long slashes
across her body. She wasn't crucified or anything, though."

After he got off the line with Robinson, Lucas called
Letty to tell her what had happened. His daughter was
not a typical teenager: she'd seen violent death, up close
and personal; she could handle the news about Henry.

Letty: "Why did somebody say they'd seen Henry up
in Duluth? It sounds to me like they were setting her up.
They're afraid that she'll talk about Henry. Dad, we've
gotta get up there."

"I can go up there," Lucas said. "You can stay here."

"Dad, I'm not going to mess with you—but you sort
of need me," Letty said. "I've met some of these people
and I can talk to them when you'd just scare them. They
don't like people like you."

Lucas said, "If I put you on a bus home, you stay on
the bus. I don't want you running around the countryside—"

"I'll come home. I will. I'll come home when you
say so."

THEY DROVE UP to Duluth that afternoon, in Lucas's truck. Lucas called ahead, to a friend on the Duluth

police force, and was told that they should check out Leif Erikson Park on the lake.

Lucas got directions, and they rolled into town a few minutes before three o'clock, on a day that had been hot in the Cities. In Duluth, an east wind off Lake Superior had kept things cool. They found a meter on East Superior Street, cut through a parking lot, and took a foot-bridge into the park.

A few dozen people were scattered around the grassy lakefront, throwing Frisbees, looking at the lake, or doing nothing at all. They didn't see anybody who looked like a traveler, but they did see a uniformed cop, and they went that way, and Lucas pulled out his ID.

"I never heard them called travelers, but we got some," the cop said. He waved off to the north. "They got a spot up there, I don't know, maybe ten minutes up the Lake-walk. There's a little beach up there. They sit around under the trees talking, mostly. Might smoke a little dope."

Lucas thanked him and they went that way. Lucas had dressed down for the trip, in jeans and a golf shirt and a light nylon jacket to cover the gun, but still, Letty said, he looked like a cop.

"And you look like a snotty college kid," Lucas said.

"Do not."

"Where'd those jeans come from? Neiman Marcus? I think I saw some Neiman Marcus on your Amex."

"Did not."

"Neiman fuckin' Marcus. La-de-fuckin'-da."

"Shut up."

————

HALF A dozen travelers were sitting in a lakeside copse. Two benches looked out over the lake toward the Wisconsin shore, where a green-and-rust-colored freighter was maneuvering in toward the docks. A couple of the travelers were smoking cigarettes—Lucas couldn't smell any weed—and two of them had tough-looking, medium-sized dogs that showed pit bull in the eyes.

They really didn't look like street people, Lucas thought, although they obviously lived outdoors. They had big functional packs, wide-brimmed hats, wore heavy hiking boots, and a couple of them had six-foot-long walking sticks. Their ages ranged from the late teens to the mid-forties. Two were women, four were men. What they really looked like, he thought, were dusty long-distance walkers.

Which they were.

They all stirred restlessly when Lucas and Letty cut toward them, like leaves rippling in a light wind. Town people tended to stay away, unless they were cops, and the big guy looked like a cop.

When they came up, Lucas said, "We need to talk to you guys. I'm a state police officer and this is my daughter. We're looking for a friend of ours, a traveler, who might be in serious trouble."

One of the men, probably in his thirties, sounded skeptical: "Well, what's up, doc?"

Lucas looked at Letty, and she took it: "We have a friend named Skye. I talked to her four days ago down in

St. Paul—we met in San Francisco in June, when she was going through. She was traveling with a guy named Henry Mark Fuller, from Texas. They were out in Sturgis at the motorcycle rally, and Henry disappeared. Somebody—she said another traveler—told her that he'd seen Henry here in Duluth, and she came up here to find him. But Henry was murdered near Sturgis. They just dug up his body. We're worried that the people who killed Henry might try to hurt Skye. They know her, she doesn't like them, and they might try to shut her up about Henry."

Another stir rippled through the group; a man said, "Shit, somebody killed Henry?" and one of the women said, "We know Skye. We knew Henry. I haven't seen them since we were in Eugene, but we were going to meet up in Hayward, Wisconsin, next weekend. There's a Juggalo Gathering. We're all going to that."

Lucas said, "You're Juggalos?"

One of the men said, "I am, these guys are just free-loaders—"

"Hey!" said the woman. "This isn't funny."

Lucas: "You didn't see her here?"

They all shook their heads: "We just got here yesterday. We were going to hang around until we left for Hayward."

One of the men said, "You know, she could have gone up to Two Harbors. I ran into Ranger yesterday when I was coming in. He said a bunch of guys were going up there. There's a county fair going on, it's supposed to be pretty good, you can get a job."

"Bet she went there with them," the woman said. "She knows Ranger, for sure, and he's a safe guy."

They had no other ideas, but one of the men asked, "Who do you think killed Henry?"

Lucas said, "We don't know anything for sure, but there's this guy who travels in a caravan . . ." He told them what he knew about Pilate and his group—none of them knew the name—then ripped a page from his notebook, wrote his cell phone number on it, and said, "Could I give my number to somebody? If you see her? Or if you see Pilate?"

A couple of the men shrugged, and Lucas asked, "How about if I wrap it in a fifty?"

"Shouldn't take money for trying to help Skye," the woman said. "Give me the number. If I see her or hear from her, or about her, I'll call you."

"You can get phones at bus stations . . ." Letty began.

The woman said, "My mom gave me a cell phone. I don't call anybody but her, but I got it, and I keep it charged up."

"Good," Lucas said. "Listen, the people who killed Henry . . . they are *bad* people. They might be killing people for the fun of it. Travelers are natural targets. Nobody knows where you're at, and if you don't show up, nobody worries, because they figure you're out traveling. Take care, until we figure out what's going on here."

They all nodded and one of the men said, "We'll tell other people we know. If we get enough of us, we ought to be able to spot this guy."

"Call us, but don't mess with him," Lucas said. "You could be dealing with the worst kind of crazy."

LUCAS LOOKED AT his watch as they walked away, and said, "Two Harbors is only a half hour from here. Maybe we can catch her there."

On the way north, Letty asked, "Have you run into any Juggalos?"

"I prefer Aerosmith."

"So you know who they are?"

"Sure. Followers of the Insane Clown Posse," Lucas said. "Most of the Juggalos are okay—unusual, even strange, but okay. They have meetings around the country that they call Gatherings. The feds say some Juggalos have formed themselves into a criminal gang. I don't know about those."

"I didn't know the gang part. I'll look them up," she said, taking out her iPad.

AT TWO HARBORS, they found three travelers, including the one called Ranger, working with a county fair cleanup crew. Ranger said, "Yeah, I seen her down in Duluth yesterday. She asked me about Henry. Nobody had seen him and she was talking about going back to the Black Hills. She thinks he might be sitting on a bench at their backup spot."

Lucas told them about Henry. They were visibly

shocked, but when he told them about Pilate, Ranger said, "Hey, that guy was in Duluth. I seen that guy. They were peddlin' puss . . ." His eyes clicked over to Letty: "No offense . . ."

She shook her head.

". . . out of that RV, up on the hill by the big mall. Tony and me—"

"Who's Tony?" Lucas asked.

"Just . . . Tony. He's one of us guys. We were walking through there, and this guy seen us, and said we could get some puss for seventy-five dollars. They were workin' it out of an RV. We didn't have seventy-five dollars, and if we did, I wouldn't have spent it on that skanky chick he had. I said no, and we kept on walking. But it was like he knew who we were. I mean, travelers."

"Where's Tony now?"

Ranger shrugged. "He was planning to go over to Hayward for the Juggalo Gathering. If he got some money, he could've gone back to the mall. He's kind of a puss hound."

"You think these women could have baited Henry in?" Lucas asked.

Ranger shook his head. "No, Henry was a nice guy, but he was kinda gay."

"Gay?"

"Yeah. He didn't really do nothin' about it, but we all knew," Ranger said. "You know, he was like from Texas, cowboy boots and jeans, but sooner or later, he was going to find out . . ."

Letty looked at Lucas and said, "Skye kind of hinted at it when I was talking to them in San Francisco. I didn't pick up on it, though."

Lucas asked Ranger, "You think they might've run into Skye?"

"I can't tell you that," he said. "She was dragging around town, looking in all the places that we hang out. We do go up to that mall, sometimes, and she probably would have gone up there, sooner or later."

"This is not good," Letty said to Lucas.

"If you guys run into Skye, or Tony, or see Pilate, you call me." He gave them his number, written on a page, and this time, he did wrap a fifty around it. "Please, don't let it go."

ON THE WAY back to Duluth, Lucas took a call from Robinson, the L.A. homicide cop. He asked, "Did you see the autopsy photos?"

"No, I've been on the road," Lucas said.

"Okay. Well, we've got them, and we got a nine-alarm fire here. The cuts are the same. Same pattern on this kid, as they were with Kitty Place. Big knife, slashes start up around the shoulder, and then go all the way down the body in one long slash. Right across the face, too. It might not stand up if they got a good defense attorney, but I personally think it's about ninety-nine percent that it's the same killer. You got a walking nightmare on your hands, my friend."

"Did they say if the kid was raped?"

"That, I don't know," Robinson said. "All I got were the pictures. They don't have an autopsy report yet."

"I'll call them, get reports for both of us."

"You chasing this guy?" Robinson asked.

"Looking for him."

"Send him to South Dakota if you get him. They got the death penalty. Unlike us, they use it."

4

PILATE AND THE disciples got out of South Dakota in a hurry, traveling in an eight-vehicle caravan spaced out over a mile or two, twelve men, seven women, leaving Sturgis and the motorcycle rally in the dust.

So far, the Great Northern Expedition had been a marginal success. They'd spent two weeks in San Francisco, buying dope, then headed east to Reno, where they peddled the weed to tourists. They ran into some Colorado competition there, but it wasn't too bad, because the Colorado dope was fairly janky, plus, it had tax paid on it, so it couldn't compete on price.

Pilate tried to use the money from the weed to step up to cocaine, but good clean coke was hard to find and they wound up with a small bag of coke and a fat bag of meth. They also lost two crew members, Biggie and Darrell, who wandered away one day and never came back.

From there, they had taken I-15 north all the way to Butte, Montana, mostly because Pilate didn't like to drive across mountains if he didn't have to. From Butte, taking their time, they'd gone to Dickinson, North Dakota, where they unloaded most of the meth, for cash, to be sold to the oil field workers, and then they turned south to Sturgis, to catch the motorcycle rally.

The meth sale in Dickinson had gone well, and they got to Sturgis with more than twenty thousand in cash and no dope at all. Pilate spent almost half the cash buying cocaine and then they'd gone through that. Then they'd gone camping up in the hills, had their fun with Henry, and then they got the fuck out of South Dakota.

"THIS IS SURE as hell the long way around," Kristen said, looking out at the arrow-straight I-90.

Pilate said, "Well, we couldn't go back through North Dakota. That cop was on us like Holy on the Pope."

"Could have pulled the trigger on him," Kristen said.

"And spend the rest of your life in a hole somewhere," Pilate said. "Those cops are wired for sound and video. We wouldn't have had a chance. Lucky you kept your fuckin' mouth shut."

They'd been hassled by a North Dakota highway patrolman. He'd been called after an argument about a restaurant bill. They hadn't been moving at the time, so he hadn't been able to give them a ticket, and he was late for dinner, but told them if he saw them driving in his state, they were going to jail. He said, "I'll get a drug dog on your ass, lickety-split. We don't care for your sort in North Dakota."

The cop had a good eye. At that point, they'd still had a pound of meth stashed in the RV, and if the cop had pushed a search, he would have gotten both the dope and the money.

"This is not our territory, and we gotta remember that," Pilate told his disciples, as they crossed the line into South Dakota, and set up camp. "We don't look like these people up here, and they don't like people who look like us. We gotta be careful when we're hauling dope. We gotta keep the dope and the money in different vehicles."

"Hate to be pushed by those fuckers," Kristen said. "Fuckin' cops. We oughta kill one sometime."

"We will," Pilate said.

As IT TURNED out, South Dakota had been as bad as North Dakota. Sturgis had almost as many cops as it did bikers, although they tried to stay out of sight. Then they got into the coke, and when they left Sturgis, they had only a little more than four thousand dollars. Pilate had another connection in Wisconsin, hooked into him through a guy they knew in L.A. He could deliver wholesale coke, which they could have retailed for enough to get them back to the West Coast; except that they'd blown the money for the coke back in Sturgis.

Then there was the whole thing with Henry Fuller.

"Maybe had *too* much fun," Pilate confided to Kristen, as they rolled on east. "I wish we'd put a boulder on top of that kid. Hold him down."

"I'm worried about Laine," Kristen said. "I could see her pullin' back."

"Well, it was her first time," Pilate said.

"If we run into some cops, somewhere, she could talk. That's what worries me."

Pilate leaned back in the passenger seat, looking out at the gray-dirt sails of the Badlands, considering the problem. He said, finally, "She's got that golden pussy. That's what I'd hate to give up."

"Pussy isn't a problem. You said it yourself: pussy is more common than TV."

Pilate yawned and said, "I'll think about it."

"We could have a really good time with her," Kristen said. She looked hungry around the eyes.

"I'll think about it," Pilate said. Kristen could be a little scary.

He did think about it, though. What he thought was, if they took Laine off somewhere and cut her up, that could damage morale; the disciples all liked her, and might start wondering who was next.

He turned his head to take in Kristen. She might be down on Laine because Laine had that golden pussy. And the fact was, Kristen was the assistant principal in the group, the one who kicked ass. If they were going to have fun with anyone, maybe it should be Kristen: that'd probably *help* morale, instead of damaging it.

He half dozed, entertaining himself with fantasies of

cutting up Kristen. The fine-woven treachery of the idea turned him on.

They'd killed a dozen people now and the numbers made him feel both powerful and comfortable. Powerful because he *could* do it, and make the others go along; and comfortable because he *had* done it, and it wouldn't be something he'd miss in life.

Most of the victims had been chosen because they were the invisible people in the world. Street people, travelers, illegal aliens. You could stop by a Home Depot early in the morning and pick out anyone you wanted to play with. They'd jump right in the car, and the other wetbacks thought them *lucky*.

He'd made one mistake, though. He'd once acted out of a powerful impulse, rather than calculation.

He'd been cruising down Sunset, stopped at a light, middle of the day, minding his own business. Okay, a little whacked on Skywalker OG. Then this blond chick, probably an actress, pulls up behind him in a BMW convertible, top down, sunglasses, red lipstick, white blouse, the whole bit. The light turned green and swear to God, she honked her horn like one split second after the light changed. He was a little doggy off the line, so what'd she do next? Dropped the hammer on the bimmer and, *BOOM!*, she was around him like he was a tourist and gone.

Pissed him off so badly that he had to hold on to the steering wheel with both hands to keep himself from shaking to pieces.

Took it as a sign.

The next sacrifice would be a woman.

A blonde. Most definitely an actress. They picked her up outside a yoga center on Melrose, hauled her up into the hills. They had a lot of fun with her before she died, begging them not to hurt her anymore.

But then . . . then the shit had hit the fan. They'd been lucky to get out of that one clean.

HE WOKE UP when Kristen said, "Look at this."

They were dropping headlong into a deep, broad river valley, with a small town on the far side. "The Mississippi River," Pilate said, in his most solemn voice. "The zipper on the United States of America."

They went on a bit, and a sign said: "Missouri River." Kristen glanced at him, but didn't correct him. He said, "I meant, Missouri," but still, it ruined it for him.

They stopped on the other side of the Missouri for a root beer and a cheeseburger, then pushed on into the evening, across the Minnesota line, camped out overnight at the Walmart Supercenter in Worthington.

From Worthington they went north on Highway 60 and then 71, running up a very long state, and pulled into Bemidji at two o'clock on a fine, sunny afternoon, ate more cheeseburgers and got some pork chops and beer and potato chips and headed north again, still on 71, to the intersection of 72, and then north all the way to Highway 11, where they ran out of state.

"That's Canada, right there," Kristen said, pointing out the window.

"Never been there," Pilate said. "The USA is good enough for me."

They took Highway 11 into Baudette, stocked up on food and beer, then turned around on Highway 11 and ran back east a few miles on the two-lane, following behind Chet on land that was as flat as a tabletop, but dark: dark trees, dark fields, past marshes, shallow lakes, small farms. Fifteen minutes out of town, Chet swerved off on a dirt track past a rusty mailbox that led through a narrow crack in the roadside tree line. Two hundred yards back, they came to a dirty white house surrounded by a dirt patch on which two dirty old Chevy pickups were parked.

Chet got out of the car and an old man came to the front door of the house, pushed the screen door open, and stepped out. He had a mustache over a three-day beard, watery blue eyes behind plastic-rimmed glasses. He was wearing overalls and rubber boots, and carrying a pump shotgun, a 12-gauge. He asked Chet, "Where'n the hell you been? And what do you want?"

"Been in Los Angeles, Pap. Worked on some movies."

The old man looked at the other cars in the caravan and said, "Must not of made any money on them. What do you want, anyway?"

"We was hoping to use the campground for a couple of days, rest up," Chet said. "We've been on the road for a while."

"Well . . . Go on ahead." The old man waved at a farther track that led away from the house into the trees. "Makes no nevermind to me."

"Thanks, Pap. Can we use the water hose when we need to?"

"Yeah, I guess. Be sure you turn it off. And don't bother me no more. And stay off the bridge."

Chet walked out to where everybody could see him and yelled, "Follow behind. Road's kinda rough."

They all followed him down through the trees to a small lake, and a puddle of cracked blacktop at lakeside, where they parked, and piled out of the cars. A single phone pole stuck out of one side of the parking lot; a single strand of wire threaded through the trees, and ended at a box on the phone pole, with four outlets. At the other side of the parking lot was an outhouse, a two-holer, the first the Californians had ever seen.

The overhead line continued to the corner of the lake, jumped over a fifteen-foot-wide creek, and disappeared into the trees on the other side. A narrow wooden bridge crossed the creek under the wire.

"NOT GREAT, BUT I can live with it," Pilate said.

They partied for the next three days. Couldn't afford any more cocaine, but they still had the weed, and all the beer they could drink. They had more women than the men could keep up with, but the women, even if not all of them were entirely happy about it, would go both ways.

They also had to deal with the question of whether Minnesotans were actually aliens. Terry brought it up: "You know what? Everybody I seen around here has big heads. You seen that?"

They did, on their runs into town for food and beer: Minnesotans all had big heads. When they spotted a guy with a cowboy hat and a small head, they asked him if he was from Minnesota, and he told them no, he was from Montana.

"Food for thought, that's what it is," Pilate said.

On the morning of the second day, a white van bumped past them, crossed the bridge, and fifteen minutes later, bumped back out.

"What's over there?" Pilate asked.

"Another campground," Chet said. "Pap doesn't want us disturbing the customers."

"I can't fuckin' believe he has customers," Pilate said.

Later that day, when he hadn't seen anybody around, Pilate walked across the bridge and found another campground, with another phone pole with outlets, and three single-wide trailers up on blocks. The trailers were locked, and nothing was stirring around them. A garbage can sat near the entrance road, half full of trash, mostly food wrappers.

THEY WEREN'T LONG for Minnesota.

The first of three Juggalo Gatherings was coming up, in Wisconsin, and Pilate didn't want to miss it. When they picked up the cocaine in Wisconsin, they could cut it by half, and still push it out to the Juggalos for twice as much as they paid for the uncut stuff. After three days, they left the campsite, never said good-bye to Pap, heading first for Duluth, then over to Wisconsin.

In Duluth, they rambled around town for a while, rodeoed at a McDonald's for cheeseburgers, fries, and malts, then stumbled over a busy mall. Pilate ordered Ellen and Kristen and Linda to set up shop, and though they were doubtful, they found a spot where cross-street foot traffic might give them a chance.

Pilate, in the meantime, went inside the mall with Raleigh, to look around. They were still there when Bell went by at a jog, spotted them, turned around and came back and said breathlessly, "You know who's here?"

"Who?" Pilate asked.

"That traveler chick who was with Henry. She's out in the parking lot."

"Shit. She could cause us some trouble," Pilate said. "She's probably looking for him. Or us."

"Yeah, after that crazy fuckin' Kristen told her that we cut his heart out," said Raleigh. "She's probably got the cops right behind her."

Pilate said to Raleigh, "She doesn't know your car, far as we know."

"So?"

"So we sneak up on her, throw a bag on her head, and toss her in the car."

"Man, she's out in the parking lot," said Bell. "There are eight million people out there."

"No, there isn't. Not really." Pilate stood up, turned

to Raleigh. "Let's get your car." To Bell he said, "Go tell Kristen to close up shop and get out of here. We'll meet them over in Wisconsin. Tell them wait on the highway."

The thing that Pilate liked about Raleigh was that after a decision was made, no matter how crazy it was, he'd go with you. To get through life, he needed someone to tell him what to *do*. If that were done, he'd do it: rob a bank, drown a guy, get the hammer and nails for a crucifix.

They got Raleigh's car and started driving loops around the parking lot, and Raleigh rambled for a while: "Back in Denver I was working on this golf course, running a mower, and I met this golfer guy who said when he was playing, and had to take a leak, he'd do it right in the middle of the fairway. He'd put his bag down and stand next to it, hold his dick with one hand and with the other hand, he'd shade his eyes like he was working out his next shot. He said nobody ever paid any attention to him. But you see a guy standing in the bushes, the women start bitching and moaning about guys exposing themselves. This guy, they had no idea . . ."

"What'd you tell me that for?" Pilate asked.

"'Cause if we yank her right off the parking lot, like we were helping her in the car, people could look right at you and never have any idea."

"You know what I like about you?" Pilate laughed. "You're fuckin' crazy. You're really fuckin' nuts."

That's what they did.

Pilate popped open the side door, grabbed her by the collar of her hoodie, and yanked her into the backseat before she even had a chance to scream, pushed her into the space below the seats, and popped her a few times on the cheekbone, with a fist loaded with a roll of quarters: *pop, pop, pop*. Raleigh rolled them out of the parking lot, and they were gone.

5

AT THE MALL in Duluth, Lucas and Letty tracked
down a security officer who told them that he'd heard of
the group attempting to sell sex out at the edge of the
parking lot, but hadn't seen them. "A guy named Larry
Royce, we've got his address and phone number, came in
here and complained. We went right out there, four of
us, but they were gone. I don't know how long they were
here, but I doubt that it was very long."

The complainant had given them a description of the
RV, but no license plate number. "It's a Winnebago Minnie, beige. Doesn't help much—maybe Winnebago can
tell you how many they made. Royce said it was pretty
beat-up. Looked like it had been pushed hard."

Royce had seen two women with the RV, no men. He
hadn't gone inside.

The security man said they'd called the Duluth cops with the story, but he hadn't heard back; and he didn't have anything more. Lucas got Larry Royce's address and phone number, and thanked him.

Back in the truck, Lucas called the sex crimes unit of the Duluth Police Department. The officer who answered knew of the call from mall security. "We had the patrol division looking for them, but nothing came back. It's possible they crossed over into Wisconsin and headed south or east. Lotta RVs out there, and we didn't have a tag number. We also didn't have any information that sex had actually been sold."

Letty had been on her iPad, and reported, "Winnebago made Minnies for a long time. They might have stopped for a while, but then they started again. Looks like they were making them for at least twenty years."

"See if you can find this Royce guy's address," Lucas said.

She found it in ten seconds: they were six or eight blocks away. "We could call him . . ."

"Better to talk face-to-face, if we can," Lucas said.

LARRY ROYCE LIVED in a bluebird-blue house in a neighborhood of white clapboard houses built on small lawns. He was home, a newer Chevy van parked in front of an older Lund fishing boat, tucked tight in the cracked driveway. A jolly, balding heavyset man with blond hair and a red face, somewhere deep in his forties, he was happy to talk about the incident, but not in front of Letty—"It's embarrassing," he said.

Lucas suggested that Letty take a walk around the block or wait in the truck. She took her iPad for a walk.

Royce sat on his stoop and said, "There were two of them, a thin blonde and a fat redhead. They were wiping the windows of this RV with some Windex and paper towels, and they said, 'Hi,' when I walked past. I said, 'Hi,' and this blonde said something like 'Sweaty day for a walk,' and I said, 'Yeah,' and she said, 'I wonder if you could wipe the top of that windshield for me.' She couldn't reach the middle of the windshield very well, so I said sure, and did that, and she said, 'Thanks,' and then 'What have you been up to?' I said I was walking over to the mall, and she said, 'Would you be interested in a party?' Well, I'm a salesman, I been around, and I knew what she was talking about, and I said, 'No.' When I got over to the mall, I told a security guy. I mean, we don't have hookers up here . . . Not in the mall parking lot, anyway. In the afternoon."

He came back with security and the women were gone with the RV: "I think my attitude might have scared them off. They guessed I was gonna call the cops."

He said he was angry with himself for not getting the license plate number, but "I wanted to get out of there." The back left corner of the RV had been hit by something, or had backed into something and was crumpled, he said. "Not bad, but there's a pretty good-sized dent."

Lucas took down a full description of the RV and

both women; the fat redhead, Royce said, had a white scar under one eye. The blonde, "There was something wrong with her teeth."

"You mean like rotten? Or missing?"

"No. They were pointed. Kind of freaks me out, now that I think about it."

LUCAS WAS WAITING when Letty got back, and after he told her what he'd gotten from Royce, she asked, "Now what?"

"Going home," he said. "There's a good chance they've all left for Wisconsin, and I need to talk to a whole bunch of people about this."

"What about Skye?"

Lucas waved his hand out at the city: "How are we going to find her? She doesn't have a phone, we don't even know if she's here. It's all too big. Best thing we can do is get back to my office and start calling. Get everybody looking for them."

ON THE WAY south, Del called and said that Honey Potts—none of the cops called her Connie Sweat—had agreed to do an interview with Daisy Jones, and Jones, in a pre-interview, had gotten her to say that she'd been sleeping with Merion all through the marriage. He hadn't been faithful to Gloria for even a week. "They're doing the interview this afternoon, and they're rolling it tonight—they want to get it done before there's any chance that Merion's attorney finds out and tries to cut another deal with Honey," Del said.

"Good," Lucas said. "Still need one more thing."

"Shrake and Jenkins are going up to Merion's cabin tomorrow, see if they can find that club," Del said. "Sounds like a wild-goose chase to me."

BACK IN ST. PAUL, Lucas and Letty stopped at the BCA office, where Lucas found that nothing had come in on Pilate, but he had gotten two sets of autopsy photos, one set on Henry Mark Fuller and the other on Kitty Place, the actress who'd been killed in Los Angeles. The L.A. cop was right: Lucas took fifteen seconds to decide that the same person or persons had killed them both.

The photos came up on his computer terminal. He pretended to be looking at something else and didn't tell Letty about them. Henry Fuller no longer looked entirely human. He looked more like a badly butchered pig.

THE HONEY POTTS interview had happened, and went on at six o'clock, after an hour of promos on the early news. About one second before the interview went on the air, WCCO reporters went looking for a comment either from Merion or his attorney. Merion refused to comment, but Raines, his attorney, said, "I want to know how she cut a deal like this. Did 'CCO pay for it? Were the police in any way involved? My client is being framed here, right out in public . . ."

———

AT ELEVEN O'CLOCK that night, Lucas got a call from a Joe Hagestrom, a highway patrolman from Wisconsin, who said he'd spoken to an agent named Bob Stern, from Wisconsin's Division of Criminal Investigation. "He said you'd called down there earlier today, looking for a beige Winnebago Minnie with a big dent on the back left corner."

"You find it?"

"I'm looking at it right now, or what's left of it," the trooper said. "It was back in the woods here . . . You know Northwest Wisconsin?"

"I've got a cabin up there, at Lost Land Lake."

"You know where Highway 77 crosses the Namekagon River?" Hagestrom asked.

"Sure. I drive across there a dozen times a year," Lucas said.

"Okay. There's an informal campground off 77, north along the river. You can get there on a dirt trail, but it's mostly for canoeists. We got a call that an RV was on fire back there, and the volunteer fire department went back, and it'd almost burned to the ground. The thing is, there was somebody inside."

"You mean—dead."

"Dead now, for sure. The firemen say the smell is unmistakable. They think the fire was deliberate. They could smell a lot of gasoline and the truck is a diesel."

"Have they moved the body?" Lucas asked.

"Not yet. The metal part of the RV sort of shrank down and encapsulated the living quarters, where we think the body is. We're waiting for the crime scene crew to get here."

"What time did it blow up?"

"Around nine o'clock—couple of hours ago. The first responders were sheriff's deputies and the fire department, and they didn't know we were looking for a Winnebago Minnie with a dent in it. I just got here ten minutes ago, when I heard some guys talking about it on the radio."

"All right. I'm coming."

LUCAS WALKED UPSTAIRS to the bedroom to tell Weather. She was working in the morning, cutting on somebody, he didn't know the details, but she'd gone to bed early.

"Don't take Letty," she said.

"I won't. I'm gonna sneak out," he said. He stuffed some underwear and socks, a couple of clean shirts, a pair of clean jeans, and his dopp kit in an AWOL bag, kissed Weather, collected his gun, a leather jacket, and a ball cap, and went back downstairs.

When he rolled out of the driveway in the Benz, he could see Letty's silhouette in the lighted window of her bedroom, looking out after him.

Lucas feared that the body in the RV was Skye's. Some things, he thought, Letty was still too young for:

like the photos of Henry Fuller, like the roasted body of
a woman she thought of as a friend.

LUCAS RAN STRAIGHT north on I-35 to Hinckley,
then east across the St. Croix River to Danbury, Wisconsin, and then farther east on Highway 77. There wasn't
much traffic and he ran with lights, but it still took him
more than an hour and a half to get to the scene. A cop
car was parked on the shoulder of the highway where it
crossed the Namekagon, lights flashing in the night.
Lucas identified himself, and the cop pointed him back
into the woods, where Lucas could see light shining
through the trees.

When he got there, he found Hagestrom, the highway
patrolman, a couple of county sheriff's deputies, and two
firemen looking at the wreck of the Winnebago. The
Winnebago had essentially melted around its core and
was blackened with soot; but it was cold now, the fire
thoroughly doused three hours earlier.

Hagestrom shook his hand and said, "I talked to
Stern again. He said this is getting to be a big deal. He
told me about California and South Dakota." Stern was
the DCI agent.

"It is," Lucas agreed. "Does this thing have a license
plate on it?"

"Doesn't have a license plate, doesn't have a VIN tag.
I can see where it was, but somebody yanked the tag off
before the fire. There should be a couple more numbers

stamped on the frame rails, but we can't get at those until crime scene is done."

As they were talking, Lucas had circled around to the left rear corner of the RV, where he saw a bowling ball–sized and –shaped dent in the rear quarter panel. He took out his notebook, found the phone number for Larry Royce, the man from Duluth, and called him.

When Royce answered, sounding sleepy and annoyed, Lucas identified himself and said, "We might have found that RV you were talking about. You said there was a dent in the back left panel. The one I'm looking at, it's like somebody might have whacked it with a bowling ball."

"That's it," Royce said.

Lucas rang off and said to Hagestrom, "We need those VINs. They can get us to California plates and that'll get us to the owner, and that'll get us driver's licenses and rap sheets and the whole thing."

Hagestrom said, "Let me call the crime scene crew. See what they say."

Lucas went and leaned against the fender of the Benz while Hagestrom negotiated. When he finished, he said, "They're not happy, but I told them that the whole thing had burned, and been saturated with water and foam, and that the firemen had trampled all over the area around it . . . They said don't mess with anything inside, but it'd be okay if we jacked up the side rails."

"You got some jacks?" Lucas asked.

Between Hagestrom, Lucas, and the firemen, they

had four car jacks, and they managed to get the RV's side rail six inches off the wet ground, along the driver's-side door. Hagestrom stretched out with an inspection mirror, which he carried in his car, and with a flashlight, looked at the bottom rail for ten seconds or so, then stood up and said, "Waste of time."

"What?"

"Chiseled it off. Looks like a while ago—the chiseled part is rusty, and the number is gone. There's another number, but we'd have to get under the engine to look at that one, and that ain't gonna happen with a bunch of little jacks like these," Hagestrom said. "Anyway, they wouldn't know about the first number unless they looked it up, and if they did, they'd know about the second one. Bet that one's gone, too."

Lucas walked around the RV one more time, then down to the dark, shallow river flowing past the impromptu campsite. He called back to Hagestrom, "One thing you might do. This is a big canoeing river, there might be more campsites downstream."

One of the deputies said, "There are. Half dozen of them, anyway."

"Soon as it gets light, you might have somebody down at the different takeout sites, see if anybody saw the RV before it burned. Or people or cars who were with it."

The deputy nodded and said, "I'll get that going."

"Good. That could be critical." Lucas looked over at the RV. It'd be hours before the crime scene crew got inside it. He was fifty miles from his cabin, less than an hour with his flashers, or twenty miles back to a motel in Danbury.

"Hell with it," he said to Hagestrom. "I'll be back tomorrow morning. I'm going to run over to my cabin, get some sleep. I can't think of anything else I can do here."

HE MADE THE cabin by three in the morning, stopping once at an all-night gas station in Hayward for gas, Diet Coke, a quart of milk, and a box of Honey Nut Cheerios. The cabin was dark and absolutely silent as he bounced up the driveway, until he triggered the motion-sensor floodlight on the garage. The only other visible light was on his neighbor's porch. He was unlocking the front door when the neighbor came out in a T-shirt and underpants and yelled, "Lucas?"

"Yeah, it's me."

"Good, I don't have to shoot you. How long you up for?"

"Just overnight," Lucas yelled back.

"Have a good one."

He went inside and had a bowl of cereal, the moon hanging low out over the lake, putting a long streak of silver on it. It was cool, almost cold. He got a spinning rod from a closet, went out on the dock and spent five minutes casting a Rapala into the moonshine, trying for bass or pike, but not trying too hard, smelling the North Woods night, looking at all the little dots of light from the cabins around the lake; then he went inside and tried

not to dream about Skye, and what might have happened
to her.

HE WAS BACK at the burned RV seven hours later.
Hagestrom was gone, replaced by another trooper, more
deputies, and a DCI agent named Mike Maddox, who'd
come in with the crime scene crew. The crew had cut
through the melted side of the RV and a tech in white
coveralls and a face mask was inside, working around the
body, which was lying on one side in the center of the
RV's cramped living area.

Lucas knew right away that it wasn't Skye inside: the
victim was male.

"All we know is that the victim is male, average
height," Maddox told Lucas. "He's too burned to get
anything else, unless we get a DNA hit. No face left,
fingers are gone, hair's gone, eyes are gone, toes are
gone . . . We'll get DNA out of the body, of course, but
it's unlikely we'll get it from anywhere else, given the fire.
Identification is . . . problematic."

"Maybe," said the tech, from inside the van.

Lucas and Maddox stepped closer. Maddox: "Maybe?
I thought you said there was no chance."

"That's before I turned him," the tech said. "I think
I can see the edge of something that might be a wallet.
He was lying on it, protected it from the fire."

"That would be pretty interesting," Maddox said.
"Fish it out of there."

"I've got some work to do before I get there," the tech said. "But I'll get to it."

WHILE ONE TECH worked inside, another was working to get at the second VIN number; and when he got to it, found that it, too, had been chiseled away.

Then they got a break. The inside tech took fifteen minutes to get at it, finally extracting a thin black leather wallet. Another tech took it to a working table and after photographing it, opened it. Inside they found a slightly melted, but still readable, Wisconsin driver's license for a Neal Ray Malin, showing an address in Chippewa Falls, Wisconsin, an expired membership card for an Eau Claire gymnasium, an insurance card for a two-year-old Ford pickup, and nothing else.

"No credit cards, no money. Whoever killed him took the money and credit cards, which means that they might be using them," Lucas said. "If one of them was a debit card, and they tortured him for the code . . ."

"We could get a picture," Maddox said. "Let me get on that."

Maddox tracked it all down in five minutes: Malin was no longer living at the address on the driver's license, but his ex-wife was. She wasn't home and Maddox spoke to the babysitter. She didn't know Malin personally, but said the ex-wife was working at a beauty parlor in Eau Claire.

"I'm going to stick here, but I'll get an Eau Claire cop

to track down his ex and give her the news, and get the credit card numbers," Maddox told Lucas.

"Wonder what a Chippewa Falls guy was doing with these L.A. freaks?"

"A question we're gonna ask," Maddox said. "Maybe he was like that guy in South Dakota—picked up and killed for the hell of it."

"Don't think so," said the crime scene guy inside the RV. "There's blood everywhere. All over the place. Why would they do that, and wind up having to burn their RV?"

Lucas stuck his head inside the RV: "Have you checked all his pockets? Did he have a cell phone on him?"

"I've checked all the pockets, no phone."

Lucas turned back to Maddox. "Have the Eau Claire cops ask his ex if he had a cell phone. People steal phones—if he had one, and they're using it, we might get a GPS location on it."

A few minutes later, Lucas, watching the slow progress inside the RV, said to Maddox, "If you don't mind, I'm going to run down to Chippewa, just to . . . observe. You know, if they locate his apartment."

"Fine by me," Maddox said. "I'll call ahead and tell them that you're coming."

CHIPPEWA FALLS WAS an hour and fifteen minutes away, rolling fast across country on back roads, then down Highway 53. When he arrived, he found that the Chippewa cops had waited for Bob Stern, the Wisconsin investigator, to arrive from Madison. Stern had gotten to Chippewa Falls a few minutes before Lucas, had stopped at the courthouse to pick up a search warrant, and then the cops and Stern had driven in a convoy over to Malin's apartment.

Lucas followed his nav system up the hill on the west side of town, and caught the Wisconsin cops as they were gathering on the lawn of an old clapboard mansion. Stern saw Lucas getting out of his truck and walked over to shake hands. "How's the old lady?"

"Cutting somebody open, about now," Lucas told him. "You divorced yet?"

"Let's not go there," Stern said. "I think she's gonna get the season tickets for the Packers."

"Man, that's . . . inhuman," Lucas said. He looked up at the house, which had an expansive front porch, including a comfortable-looking swing, and a bunch of white, life-sized, wooden-chicken flower boxes showing off bunches of geraniums, marigolds, and petunias. "Nobody's gone in yet?"

"Doing that now," a deputy said.

They watched as a sheriff's deputy with the search warrant climbed the porch and knocked on the door. A minute later an elderly woman in an apron answered, nodded a few times, and then pushed the screen door open.

"Let's go," Stern said. As they crossed the porch he said, "Ugly chickens. Ugly."

THE OLD LADY was the owner of the house. Her name was Ann Webster, and she hadn't seen Malin in two days. Malin, she said, rented the top floor of the house, and had a separate exit out back. One of the deputies was sent around back to cover it, and the rest of the cops climbed a wide oak-floor stairway to a second entry, apparently added when the top floor had been converted into an apartment.

"I was never using it, the stairs are too high, so I thought maybe somebody would rent it," Webster told them. "I had the nicest family here for three years, and then Mr. Malin. He's very quiet. No wild parties or anything like that."

She opened the apartment door with a shiny new key, and they all pushed inside. The apartment was huge, as apartments go, and oddly shaped, as it once had contained an oversized master bedroom, with four more bedrooms down a long hallway, plus two bathrooms. The former master bedroom had been converted into a living room, with a cook's kitchen at the far end, behind a newly built partition.

One of the four bedrooms had been converted into a den, with a comfortable couch, and a compact bar, a stereo system, and a fifty-inch television; another had been converted into an office. The other two were still used as bedrooms, although Webster said she was unaware of any overnight visitors.

"Hell of an apartment," Stern said.

Webster said Malin paid two thousand eight hundred dollars a month for it, and one of the cops said, "That might be the most expensive apartment in Chippewa."

Webster watched as the cops probed the place; she was rolling her hands together as if washing her hands of her tenant. He was a salesman, she said, for horse barns and pole barns, at a place called Collins Metal Buildings in Chippewa.

Lucas and Stern walked through with the cops, looking behind books and under desks, and then the cops got serious about the search, and began pulling the place apart. They found four guns hidden in various drawers, all compact .38 caliber revolvers, fully loaded; and in one drawer, under the revolver, found a couple hundred packs of orange and double-wide Zig-Zags.

The main room had wall-to-wall carpeting, but one of the cops found that it hadn't been tacked down. They rolled it one way, found nothing, rolled it the other way and found several loose floor planks. Under the planks they found twenty tightly sealed, highly compressed bags of marijuana, probably a pound each, and two kilos of cocaine.

"So it wasn't entirely metal buildings," Stern said.

"This is good," Lucas said. "This gives us a contact point for Pilate, a reason for the two of them to be seeing each other."

"Wonder if they took his truck?" Stern asked. "We got people looking for it, haven't heard anything back." He checked with his office, shook his head, and said to

Lucas, "Nothing. If you see a two-year-old blue Ford Explorer pickup . . ."

The search continued: a half hour into it, Stern took a call, wandered into a corner, looked over at Lucas, hung up.

"Malin had a debit card with Wells Fargo. It was used twice, once just before midnight last night, then again a little while after midnight. You know, two separate days, maximum withdrawals both times, six hundred bucks each. There are recognizable photos of the woman who put the card in."

"Excellent," Lucas said.

"Better than that, big guy," Stern said. "You know where they used them at?"

"Where?"

"St. Paul," Stern said.

Lucas stepped back: "Ah, man. I probably passed them on I-35 last night. They were heading south and I was going north."

"Ships in the night," Stern said. "Anyway, Wells Fargo moved the photos to the St. Paul cops, and they sent them down to us. Let me get my iPad, we'll take a look."

He was back in two minutes with the slate. "Got her," he said.

He passed it to Lucas.

Skye was looking straight into the ATM camera, hoodie back on her shoulders. She looked scared to death.

"Skye!"

"That's—" Stern began.

"Oh, boy, oh boy . . . I'm going," Lucas said.

6

THE NIGHT BEFORE:

Neal Ray Malin felt crowded in the RV, like a big dog in a small kennel. When he shifted his weight, he could feel the RV move. He was on his feet, his hair like a haystack, fat cheeks with a bristling beard, facing Pilate, both of them angry, and he said, "I told you what the terms was: the terms was cash on the barrelhead. I don't want to hear this bullshit about promising to pay. That's not how we do business."

"That might not be how you do business in the backwoods, but it's how we do it in L.A.," Pilate said. "I got contacts all over the movie business, we get top price—"

"Excuse me," Malin said, looking around the RV. He was a bulky man with skinny legs. Cowboy boots poked out from under his boot-cut jeans. "I gotta say, this don't exactly look like a big-time director's place."

"Hey! We're good for the money. I got a reputation in L.A.—"

"Look out the window, you fuckin' moron, you see any skyscrapers out there?" Malin asked. "Does that look like Rodeo Drive?"

He said, "Rowdee-oh Drive," and Kristen smirked over her pointed teeth and said, from behind him, "That'd be Rodeo Drive, dumbass. Row-Day-Oh."

"Fuck a bunch of roads, I'm going," Malin said. "If you actually get the cash, I'll be in Chippewa. You got my number."

Pilate put his hand up, toward Malin's chest: "Wait a minute."

"I ain't waiting," Malin said. He was wearing one of those loose Tommy Bahama Hawaiian shirts and now dropped his hand down to his side, slipped it under the shirt, dropped it again, now showing a compact revolver. "I'm going."

"So now you're showing a gun and we're supposed to be business partners?" Pilate said. "That's really fucked up, man."

"Yeah, well . . ." Malin stepped toward Pilate, who didn't step back.

"Get the fuck out of the way," Malin said.

KRISTEN WAS STANDING behind him, and she was such a thin woman that Malin ignored her, despite the filed teeth and all the apocalyptic-themed ink. As Malin pushed toward Pilate, she picked up a ten-inch Henckels chef knife that had been lying under a towel on a sideboard, and *stuck* it in his back.

Nothing tentative about it, she stuck it in him as hard as she could, with a hundred and ten pounds of weight behind it. The knife went through the peachy silk shirt, deflected off Malin's spine, missed his heart to the right, took out a piece of lung, and emerged on the other side of his body, inside his right nipple.

Malin grunted, "Oh," and with an astonished look on his face, turned to her, the gun momentarily forgotten in his hand. Kristen wrenched the knife free and stabbed him in the neck, the razor-sharp blade sliding off to the left, slicing neatly through Malin's carotid artery.

He tried to scream but failed, turned to run from the flailing knife, blood pumping from his neck like water from a hose. He crashed into Pilate, almost fell, then threw an arm at Kristen: she fumbled the knife, flipping it up in the air, and it came down on her arm, between her elbow and hand, slicing it open. She tried to snatch at the blade and cut her hand, badly, through the palm, and Malin hit her in the face and she went down and he rumbled toward the back door, blood still pumping from his neck, his vision going gray like an Apple computer with a bad video card, and then black.

He missed the side door to the outside and crashed through a door at the end of the short hallway, into a bedroom where a young woman lay on the bed, wrapped in silver duct tape.

He never saw her, simply crashed on the bed, pushed himself up, and as Kristen followed him with the knife, blundered into Skye. Kristen stabbed him in the eye, and he managed to backhand her, then plowed all the way through the RV, almost to the front door, where Pilate whacked him with his scepter, and Malin finally went down, the flow of blood from his neck slowing to a gurgle.

Then everything stopped for a few seconds, and finally Pilate said, "Jesus H. Christ."

Six quarts of Malin's blood had painted the inside of the RV: the carpet, the couch, a bolster, an ottoman, the woodwork, towels, the mattress on the bed. The blood had painted all three people in the RV: Pilate, Kristen, and Skye, whom they'd picked up in Duluth.

Kristen spit on Malin's body and said, "Suck on that, asshole."

Pilate said, "Make sure that bitch is still taped up back there." He felt Malin's hip pocket, took out his wallet, extracted three hundred dolllars in twenties and his credit cards, looked at a half-dozen other cards and slips of paper, and found one with four numbers: held the paper up to Kristen and said, "Does that look like an ATM code, or what?"

"I'm bleeding bad," she said. She held her hand out, showing the bloody cut, and wrapped a towel around her forearm. "I need a hospital."

"Not around here," Pilate said. "Not with Malin all carved up like that."

"I need a doc—"

"We'll get you one," Pilate said.

———————

PILATE DROPPED THE wallet on the floor and said, "We need to get his keys. Can you use the phone?"

"Yeah."

"Call the guys, tell them we're heading down to St. Paul. We'll get you to a doc, tell them it was Saturday-night fights at the local parking lot, and some black dude cut on you. You don't know who it was . . ."

As she called, Pilate rolled Malin's body, dug in his pants pocket and came up with the truck keys. Didn't notice Malin's wallet disappearing under his butt. When Raleigh came up on Kristen's phone, Pilate took it and said, "We got a situation. You need to go to a gas station, tell them your buddy ran out of gas, get a five-gallon can if they got one, or a couple of two-gallon cans, get over here to the campground. Gotta be fast: we're heading down to St. Paul."

He rang off and Kristen, who was rewrapping the towel around her arm and hand, asked, "What are we doing?"

Pilate looked around the RV. "No way we can keep this—no way we can clean it up enough. There'll always be blood in it, and if we ever get seriously pushed by the cops, they'll find it. And in a couple days, it's gonna stink real bad. We're gonna drive it out in the woods and burn it. In the meantime, you lay towels on the floor so we can walk on something clean, and get in the shower and hose yourself off. I'm going out, I'll be back in a minute."

"My arm is really hurting—"

"Yeah, yeah, we'll take care of it."

———

PILATE WENT OUT in the cool night air, walked over
to Malin's pickup. Took a while, but in the end found a
kilo of cocaine—the coke he was supposedly buying that
night—and two pounds of weed.

He went back in the RV and said, "Lookee what I
got."

Kristen was just out of the shower. She still had the
towel wrapped around her arm, blood was showing
through. She said, "Oh. My. God. I might be hurtin',
but I'm not gonna be hurtin' long."

Pilate laid out a few lines, and they snorted them up,
then Pilate, high as a kite, went to shower and change
clothes. When he was out, they piled all the bloodstained
clothing on top of the body, then walked around to the
cab, and rolled off into the dark. Raleigh called ten minutes later and asked, "Where you at?"

"Coming down to 77. We're gonna go west on 77
until we find a good spot. You got the gas?"

"Four gallons. I'll be up behind you in three minutes.
The rest of them are coming along behind me. What are
we burning?"

THEY GOT READY to burn the RV in the campground by the river. Skye was still taped up in the back.
The tape wrapped round and round her body, pinning
her arms to her sides, but left her hands free. They cut
the ankle wraps so she could waddle out, but left the

wraps around her knees and thighs, so she couldn't run. As she was edging past Malin's body, she saw his iPhone lying on the blood-soaked couch, almost slipping through the couch cushions. She faked a fall.

"What the fuck are you doin'? Get up, bitch."

"I fell . . . Don't hurt me." Skye managed to get the phone between her hand and her thigh, and hold it there. She struggled to her feet and waddled outside.

They put her in the back of Bony's station wagon, and threw a wool blanket over her. Bony said, "You move that blanket, I'll get the tire iron out and beat the shit out of you."

Skye never saw the RV burn, but she heard the *whump* when the fire started. The four remaining cars in Pilate's convoy fled west on 77, crossed the river into Minnesota, hit I-35, and turned south toward the Twin Cities. Skye could move her hands, from her wrists to her fingertips, but not her arms; nor could she see what her fingers were touching. The back of the old station wagon smelled like dog shit and hay and oil, and the car's shocks were so bad that lying under the blanket was like rolling down a hill in a garbage can.

She was afraid the phone would ring and give her away. The rattling car gave her the cover she needed to turn the phone in her hand, find the power button with her index finger, and hold it down until she thought it was turned off. She then twisted around enough to see that the phone's screen had gone dark.

Then she folded her legs at the knees, and managed to shove the phone into her sock.

In St. Paul, the convoy rolled into Regions Hospital. Kristen went in alone, and told the duty nurse a story about a fight on the Capitol lawn between a bunch of drunk street people. The cops came and took a statement, and three hours later, she was sitting on a wall outside the hospital when Pilate came back.

"Didn't cost me anything, but I had to promise to pay," she said. She'd used Skye's ID, and nobody had looked too closely at the photo.

WHILE KRISTEN WAS being sewn up, Bony took Skye around to two Wells Fargo ATMs, gave her the card and the number, and they pulled out six hundred dollars before midnight, and another six hundred after midnight, the single-day limit on the card. Then they taped her up again, threw her back into the station wagon, and covered her with the blanket. Skye heard Kristen talking outside the car before they were moving, and so knew the other woman had gotten out of the hospital. She felt the car take a couple of turns, then it accelerated: they were back on the freeway. Which one, she didn't know, but she didn't care.

She had one chance: the cell phone. She resolved to wait to use it, until she was sure it would pay off. She knew one cell number for sure: Letty's. She mumbled it over and over as she lay under the blanket, hoping for a break.

She didn't get it that night. They drove for no more than fifteen minutes, then pulled off and parked. Bony rolled down his window and Pilate said, "We'll stay here for the night. We can get water and food, and they don't give a shit how long we stay. And no cops. Give Skye some water, don't have to waste any food on her."

"I'm gonna go ahead and fuck her—"

"Not here, you asshole. Somebody would see the car bouncing up and down, and then we could have trouble. You can fuck her tomorrow."

"You said we were all gonna party, we were all gonna fuck her tonight."

"Well, you might've noticed we had a little problem," Pilate said. "We don't need to attract no cops."

SKYE HAD NO idea what time it must have been, but it was late. People were getting in and out of the car, talking, paid no attention to her. At some point, Bony remembered that he was supposed to get her water, and so came back and ripped some tape off her mouth and let her drink a bottle of spring water. He said, "We're gonna get you airtight, tomorrow, bitch. Think about that."

She slept for a while, or passed out, or something.

SHE GOT HER break the next morning. They were in Hudson, Wisconsin, where the convoy stopped for gas at a Kwik Trip convenience store, and breakfast at the McDonald's next door. Before Bony got out of the car, he said, "You move and I'll kill you. I'll cut your fuckin' throat."

He got out of the car and Skye managed to pull the phone out of her sock and turn it on. When the screen lit up, she lay the phone on the floor and, using her thumb, managed to punch in Letty's number.

Letty answered on the second ring. "Hello?"

"Letty. Pilate's got me. They're going to kill me. I think they killed Henry. They killed a man up by Hayward, they murdered him in the RV and set it on fire. They've got me in the back of Bony's car, they're getting gas, I stole this phone—"

"Skye! Hide the phone, but leave it on. I think they can track cell phones. You have to turn off the ringer. Do you know how to turn off the ringer?"

"No."

"Do you know what kind of phone it is?"

"I think it's an iPhone."

"There should be a button on the side of it . . ." Letty talked her through it, and Skye found the button and pushed it until the ringer-tone indicator was down as far as it would go.

"Okay, I think it's off," Skye said.

"Look in the upper left corner of the screen. Does it say AT&T, or Verizon, or—"

"It says Verizon."

"What kind of car are you in?"

"A station wagon, an old one, it's black and it's funny-looking and it stinks. But I don't know where I am, I think we drove out of the city we were in."

"Okay. When they come back, hide the phone in the

car, in case they search you. Leave it turned on. Now, tell me what happened."

"They picked me up at a mall in Duluth," Skye said. "I was walking in and this car pulls over to the side, and this guy gets out and picks me up, just picks me up and throws me in the back of the car, and Pilate was there and they beat me up and then they taped me up . . ."

They took her to Hayward, she said, where they told her that they were going to take her out in the woods for a party. She didn't believe she'd survive it.

"Then something happened and they killed the man in the RV, where they had me. There was a fight, and Kristen got hurt. Got cut. We drove for a couple of hours, for a long time, anyway, and then they stopped at a hospital. I think we were in Minneapolis or St. Paul, we were at some ATMs and I could tell it was a big city."

"Okay. Hide the phone. I'm going to call my dad."

LUCAS WAS ON I-94, heading back to the Twin Cities, when Letty called. "Skye called me. Pilate's got her, she thinks they're going to kill her . . ."

She gave him the details of Skye's call, and Lucas said, "She's right. They're going to kill her. I gotta call in. Good-bye."

He got the BCA duty officer on the phone and told him the problem. "Get to Verizon, find out where they're at."

He gave the duty officer the number that Skye had called from, then called Stern, the Wisconsin DCI agent, and told him what had happened. "It's possible they came back this way. We'll know in a few minutes."

"Keep me up."

Lucas turned on his flashers and went past the town of Menomonie at a hundred and ten. The duty officer called back and said, "The phone's on Highway 63 in Wisconsin, headed north, they're south of Clear Lake."

"I went through Menomonie a few minutes ago. I'm gonna take County Q, I think it goes north—"

"No, no. I'm looking at a map. Keep going past Q, just a couple more miles up to 128, you'll be faster and closer."

"Okay, you get onto the county sheriffs up there, I don't know what counties they are, tell them to look for an old black station wagon, maybe California plates. You should be able to vector them in pretty close, tell them it might be part of a convoy, everybody in it is wanted for multiple murder . . . You gotta get me there as quick as you can. I'm going to call my guy at the DCI."

Lucas got Stern on the phone again. Stern said, "I'll get my duty guy on our net up there, we need to talk to your guy about what Verizon is telling them. You say this girl is a witness to the Malin killing?"

"Apparently. And I gotta go, my turn's coming up."

Lucas took the off-ramp, took a fast right past the convenience store, drove past a half dozen cars on the wrong side of the road, punched up the duty officer again, and said, "I'm on 128."

"Take it right straight north to 64. They're in Clear

Lake right now. Okay, we got nothing going yet in Clear Lake, but we got a highway patrolman coming south on 63, he's in Turtle Lake. Hang on, hang on . . . Okay, I'm talking to a guy in Madison, he's saying that the patrolman is talking to the sheriff's department up there, there's a lake, right on the highway, Magnor, everything squeezes down."

"I know it."

"They're going to take him there," the duty officer said.

Lucas went past Glenwood City about as fast, he suspected, as anyone had ever done that, watching his nav system for a jog in the road, got through it just fine, then almost drove right through a T intersection, got straight, and went on.

"Lucas, the phone's north of Clear Lake, they're heading for a collision up at Magnor. We got two deputies coming up behind him, too."

"Okay. You told them about the girl? The hostage?"

"Yeah, they're all clear on that," the duty officer said. "They're only three or four miles out."

Lucas came up on Highway 64, took a left, and ran hard the three or four miles to the intersection of 63. Now he was behind them, but still well back, out of the action.

"What's happening?"

"I don't know, I don't know . . . Verizon . . . ah, heck, Verizon said the phone's turned left on a back road. Turned left. They were only two miles out of Magnor, the deputies coming up behind saw him make the turn. They say he's moving fast now, they're strung out behind him, they're all running behind him, chasing him."

"Shit, one of the other cars in the convoy saw the cops and they called him."

The duty officer went away for a minute, then came back and said, "They didn't see anything that looked like a convoy. They're all over this guy, they're right behind him."

"I'm coming, I'm coming."

"Where are you?"

"Coming up on Clear Lake, a couple miles out," Lucas said.

"Okay, if you see a JJ road just on the north side of Clear Lake—"

"I see it on the nav."

"That'll take you . . . Okay, the guy's off the road, he ran through an intersection, he's off the road in the ditch."

"What about the girl?" Long silence, and Lucas repeated it, "They got the girl?"

"No. I'm hearing that the guy's still in the car, he's got a gun and he's going to kill this girl if they don't get him another car."

Lucas took the corner at JJ and headed north. "I'm north on JJ, get me in there."

He saw them from a mile away, what looked like ten cop cars with their flashers going. He came up fast, saw cops behind cars, saw an ancient Chevy Cavalier station wagon in a bean field at the intersection of a narrow side road. It looked as though the driver of the station wagon had tried to make the turn, but missed it, ran through a fence out into the bean field, where he bogged down.

Lucas pulled up behind the last sheriff's patrol car, climbed out, and jogged down to the lead car, where the Wisconsin patrolman and a couple of deputies were crouched. The patrolman said, "You're Davenport?"

"Yeah."

"Stern is on the way. He'll be a while, though."

"You talking to the guy?"

"Off and on. He'll roll down that side window and scream at us, then roll it back up. He seems . . . I mean, nuts. I mean like, you know, he needs a doctor and medication. Or maybe he's just high. He was yelling some stuff at us, like the Fall is coming, and we're all scared shitless, and it won't do us any good because we're all going down . . . Sounds crazy to me."

"Did he say what he wants?"

"He said he wants a patrol car or he's going to kill her. We told him a guy was coming to talk to him, and we could work something out."

"He shoot at anybody?"

"Not yet, but he's got a gun. Randy's got some glasses, he's looking at him."

He pointed over at another car, where a deputy was sitting behind a rear wheel, looking at the car in the field with a pair of heavy binoculars. "Looks like a big old revolver."

"I'll go look. But what do you think?"

"Well, honest to God, you know, Phil over there is on

the regional SWAT team, he's got his rifle, he could take him out." Lucas looked back to where a guy had a rifle propped on a sandbag over a patrol car's bumper. "But we're shooting through that window glass. My inclination is, if it looks like he's going to do something . . . I'd try to take him out. I mean, if he freaks out and shoots the girl, then it'll be too late, and he seems to be freakin' out."

"Let me go look," Lucas said.

"Sheriff's coming down, he'll be here in five, ten minutes."

Lucas duckwalked over to the car where the deputy was keeping watch with the binoculars. "Can I look?"

"He's waving the gun around. Looks like he's arguing with whoever's in the back."

Lucas took the glasses, focused. The car was only a hundred feet away, and with the big image-stabilized Canons, he could see individual hairs in the man's beard. He looked like he was in his late twenties, had what appeared to be a propeller-shaped tattoo, or maybe an elongated infinity sign, on his forehead. He was shouting into the back, kept poking the gun toward the back, then swiveling to look out at the cops.

"Doesn't look good," he said.

"No, it doesn't."

Lucas handed the binoculars back to the cop, sat with his back to the car, and called Letty. "If I message Skye, will the phone make a sound?"

"I don't know. I think so. But you could call her—the phone won't ring, and she should see the screen light up."

"Give me that number again," Lucas said.

Lucas took the number, then crawled over to the car's bumper, whistled at the highway patrolman, and waved him over. When he got there, Lucas said, "You're running this scene—I've got no jurisdiction. I think I can call her without tipping the guy off. What do you think?"

"I don't know. What do *you* think?"

"The guy's not just *acting* crazy—we've got good reason to think he *is* crazy. I think if we put the rifle on him, and if I call and he reacts, then if it looks like he's going to use the gun, we take him."

The cop bit his lip, thinking, then said, "We've got to do something. I'm not sure we can wait until the sheriff gets here."

"The question is, can our shooter hit him through the window glass?"

"I asked him that, and he said he's shooting solid core. He says he's pretty square to the window glass, and if he shoots at the guy's head, the bullet might deflect a bit, but he'll still hit his head somewhere. A smaller target would be more of a question."

Lucas nodded. "Okay. I'm gonna call her. You tell the rifle guy to be ready, but don't shoot unless it looks like he's about to pull the trigger on her." To the cop with the glasses, he said, "Watch him. Tell me what he does."

He called. When the phone stopped ringing, there was silence. He said quietly, "This is Lucas, Letty's dad. If you push the round button at the bottom of the phone, the main screen will come up. Then push the green button on the screen, too. It'll switch you to phone mode. Could you do that?"

The cop with the binoculars said, "He's just sitting there. Looks like he's talking to himself."

Lucas said into the phone, "On the bottom line, there's a square with a lot of dots in it—the keypad. Push that button. When the keypad comes up, push the bottom of the phone against your body—that's where the keypad sound comes from. You need to muffle that. If you've done that, tap any button. Don't hold it down, just tap it quick."

A second later, he got a beep.

"Good. We're talking. Are you hurt? If you're hurt bad and need an ambulance right now, tap a button."

Silence.

"Good. You're not hurt. If you think this guy is going to shoot you, that he's seriously going to do it, tap a button."

Beep.

The patrolman said, "Damnit."

Lucas said into the phone, "If you think there's any chance that you can talk him down, give me a beep."

Silence.

Then a man's voice: "This is it, this is it. No way out. No way out now. They ain't coming back for me, they ain't comin' back. Piece-of-shit car, piece of shit. *You* ain't goin' no place, don't even think about it, bitch. I'll blow your fuckin' brains all over the car, that's for sure."

The guy with the binoculars said, "That's him. I can read his lips when I hear the words, she's holding the phone so we can hear him."

A cop called, "The sheriff's here."

———

A MINUTE LATER, the sheriff scuttled up, half bent over, crouched next to the patrolman. He was a short, thick man with sandy hair, a brush mustache, and round, gold-rimmed glasses. "Are we talking to him?"

"We're yelling at him, but we're afraid to make a move any closer," the patrolman said. "Says he'll kill the girl if we do. We're talking about having Phil take him out."

The sheriff looked back three cars, where the shooter was sitting behind a patrol car, looking at the fugitive car through a scope. "If we have to."

"I'd really like to talk to this guy—he could probably give us all the rest of them," Lucas said.

The sheriff looked at him and asked, "Who are you?"

Lucas gave him the five-second version, and explained the phone connection with Skye, and the sheriff said, "Phil could probably actually shoot him in the shoulder of his gun arm. I mean, shooting normally, Phil could put three shots through a dime at that range. With the window, it's more of a problem. But if he could take that shoulder out, we could rush him—"

The phone beeped, then beeped again and Lucas said, "If there's a problem, beep me again."

Beep.

Then the man's voice again, "Say good-bye, bitch, 'cause you're going first. They're gonna shoot me, but I don't give a shit no more, I don't give a shit no more . . ."

The man sounded frantic, whipping himself up for it. The deputy with the binoculars said, his voice calm enough, "He's turning around in the seat, he's kneeling on the seat looking toward the back . . ." and the sheriff scrambled away, toward the car where the rifleman was set up.

From where Lucas was sitting with the phone, he couldn't see the shooter, but the patrolman could, and Lucas called, "Is he—?"

BAM!

7

LUCAS SAW THE sheriff bolt toward the target car, pistol in his hand, and Lucas followed, well back. The sheriff stumbled through the beans and almost went down, and Lucas worried that he'd shoot himself, or somebody else, but he didn't, and a few seconds later, they were looking through the side window at a dead guy in the front seat of the car. The rifle round had struck him in the cheekbone and gone through his head, knocking him back into the front seat.

Lucas said, "The girl's in the back," and a deputy arriving at that moment yanked on the back hatch, but it was locked, and the sheriff pulled open the driver's-side door and reached across the dead man's legs to pull the keys out of the ignition, and they all went around to the back of the car and unlocked the hatch.

They could see the unmoving body in the back, covered with a green woolen blanket. Lucas pulled it off and Skye was looking up at him, eyes wide with fear.

Lucas said, "Skye: you're okay."

The sheriff said, "Don't let her see that," and tipped his head toward the front of the car. And, "Tom, get that tape off her."

A deputy produced a switchblade and began cutting the tape off Skye's legs and she said, "They were going to kill me. Last night Pilate told Bony to give me some water but he wouldn't have to bother with feeding me, they were going to kill me today . . ."

"Gonna get you to the hospital, honey," the sheriff said. "You gotta be pretty shook up." To Lucas he said, "We called in an ambulance, they're on the way, oughta be here . . ."

THE DEPUTY FINISHED taking off the tape that bound her arms to her body, and Skye tried to get out of the car, but when she put her feet down, nearly collapsed. Lucas caught her under the arms and pushed her back until she was sitting on the edge of the trunk. He said, "Letty told me that you were a witness to a killing last night."

"Who's Letty?" the sheriff asked. Lucas gave him another five-second explanation, and then Skye said, "I heard it all, and saw the end of it. I was taped up in the back bedroom and the doors on that thing were about as thick as tinfoil. Pilate got connected to some dope dealer here and was going to buy some cocaine from him, but when the dope dealer got here, Pilate didn't have the money. He was trying to buy on credit—"

"On credit?" the sheriff said. "Dope?"

"That's what he tried, and the guy tried to get out. I guess he had a gun. Pilate said something about him having a gun, but then there was a fight and this guy came crashing through the bedroom door and there was blood gushing out of his neck, like they cut his throat or something, and Pilate told Kristen—Kristen got cut bad, they talked about that, they took her to a hospital, I think in St. Paul, last night. Anyway, Pilate said that the RV wouldn't be safe anymore because there was no way they could clean up all the blood. I mean, there was blood everywhere, you wouldn't believe it, so he decided to burn it . . ."

She told the story, sitting on the edge of the car, of how she got the phone, and how she called Letty, and how they took her off the street in Duluth. Then she turned her eyes up to Lucas and said, "I think they might have killed Henry. Have you heard?"

Lucas shook his head. "Henry . . . didn't make it."

She'd been stressed and talking fast but showing no tears . . . until Lucas told her that Henry hadn't made it, and then she suddenly began leaking tears and flopped backward into the trunk space, sobbing. The sheriff pulled on Lucas's sleeve and Lucas stepped back and the sheriff whispered, "We gotta talk. Who in the heck is Henry?"

"Her companion. They killed him in South Dakota. Let's get her on the way to the hospital, and I'll fill you in."

THE AMBULANCE ARRIVED, and though Skye said she wasn't hurt, Lucas put her in the ambulance and told her, "Just ride along with this. You don't have to be bleeding to be hurt."

She no longer had her pack—she thought it might have burned in the RV—but her walking staff was in the backseat of the car in the bean field.

"If I could get that . . . I've had it a long time."

"I'll see to it," Lucas said. "They'll probably want to take fingerprints off it, in case one of the other people handled it. So, it could be a while."

"Okay. Call Letty," Skye said. "Tell her what happened. She saved my life."

"I will," Lucas said.

The ambulance left for the hospital in Menomonie and Lucas stepped away from the deputies and the post-shooting bureaucracy, and called Letty. Letty answered halfway through the first ring and Lucas said, "We got her. The guy she was with was killed."

He told her what had happened, and Letty said, "I'm coming to the hospital."

"Not a bad idea, you might be her only friend. Uh, take your mom's car."

"Mom's not here."

"Letty . . ."

"I'm coming," she said.

She hung up and Lucas looked at the phone and said, "Ah, shit."

She'd be coming, all right, in his Porsche.

She had a right foot like a ship's anchor.

LUCAS GAVE THE sheriff everything he knew, from the murder in Los Angeles to the crucifixion in South Dakota, to the murder of Malin the night before, the search of Malin's apartment, and the phone call to Letty.

The sheriff stuck a wad of Copenhagen under his tongue as he listened, chewed, spit once, and then said, "Those sonsofbitches come to *this* county, they won't be walking away."

"I don't think they're looking to walk away," Lucas said. "They're like a tornado: they don't think about too much at all. They just kill and move on."

"So we're shifting this basically over to the DCI? To Stern?"

"I guess. Nobody knows exactly where these people are, or what their cars look like. Probably get Skye to do some identikits."

Another car came rolling fast from the south, grille lights flashing, and the sheriff said, "That's probably Stern now."

IT WAS. STERN looked at the body in the car and said, "One down. Would have liked to have talked to him."

"I made the call," the sheriff said, spitting again. "We thought he was about to shoot the girl."

Stern slapped him on the shoulder and said, "I'm not criticizing, Jim, we all would've done the same thing." He turned to Lucas: "Did the girl give us anything useful?"

"One thing. There were two people present at the murder last night, this Pilate guy, and one of the women, named Kristen. Skye said she got cut pretty bad and she was treated at an emergency room, probably in the Twin Cities. We should get some video of her."

"We need that right now," Stern said.

"I'll call on my way down to Menomonie," Lucas said. "About Skye. You guys are going to want to wring her out, but when you're done . . . she's sort of a friend of my daughter. If you want, I'll put her in a hotel in St. Paul and we'll keep an eye on her."

"Probably as good as it's gonna get, if she doesn't have an address," Stern said. "Appreciate the offer."

Before Lucas left, he took the highway patrolman aside and asked, "Are you guys running any speed traps down on I-94?"

"Just curious?"

"Well, my daughter's coming over, she's a friend of Skye's. She's probably upset and driving too fast, because she's kinda freaked out. If I could slow her down a bit . . ."

The patrolman checked and found a trap near Exit 10, at Roberts, Wisconsin, not far from the Minnesota line. Lucas called Letty from his truck: "Where are you?"

"I-94."

"But not in Wisconsin, yet," Lucas said.

"Not yet. Not quite."

"The Wisconsin highway patrol is running a trap near Exit 10, that's ten miles on the other side of the river. Watch the mile signs."

"Got it. I'm driving slow. I'll tell you, though, a seven-speed manual seems a little overcooked for this bitch. You can keep it in fifth and still blow the doors off anything else on the road."

"Letty, goddamnit . . ."

"Just honking your horn, Dad. I'll see you in Menomonie."

LUCAS HAD JUST gotten in the Benz when he saw Stern jogging toward him. He rolled down the window, and Stern came up and said, "He had a cell phone. We looked at the recents and he had a call just a minute or so before he got off the highway. That had to be somebody else in the caravan who spotted the roadblock being set up."

"Had to be," Lucas said.

"I'll get the numbers down to Madison and we'll start pinging them," Stern said. "We oughta have a location pretty quick."

LUCAS WAS ALMOST as far from the hospital as Letty was, the difference being that she was driving a Porsche on an interstate highway and he was driving an SUV on back roads. On the way down, he called the BCA duty officer and told him about the woman who'd been treated for knife cuts, and asked him to check the local hospitals.

"Sometime right before or after midnight, probably," he said.

"We'll get it going."

LUCAS WAS NOT surprised when he pulled into the hospital parking lot and saw his Porsche already there. When he walked past it, he could hear the ticking as the engine cooled. Inside the emergency room, Skye was sitting on a bed, talking to Letty, who was sitting in a visitor's chair.

A nurse called to Lucas, "Are you a relative?"

"I'm a cop," he said.

She nodded and he got a chair from an empty bay and put it next to Letty's. He asked Skye, "You okay? I mean, more or less?"

"Yeah. They gave me some dope. Said it would help relieve my anxiety, which is good, because I'm pretty anxious. How did Henry die?"

"Stabbed, I think," Lucas lied. "I haven't seen the autopsy report, they're doing that in South Dakota. I'm sorry. I know you guys . . ."

Skye said, "Yeah," and "His folks still live in Johnson City, Texas, if that makes any difference to anyone."

"Somebody will contact them. Probably already have," Lucas said.

"He was a good guy," Skye said. "Good traveler. I

think the dope is taking the edge off, but I'm . . . awful sad."

"Proves you're a human being," Letty said.

Lucas said, "Some Wisconsin cops are going to talk to you . . ."

STERN AND THE sheriff's chief investigator arrived together twenty minutes later. They interviewed Skye for an hour, with Lucas and Letty chiming in from time to time. Pilate and his disciples had taunted her, talking about *playing* with her, which she understood to mean rape and murder. She'd not been raped, because the disciples had been too busy. If the dope dealer from Chippewa Falls hadn't shown up, she said, she'd already be dead, but his murder had sidetracked Pilate's plans.

Skye only had first names for Pilate's crew, and not all of those. She thought they might be on the way to a county fair somewhere, and then on to a Juggalo Gathering at a farm near Hayward, Wisconsin.

Lucas volunteered a BCA artist to create portraits of Pilate, Kristen, and the others, and Stern accepted the offer.

When they were done talking, a social worker and a doctor took Skye for a private interview.

While she was being interviewed, Stern got on the phone with the sheriff at the shooting scene, and to California. He came back with a notebook and said, "The dead guy's name was Arnaty Roscow, which might be short for some longer Russian name. But that's the name on his driver's license. He's done time twice, in California, both times for burglary. The L.A. cops said he was in the commercial burglary business for years, probably knocked over a couple hundred places, mostly houses on the Westside of Los Angeles, and Malibu and Santa Barbara. There's quite a bit on him—they'll run down his known contacts for us, because of that Kitty Place murder. They're hoping we'll clear it for them."

"If we can get our hands on Pilate, we will," Lucas said. "That murder out in South Dakota was like a fingerprint."

Skye was released a few minutes later and came out clutching an amber bottle with thirty blue pills.

Lucas had already suggested that they put Skye back in the Holiday Inn, and Letty said she might see if she could get an adjoining room just for the night; "and we need to get you some clothes."

"I need everything," Skye said. "They just burned all my stuff."

"Macy's, and then over to REI," Letty said.

"Don't need the Macy's," Skye said. "REI is good enough."

"Get what you need, you'll have lots of room in the Benz," Lucas said. He held out his hand to Letty. "The keys."

IN THE BENZ, Letty asked Skye, "How are you? Really?"

"Screwed up," Skye said. "I was bouncing around in

that car like a loose tire; everything hurts. They gave me some pretty good dope, though. If I didn't have it, they'd probably have to put me in a rubber room somewhere. Poor Henry. Poor, poor Henry. I hope he didn't suffer."

Letty said, "He was too young to die."

When Letty had determined that Skye was functioning, she took her straight out of Wisconsin, to an REI store in Roseville, a suburb of St. Paul. "Go ahead and get whatever you need," Letty said. "Dad gave me an American Express, I don't even think he looks at the bills. Besides, he already said it was all right."

Skye got underwear and shirts and cargo pants and six pairs of pumpkin-orange socks, and at Letty's urging, a new pair of boots, a decent pack, a top-end three-season sleeping bag, heavy long johns, and a variety of cooking and eating gear: a compact stove, fuel bottle, camping silverware, a lightweight parka, and gloves—"I'll be down south before I need them, but it can get pretty frosty even way down south, in Mississippi and Texas."

And, "I need a knife."

"Well, let's find a good one," Letty said.

They settled on a Gerber survival knife, with a five-inch blade, for sixty bucks.

When they left the store, Skye said, "I owe you. This isn't just a donation. I owe you."

"I'm okay with that," Letty said. "You can owe us. Someday you'll do good, and you can pay us back. I'll get you some cash—you're going to need to eat until everything is done with."

_____

LETTY GOT TWO rooms with a connecting door, at the Holiday Inn, and they wound up staying two nights. Skye was an interesting talker and an interested listener, and got Letty talking about her younger days as a trapper and a shooter of crooked cops and cartel killers.

"I'd never ever shoot anyone if it wasn't self-defense, but that's what it was," Letty said. "I sometimes think I might have a touch of the sociopath, or more than a touch, because none of it ever made me feel the least bit bad."

"But if you were a sociopath . . . wouldn't that mean when those cartel killers came after the family, you would have taken care of yourself first? Instead, you got between them—the Mexicans and your family."

Letty smiled: "I never thought of it that way. Thank you. I guess I'm not a sociopath, and I'd kinda started to worry about it."

"I don't know how killing somebody would make me feel, but I guess I might feel bad after a while," Skye said. "I can see how if it was kill or be killed, I'd rather be the one who stays alive. But I believe I'd lose a lot of sleep over it."

"Then you're a nicer person than I am," Letty said. "I never missed a minute's sleep."

THE NEXT MORNING, Letty drove Skye to Lucas's office. Lucas had just gotten copies of a video taken at Regions Hospital. He'd looked at it once, and had been about to call the support services to cut some frames out of it, when Letty and Skye walked in.

"Is this the woman you call Kristen?" Lucas asked Skye, putting the video back up on his computer.

Skye crouched over the screen, watching, then said, "Yes! That's her. For sure."

"The video's not so good."

"I don't care. That's her. You can't see it, but she's got these pointy teeth. She filed them down herself."

"All right. I'll have the best stills printed out, and you can talk to our artist, help him make some pictures of the other people." To Letty, he said, "This will take a while."

"I don't care. I want to watch."

SKYE DID FOUR identikits, of Pilate, Bell, Raleigh, and a woman named Ellen.

While she did that, Lucas had gone to check on his other cases. Jenkins and Shrake were at Ben Merion's cabin at Cross Lake, and told him that there'd been no problem finding places in the woods that looked dug up, but, "There are about a million of them. We saw a squirrel actually making one of them, burying acorns, and there are squirrels all over the place. The idea was good, but the execution is impossible."

"So, you're coming back?"

"Yeah, we'll see you tomorrow, I guess. Go back to looking for computer chips."

Del had not yet found the guy with the safe full of diamonds.

He called Stern, who said, "We got something weird on that Roscow's phone . . . that Bony guy."

"Weird's usually not good," Lucas said.

"Not good in this case," Stern said. "We pinged them all, and the only returns we've gotten so far are from California. On the most recent calls, we got nothing at all. Our guy here says they may be pulling the batteries on their phones."

"That doesn't help," Lucas said. "They'll use them sooner or later, though. Keep pinging them."

When he came back to Letty and Skye, he checked out the identikits and said, "Not bad. We could get something from these. I'll send them over to Stern, he said he'd plaster northern Wisconsin with them, get them in all the papers up there."

"Are you sure they're up there?" Skye asked.

"We're not sure of anything, but that's where they were headed. By now, they could be in New Orleans."

After a fast lunch, Lucas, Letty, and Skye went over to Swede Hollow Park to look for other travelers. They found three, sitting together, passing a joint, and Skye told them about Henry—one of the three knew him—and asked about Pilate. None of them knew him, or had heard about him.

Skye caught up on gossip, then Lucas went back to work and Letty and Skye drifted off, caught a movie at the Mall of America, bought a burner phone for Skye with twenty-five hours of talk time, bought a hat for Letty, ate again, and went back to the Holiday Inn. Letty broke out her laptop to check her Facebook for news from her friends, and punched in "Pilate," and got nothing but the wrong one.

Skye always carried one big fat paperback novel with her, and she'd spent some of the money Letty gave her on a Diana Gabaldon Outlander novel. In between spates of talk, she'd read the book, and she was reading it when Letty took a bathroom break.

During the day, nobody had wanted to talk to Skye about Henry, and she'd begun to feel that something was being hidden from her. When Letty went into the bathroom, she put the book down, stepped over to Letty's laptop, which was showing the Google page, and typed "Henry Mark Fuller" into the search field.

The front page of the *Rapid City Journal*'s blog page popped up, with the headline "Murdered Man Was Crucified," and beneath that, a bad picture of Henry, taken from his high school yearbook.

With increasing horror, she read through the news story, based on the autopsy done by a South Dakota medical examiner. Henry had been crucified, castrated, and slashed nearly to pieces.

She barely heard the toilet flush, and the bathroom door open, and then Letty, behind her, blurt, "Oh, shit."

Skye turned around, tears streaming down her face: "You didn't tell me."

"You were already screwed up. You didn't need to know the details," Letty said.

"I needed to know . . ." Skye said. "Could you . . . uh,

I want to read everything I can find, but I don't want you here to watch me. I'm gonna cry a lot. Could you go out and get some Cokes or something? I won't be real long."

"Sure. Half an hour?"

"That should be enough. I want to see what all the papers say."

When Letty was gone, Skye went to Craigslist and dropped an ad: "Going to Juggalo Gathering near Hayward? I need ride, will pay $50."

She listed the number for the burner phone, then dropped back to Google and typed in Henry's name again. All the daily papers in South Dakota had the story, and a couple across the border in Wyoming and down in Nebraska. They were all the same, reprints of an AP story based on the *Rapid City Journal*'s initial report. She read them all anyway.

When Letty got back, Skye gestured at the laptop and said, "Nobody cares. They wrote one story and everybody copied it, and that's the last we'll hear about Henry Mark Fuller, because nobody gives a shit about people like him. Like us."

"That's not true," Letty said. "A lot of people give a shit, which is how you got pulled out of the back of that car."

Skye dropped onto one of the beds and cried, "Ah, jeez . . ."

THEY TALKED OFF and on until midnight and then Skye went off to her room and flopped on the bed and failed to sleep. Letty managed to sleep, after two o'clock. Skye got a phone call at seven, a male voice: "This is Juggalo Central, two of us going today. We've got two seats."

She arranged to get picked up at nine, at Mears Park, said she'd buy both seats, got them for thirty-five dollars each, but she wanted to take a pack. "We got that much room." Skye slipped out and ran to Swede Hollow, where she found some friends, including a reliable guy named Carl. When she asked if he wanted to go to the Juggalo Gathering, he said, "I was thinking I might."

"I've got two seats," Skye said. "I got a motel room, you can take a shower so you don't smell too much."

Carl said sure, and they hurried back to the motel. Carl showered with the motel's perfumed soap, put on his cleanest clothes, and at eight-fifteen, they were gone. Skye left a note for Letty that said: "Thanks for everything, I will pay you back someday. You're a good friend, but I just can't handle this. I got to travel on."

Letty found the note when she walked through the connecting door at nine o'clock, as Skye and Carl loaded into the ride.

Carl said, "This is gonna be great, huh? Jug-A-Lo, know what I'm saying?"

LETTY RAN DOWN to the Benz and headed to Swede Hollow. She spotted a guy they'd talked to the day before, sitting on a sleeping bag playing a recorder, and hurried over. "I'm looking for Skye. Has she been by?"

"She's gone," the guy said. "She came down and got Carl, said she had a ride waiting. Don't know where they were going, but they were in a hurry."

"Goddamnit." Letty walked back to her car, sat and called Lucas, and told him that Skye had taken off.

Lucas said, "How'd she arrange a ride?"

"Well . . . I don't know. Maybe she knew somebody."

"I thought you were with her."

"I was, until midnight. She found an online newspaper article about the autopsy on Henry and kinda freaked out. Anyway, she's gone."

"Damnit, we need her here," Lucas said. "If you're down there anyway, ask around. Maybe somebody else knows where she went."

"All right."

"Be careful."

Letty got fifty feet back into the park, when a thought struck her, and she turned, went back to the car, turned on her laptop and called up the browsing history. The link was right at the top: Craigslist. She drove five minutes to a Caribou Coffee, got online, went to Craigslist and to Rideshare, and found Skye's advertisement from the night before.

She called Lucas back: "I know where she went."

She told him how she found out, and he said, "Good. Stern will be up there, or at least have some guys up there and they know what she looks like. I'll get them to track her down."

"They won't recognize her if she goes as a Juggalo," Letty said. "I've been doing some research on them.

They wear costumes and clown faces. It's hard to recognize anybody."

"Well, we gotta look," Lucas said. "We really need her back."

"That's your last word? 'We really need her back'?"

"Well, what the heck am I supposed to say?" Lucas asked. "We do need her back. And we'll find her."

Letty was fuming when she got off the phone. Lucas had gone bureaucratic on her and Skye was headed for serious trouble. She didn't want to do it. She knew Lucas would go ballistic—but she pulled out and headed for I-35.

The Juggalo Gathering was two and a half hours away.

8

PILATE AND HIS crew freaked when they learned what had happened to Bony and that the cops had gotten Skye back.

Chet found out at a convenience store, where a television was tuned to a Duluth station. The shooting and rescue were big news. He drove back to the new campground at eighty miles an hour, about all he could get out of the aging Corolla, to tell the others.

Pilate was gone when he got there—the rest of the crew said that he and Kristen had gone to cruise used-RV lots, planning to trade a half kilo of lightly cut cocaine for an RV, if they could find the right guy.

The crew stood around remembering Bony and some of the stunts he'd pulled. Like the time he screwed this lady teacher and then told her that he was a student at her school—he looked young enough—and blackmailed her into what he called Stupid Teacher Tricks. And he did mean tricks.

The new campground was fifteen miles east of Hayward, Wisconsin, and was mostly empty, except for a carnival crew setting up a Tilt-A-Whirl in one corner of the open field, getting ready for the Juggalo Gathering that would start the next day. They were still standing in a semicircle, talking about Bony, when Pilate and Kristen pulled in, Pilate driving what turned out to be another Winnebago Minnie, this one a 1999 model with eighty-six thousand miles on it, but otherwise, cherry.

He got out, grinning, picked up on the vibe and the grin drained away: "What?"

"The cops shot Bony. He's dead," Laine said. "Chet saw it on the TV."

"What!"

"Dude, they shot him. It's on TV," Chet said. "The cops got that chick back, and she's gonna tell them everything."

"He was my main *man*," Pilate wailed, spittle flying around the semicircle of disciples. "They gunned him down?"

PILATE, RALEIGH, AND Richie piled into Chet's car, and they went back to the gas station, where the story never did show up again. They waited so long that the guy behind the counter finally asked them what they were watching for, and Pilate told him that they thought they might have known the girl rescued by the cops, who was a Juggalo. The counter man pulled an iPad out from behind the cigarette rack, called up the TV station's website, and let them look at the cached news story.

The reporter had heard from a sheriff's deputy that the kidnapping victim had managed to conceal and turn on a cell phone, which the authorities had then tracked to the ambush point. The victim had told them that her kidnappers had been responsible for murdering a Chippewa Falls man who'd been found dead in a burning RV.

"You know what this fuckin' means?" Pilate asked, back in the car again. "That bitch is gonna tell them what we look like. They're gonna make those drawings of us, and plaster them all over the fuckin' state."

"We gotta get out of here," said Richie. "Like way gone."

"We gotta do something," Pilate said, toying with one of his beard braids. "But they don't know we're at the Gathering. We put on some clown makeup, nobody'll recognize us and we'll be good for a while. Move the rest of that cocaine and we'll have the bucks to get on up to the Michigan Gathering, that's a long way from here. Put on the clown faces again, and by the time that's over, nobody'll remember us."

"I don't know—I think they'll remember, at least around here," Chet said.

"If I could get my hands on that bitch Skye, I'd skin her alive," Pilate said. And, "Who's got the Cheetos? Pass them up here."

"What are we going to do about Bony?" Raleigh asked.

"Nothin'. He's dead," Pilate said. "He's outa here. No point in doing anything."

"It seems like—"

"Nothin'," Pilate said. "Dead gotta take care of themselves."

"I was thinking some kind of . . . words," Raleigh said.

"Leave the thinking to me, dickwad," Pilate said. Then he nodded. "But yeah. That's a good idea. Words is good. I'll talk tonight."

That night they did almost half of the remaining cocaine, getting high with Bony, and Pilate said his Words.

"Bony was our friend. He was an outlaw. Y'all remember the time he got that .22 and went up Malibu Road shooting cats out the window of his car, and about fifty cops came and how he didn't give a shit, he just turned right around and did it again? Remember how he rolled that guy's antique Porsche down that boat ramp into the ocean? We were sitting up there laughing our asses off and the guy was down there crying tears about his fuckin' Porsche?"

And so on.

They were up late that night and got up late the next morning, and the first thing Pilate saw when he climbed out of the new RV was an enormous fat man riding past in the back of a John Deere Gator.

He was shirtless, with black rings painted around his

tiny pink nipples, and was wearing a black, white, and red clown face, and was throwing bottles of Faygo to bystanders. Another clown was driving the cart.

The Juggalos were coming in.

THE JUGGALO GATHERING was on a run-down farm east of Hayward, off Highway 77. Roughly the size of a football field, the site had until recently been used to grow alfalfa. At one end, Juggalos were unloading cardboard boxes full of firewood from a flatbed trailer, to be used to construct a huge bonfire. At the other end, more Juggalos were setting up a stage, for music groups. Between them, but closer to the fire, a carny crew was setting up a low-rent Ferris wheel beside the Tilt-A-Whirl.

Designated parking areas were set up on both sides of the field, marked with red plastic tape stretched between poles; and rows of blue fiberglass porta-potties were set up on the far sides of both parking lots.

Pilate and his disciples had set themselves apart, in a circle at the far end of one of the parking areas—the end zone of the field, to the left and slightly behind the stage.

Skye got to the campground at ten o'clock. She'd ridden up with her friend Carl and two guys, named Siggy and Ivan, both Russians. The Russians had been cool guys, and had face paint that they were happy to pass around. Carl helped make up Skye's face as a sad clown and she did his as a happy face, but when they got out of the car and collected their packs, Carl said, "We don't look like Juggalos. We look like travelers with clown faces."

Skye nodded. "Let's see if we can find some guys and ditch the bags."

"Get something to eat," Carl said. "You got money?"

"Yeah. We're good."

There were already a couple of hundred people at the Gathering, with more coming in. A white TV truck rolled past them, toward the stage, and a fat guy in a John Deere Gator went by and tossed them bottles of Faygo.

Skye had never heard of it and gave hers to Carl as they made a quick loop around the field. As they walked, they passed through invisible clouds of marijuana smoke, like old autumn leaves being burned. Halfway around, they found a cluster of travelers, sitting under a tree. Skye knew two of the women, and trusted one of them, who was named Lucy, and who agreed to watch her pack while Skye scouted the field.

"Gotta need for weed," Lucy said.

"Got ya covered," Skye said. "We'll spark up when I get back."

"Then hurry back," Lucy said.

FIFTY OR SIXTY cars dotted the two parking areas, along with a few campers and RVs, but a cluster of vehicles that seemed to be parked together caught her eye, and she went that way. Not much was moving around the cluster;

freshly burned log remnants were still sputtering in a fire ring. She moved closer, trying to shelter behind groups of Juggalos and the random cars in the parking lot.

She was thirty or forty yards away, standing behind an aging Volkswagen van, when a woman staggered out of the RV. She was wearing cut-off jean shorts and nothing else, though she was carrying what looked like a T-shirt, and one of the nearby Juggalos yelled, "Yay, tits," and the woman laughed and gave him the finger, and a minute later, wiggled the shirt over her head.

Skye didn't know her, but she looked like a disciple. Skye edged closer as the woman went to one of the cars in the cluster, opened the door and emerged with a pair of sunglasses, a pack of Marlboros, and a Zippo lighter.

Skye called over, "Hey: tell Pilate that Carly said hi!"

The woman finished lighting a cigarette, blew smoke, and called back, "I think he's still asleep."

"I'll talk to him later," Skye called. She waved and walked away. Back with the travelers, she recovered her pack, took out the Gerber survival knife, and slipped it into the leg pocket on her cargo pants. Across the field, another carnival ride was pulling in. She'd lie around with her friends, Skye thought, until dark.

Then she'd spot Pilate and she'd stick him.

She had no qualms about it: thought about Letty, and her feelings about killing. Ridding the world of Pilate was a public service, Skye thought, and would probably save a lot of lives. Still: the cops would call it murder, and if she went to prison, there'd be no more traveling. She could feel the tension growing in her gut, and let it build, not trying to deny it. She was talking to Lucy, passing a joint back and forth, watching more and more Juggalos pulling in, when she spotted Letty: "Gotta go," she said, getting to her feet. "Gotta run."

LUCAS'S CABIN WAS less than twenty miles from the Juggalo campground and Letty knew the route well. She'd started north an hour or so behind Skye and closed the gap on the way up, arriving forty-five minutes after Skye had.

When she pulled the Benz into the campground, she gave a guy standing next to a barrel five dollars to park, got a date-stamped ticket, put it on the dashboard, and said, "Thanks," when the guy said, "Nice ride."

When she'd parked and got out, a tough-looking, bare-faced guy in work clothes, who was probably a cop, walked by and muttered, "Not a place for college girls."

Letty winced: the ticket seller and the cop, if he was a cop, had picked her out in seconds. She made a quick circuit of the field, looking for Skye, then drove back to Hayward, found a yoga place, bought a pair of black yoga tights and a bright red crop top and black jacket, went over to the Walmart for a pair of high-top hunting boots and cotton socks.

She changed out of her Neiman Marcus jeans, blouse, and wedge sandals in the car, into the new stuff, drove back to the campground, reparked, got out, and decided she more or less fit, except for her hairdo and bare face. When she walked onto the field, where the crowd was still a little sparse, a short, thin, balding man with a box said, "You need a face. I'll paint your face for free if you show your tits."

Letty grabbed the front of his shirt and said, "You'll paint my face for free or I'll beat the shit out of you."

"Violence. That's so hot," the guy said. "Gives me a little woody."

"'Little' being the key word," Letty said. "Now, you gonna paint or get beat up?"

"Can we do both?" he asked.

DESPITE THE PAINT—a dog face with a droopy red tongue—Skye picked Letty out instantly.

Had nothing to do with the way Letty dressed, or the face paint: had something to do with the way she walked, like she owned the place. She said to Lucy, "Watch my bag again, okay? You see that girl over there? The one with the red nose in the black tights? I gotta stay away from her. She's gonna come here and she'll see my pack. Tell her that I went to Hayward with a friend."

"Whatever," Lucy said, in a voice that sounded like a gravel road. "Gimme a last good hit."

"Finish it," Skye said, passing the joint. "Tell her I won't be back until after dark."

LETTY SPOTTED THE travelers, but nobody shaped like Skye. She went that way, and asked for her, and Lucy said, "She's gone off to that . . . that town, I can't remember it. She went off with Carl, they're not coming back until night."

"Hayward? She went to Hayward?"

"Who?" Lucy was confused. "Man, that shit just crawled right over me."

"Skye. Skye went to Hayward?"

"Who?"

Letty knew that Skye would be back, because she'd left her pack, and all her gear, with her friend. It was a matter of waiting, but the waiting nearly drove her to distraction: nothing to do. Even the Juggalos seemed uninteresting, after she'd seen a few dozen of them. A really bad rap band got going on the stage and a guy ran past wearing nothing but a jockstrap. She began to feel stupid in the face paint. The hours crawled by, until dinnertime; she got two hot dogs with lots of onions.

Then Weather called: "I don't want to pry, but are you in Hayward?"

"Not exactly," Letty said.

She heard her mother turn and tell Lucas, "She says, 'Not exactly.'"

Lucas said, "Goddamnit, she is. That Juggalo thing is east of town, that's why it's 'not exactly.'"

Weather asked, "At this Juggalo thing, right? Looking for Skye?"

"Maybe," Letty said.

Weather said, "Your father is seriously annoyed."

"I believe it," Letty said. "Not for the first time, though. He'll get over it."

"Yeah, well . . . he just went steaming out of here. I

think he'll be telling you how annoyed he is, personally, in about two hours."

"He doesn't have to—"

"He thinks he does," Weather said.

When Letty got off the phone, something in her spine relaxed. Lucas was on the way up: that was a good thing. A Juggalo went by, looking for volunteers: "We're putting up the fire and we need somebody to help. Could you help?"

She was doing nothing else, so she went to help. The Juggalos were building a fire stack out of cardboard boxes stuffed with stove-length pine logs. From the fire site, Letty could keep an eye on the travelers, and Skye's backpack.

LUCAS WAS BOTH furious and frightened. Letty thought she was tougher than she actually was, and she didn't know enough about crazy. He changed clothes, got his gun, climbed into the Porsche and took off. He drove the route so many times during the year that he could almost do it with his eyes closed. He stopped once to pee and stuff the footwell cooler with Diet Cokes, and flew on into the evening.

SKYE GOT BACK to the campground just after dark, looked for Letty, didn't see her in the milling mass of bodies. When she'd left that morning, there might have been dozens of people. Now there were hundreds, and at the far end of the field, a moderately good rap group was performing, the music pounding over the heads of the crowd. The organizers had strung long lines of Christmas lights down the length of the field, on both sides. A dozen campfires were going on the edges of the field, and the smell of roasting meat mixed with the odor of marijuana.

Lucy was lying on her sleeping bag, staring at the stars. Skye crouched next to her and asked, "That chick show up? Letty?"

"Who? Oh . . . yeah. Just for a minute."

At that moment, Letty walked up: "Skye."

And Skye looked up and said, "Ah, shit."

Letty: "What are you doing? Are you looking for Pilate? And if you find him, then what?"

"I'll figure that out when I find him," Skye said. She didn't look toward Pilate's encampment. She squared off with Letty, and added, "Letty, I owe you, I appreciate the help, but you're not my mom."

"I know I'm not your mom, but if you try to go up against Pilate and those guys who had you . . . I mean, Skye, that's crazy," Letty said. "You can't do that. You'll get hurt. My dad's coming up here. If you can spot Pilate, he'll bring in the cops—"

"Yeah, yeah, and then what'll happen? There'll be some kind of bullshit legal stuff and Pilate will blame everybody else and he'll walk. You watch, you'll see. He's the devil."

"He's just an asshole," Letty began. "My dad's handled a lot worse than him."

"There *is* no worse than him," Skye said. "That's what nobody gets."

She turned and looked out at the growing crowd and then asked, "You bring your car? Could you lock up my pack?"

"Yeah, sure. I'm just down the field."

Skye picked up her pack, said, "Thanks," to Lucy, and to Letty, "Let's go. This stuff is too good to get ripped off."

They dropped the pack at the car and Letty asked, "So you'll wait for Dad?"

Skye shrugged. "Might as well. What are they doing over there? Building a teepee?"

"Fire stack. They're going to torch it off at midnight," Letty said.

"Jeez, you'll be able to see that from outer space," Skye said.

"Not done yet. Once they get it built up to the point, they start another ring of boxes and build that up. They got a lot of boxes left. I was over helping to build it."

"Then let's go help . . . at least until your dad gets here."

THEY WORKED STACKING fire boxes for ten minutes, then Letty turned away, caught up in the construction, and when she turned back, Skye was gone. She looked around, like a mother for a lost child, then stepped outside the ring of workers, still didn't see her. Stepped farther outside and looked down the field, and caught a flash of Skye's face, forty yards away, looking back at her. Their eyes touched, then Skye juked and disappeared into the crowd.

"Goddamnit." Letty jogged after her. When she got to where Skye had been, she couldn't see her. She wandered through the crowd, turning, but the lights, the painted faces, were like something out of a nightmare. The Juggalos were dancing to the rap music now, long chains of them . . .

THE DISCIPLES HAD built a fire in the middle of their camp circle. They were all sitting around or lying around, talking, smoking, but nobody was singing "Kumbaya." Most of them were wearing clown faces, including Pilate: Laine had painted a half dozen faces on him, wiping them away and redoing the work, until he was satisfied. The white paint was fluorescent, and she'd outlined his face with it, and put a dab on the tip of his nose. He was wearing a Catholic priest's black clerical suit, including the white collar, which, he thought, made a proper Juggalo statement.

Raleigh, Bell, and Chet were also in costume, and were moving the last of the cocaine. They'd already figured out that there wasn't much around, and they stepped on it again with dry baby formula, and still got premium prices. They wouldn't get rich, but they'd have enough cash to get back to L.A.

———

SKYE SAW A priest with a clown face, but didn't recognize him as Pilate because of the costume and face paint. She stood in a clump of trees behind the circle of cars, in the dark, waiting for him, handling the knife, calm, quiet as a hunting cat. Thinking about Henry. About Henry's baby face, and how he'd always go off somewhere to pee, so Skye couldn't see him, even though they'd been together for months.

At eight, a decent rap band broke out on the stage, and the crowd got tighter; several people in Pilate's campground moved out toward the stage, and the new band set off a series of powerful strobes that flashed red, white, and blue at the crowd.

From her stand in the clump of trees, Skye saw the clown-face priest amble off toward the bonfire structure. She fumbled a joint out of her breast pocket, lit it, and with most of the disciples gone, she went looking for Pilate, moving into the circle where three remaining disciples were sprawled on blankets.

She said, "Dudes."

One of them said, "Whatcha got there?"

"This shit from Oregon." She lifted her chin and blew a smoke ring.

"Pass it?" asked one of the disciples, a woman in a phosphorescent green Hulk mask. Skye passed it and the woman took a hit and handed it down to one of the guys on the ground. They were standing behind the fire ring, and Skye asked, "Anybody seen Pilate?"

"Think he's out at the show," said one of the men.

"Naw, he went down to the fire thing," said the other man.

The woman pointed down to the end of the field and said, "That's Pilate, you can just see him, the guy in the dark suit, he's dressed like a priest."

Skye turned to look, and the woman stooped and picked up one of the logs next to the fire ring and hit Skye in the back of the head. Skye dropped as though she'd been hit by an ax and the woman said, "C'mon, we got to hide her." She stooped and got Skye by the wrists and started dragging her between a car and the RV.

"What the fuck are you doing?" a man asked. He was on his hands and knees, looking out at the Gathering grounds. "There are people all over the place." He looked at Skye and said, "Shit, she looks like she's dead."

"Not yet," the woman said. "This is that Skye chick. She didn't recognize me, but I recognized her and her voice. She was looking for Pilate. I bet she's got a gun."

Skye was on her side, her breathing rough, bubbly. The woman patted her down, found the REI knife in her leg pocket. "Gonna cut him," she said. "Gonna kill him. Richie: go get Pilate."

Richie got unsteadily to his feet, but started down toward the bonfire, found some momentum, and went off at a trot. The woman said to the other man, "Let's get her over in those trees across the road. Pick her up, put your arms under her armpits, like she's drunk and you're trying to help her out."

"Jesus, she's hurt bad," the guy said. Skye's head swung around, loose.

"Not as bad as she's gonna be, if I know Pilate," the woman said. She looked out at the field: "Nobody's watching. Let's go."

LETTY WAS AT the back of the music crowd, twenty-five yards from the stage, turning, looking for Skye. A priest in a clown face went by, and a moment later, somebody called, "Pilate! Pilate!"

Pilate turned, stepped around Letty, and called back, "What?"

"Gotta come back, man." He poked his thumb back over his shoulder, back toward the ring of cars.

"What?"

"Just . . . you gotta come, man, like right now."

Pilate could see he didn't want to say why, but could feel the urgency in his voice. He nodded and started after him.

So did Letty.

SHE LET THEM get twenty yards ahead, then took out her cell phone, called Lucas, and asked, "Where are you?"

"I'm half an hour out. Where are you?"

"I'm at the Gathering. I found Pilate."

"What? Get the fuck away from there. Letty—"

"He doesn't know I found him," Letty said. "I heard somebody call him that. I mean, how many can there be?"

"*Stay away from him.* I'm coming. I called Stern, he's talking to the sheriff up there, about getting some people together. We're hooking up in Hayward, we're coming out in a convoy. You see any cops there now?"

"I saw a guy who I thought was a cop, but there aren't any uniforms or squad cars around . . . I could look for that guy." She was on her tiptoes, trying to follow Pilate as he pushed through the swirling crowd.

"If you can find a cop, it'll probably be a sheriff's deputy. Tell him we're coming. He'll have a radio, have him get in touch with the sheriff. And stay the hell away from those people."

LETTY RANG OFF. Pilate and the man who'd come for him were now thirty or forty yards away and headed behind the stage, and she jogged in that direction. Somebody yelled, "Show your tits," but not at her, though it was about the two hundredth time she'd heard it that day, and from the round of applause, she suspected that whoever yelled had gotten his wish.

She lost track of Pilate and the second man in the scrum around the stage, where the rap was getting better and hotter; the enormous fat man in the John Deere went by again, wearing a shirt now, still passing out bottles of Faygo. Somebody ran past and shouted, "Fart-lighting contest . . . Follow me!"

Letty stayed on track; the urgency of the man's call to Pilate suggested that they'd go wherever they were going in a straight line. From one of the parking lots, looking over the hoods of parked cars, she saw them again, at the far end of the parking area. The priest and five or six other people were walking past a circle of cars into a stand of trees. There was some light from the stage, and various other sources, including headlights of cars coming and going, but the strobes broke everything up, and she couldn't get close enough to see what Pilate and the disciples were actually doing, until they seemed to break into an odd dance.

She muttered to herself, "What the heck?" and edged closer, but worried about breaking out of the parking lot. The dancing stopped and they drifted out of the trees, back toward their cars, where they stood around talking.

Letty watched for another five minutes.

Then, afraid they could spot her if she stood in one spot too long, she faded back into the cars and looked around for a cop, or a cop car. She didn't see one immediately. Where was Skye? Had she found Pilate? Did they have her?

Her phone rang, and she looked at the screen: Lucas.

"Yeah, Dad?"

"Where are you?"

"Uh, in a parking area . . . When you come into the field, I'm in the parking area that's to the left of the entrance."

"Are you leaving? Are you getting out?"

"Not yet. I think Skye . . . I don't know, I think Skye was looking for Pilate. I don't know if she found him, but I can't find her."

"Don't look! Don't look! Get out of there!"

"Okay, I'm backing off. When you come in, Pilate's in a circle of cars at the far end of the field, off to the left of the stage and a little behind it. I can't see him now, I'm too far away."

"Get out of there!"

HAD SKYE GONE back to the other travelers? It was possible, Letty thought—and they were directly across the field from where she was. She looked back toward the circle of cars. Pilate's people were talking, Pilate was gesturing, and a fire was burning hot in the middle of the circle. Looked like they'd be there for a while. Even if they broke up, and moved into the crowd, she'd seen only one person with a priest costume, so finding him again shouldn't be too hard.

She looked toward the spot where the Juggalos had been, and decided she had time to run across the field. She did that, jogging past a group of people with a circular blanket; they were using it to throw a half-naked woman up in the air, the woman laughing, kicking and screaming as she went up. There were only two travelers where Skye's friends had been. No sign of Skye.

Lucy was there: "Where's Skye? Did she come back?" Letty asked.

The girl shook her head. "Didn't see her after you guys left."

Letty turned and looked back toward the circle of cars. She couldn't see it from where she was, thought about it for a moment, jogged back that way, detoured around the growing crowd at the stage, pushed past a couple of drunks, one of whom grabbed her ass. She slapped him away and kept going, out to the side of the crowd, and then back toward the circle of cars.

The priest was there, pointing his finger at his various disciples, snapping out orders. The disciples were scrambling around, dragging stuff into cars and the RV. Getting ready to move. Fire still going hard.

Letty pushed past the last of the dancing Juggalos— not so much dancing, she thought, as bouncing up and down in place—and walked up to Pilate, who saw her coming, tipped his painted face toward her.

"Where's Skye?" Letty asked.

"What?"

"I saw her coming over here—"

He was *so* fast. She never saw the fist coming and it hit her like a meteor, below her right eye, to the right of her nose. She went down, dazed, and Pilate kicked her in the ribs and she felt a knifelike pain and he tried to kick her again but she managed to push away and caught the blow on her arm and rolled and tried to get up but he kicked at her again and she couldn't see very well and then somebody screamed, "Hey-Hey-Hey quit that shit, quit that shit . . ."

Pilate shouted, "She tried to stick me with a knife . . ."

And the other person shouted, "Quit that shit, quit that shit . . ."

Pilate shouted back, "Fuck it, get the fuck out of here."

He picked up one of the fire logs and waved it in the

face of the fat Juggalo in the John Deere, who threw a bottle of Faygo at Pilate's face and at the same time screamed, "Help a Juggalo!"

A group of Juggalos turned and broke off from the dance crowd and started toward them and Pilate went away.

Letty was on her hands and knees, the pain rippling up her side, and she thought that maybe Pilate had hit her harder than she had realized, but she got to her knees. The rap music was so loud she could barely hear anything, but she did hear the fat man shout, "Get in here," and he pulled her into the back of the John Deere and shouted, "Roll it," to the driver and they rolled away down the field and Letty shouted, "Wait, wait."

The fat man shouted to the driver, "Keep going," and took her to the middle of the field, where the crowd was thinnest, and told the driver to stop, and said, "Babe, you got a bloody nose, your nose is really . . ." Then he turned to the driver and said, "Dave, we got to get her to the med tent."

They started driving again and after a dozen bumps that sent pain screaming up Letty's rib cage, they got to a med tent where a Juggalo in full makeup, but with a fingerwide Red Cross on his forehead, said, "That's gotta hurt. Let me get you a gauze pad."

He pressed the pad to Letty's nose, and he said, "Might help to tilt your head back," and she did that, and said, "I gotta go back there."

"That's not the brightest idea I've heard tonight," the fat man said.

"They might've hurt a friend of mine," Letty said.

The fat man wouldn't move until she'd thrown away the first gauze pad, now soaked with blood, and the medic had given her another. "Should stop now," the medic said. "Where else did you get hit?"

"Kicked me in the side . . ."

The medic asked her to lift her arms above her head, but when she did, the pain shot through her, and she jerked her arms back down and leaned forward to groan.

"You got some busted ribs," the medic said. "You need to get into town, go to the hospital."

"Gotta go find my friend," Letty said. The second nose pad was now soaked with blood, and the medic gave her a whole pack of them. "Keep pressing them against the side of your nose."

"Gotta find my friend . . ."

"Dave and me'll give you a ride down there," the fat man said. And, "My name is Randy. I'm your friendly fat guy."

WHEN LETTY WAS taken out of Pilate's circle, a number of Juggalos stood around looking at them, and one of them, maybe drunk, asked, "What'd you hit the chick for, asshole?"

"Caught her fuckin' around on me," Pilate improvised. He turned away—no place to get in a real fight, not with Juggalos, they'd swarm you—and he said to Kristen, "Keep moving, we gotta get out of here. Too many people here. The cops could be coming."

They started moving and Bell slipped off into the

stand of trees where they'd left Skye, half buried in brush. He gathered up as many downed tree limbs as he could easily find, threw them on top of her, broke a few more off the evergreens and added those. When he was done, he thought Skye's grave looked like an ordinary pile of brush. Somebody might find her eventually, but not until they were long gone. He hurried back to the circle, where they were throwing stuff in his car.

Pilate pulled Raleigh aside; Raleigh was in full Juggalo dress. "You got Colorado license plates, so nobody will be looking at you. I want you to hang out here, see what happens. Stay all the way to the end. Anything too weird happens, call me."

"Got it."

Pilate said, "You can have Linda to ride with you."

Raleigh gave him a thumbs-up: "Most excellent. I will pound her like a fuckin' big bass drum."

Pilate patted him on the cheek, then pulled the others together for one last-minute pep talk: "This isn't working out as well as we thought. That fuckin' Skye might have fucked us up—we don't know what she told the cops after Bony got killed. Let's meet up next week at the Gathering in Sault Ste. Marie. Kristen's dividing up the money, giving some to everybody. Save as much as you can. We can't go in a convoy, because Skye probably told them that's how we travel, and that we're from California, and we've all got California plates. So when we head out, split up. Everybody go their own way. Go to town and get maps, and, you know . . . stay out of sight. See you at the Gathering next week. Remember, we rule."

Everybody muttered, "We rule," and a minute later Pilate rolled out in his Pontiac, followed by the RV, and then the others.

THE FAT MAN and his driver took Letty to where Pilate had been, but when they got back behind the stage, the circle of cars was gone.

She unconsciously grabbed the hair above her ears and squeezed her fingers tight: "Oh my God, I let them go . . ."

She stood up in the back of the cart, turned and looked down the length of the parking area, hoping to catch sight of the convoy before it got out to the highway. If she could get a tag number, any tag number . . . She saw taillights of cars turning onto the highway, but they were too far away to read any tag numbers and even if she had been able to see them, she couldn't be sure they were the right cars.

She got on the phone and Lucas answered instantly: "Dad, I found them, Pilate—and then I lost them. I think they're on the road."

"Are they in one tight convoy?"

"I don't know. There are all kinds of cars coming and going," she said.

"You okay?"

"Not exactly," she said, pressing the gauze pad to her nose.

———

LUCAS GOT THERE fifteen minutes later, along with three sheriff's cars and six deputies, all in plain clothes. Letty was waiting at the entrance to the parking lot, and when he got out of his car, Lucas said, "Aw, Jesus Christ, Letty . . ."

He reached for her, to hug her, but she flinched away and said, "Don't do that—I might have a cracked rib or something. Pilate kicked me. It hurts."

"Need to get you to the hospital, need to get you going."

Lucas looked frightened, something she really hadn't seen before. Frantic, yes; frightened, no.

Letty said, "I'm not gonna die, I just don't want to be squeezed."

"Let me see your face."

After they did all the father-daughter stuff, Letty told Lucas and the ring of cops, "They were parked right here."

She told her story, about the disappearance of Skye and the attack by Pilate, and how the man in the John Deere saved her, and how just before they left, Pilate and his disciples had been in the trees across the entry road. She pointed past the parking area, to the straggly stand of pine and aspen. ". . . and they did a little dance, jumping up and down."

By the end of the story, she was shouting at them. The music had stepped up another notch, now as loud as a jet plane at takeoff, loud enough to feel it scratching at your face. The group onstage had set off whirling green laser lights that flashed up into the trees around the field, and made the branches seem to sparkle with thousands of emeralds.

Lucas took a moment to walk away to the fat man in the John Deere and say something to him, and then slap him on the back, and say something else, and then he walked back to Letty and the deputies and said, "I'll talk to that guy again. Now, where were they parked exactly? And you say there was another RV?"

Before she could answer, he said to one of the deputies, "And I need one of you guys to run Letty into the clinic."

"Not yet, not yet," Letty protested. "In a minute."

"Yet!" Lucas said. There was a copper taste in the back of his mouth, like blood. Letty was still bleeding from her nose and would have a major black eye: he could see it already.

"In a minute," she said again.

Another cop car had come in and a seventh deputy joined them, this one in a uniform. They all had flashlights and they walked across the circular parking area inch by inch, and dumped out a plastic trash bin that sat at the edge of the parking lot, thirty or forty yards away, checking the contents under the flashlights.

As the deputies were doing that, Lucas scuffed around the fire, his own flashlight probing the dirt, looking for something, anything—a charge slip would be good, something with a credit card number—that might tell them something about Pilate's group, and at the same time lecturing Letty. "Goddamnit, Letty, I know you're grown up and all of that . . ."

Letty pointed to the clump of trees. "I'm going over there, where they were dancing."

"You're going back to town."

"In a minute."

He followed her and rolled on through the lecture as they got into the trees. Nothing there but a pile of brush, and some scuffed-up dirt. The strobe from the stage was flickering off the tree branches and aspen leaves and made it hard to focus on anything.

Lucas walked back until the brush got dense enough to drag at his jeans, then shone his light deeper into the trees, saw nothing interesting, and walked back toward Letty. To get to her, he had to circle the edge of the pile of tree limbs, and caught a flash of yellow-white: the stump end of one of the tree limbs was fresh, recently ripped off a tree. He stopped and shone the light into the pile, and saw more fresh breaks.

Letty asked, "What?"

"These branches. Looks like somebody just broke them off the trees." He shone the flash around the clump of evergreens and spotted a couple of places where the limbs had been pulled off, leaving a white gash in the bark. They moved the smaller branches and Letty, one arm clutched to her injured side, tugged away a bigger one. As she dragged it out, she spotted a streak of deep pumpkin orange, in the light of the flash. Her hands went to her mouth and she said, "Oh, no. No."

"What?"

"Skye bought some orange socks at REI. We joked about it."

Lucas shone the light deeper into the pile, caught the flash of orange. "Okay. Get back. Get out of the trees." Letty backed away and Lucas shouted at the deputies, who hurried over.

Lucas said, "We might have something here. We don't want to move any more stuff than we have to, if it turns out to be a crime scene. But there's an orange . . . something . . . under these tree limbs. Might be a sock. Somebody hold the light."

They spotted the streak of orange again, and two of the deputies lit it up from different sides, and then the third deputy held Lucas's belt, at the back, so he could lean far into the pile without touching anything, and he pushed aside some bark and pine needles and said, "It's a foot. There's a body under here."

"We gotta get her out," Letty cried. "It hasn't been long. She could still be alive."

"Don't think so," Lucas said. "Can't take the chance. Let's see if we can spot how she's oriented under there."

They pulled out a few more tree limbs, discovered a lower arm, and Letty, standing next to Lucas, with both hands now clutching her chest, saw the plastic exercise bracelet she'd given Skye in San Francisco.

"Oh my God, it's her, it's her, it's her . . ."

She was babbling, and knew it, but couldn't stop. One of the deputies put an arm over her chest and pulled her away. Lucas decided where Skye's head must be—the body was hardly buried, mostly just covered with damp leaves, pine needles, and brush. When Lucas found Skye's face, the first thing he saw was one dead blue eye, nearly popped from its socket, behind a crushed zygomatic bone.

WHEN HE SAW it, and the graying flesh behind it, the anger finally ripped through him. It had been a year since he'd felt anything like it: since the fight in a madman's basement. Letty's actions had frightened him, but he'd always known, through the series of phone calls, that she was all right.

But Skye . . . a young woman who had no parent or anyone else to look after her, except his daughter; and this could have happened to Letty, if a fat man hadn't been there.

If they'd dragged her off between the cars . . .

For a whole year, he'd been stuck in bureaucratic mode, running down little ratshit criminals. Even in the larger cases, like the Merion murder case, the trial would turn on sleazy money-conflicted witnesses. This was different. This was a kid . . .

He backed away: "She's gone. She's gone. Goddamnit. We need to get a crime scene crew out here . . . Ah, Jesus Christ . . . she's gone."

He wrapped an arm around Letty and one of the deputies went running to his car, to call more cops. In the background, the rap went on, and the strobe bounced its wicked multi-multicolored light off all the clown faces around them.

Letty started to cry into Lucas's shoulder.

9

LUCAS TOLD THE deputies that he had to take Letty to the hospital, right now, and he pried Letty loose from the murder scene and half dragged her across the parking lot to where she'd parked the SUV. The only thing Letty said on the way out of the parking lot was "Take it slow."

Her nose was bleeding again and she tipped her head and pushed Kleenex into her nostril.

"What was I thinking about?" Lucas asked, pounding the steering wheel as they headed onto the highway toward town. "What the fuck was I thinking about?"

He had his flashers on, but the highway was crowded with people heading into the Juggalo Gathering, or leaving it, and he never got any speed.

"You should have been at the goddamn hospital a half hour ago," he groaned. "What the fuck was I thinking about . . . ?"

"Had to find Skye."

"Somebody else could have found her," Lucas said. He turned sideways: "Tell me the truth. How bad?"

"It hurts, but he never hit me or kicked me square, except that first punch, and that didn't knock me out or anything, I kept moving—"

"Get the fuck out of the way, you asshole," Lucas shouted at a slow-moving car ahead of them. "Get the fuck out of the way." He crowded the car until it pulled off onto the shoulder, then accelerated away until he caught the next slow-moving vehicle.

"He could have killed you if that fat guy hadn't helped you," Lucas said. "Letty: you're not a cop. Maybe you will be, but you're not now. What you did . . ."

He trailed off, and she said, "Stupid."

Lucas banged the steering wheel with the heels of his hands: "Motherfuckers. Get out of the fuckin' way."

AS THEY GOT close to Hayward, Letty said, "You're mad now."

"Yes," Lucas said.

"I don't want to . . . sound like a jerk, but I don't think the sheriff's deputies up here will find Pilate. They don't do that kind of thing. They don't track people. They've got their county and that's it."

Lucas nodded. She was right.

"So you're gonna have to do it."

He didn't have an answer to that.

They crossed Highway 63 and pulled into the hospital

emergency room, and Lucas led her in. A nurse went to wake up the night doc and a couple minutes later he came in and took Letty away, while Lucas went to fill out some paperwork.

The doc was back in five minutes and said, "We're going to do some X-rays. She got hit hard, by that eye, I want to make sure nothing's broken, and I want to take a look at her ribs. I think she's probably got a cracked rib or two, we need to make sure there's nothing sticking into a lung."

"What are the chances of that?"

The doc shook his head: "Small. The X-ray's more of a precaution, than anything. We'll know right away if there's a problem."

HALF AN HOUR later, Letty was back. The doc was with her, and said, "She's got two cracked ribs, but they're not displaced at all. Judging from the placement of the bruise where she was kicked, I don't think there'll be any complications: it was well away from the kidneys or liver. We already talked about it, she knows what to do, and what to look out for. And there's not much to do, except try not to sneeze or cough or laugh too hard."

"What about her face? Her nose?" Lucas asked.

"Nothing broken, but she's got a small natural bone spur inside the nasal vault." The doc tapped the bony top of his own nose to show Lucas what he was talking about. "When she got hit, the spur apparently cut through a part of her nose lining, and that's where the blood is coming from. It didn't look like it was going to stop, so I put a little dab of chemical cautery up there, to seal it up. It won't bleed anymore, but it's going to hurt when the anesthetic wears off. I got her some pills for pain, more for the nose, than the ribs."

"How long to heal up?" Lucas asked.

"Maybe three days for the nose to stop hurting. The ribs are going to hurt for a while. She's got a big bruise on her rib cage, and that'll add some pain in addition to the ribs, and she'll have a heck of a shiner. She's gonna be creaky in the morning. Nothing dangerous—but it's gonna hurt." He looked at Letty and said, "Remember what I told you about, mmm, the side effects."

"What side effects?" Lucas asked.

"Side effects of the drugs," the doc said.

Out in the truck, Lucas asked, "What side effects? The doc was tap-dancing back there."

"He was afraid he'd embarrass me," Letty said. "If I use the pain pills, I might not be able to poop. He said I should get something called a stool softener."

"Does that embarrass you?"

"No."

"Good. If you get to be a cop, and things get rough— they stick tubes into all kinds of places that could be embarrassing, if you're the embarrassing type. I've had a few of them," Lucas said. And, "I'm gonna call your mom."

"She's gonna scream," Letty said.

"Yeah, well—it's her turn."

LUCAS CALLED WEATHER, then gave his phone to Letty, who talked to her mother for another five minutes, telling her the whole story, downplaying her injuries. A cop car with flashing red lights whipped past them as they drove back toward the Juggalo campground.

When Letty was finished talking, Lucas took the phone back and said, "She's hurt more than she told you. She's not feeling too bad right now, but she will in the morning. She's not going to be driving anywhere. We're gonna need somebody to come up here and get the truck, or the Porsche."

Weather said that Letty should stay at the cabin until the next afternoon, then she'd be up with either Lucas's old friend Sloan, or with Del's wife, to get the extra car.

A minute after he rang off, Lucas took a call from Stern.

"Clark Chapman called, he said you've got a body," Stern said. Chapman was the county sheriff.

"Yeah. Skye. Pilate apparently killed her by kicking her to death. My daughter might actually have witnessed the murder. She didn't know it at the time, only found out later."

"Jesus. Is Letty okay?"

"More or less. Got beat up," Lucas said. He described the scene, and how Letty was assaulted by Pilate.

"Oh, boy. Okay, we're blocking off all the major roads around there, making people go through the checkpoints. I understand we're looking for a guy dressed as a priest."

"Might not be, anymore," Lucas said. "After they killed Skye, they left in a hurry. They're running."

"I'm rolling the crime scene crew," Stern said. "But, uh, what are you doing up there?"

"Letty came up after Skye, and I got worried," Lucas said. "I'm sort of up here as her dad. I'm gonna stand back now and let the deputies do it."

"Don't stand too far back," Stern said. "They might need a little advice. Weren't you technically a deputy sheriff up there once? Seems like I remember something like that."

"Yeah, but that was years ago, a different county, and it was pretty technical. Didn't get paid, or anything."

"Okay. But hang around for a while. I'm still in Madison. Talk them through it, until I can get up there."

Lucas said he would.

THEY CAME UP to the Gathering site, and Lucas asked Letty, "How bad do you hurt right now?"

"Not terrible."

"I need to pull in here for a minute. Kick the seat back and sit here. Don't get out."

"'Kay."

Lucas parked and said, again, "Do *not* get out."

THE DEPUTIES HAD taped off the area of the murder and Pilate's encampment, and were waiting for the crime scene crew.

Lucas had one of the plainclothes deputies interrupt the rap concert. The deputy went onstage and told the crowd that a Juggalo woman had been murdered by some outsiders from California and that if anyone had taken any photos that showed a circle of cars parked over there—he pointed—"we would be desperately anxious to see them."

The announcement cast a temporary pall over the concert—the pall lasted for more than twenty minutes, before the music got back to where it'd been—and a half dozen Juggalos wandered over to the cops to show off cell phone photos.

One of them, by a Hayward Juggalo named Betty Morrow, had a snapshot that showed her girlfriend in the foreground, and a license tag in the background, on a car that appeared to be in the Pilate circle.

They couldn't make out the tag on the phone screen, but a deputy had Morrow e-mail the photo to a friend of his in Hayward, an amateur wildlife photographer, who ran the shot through Lightroom and two minutes later came back with both the license plate number and a make and model on the car, an aging Subaru Forester.

"Here's the thing. The plate's not from California," the deputy said. "I'll give you one guess where it's from."

"I don't want to guess," Lucas said. "Where's it from?"

"Would you believe . . . Minnesota?"

"Goddamnit—they're from California," Lucas said. "If it's a Minnesota guy, he might not be related."

"He was parked in the circle," the deputy said.

"Give me the number—I'll call the office and have them run it," Lucas said.

Lucas called the BCA duty officer in St. Paul, and said, "Everything you've got. E-mail it to me."

The duty officer could give him one bit immediately: the car was registered to a Chester Tillus, who lived east of Baudette in Lake of the Woods County.

"I'll get you a driver's license photo in ten minutes, if he's got one."

"Hang on." Lucas got an e-mail address for the sheriff's office from the deputy, and passed it on to the duty officer. "Send copies of everything to both me and the sheriff's office. They're looking for the guy over here in Wisconsin, could be a murder charge involved."

"I'll do that. Are you at the scene?"

"Yeah, but I'm going over to my cabin," Lucas said. "Right now, it's a snake hunt, and the cheeseheads got it."

The deputy said to Lucas, when he rang off, "Nothing I like better than a nice Brie."

"I believe it," Lucas said. He called Stern to fill him in, and said, "I can't think of anything else. I'm gonna get Letty back to my cabin and get some sleep myself."

"See you in the morning," Stern said. "I'm catching an early plane out."

LUCAS DROVE OUT to his cabin, lit it up, offered to put together a cheeseburger, but Letty declined and said, "I'm gonna go sit on the dock for a few minutes."

"You're sure?"

"Yup."

When Lucas followed her out, carrying a beer and his iPad, she'd unfolded a second deck chair for him. He sat down and sighed and said, "You do have the ability to piss me off from time to time."

"I know," she said. "I don't think I can be any other way. Or you, either."

"Probably not," he said.

"You know how she was killed?"

"We'll know in the morning, when crime scene gets a look," Lucas said. "From what you saw, and what I saw, I believe she was probably kicked to death."

"Ah, jeez." She was quiet for ten seconds, then said, "I've been sitting here, wondering if me meeting her had anything to do with her getting killed. The closest I can get is, if I hadn't given her my phone number in San Francisco, she might never have found out that Henry was dead. Or she might have stayed in South Dakota looking for him, and she never would have run into Pilate at all. You follow all the bread crumbs through the woods, that's what comes out."

"That's a good way to drive yourself crazy," Lucas said. "I talked to Bob Shaffer before he went off and got murdered last year. We could have done twenty other things that day and he'd still be alive. I believe there was one second, one tiny moment, that decided whether he'd live or die—if he hadn't gone into a supermarket for a jelly donut, he'd have lived. He was a pretty good husband and father, and he still would be."

"Yeah, but if he'd lived, you wouldn't have been so involved, and maybe Catrin Mattsson would have died."

"I don't know. She might have, or maybe Shaffer might have found her sooner," Lucas said. "Impossible to know. The thing is, you take a fork in the road, it doesn't always work out for the better . . . but sometimes it does. It must."

They were quiet for a couple of minutes, then Letty asked, "You get the e-mail yet? From the office?"

"Let me check." He turned on the iPad to check his mail. The download was slow, with only two bars on phone reception, but in five minutes he had a long file on Chester Tillus. Lucas scanned it and said, "He's with them. With Pilate."

He got on his cell and called the sheriff's office, talked to the duty sergeant and told him the same thing. "You find him, hold him, because he's part of the bunch. He's got two burglary convictions and two assault convictions in Minnesota, and a fighting charge in California, and that was only two months ago. He's been out there, he just didn't buy the California plates."

"We're looking for him," the deputy said.

AS LUCAS AND Letty sat talking on the dock, Pilate was on a back highway crossing into Michigan. The rest of the crew had scattered. Skye had been with the cops for a full day before the disciples killed her, and they had no idea what she might have told them. But she knew some names, for sure.

After kicking her to death, they'd gotten scared: Pilate pretended he wasn't, but he was. All the other murders had been in quiet spots, with nobody around but the disciples. This time, they'd killed a woman next to a large crowd.

Then the dark-haired Juggalo chick had shown up and started yelling at him about Skye. Pilate had punched her: couldn't help himself, chicks *did not* get up in his face like that, and walk away.

He was lucky, in a way, that the fat guy had shown up, because he was so buzzed on kicking the first girl to death that he might've killed the second one, right there in front of the crowd.

But the fat guy did show up and the Juggalo chick was taken away and they'd hauled ass.

WITH EVERYBODY ELSE going every which way, Pilate headed east in his Firebird, followed by only one other vehicle, the new RV, driven by Terry and Laine. They stuck to back roads but hurried to get across a state line. In Pilate's experience, which mostly came down to watching *Cops* on television, the police did not talk well across state lines.

Once in Michigan, at midnight, they found . . . almost nothing. Trees.

"Jesus, it's dark. Aren't even any cars," Kristen said, peering into the darkness through the Firebird's windshield. "It's like somebody's pulled a black sack over your head."

Dark as the L.A. people had ever seen the world; even the cars' headlights didn't seem to punch much of a hole in it. A few miles into Michigan, they saw a narrow dirt track in their headlights, heading off to the left, with a sign and an arrow that said something that they were going too fast to read. They took the turn, and found that it led to a boat landing. They couldn't see anything of the lake, but there were no lights anywhere. They got flashlights, found a spot where people had camped out, and rolled the two vehicles back into the trees.

"Now what?" Laine asked, when Pilate and Kristen joined Terry and her in the RV.

"Just gonna sit and wait," Pilate said.

Laine peered out a window. "Bears out there, I bet. Maybe wolves."

"Wolves don't eat trucks," Pilate said. "It is really fuckin' dark, ain't it? Lots of stars, though."

LETTY WAS HURTING when she got up in the morning, at nine o'clock. "Everything hurts. The nose hurts worst. Not the bruise, the place where the doctor cauterized it."

"Take some pills," Lucas said.

"I've already taken four of them," Letty said. "The max is two."

"Uh-oh," Lucas said. "You're gonna have to stop at the drugstore."

"I always thought stool softener was for old people," she said. "Maybe you could get it for me."

"Screw that," Lucas said. "I'm not doing it."

A few minutes later, she said, "The nose . . . it really hurts. It feels like somebody stuck a blowtorch up there."

Neither one of them felt like eating more Cheerios, left over from Lucas's first night at the cabin, so they drove back to the Juggalo Gathering site, which had sprung a hundred tents, and more people sleeping in cars, and, on one side, a big no-go zone defined by yellow crime scene tape and a bunch of sheriff's patrol cars and a Wisconsin crime scene truck. A group of Juggalos was disassembling the stage, and when Lucas asked, a deputy said they were going to move the stage to the other end of the field, where the bonfire had been.

The crime scene crew had exposed Skye's body; her head was misshapen, like a partly deflated soccer ball. The leader of the crime scene crew said he'd heard that Lucas thought she'd been kicked to death, and he said, "I think you're probably right. Doesn't look like clubs, no bark or anything in her face or her arms. Skull was crushed, with impact marks everywhere. Dollars to donuts, they kicked her to death."

"DNA?"

"We're sampling everything that looks possible."

The deputies said that there'd been no convoys spotted overnight, but they did have tag numbers for a half dozen vehicles from California, which had been run when the cars were stopped. None of the people stopped were wearing Juggalo makeup. Nothing had come back that would allow the Wisconsin cops to hold the cars.

The deputy said: "What are we gonna do? We got nothing to go on, but that one tag from Minnesota, and we never did spot him."

Lucas said, "Gimme what you got. All the California tags you stopped."

BOTH LUCAS AND Letty had to go into Hayward to make formal statements for the sheriff's department, so they continued into town.

The guy who would take their statements wasn't in yet, and wasn't expected for half an hour, so they walked over to Main Street, looking for breakfast. The Angler's Bar and Grill, where Lucas usually ate, wasn't open, so they settled for coffee and scones from a coffee shop around the block. Then they weren't far from the Walgreens, so they walked across the highway, and Lucas lingered by the book rack as Letty was checking out with the stool softener.

Outside, Lucas asked, "You got it?"

"Yeah. I told the checkout lady that it was for you, but you were embarrassed to ask for it."

Made him laugh.

AS THEY WALKED back toward the sheriff's office, they talked about the murder. Letty told Lucas, "Skye was going to stop at three Juggalo Gatherings. One here, one in the UP, and one down by Detroit somewhere. She thought Pilate might be going to them, too. All the people I saw with Pilate were wearing Juggalo gear, like they were really into it."

"Where is it at? And when? The next meeting?"

"Let me look at my phone . . ."

A half block farther along, she said, "It's in Sault Ste. Marie. The American one. Actually, on a farm south of the town. It's next weekend, and the Detroit one is two weeks from now."

"Sault Ste. Marie is a hell of a long way from here," Lucas said. "I drove it once, years ago, on my way to New York. If I remember, it's a six- or seven-hour drive from here. Eight hours or more from the Cities."

"You think you might go?"

Lucas scratched his cheek, where a mosquito had bitten the night before, then said, "I don't know. Maybe, if these guys haven't turned up by then. The fastest way to get out of this area would be to go south. Once you get down to I-94 you could head down to Chicago or start back toward California. They'd have a whole choice of routes. If they drove all night after killing Skye, switching off drivers, they could be . . . through Omaha, through Kansas City, down to Chicago. Unknown California license tags would be meaningless in the big cities. Tomorrow morning, they could be damn near to Phoenix, or Vegas, or out to New York. We'll put out watches, but our best chance of finding them would be when they go back to L.A. The California cops are really hot for Pilate."

"So they're gone. As far as we're concerned," Letty said.

"They might be. But if they went south, they'd be in Wisconsin for a long time, where everybody was looking for them and not finding them. So they might have headed for the nearest state lines—back to Minnesota, or east to Michigan. Depends on what this Pilate guy wants to do, I guess. If he's really a Juggalo freak, he could show up in Sault Ste. Marie next week, and then Detroit. I'll tell you something—you could hide a jumbo jet in the UP so nobody could find it. There's not a lot up there. If I were them, that's where I would have gone."

"What are we gonna do?" Letty asked.

"What are *we* gonna do? I've got the Merion case hanging over my head, and a bunch of other stuff."

"You can't just drop this . . ."

"I won't. I might ditch you at the cabin, to wait for your mom. If I leave right now, I could get over to Baudette, where those Minnesota plates came from, by early afternoon. See what I can see. Make it down to the Cities by late tonight. Then, if nothing turns up, I might zip over to Sault Ste. Marie and sniff around. Between you and me . . . if this thing is outside Sault Ste. Marie, that means the city cops won't be covering it, and the county cops are gonna be way overloaded."

"But I—"

". . . Will not be going to Sault Ste. Marie. I've had busted ribs and you're not going to want to walk around a lot. Or even hit potholes, as you'll find out this afternoon when your mom takes you home. She's never met one that she didn't hit. So basically, you'll be hanging out with your yuppie friends, trying to decide what kind of obscenely expensive hipster hi-tops you'll wear back to your obscenely expensive college in the fall."

"You know I'm not like that," Letty said.

"You're like that a little bit," Lucas said. "Like me, though not as much."

"Thank Jesus. I really don't know where you get the time to shop."

"It's more important to look good, than to feel good," Lucas said.

"What?"

"Never mind. Before your time," Lucas said.

THE STATEMENTS TOOK an hour, starting with Letty's meeting with Skye and Henry in San Francisco, through the discovery of Skye's body. Lucas filled in bits about the discovery of Henry's body in South Dakota, the relationship to the probable L.A. murder of Kitty Place, about the shooting of Bony.

As they were finishing, a deputy came in and said, "They found an ID on that girl. Her name wasn't Skye, it was Shirley Bellows. She was from Indiana, had a couple of arrests for shoplifting and minor possession. We're trying to get in touch with her folks now, but we're having trouble locating them."

Letty and Lucas looked at each other and Letty teared up, didn't try to hide it, and Lucas said to the deputy, "Thanks for letting us know."

When they got out of the sheriff's office, they walked down the street to the Angler's Bar and Grill and got cheeseburgers for breakfast, then Letty wanted to stop at the bookstore on the corner and get newspapers, to see if there'd been any coverage of the murder the night before.

There had not been: "Too late," Lucas said. "We'll see it tomorrow."

Letty went to get a magazine for the trip home, and Lucas took a minute to browse the hunting and fishing books. Somebody had left a book, facing out, about cadaver dogs. He read a few pages of it, until Letty was ready to go.

Outside, she asked, "Are you going to Baudette?"

"Yeah, but I won't get there until late in the day— four o'clock, if I leave the cabin as soon as I get you back there."

"Wish I was going," Letty said.

"But you're not. You're gonna sit on your butt until your ribs heal up," Lucas said. "Even if I gotta handcuff you to a chair."

10

WEATHER WAS UNHAPPY that Lucas was leaving Letty at the cabin alone, but Lucas said, with a crackle of impatience, "Listen. Nobody's gonna find her at the cabin. We give highly detailed maps to friends and they still can't find it. She'll be alone for four hours, watching TV. If you insist, she can go up in the attic and pull out the shotgun. But if I've got to sit here, staring at her for four hours, and then go over to Baudette, I'll have to stay overnight. I was hoping to get home tonight."

"All right. All right. We'll get there as fast as we can," Weather said. "I'll be righteously pissed if you don't make it home tonight, though."

So he left Letty at the cabin with a kiss on the forehead, with easy access to food and a Beretta 12-gauge, and headed west. He passed the Juggalo encampment, which had grown even further, still with a cluster of cop cars around the murder scene.

As he went through Hayward, he got on the phone to Virgil Flowers: "Are you still in Fergus Falls?"

A moment of silence: "Where the hell else would I be?"

"Hey, you don't have to be rude about it."

"Fuck you, I'm hanging up."

But he didn't, not quite quickly enough. Lucas asked, "How fast can you get to Baudette?"

"Are you kidding me? I can leave in one minute," Flowers said. "If I have to stay here for more than another *ten* minutes, I'm going to start shooting at a state senator's cousins."

"Use your pistol. At least that way, you won't actually hit anyone." Lucas and Flowers had once been in a shoot-out in which Flowers attempted to shoot a woman in the chest. He hit her in the foot.

"I'm laughing inside," Flowers said. "Of all the miserable, rotten, corrupt, useless, political-payoff assignments in the universe . . . I'm out spying on sheep in the middle of the night, I'm talking to a guy who says he was taken up in a flying saucer and had sexual experiments done on him—which, I got to say, is probably the only sexual experiments he's ever had done on him, that didn't involve a heifer, because he's the single least likable motherfucker in the state of Minnesota."

"Yeah, yeah, yeah. You weren't really supposed to investigate, Virgil, you were supposed to *pretend* to investigate. You knew that. Anyway, this is serious. I'm headed over to Baudette . . ."

He explained the situation, and Flowers asked, "Letty's really okay?" Despite their difference in ages, there'd always been an electrical buzz between Letty and Flowers. And Flowers wasn't *that* old.

"She's fine. She hurts, but I have to say, a little pain will probably be good for her," Lucas said. "She walks up to an insane killer—literally insane—and gives him shit, and gets off with a black eye and some cracked ribs. I'll take that."

"I wouldn't, if I had a daughter," Flowers said. "I'd hunt him down and shoot him. With a rifle. Or maybe just beat him into tomato paste."

"From what I've heard about Frankie, you probably will, sooner or later, have the chance to do something like that, and probably sooner. Then you'll be begging for daughter-raising advice. Like the first time she comes home with her bra on backwards."

"Whatever. See you in Baudette. If I get there first, I'll check at the courthouse and find out where this guy actually lives."

"See you there," Lucas said.

LUCAS WORRIED ABOUT Letty all the way through Duluth, heading west and then north in the Mercedes until Weather called and said, "We've got her. She's still alive. But jeez, that's a black eye for the ages."

"Tell her to remember to take her stool softener," Lucas said.

———

WITH LETTY SAFE, he worried about Flowers for a while. Flowers was one of the best investigators he'd ever met, or even heard of, and had gotten himself tangled up in some strange cases: but he'd been right about the Fergus Falls assignment. The assignment had been phony from the start and Flowers was in Fergus Falls basically as a sop to a state senator who had some influence over a piece of the BCA budget.

The fact that the senator was crazier than a bedbug and dumber than a crescent wrench hadn't changed that one salient fact: he had some influence.

So Flowers had gone . . . and Lucas had been dragged under another inch.

THE DRIVE TO Baudette was fundamentally boring, through low, swampy country for the most part, though the straight sections of the empty highway gave him a chance to blow the excess oil out of the Benz's cylinders—he could get it to 121, but then it started to make some strange noises, and the road was rough enough that the truck was hopping around like a grasshopper on a griddle. Lucas was closing in on Baudette when Flowers called: "I've got the address, some satellite photos, and a search warrant. Supposedly an old farm gone to seed. Where are you?"

"The nav system says I'm fifteen miles out," Lucas said. "What's this about a search warrant?"

"The sheriff knows the place and the kid you're looking for. Says he's no-good white trash and probably heavily armed. I told him the situation and he took me over to a judge's house and got us a search warrant. I didn't see any reason to say no," Virgil said. "If you're fifteen miles out, you probably just passed the farm. We can either come that way—me and the sheriff's deputy, with the warrant—or you can come on into town. I'm at a Holiday station."

"I need gas and something to eat. I'll meet you there."

"Look for the giant walleye," Flowers said.

LUCAS EASED OFF the accelerator as he came into town, eventually crossed a bridge, and simultaneously spotted the giant walleye, the Holiday station, and Virgil Flowers. Flowers was sitting on the hood of his 4Runner, in the Holiday parking lot, wearing a tan straw cowboy hat and eating an ice cream cone; his boat was hooked to the back of the truck. Seated next to him on the hood was the deputy, also licking an ice cream cone, and the first thing that Lucas noticed about her was that she was noticeable, and she was laughing at something Flowers had said.

"Fuckin' Flowers," he muttered to himself.

Lucas parked and got out of the truck, and Flowers introduced the deputy as Nancy Mahler. Mahler hopped down and shook his hand and said, "Virgie has been telling me all about you. I'm honored."

Lucas said, "Jesus, Virgil, what'd you tell her?" though he didn't mind the attention.

"About how you rescued that deputy last year," she said. She had eyes the color of new-mown hay and blond hair cut close. "He said if you hadn't kicked down the door and gone in there alone, she'd be dead now."

"Well, we don't really know that," Lucas said. But he clapped Flowers on the shoulder and said, "Good to see you, guy. Let me get something to eat and we'll figure out what we're doing."

LUCAS GOT A suspicious-looking egg salad sandwich, a pack of Sno Balls, some strips of beef jerky, and a Diet Coke. They all got in his Benz, with Mahler peering over their shoulders from the backseat as they thumbed through the aerial photos Flowers had downloaded at the sheriff's office.

"The owner's name is George Tillus, and the kid's name is Chet, or Chester," Flowers said. "Supposed to be a farm, but Tillus never farmed it. He always rented it out. Then, a few years ago, they quit farming altogether: don't even rent it out anymore. He's been on welfare, off and on, gets some medical aid, and that's about it."

"Chet Tillus is a jerk, I can tell you that. We were glad to see the last of him. Likes to fight, at least, when he won't lose—he's a classic bully that way—and he's been in trouble since he was a kid," Mahler said. "All crappy stuff. Got caught doing a couple of small-time burglaries. One time, four or five years back, he broke into this guy's house and stole a sackful of computer equipment and some other stuff, and the vic's hat. The vic had a black cowboy hat, pretty expensive for a hat. Bought it in Denver. Chet, who's got all the brains of an oyster, was wearing it around town. The vic sees him, called us, Chet told us he'd had the hat for years, and when we took it off his head, here was the vic's name stamped on the hatband. Hadn't even bothered to scrape it off."

"So we're not talking about Einstein," Flowers said.

"We're talking about a mean little jerk who, if you told him you were a cop, he'd spit on your shoe," Mahler said. "The general feeling around the office was that sooner or later, he'd kill someone, or one of us would kill him. We were just waiting for it to happen. Then one day, he picks up and leaves town. This was maybe a year ago, and we haven't seen or heard from him since."

"Well, you might have your murder," Lucas said. He'd never in his life called a victim a "vic," and it made him think that Mahler might have spent too much time looking at the TV.

"Virgie told me about it," Mahler said. "You think he's back at the farm?"

"Could be, if he thinks it'd be a good place to hide," Lucas said. "What I'm really hoping is that he's still running with Pilate and his gang, and we can get a cell phone number. If we can get a number for him, we can probably figure out where he is, and where the gang is."

Virgil squared up the photos, tapped the top one, and said, "The farm's this fuzzy square you see here. They were fields once, but now they're getting overgrown with trash trees. You can still see the outlines. At some point, I was told that George Tillus . . ."

"He's called Pap," Mahler said.

". . . tried to start a cheap RV campground down there, but that went nowhere. He'll still get a camper now and then, but it's the bottom of the campground heap." He touched the map: "Here's the house, it's pretty far back, a couple hundred yards, so he'll see us coming. And then way back, by this pond, there are actually two campgrounds. The back one looks like it's got four single-wides. I don't know what they're about. They're not RVs."

Lucas looked at the photos, and touched a wide, dark stream that showed up a few hundred yards north of the farm. "Is that the Rainy?"

"Yeah, it is," Mahler said.

Lucas said to Mahler, "Virgil once illegally shot a guy, I think it was across the Rainy, wasn't it, Virgil? You were in Minnesota, the guy was in Canada?"

"Purely self-defense," Flowers said.

"Gee, I'd like to hear about that," Mahler said to Flowers. She was close enough to him, leaning over the backseat, that she could have stuck her tongue into his ear.

"We better get going. I want to get back home tonight," Lucas said. He added, "I suspect Frankie's probably pining for you, too . . . Virgie."

THEY WENT OUT separately, led by the deputy, Lucas behind her, Flowers trailing with his 4Runner and boat. The farm was fifteen minutes east of Baudette. Mahler signaled the turn well before they got to it, and they followed her bouncing down a dirt track into what looked like a forest, but was actually a fairly thin tree line that opened out into swampy-looking onetime fields now dotted with short evergreens.

Farther back, a weathered, dirty two-story farmhouse dominated the fields, with crumbling outbuildings off to the left side of the dirt patch that surrounded the house. Lucas could see that the driveway led past the house, back toward the campgrounds.

They pulled into the dirt parking area, and a few seconds later, an older man stumbled out of the house: George Tillus had hair longer than Flowers's, and hadn't shaved for a week or so, the gray beard making him look even older than he was. He was wearing overalls over a stained white T-shirt, and rubber boots. "What the hell's going on?"

Mahler said, "Pap, we've got a search warrant for the house. Looking for that boy of yours."

"He's not here and I ain't seen him. What'd he do?" He was talking to Mahler and Lucas, but his eyes kept sliding over to Flowers. Flowers was standing next to the open driver's-side door of his truck, watching the confrontation across the hood. He had a shotgun lying across the front seat.

"Might be involved in a murder," Mahler said. "We're gonna have to take a look inside."

"Well, now, I'd have to talk to my attorney about that." His eyes shifted again.

"As far as I know, you don't have an attorney," Mahler

said. "We'll get one for you, but we get to look inside right now. So, if you'll show us the way . . ."

She stepped forward, toward the house, but Tillus moved in front of her and shouted, "Is this what America has come to? The cops—"

Lucas looked at Flowers and called, "He's stalling."

"I'm gone," Flowers said. He grabbed the shotgun and jogged down the far side of the house and disappeared.

Tillus stepped back and shouted, "What's going on? I know my rights. I want an attorney—"

Mahler: "You'll get an attorney—"

Lucas hooked her by the arm, said, "Get behind my truck, pull your firearm, I've got to cover Virgil."

"What?"

"Just do it."

Lucas pulled his gun and ran past Tillus, down the near side of the house. At the back, he saw a line of people running, seven of them, strung out toward the campgrounds. Flowers had passed two of them, women wearing long dresses and head scarves, and then slowed and pointed his shotgun into the air and fired a shot.

BOOM!

The 12-gauge sounded like an artillery piece, and the five runners ahead of Flowers slowed, and looked back, and one cried out something that Lucas didn't understand, and they slowed and finally stopped on the dirt track. Far down the track, Lucas saw two young children and a woman run into a clump of trees.

Ahead, Flowers was shouting, and the runners now had all their hands in the air. They were tall, thin people, frightened. Lucas came up and Flowers said, "Illegals. He's running a campground for Somalis coming across from Canada. Goddamnit."

They got the Somalis back to the house, checked them for weapons, had them sit on the porch with Tillus, who'd gone silent, and left them with Mahler, who said more cops were on the way.

FLOWERS GOT AN M16 out of the back of his truck, gave it to Lucas, and the two of them walked back to the campground, where they found seven more Somalis, four women and three children, hiding in the single-wides. No guns, anywhere. They waited until the women had packed up some clothing, then escorted them back to the house.

On the way, Flowers said, "They come in by ship, get dropped off on the Canadian North Shore, get trucked over here, and cross the river at night. Next day, they're in Minneapolis."

"How do you know all that?"

"From a story in *Musky Hunter* magazine," Flowers said. Then: "Just kiddin'. Saw it on Channel Two."

At the house, two more sheriff's cars had arrived, and the late-arriving deputies were chatting with Mahler, and watching the Somalis.

Mahler asked, "That all of them?"

"Might be some hiding out in the weeds, I don't know," Lucas said. He didn't much care, either.

"I called the Border Patrol. Ought to have somebody here in ten minutes," Mahler said. Another sheriff's car turned in the driveway.

"All I want to do is look in the house," Lucas said.

"Fuckin' Nazis," Pap shouted at them.

HE AND FLOWERS went into the house, stepping through the Somalis now clustered despondently on the porch. One of the kids was crying and Flowers said, "I kinda wish we hadn't done this."

Lucas nodded. "Didn't want to. As far as I'm concerned, they can put them in a bus and haul them down to Minneapolis and turn them loose."

Not going to happen; they were now in the system.

"Stinks," Flowers said, as they stepped into the house.

The interior of the house was old, moldy, and poorly kept. The kitchen appeared to have been built in the 1930s, and not cleaned since, smelling of bacon grease, fried eggs, and flatulence. The refrigerator was full of ready-to-microwave frozen food, in the top compartment, and a dozen eggs and the remains of a pound of butter in the lower. An overflowing trash can smelled of rotten coffee grounds.

Tillus had used what had once been a parlor as storage for every kind of paper—bills, magazines, catalogs, newspapers; the rug on the parlor floor was not much thicker than a sheet, most of the nap worn through. The living room featured an oversized television, two chairs facing it, and probably thirty fox tails pinned to the crown molding, so that they hung down all around the room like fuzzy red icicles.

As they walked around, pulling drawers, looking in corners, they found a half dozen guns—three rifles, three revolvers, ranging in age from old to ancient.

A wired telephone sat on a side table in the living room. Lucas went there while Flowers, still with his shotgun, crept up the stairs, ready for trouble if any was up there.

Lucas found a sheet of paper under the phone and the stub of a pencil off to one side. A dozen phone numbers were written on the paper, a doctor, the "county," a few names that meant nothing to Lucas, and one that might have said "Chet."

Lucas wrote down the Chet number, and started for the door, when Flowers called from the second floor: "Hey, Lucas. You better come up here."

Lucas turned back and climbed the stairs. Halfway up, a long strip of wallpaper had fallen from the wall, and now seemed to be mostly held up by spiderwebs. At the top of the stairs, he found two bedrooms and a bathroom. Flowers was standing in the front bedroom, shotgun over his shoulders, next to an antique single bed with flat springs and a two-inch-thick mattress, like an army bunk. It was covered with a dirt-gray sheet, flocked with dust bunnies.

Lucas recognized the symptoms: "What have you done, Virgil?"

Flowers said, "There's a roll of carpet under the bed."

"What?"

"A roll of carpet under the bed." Flowers was smiling, sort of, but his voice wasn't.

Lucas knelt next to the end of the bed, saw a carpet roll—and in the middle of the roll, a fold of clear plastic, maybe Saran Wrap, now as dusty as the top sheet, but very clearly wrapped around the bones of a human foot, which were held in place by the wrapping plastic.

Lucas stood up and brushed off his knees and said, "You know what? We ought to sneak out of here and let the deputies find the body."

Flowers said, "Even if we could work it . . ."

"Yeah. We're too straight," Lucas said. "Goddamnit, all I wanted was a fuckin' phone number."

"You get it?" Flowers asked.

"Maybe. Gotta check."

Flowers said, "We better go tell them."

LUCAS LET FLOWERS handle that, while he walked to his car and got on the phone to the BCA duty officer and asked him to check the owner of the phone number he'd found. As he waited, he saw a couple of deputies, including Mahler, follow Flowers into the house. Tillus was still sitting on the steps with the Somalis; a moment later, a Border Patrol truck rolled into the yard, followed by another sheriff's car.

The duty officer came back and said, "Goes to a Chester Tillus, on Verizon."

"Good. Get onto Verizon and tell them to ping it. We need to know where the phone is, right now. And tell them that this is official business and the phone owner is not to be notified . . . however you do that. As soon as you hear back, call me."

That done, he got out of his truck, met Flowers coming out the door.

Flowers asked, "Now what?"

"I'll call Sands and see if we can unload this on the Bemidji guys, and get the hell out of here," Lucas said. Sands was the BCA director. Bemidji was the BCA's northern outpost.

Flowers looked around the yard: there were now five or six deputies and a couple of Border Patrol guys wandering around.

"Quite the little party you got going here, Lucas," Flowers said. "Reminds me of the stuff I do every day."

"Thank you."

A little while later, the sheriff arrived, followed by a white bus-like conversion van to transport the Somalis. Lucas and Flowers chatted with the sheriff for a few minutes, and the sheriff went up to look at the foot in the carpet roll.

A few minutes later, he came back and said he suspected that it was George Tillus's mother, who hadn't been seen for a couple of decades. She supposedly had gone to California to live with her sister; but now, it appeared, might not have gotten out of the driveway.

They were still chatting when the duty officer called back and told Lucas, "He's off the grid right now, but they had him last night, first in Ironwood, and then a few minutes later, in Bessemer. Looks like he was heading east into the UP."

"Tell them to keep pinging him. I want to know if he comes back up," Lucas said. To Flowers: "My boy is on his way to Sault Ste. Marie. I will see you later."

"I'm not going back to Fergus Falls," Flowers called after him.

"You got *anything* else to do?" Lucas asked, turning back around.

"Lucas . . ." Flowers always had things to do. He covered roughly one-third of a large state.

"Then go do them. If Moore calls, I'll personally tell him to go fuck himself," Lucas said. Moore was the state senator who had influence on the budget.

LUCAS HEADED HOME, driving fast, stopped once to pee and buy an ice cream cone, cut I-35 at Moose Lake, and made it into St. Paul a few minutes before eleven o'clock. He'd driven a little over six hundred miles since leaving the cabin that morning, and he was beat.

Letty was still up: she met him at the door from the garage, and he looked at her face and said, "Wow."

"Yeah, he really plugged me," Letty said. Her black eye extended probably two inches down from her eye, and was a deep blue-black. "Mom's in bed. She's working early tomorrow."

"And you're okay?"

Letty nodded. "Mom took me all over the place, an

eye doctor because she wanted to make sure I wasn't going to have a detached retina, which I don't and won't have, and an ENT guy. The ENT guy said it'll be three days before the nose stops hurting inside and three weeks before the black eye is gone."

"Sounds about right. At least he didn't break your nose. I can tell you, *that* hurts."

"What happened in Baudette?" Letty asked.

Lucas told her about it as he led her into the kitchen, where he stuck his head into the refrigerator looking for something substantial to eat. He told her about the phone number and the body under the bed. "Beneath its blond exterior, Minnesota is a very weird place," Letty said.

"On the basic weird-shit-o-meter, you're going to college in a state that's probably an eleven. They don't notice it so much, because they've gotten used to it."

"Are you going to Sault Ste. Marie?" she asked.

"Don't know. I'll talk to some people in Michigan, but I might run over there, depending on what the Michigan cops say. Put more of a point on things."

"Not because Pilate punched me out."

"A little bit because Pilate punched you out," Lucas said. "The main reason is, everything is now so bureaucratic, so much talking on telephones and sending e-mails, that I don't know if anybody else has . . . the feeling . . . I've gotten about this. This guy is a major-league wacko. There are three dead in Wisconsin, counting that Bony guy, and even Stern is acting like it's another day in the flour mill. And Stern's a good guy."

WEATHER GOT UP at six o'clock, moving quietly by habit, but Lucas woke up and caught her naked in the bathroom for a little squeeze. "Letty is hoping you're going to Michigan," she said.

"Maybe. I'll check at the office first," Lucas said.

"You're gonna fly?"

"Probably not. I looked online last night, and the absolutely fastest way I can fly there from here goes through Detroit, and from the time I have to be at the airport, until I get off the plane, is going to be seven hours or more. I can drive it almost as fast, and take all my gear."

"You mean your guns."

"Maybe."

"Don't get shot, it'd be really inconvenient for everybody."

LUCAS GOT CLEANED up and slid out of the house before seven o'clock, Letty still sound asleep. At the office he checked notes and e-mails from his agents, got a note from Flowers that had come in before seven, saying that he was heading back to Mankato, where he lived.

Lucas called him, caught him in a diner: "What about the body?"

"Tillus said it was his mother. Said he went up to her bedroom one morning when he didn't hear her stirring around, and she was dead. He was planning to bury her there on the farm, but never got around to it.

He eventually got tired of looking at her up there, wrapped in a sheet, so he rolled her up in that rug."

"You believe him?"

"Yeah, I guess. Ol' Mom was just another pain in his ass. Tillus also mentioned something about her Social Security checks—he might still have been cashing them."

"Good ol' Mom, the gift that keeps on giving."

"Yeah. Her arms and legs were mostly gone, but there was some mummification around her head and chest, so they're shipping her down to the medical examiner to see if there are any wounds," Flowers said. "But I kinda believe him."

"Okay."

"What about you?" Flowers asked. "What are you doing up at this time of day?"

"Going to Sault Ste. Marie, if I can get out of town. Gonna talk to Michigan about meeting somebody up there."

"Yeah, good idea. It's just a teeny bit out of your jurisdiction," Flowers said. "You've cleared this with Sands, right?"

"Not exactly."

"Lucas: clear it with Sands. Please, I'm beggin' you."

"I'll think about it," Lucas said.

LUCAS FIGURED THAT if he could get out of the office before eight-thirty, he could make it into Sault Ste. Marie before five, which would give him some office hours' time to talk to the local sheriff and scout the site of the Juggalo Gathering.

Michigan was an hour later than Minnesota, but when he called State Police Headquarters in Lansing, he got kicked around between offices for a while, and finally gave up. He'd call from the truck, he thought.

Jon Duncan, one of the senior case coordinators, was in his office, and Lucas told him about the situation in Baudette. Duncan said he'd tell the Bemidji office to get in touch with the local sheriff, and see if any BCA help was required.

He left a message at Hennepin County Medical Center for Weather, telling her he was on his way to Michigan, and was on his way out the door when he ran into Henry Sands, the BCA director, coming up the steps.

Sands was unhappy: "Senator Moore got me out of bed this morning. He said Flowers ditched them for some other case."

"I had to pull him off—not Virgil's fault," Lucas said. "Something came up, up in Baudette, and he was the closest one of my guys."

Sands said, "Lucas, I don't think you understand how important the Fergus Falls case is. Moore is really unhappy. He said Flowers was dragging his feet anyway, like the whole case really didn't interest him."

Lucas leaned into Sands and said, "Henry, the whole Fergus Falls case is bullshit. Moore is a bullshitter. Not only are we wasting our time, we risk becoming a laughingstock out there."

Sands's face flushed, and he said, "I don't care what some hick farmer out there thinks, I care about what Moore thinks. He's on the finance committee, and he can fuck us."

Lucas said, "I gotta go," and walked away, heading for the front doors.

"Where are you going?"

"Michigan."

"What? What? What about Flowers?"

Lucas turned and said, "Flowers is working. He's got real work to do. Leave him alone, Henry."

11

THE DRIVE TO Sault Ste. Marie was tedious. Lucas stopped twice in small towns to stretch and get a bite to eat, and along the way, made a few phone calls. He couldn't drum up much interest from the Michigan state cops, who suggested that he talk to the local sheriff, and then *he'd* talk to the state cops, if that were really necessary. But the UP was *such* a long way from anywhere . . .

He talked to Del and Shrake, his agents, about their ongoing cases in Minnesota, and to Letty, who was spending her time in an easy chair in Lucas's home office, reading and doing research on the Internet when he needed it.

Lucas had been told by several people, including Letty, Skye, and other Juggalos, that the Juggalo event was in Sault Ste. Marie. Now Letty told him that it actually wasn't in the city itself, but at a county park in Barron County, southwest of Sault Ste. Marie.

"I think everybody says Sault Ste. Marie because it's the closest real city," Letty told him on the phone. "You're not going to like what you find in Barron County. The county seat is Jeanne d'Arc, which is the French spelling of Joan of Arc. According to the Wiki, the population in 2000 was two thousand forty-six, and in 2010 was one thousand eight hundred and four, which means the place lost ten percent of its population in ten years. It's on Lake Michigan."

"The local beaver plant probably closed," Lucas said, looking out the window at the passing landscape, which consisted of a two-lane highway, an unrelieved wall of dark green oak trees, a scattering of pines, and the tail-lights of a single car, far ahead of him.

"What?"

"Nothing. Who's the sheriff?"

"A guy named Roman Laurent. Here's another non-great thing. The county website sucks and I'm not sure about this, but he appears to have six deputies and a po-lice dog. Total. There might also be some clerks and part-time help. They don't have a jail—if they need to put somebody in jail, they rent space from Chippewa County, which is Sault Ste. Marie."

"Ah, boy. What about Jeanne d'Arc city cops?"

"Let me look . . . Okay, there's a picture, looks like they've got at least seven cops. But the Gathering isn't right in Jeanne d'Arc, either. It's ten or twelve miles out of town, at a lake at Overtown Park. I don't know if the city cops would go there."

"There's gotta be some kind of mutual aid program, if they need it," Lucas said. "What about motels?"

"Let me look . . . There's a Comfort Inn and a Holiday Inn Express, both on Lake Michigan. Then there are a couple local places, it looks like."

"See if you can get me a room in whatever looks best . . . and find me the fastest route into Jeanne d'Arc."

A WHILE LATER, remembering his stop at the bookstore in Hayward, with Letty, he called Shrake back and told him to see if there was a cadaver dog in Minnesota. "A what?"

"A cadaver dog. I was just reading about them—about how they can sniff out even small traces of blood. Even after somebody's been dead for a while. If there's a bloody club buried somewhere . . ."

"You want us to go back up to Cross Lake?"

"We gotta try. If you find a cadaver dog, you can go play golf while the dog works," Lucas said. "And if you find one, check around Merion's house, too."

Shrake still sounded doubtful: "I suppose we could try. We're not getting much talking to these computer-chip guys."

LUCAS PULLED INTO Jeanne d'Arc a few minutes after four o'clock and followed the highway along the Lake Michigan waterfront to Main Street. Letty had said that the county courthouse was on Main, several blocks back from the water.

Lucas turned up a shallow hill, between Main's double line of early-twentieth-century two-story brick buildings, and found the courthouse above a narrow green lawn six blocks from the lake. A newer building, of metallic-looking purple brick, with a steel roof, the courthouse was half wrapped by a parking lot. Lucas found an empty slot, parked, and went inside.

A guard was sitting at a desk in the lobby, doing nothing, although he seemed content. He nodded and Lucas said, "I'm an investigator with the Minnesota Bureau of Criminal Apprehension. Can you tell me where the sheriff's office is?"

"Yup. You go all the way to the end of the lobby, take a left, go down that hall. You'll see the door. Roman's in there, because I just saw him come back from Pat's with a sandwich and a soda."

"Pat's is decent?" Lucas asked.

"The best around here, if you just want a sandwich," the guard said.

Lucas thanked him for the tip and walked down the lobby past the county clerk's window—the clerk was sitting on a stool, doing nothing, and said, "Hi, there," as he walked by. He nodded at her, turned the corner, and found the door to the sheriff's office at the back of the building.

Inside the door, he found himself in a small room with an empty desk, two closed doors apparently going back to other offices, two paintings of fish, one of ducks, and a DARE poster. Not exactly sure what to do, he waited, and a minute or so later, an older lady came bustling through, stopped when she saw him, and said, "Oh! I didn't know there was anybody here."

Lucas identified himself and said, "I'd like to talk to Sheriff Laurent if he has a minute."

"I think he's over at Pat's."

"The guard at the door said he just came back."

"Oh!" Surprised again. "Just a second, then." She went to one of the closed doors, opened it, stuck her head through, and called, "Hey, Rome? You back there?"

"Yeah, I'm here."

"You got a fellow here to see you. He's an investigator from Minnesota," she said.

"Minnesota?"

"That's what he says."

"Well, send him on back."

ROMAN LAURENT WAS a tall, thin man with steel-colored hair, gray eyes, and high cheekbones; he looked like he might run marathons. He was wearing a tan sheriff's uniform, and when he stood up to shake hands, Lucas noticed that while he was wearing a holster, it was empty.

"Sit down, sit down. You don't mind if I finish a late lunch? Or early dinner?" Laurent asked.

"Go ahead. I might stop over there myself," Lucas said, as he took a visitor's chair. "Did you get a call from the state police this morning? About what I'm doing?"

Laurent paused in mid-chew and shook his head. "The state police don't call me about anything. We could have an asteroid about to hit the town and the state police wouldn't call me."

"Ah, jeez. Well, I got some news for you, then. You've got a crazy killer on his way, with a whole bunch of assistant killers, if they're not already here."

Laurent stopped eating as Lucas explained about Pilate, about the probable murders in Los Angeles, the for-sure murders in South Dakota and Wisconsin, and the peculiar findings in Baudette, Minnesota.

He concluded by saying, "We heard they were headed here for the Juggalo Gathering. Then, when we pinged the one guy whose phone we knew, we spotted him in Ironwood and a while later, in Bessemer, so he was coming this way."

"Pretty interesting," Laurent said. He ate the final chunk of his sandwich, balled up the wrapper, bounced it off the wall and into a wastebasket. He sighed and said, "You know, I believe every word you've said, but I don't need this. I've got six officers working for me full-time, plus reserve deputies and a dog, and the dog got his feet cut up on broken glass yesterday and he's out of it for a week. That means two guys for busy shifts, one guy for others. The dog has the most experience. Not counting the part-timers, he might even be the smartest. I include myself in that. I've never investigated anything more complicated than mailbox theft."

"How about the city cops?" Lucas asked.

"About the same, except dumber than the dog, for sure."

They stared at each other for a few seconds, then Lucas asked, "No offense . . . but how'd you get to be sheriff?"

Laurent grinned at him and said, "I wanted to live up here near my family, my folks and brothers and sisters, and my ex-wife. This was the best job around. I was a Ranger officer in the army with three tours in Iraq, I know some things about guns and don't mind the occasional bar fight . . . and that was good enough for the folks in Barron County. The last sheriff was both incompetent and a crook. I'm neither one. So, basically, I'm good for the job, at least in Barron County. We just don't do what you might call your high-end investigations."

"I'm not sure we'd really need that here," Lucas said. "What we need is to go out to the Juggalo Gathering and bust a few guys, if they show up there."

Laurent shrugged and said, "We're good for that, if you can point them out. I've got a couple muscle-heads working for me who'll do the job."

Lucas said, "All right. I can get you warrants from both Wisconsin and South Dakota. The Gathering starts tomorrow."

"It's already started," Laurent said. "The early birds are setting up their camps right now."

"Then we ought to go up and take a look. The way this wacko operates, he might be picking out a victim right now. He got pissed at this girl in Wisconsin and kicked her to death right there in the Gathering field, about a hundred feet from the bandstand."

"Jesus. That's not something you see every day," Laurent said. "You want to ride with me or go separately?"

Lucas didn't usually want to ride with another cop, because they'd often wind up having separate things to do. At the same time, he needed to talk more with Laurent, to figure out what the other man could do and not do. "I'll go with you tonight," Lucas said. "We're just looking around."

"We can stop at Pat's, if you want, get you a sandwich."

LAURENT GOT HIS gun from a desk drawer, a black Beretta of the type he probably carried in the army, and they walked out to his truck, stopped at Pat's, where Lucas got a roast beef on rye with mustard and onions, on Laurent's recommendation, and a Diet Coke, and they headed out to the county park.

"Let me tell you a few things about this place, the UP," Laurent said, as they drove out of town in his Silverado pickup. "The UP is about the most remote place in the lower forty-eight—other people make the same claim, but they don't know about the UP. The people down in Lansing don't give a rat's ass about us—we've only got three percent of the state's population and don't have enough votes to worry the politicians who don't live here, so why should they care? The UP is about the size of Massachusetts and Connecticut put together. The biggest town's got twenty-one thousand people. It's better than three hundred miles from one end to the other, from Ironwood to Sault Ste. Marie, and no four-lane highway, except I-75, which runs up from the south across the Mackinac Strait to Canada. That's no more than sixty miles long, and only affects the far east part of the UP. If you want to drive from east to west, the way this guy is coming, it'd take you at least five hours. Covering that amount of territory, sixteen thousand square miles, you've got no more than a few hundred cops, working three shifts plus weekends, most of those concentrated in maybe a dozen towns. So, if you want to enforce the law in the UP—well, you're on your own."

"If it's so remote, why do the Juggalos come up here?" Lucas asked.

"Because it's nice in the summer. Most of them come up from the Detroit area, where the Insane Clown Posse comes from, which is not nice, in the summer or mostly any other time. We got good lakes and, like I said, no cops—we leave them alone," Laurent said. "They want to smoke a little weed, no problem. Besides, everybody up here wants them to come. They've been up here for four years now, don't cause us a lot of trouble, other than hauling some trash out of the park. They've got their own medics and if somebody ODs, they haul them off to Sault Ste. Marie—no hospital in Jeanne d'Arc. And the Juggalos probably leave a quarter million dollars behind. In Barron County, that's big."

After a while, Laurent asked, "How many guys traveling with this fruitcake?"

"Well, we killed one of them. So, not more than twenty," Lucas said.

Laurent said, "Wait a minute. There are *twenty* crazy killers coming up here?"

"At the most," Lucas said. "As far as we know."

Laurent laughed; and that reassured Lucas. He wasn't working with someone who was easily frightened. Or maybe, Lucas thought, he really *was* dumber than the dog.

THE ENTRANCE TO the county park was a gravel road that broke off the highway, followed a winding road through a stand of oaks, and then plunged into a pine forest and emerged at a series of campgrounds spread around a lake.

A few local families were in the nearest campgrounds, set up around picnic tables. Two small boats bobbed in the lake; judging from his own lake, at his cabin, Lucas thought it might be five hundred acres or so.

At the far end of the road, at the end of the lake, the park opened up into a field with a baseball diamond at one end. Fifty cars and pickups and a few RVs were already scattered around the field, and a flatbed truck was unloading green fiberglass porta-potties. Laurent left his truck at the near end of the parking area, and as Lucas got out, the scent of pine trees, wood smoke, and roasting weenies hit him in the face.

Laurent asked, "Now what?"

"We know that they had an RV when they left Wisconsin. Let's kinda cruise those. We're looking for a tribe of people, who hang together. Probably look a little more California than the locals. The Pilate guy dressed as a priest at the Wisconsin Gathering. As I understand it, the RV was at the center of a cluster of cars in Wisconsin."

They cruised the RVs and found no cluster of cars, or

anyone dressed as a priest. In fact, they found only a few people in Juggalo makeup: most of the people were involved in setting up. They'd just taken a look at the last of the RVs when Lucas spotted a green John Deere utility cart bouncing down the field with the fat man in the back.

Lucas headed them off, flagged them down. "You remember me?" he asked the fat guy.

The fat guy pointed a finger-pistol at him and said, "The cop from Minneapolis with the daughter. How is she?"

"Got a big black eye and some cracked ribs. Listen— it's Randy, right?—we're looking for those guys who killed the girl down in Wisconsin. You see anyone like them?"

"Not yet—I've been too busy setting up. Give me your cell phone, and if they come in, I'll call you."

"We especially want the guy who dressed like a priest," Lucas said, as he scribbled the cell number on the back of a business card.

"I will do that," the fat man said.

AFTER A LAST walk-through, Lucas and Laurent left the park. "You think they'll still show up?"

"Don't know," Lucas said. "We'll catch up with them somewhere, but it'd be nice if we could take them down right now. I'll tell you, Rome, the ideal thing would be to bust a bunch of them, and get one to turn."

"Did anyone turn in the Charlie Manson bunch?"

"Yeah. One woman, big-time. And a few other people who knew about Manson, but weren't part of the gang. These guys are not quite the same thing. They're a little more careful, even if they're not a lot smarter. But from what the L.A. cops tell me, they're off in the same direction."

"Oh, boy." Laurent scrubbed at his upper lip with a knuckle. "Let me call some folks, my reserve deputies. They'll help. Why don't we get together at my place, tonight, see what we can figure out. You know, scenarios."

"Why the reserves?"

"Because they're all smart guys," Laurent said. "I think we need smart guys for this."

LUCAS GOT THE last room at the Holiday Inn Express, which turned out to be a handicapped room. That was fine, because it had a better shower than the standard rooms and apparently there were no handicapped people who really needed it. He got cleaned up, and took a phone call from Del about the guy who stole the safe full of diamonds.

"I found Cory."

"Where is he?" He was looking out a window, at cold, steel-gray waves marching across Lake Michigan.

"In a house out in the sticks west of Wyoming, backing up to Carlos Avery. Since that's public land, I snuck up on his place, from the back, with a pair of binoculars. Never saw him, but guess what: there're two standard oxygen tanks lying on the back porch. I think he's running an oxyacetylene torch in the garage, trying to cut the safe open. Since he technically became a fugitive when he stopped talking to his PO, we don't even need a search warrant."

"Goddamnit. I'm over in the UP," Lucas said. "You're gonna have to talk to Jon, organize a raid on the place."

After a long silence, Del said, "I'm not sure that's a good idea, Lucas."

"We can't wait, Del. It might already be too late," Lucas said. "If he's cutting that safe open, he could get through it anytime, and once he does, the diamonds are gone."

"Yeah, but . . ."

"What?"

"Sands is really pissed at you for going up to the UP and at Flowers for dumping that state senator's investigation," Del said. "He called Flowers and jacked him up, and Flowers apparently told him to suck on it. What I'm saying is, this is a fairly high-profile case and you guys could use the credit for busting it. If we get Jon involved . . . I mean, he's not a bad guy, but if he sees a commendation coming down the road, he'd be the first guy to jump in front of it."

Lucas laughed: "You really think I need to blow Sands?"

"No. He's got his own political problems. What I'm saying is, *Davenport* could use some . . . some . . . image-building. Flowers will be okay: everybody loves Virgil. But you've got a U.S. senator who hates you, you've got a big newspaper that'd fuck you any way they could . . ."

"Governor sort of likes my ass."

"Yes, he does. That's why you're still working here," Del said. "But he's gone in a year and Rose Marie goes with him, and then you're out there naked. So . . ."

"Del, I appreciate what you're saying—but fuck it. I don't care much about the credit," Lucas said. "Talk to Jon. He can have Jenkins and Shrake help, if you can hit Cory tonight, but tomorrow, Jenkins and Shrake might be out-of-pocket on another thing. If Jon gets you and Jenkins and Shrake to go on the raid, then everybody will know it's our group who took Cory."

Another silence, then Del said, "This feels bad to me."

"Do it, okay? I've got a real headache over here. So just do it."

"I'll try to get Jon to do it tonight, and I'll call Jenkins and Shrake," Del said. "Goddamnit, man . . ."

"Yeah, I know, Del. Call me when it's done."

LUCAS HAD WORN tan slacks, a Façonnable shirt, and a blue knit sport jacket on his drive over to the UP, an effort to look somewhat official when meeting out-of-state cops. Having checked out Laurent, he decided that wasn't necessary, and changed into jeans, a pull-over shirt, and a light leather jacket that hung down over his .45.

Laurent had given Lucas directions to his house and Lucas arrived a couple of minutes after seven o'clock, as a pizza truck was pulling away from the curb. Laurent lived in a fifties ranch house, with an add-on three-car garage at one end. Two guys in casual dress were standing outside Laurent's side door, drinking beer from bottles, and when Lucas got out of the Benz, one of them said, "Must be the guy," and the other called, "Wish I was a Minnesota cop, get a Benz like that."

"I was too tall for the sports cars," Lucas said. He came up and one of the men, a short bald guy, stuck out his hand and said, "Jim Bennett," and the other said, "Doug Sellers." They shook hands and Sellers said, "Rome is down the basement, probably suckin' down those pizzas already."

Sellers ran a hardware store, he said, and Bennett ran the post office.

Lucas followed them through the door and down to the basement, which had been converted into a recreation room. Along one wall were a number of photos, Laurent on deployment with the army, most of the photos showing him with camo'd-up guys with M-4s.

Laurent, as Bennett and Sellers had suggested, was loading up a plate with pizza from three boxes sitting on a Ping-Pong table. Three other men were sitting on a couple of couches and a La-Z-Boy facing a TV, and were eating or drinking beer.

Laurent saw Lucas and the others come down the stairs, and said, "Beer and Pepsi in the fridge, pepperoni and mushroom pizza. Come on over and meet the guys."

Lucas shook hands with Barney Peters, a lawyer; Rick Barnes, who ran a Subway store; and Jerry Frisell, a high school teacher and coach. The guys turned out to be friends of Laurent. All of them were military veterans, all of them had been deployed in Iraq and were familiar with weapons, but only two, plus Laurent, had seen any combat. Another member of the group had gone south across the bridge to a family affair, and couldn't come.

"This is my posse," Laurent said. "They're all deputized, they've all taken law enforcement courses, they've all qualified with handguns. We don't want any shootouts, but I thought we could put them in the Gathering, in plainclothes, walking the place, looking for this Pilate guy. The main thing being . . . they don't look like cops. You and I do."

Lucas looked at the group and said, "Guys, I appreciate it, but are you sure you want to do this? Pilate is major trouble. He's dangerous, almost certainly a psycho."

Peters peered at Lucas through thick glasses and said, "We know we're not exactly combat troops anymore, but that's the point, isn't it? If somebody has to go after Pilate mano a mano, that would be you or Rome. We're sort of . . . pointer dogs."

Laurent said, "One of the perennial problems with the Gathering is the trash that gets thrown around. We thought we could put one of the guys in there with paper pickup sticks, you know, those things with nails on the end, and some bags. A garbageman. Nobody'll look at him twice. You and I, they'll make us as cops, if they see us . . . but they won't make these guys. The park is close enough to town that we'll have cell service, so we can stay in touch."

"Let's talk about it," Lucas said.

———

THEY DID THAT, and Lucas felt himself nodding. They were serious guys: smart and reasonably tough. They agreed that they wouldn't initiate any action, even if they saw Pilate. They would carry guns: they all had concealed carry permits and Laurent had set up a combat shooting course at a local landfill.

"When we get tired of punching paper, we go after the rats," Sellers said. "Rats are hard to hit with a pistol, but we do it."

"Sometimes, anyway," Frisell amended.

"We don't want anybody shooting anybody, if we can avoid it," Lucas said. "What we want is to spot these guys and drop a net on them."

"We all agree on that," Laurent said. "But we've got to work with what we've got and this is what we've got. My regular deputies—two of them, anyway—will be on duty at the park just as a regular thing. They'll know what's going on, so we'll have four full-time cops, including you and me, right there. The posse will purely be for recon and backup."

Lucas said, "Well . . . let's get another beer."

WHEN LUCAS LEFT, he felt that they had a plan: his biggest worry was that one of the part-timers would get hurt if there was a confrontation. They weren't worried, though, and Laurent was confident that they could handle it. They agreed to rendezvous at Laurent's house at nine o'clock the next morning, for a last talk, and then go on out to the park.

Back at the motel, Lucas got on the phone and talked to Letty and then to Weather, who said that Letty was doing all right, but getting cranky about it. "I don't think she's sat in one place longer than an hour in her whole life—those cracked ribs are getting her down. It's gonna be a few more days before even the ibuprofen helps."

"Every once in a while, without being a jerk about it, remind her of what can happen if you rush in on something without thinking. If she'd handled this better, she wouldn't have gotten hurt, and the entire Pilate crew might be in jail. Instead of getting in Pilate's face, she might have gone around their camp and written down all the numbers of the car tags—"

"Lucas, that would be mean."

"And the experience, and the results, and the after-action analysis might just save her life sometime. Our little sweetie thinks she might want to become a cop, or an intelligence agent, or something. Something exciting. The thing is, if you really want to do something exciting, then you gotta be conservative about it. Be cautious-crazy. It'll keep you alive. Any asshole can get an exciting job that kills him."

"I'll think about that. You might be right. I mean, if she doesn't go to medical school . . ."

"And as far as medical school is concerned, you've got

a couple of other kids to work with," Lucas said. "Letty's a lost cause. Unless there's a job like Navy SEAL doctor."

Silence, for a few moments, listening to Weather breathe, then she said, "Okay."

DEL CALLED AN hour later, as Lucas was watching a West Coast baseball game. "I'm standing in Cory's bedroom," he said, his voice pitched low. "We got Cory, his wife, and his son, who's legally an adult, though he's telling us he never looked in the garage. The safe was in the garage and it's seriously screwed up—I don't know if anybody'll *ever* be able to open it. Cory learned how to use a cutting torch by watching videos on YouTube. He managed to weld it into a blob."

"That's not our problem. Our problem was finding the safe. Hoist it up on a truck and get it downtown."

"They're doing that right now," Del said. "I'm hiding in the bedroom so the TV cameras don't see me."

"TV?"

"I told you. Jon's okay, but his idea of a raid is ten people with M16s and camo and helmets and three TV trucks. We could've gotten the same results by knocking on the door."

"Well, the important thing is the safe."

"What have I been telling you, Lucas? The important thing *isn't* the safe," Del said. "Who really gives a fuck about the safe? Nobody gives a fuck about anything but the entertainment media, of which we are now a branch."

"Del . . ."

"Wake up and smell the coffee, dipshit. You should have been here. You should be out there talking to the talking heads," Del said. "Instead, you're up in the UP with your dick in your hand."

"Good night, Del . . ."

12

LUCAS, LAURENT, TWO regular uniformed depu-
ties, and five part-timers met at Laurent's house the next
morning at nine o'clock, went over their assignments one
last time.

"The basic idea is to find them, watch them, isolate a
few of them, who we can pick up. We talk to them about
being sent back to South Dakota, where they have the
death penalty, and see if that produces anything," Lucas
said. "Right now, if every one of them kept their mouths
shut, we'd have a hard time proving anything—our main
witness got kicked to death in Wisconsin. So, we need
somebody else to turn."

Laurent repeated the essence of it as they went out the
door: "Find, isolate, detain." Before they got to their vehicles, he said to Lucas, "I looked you up on the Internet

last night. There was a story there that said you were a deputy sheriff in Wisconsin one time."

"Yeah, for about fifteen minutes. I didn't get paid or anything. They made me a deputy to give me some legal status."

"And Barron County is happy to do the same, including the part about no pay," Laurent said. "Raise your right hand and repeat after me . . ."

THEY DROVE OUT to Overtown Park separately and several minutes apart. When Lucas arrived, the plainclothes deputies had already disappeared into the growing crowd. The night before, there'd been a few dozen people working in the park. Now there were a hundred, and half of those wore Juggalo clown faces. The paint, mostly black and white, made it difficult to pick out individual features. A bandstand was going up, just as it had at the Wisconsin site, and Lucas spotted Sellers, the guy who owned the hardware store, apparently giving instructions to the workers putting it up.

He didn't find a circle of cars pressing around an RV and none of the RVs he surveyed showed any activity that might be suspicious. Frisell, the teacher, ambled past, shook his hand, smiling, slapped Lucas on the shoulder with his other hand, and said, "There are two California plates down in the far corner, to the left, as you walk down there, right in front of all those pop-up tents. There's only one car in between them. No RV."

"Thanks, I'll take a look," Lucas said, smiling back.

Old pals, bumping into each other in the park: Lucas thought Frisell had done it well.

Lucas wandered down to the far corner, took a look at the cars. One was a five- or six-year-old Subaru, the other an older Corolla. From what Skye had told them about Pilate's group, that sounded right—but then, most of the cars in the parking lot were older. The Juggalos were not an affluent demographic.

He wrote the tag numbers in his notebook, then wandered off, fifty yards or so, and sat under a tree to watch them. Fifteen minutes later, a youngish woman—maybe thirty?—walked up to the Corolla, popped the trunk, took a daypack out, slammed the trunk lid, and walked away.

Lucas followed. She was slender and narrow-shouldered, with dark hair bent around her head like a bowl. He hadn't been able to look directly at her face, but got the impression of delicate features, thin bow lips, and dark eyebrows. She was wearing a white blouse, form-fitting jeans, and rubber-soled slippers. No face paint.

They'd gotten a few general descriptions of Pilate's disciples from the people at the Hayward Gathering, but nothing specific enough to be really identifying. One of the descriptions was for a slender dark-haired woman . . . but even standing where he was, he could see fifty of those.

The woman angled diagonally across the park to where two stoners were sitting on the grass, sharing a joint. She unzipped the pack, pulled out a thin blanket, and she and the stoners spread it. One of the stoners dropped onto his back, staring up at the sky, while the second guy sat down with his arms wrapped around his knees. The woman continued digging in the pack, chatting with the second guy, then pulled out a plastic box. She opened that up, took out a couple of tubes and a cloth, and started spreading paint on the second guy's face.

A happy clown, but a frightening happy clown, nothing you'd want to show a little kid, in red, black, and white face paint.

Lucas watched for ten minutes and nothing more happened except that a woman wearing a cat mask and a bikini bottom, but no top, asked him if he were a cop. Looking steadily into her eyes, he said, "No. I'm actually a fashion photographer with *Vogue* magazine."

"You liar."

"Really," Lucas said.

"How come you don't got no camera? And why would you come here?"

"Camera's in the van," Lucas said. "It scares some people, who think we might be spies or cops. We want to make contact with fashion-forward young people, and arrange for the shoot later on."

"Oh," she said. She still looked suspicious as she faded into the crowd.

PETERS, THE LAWYER, went by carrying a canvas bag slung over a shoulder, and a paper-pickup stick. Lucas said, "Hang on a minute, but don't look at me."

Peters speared a gum wrapper and looked away from Lucas, and said, "Yeah?"

"I want you to walk down past the bandstand, over on the left side but behind it, maybe twenty yards, and then yell, 'Pilate! Pilate!' Twice like that—like you were calling to him across the field," Lucas said. "When you're walking away from me, off to your right, you'll see two guys and a woman sitting on a blanket. She's painting their faces. They're the ones I'm interested in. When you call for Pilate, I don't want them to be able to see you, but I want them to hear you. As soon as you call, get into the group around the bandstand, so they can't figure out who was calling. Got it? I want to see if they look for you."

"I got it. Give me a minute or so."

Peters walked off and twenty seconds later, disappeared behind the bandstand. Another fifteen seconds and Lucas heard him call, "Pilate! Pilate!"

The woman immediately looked up from her nearly finished mask and the supine man rolled up on his side, then pushed himself up, both of them looking toward the bandstand. The second man, with the half-painted face, turned and said something to them, and then got up and walked toward the bandstand, looked behind it, apparently didn't see anything that interested him, and walked back to the first two, shrugged, and sat down on the blanket again. The woman took another long look at the bandstand, then sat down again and went to work on his face mask again.

And Lucas thought, *Gotcha*.

He called Laurent on the phone, and told him what had happened.

"Do we pick them up now, or wait until Pilate gets here?" Laurent asked. "It sounds like they don't know where he is and are waiting for him. If we wait, they might take us straight to him."

Lucas had to think about it for a moment: "If we wait," he said, "and they take us to him, it might be impossible to isolate them later. If one of them starts screaming for a lawyer, they'll all start. We need to get something from them, almost anything, to really go after him. As soon as they lawyer-up, though, we could have a problem."

"What do you want to do?" Laurent asked. "You tell me."

Lucas said, "I guess I'd really like to split the difference: watch them, and wait until one of them splits off from the other two. Pick up that one, see if we get anything, then see if the other two take us to Pilate when he shows up."

"That's a plan," Laurent said. "I'll tell the guys."

"If we pick up one, you guys don't have a jail . . . am I right?"

"No, but we have a holding cell and an interview room."

"Good enough."

LAURENT GOT A spot at the end of the field, where he could look down at the three people on the blanket, while Lucas watched from the other side. The two uniformed cops stayed down by the end of the field, near the car where the woman had gotten the backpack.

The woman finished putting the mask on the first man, put one on the second man, then packed up her makeup kit and put it in the backpack. She said something to the men, one of them nodded and dug into a bag he'd had beside him, and sparked off a fatboy.

The woman took a long drag, then another, passed the joint back, said something else, and started back toward her car. Lucas's phone beeped: Laurent. "She's moving, you see her?"

"I got her. She's going back to her car," Lucas said. "Let's close in on her, see if we can grab her without too many people noticing. Let's you and I do it. Tell the uniforms to get a car ready, but not to move until they see us grab her. We want her in the car, cuffed and gone in ten seconds, no muss, no fuss."

"Got it." Laurent rang off, and Lucas ambled down the field, twenty or thirty yards in front of the woman. She was moving a bit faster than he was, and he slowed enough that she'd catch him about the time she got to the car. As he came up to the car, he glanced back and saw Laurent moving up on the woman. Lucas angled toward the car. From where he was, she'd walk down the far side of it; he touched the call button on his phone, and Laurent said, "Yeah?"

"Follow her as she goes around the car. I'll be on the other side, we'll have her between us. Roll the patrol car."

The woman never saw them until they were right there. She popped the trunk lid, and Laurent came up beside her, and Lucas slightly behind her. The cop car was already rolling up, and Laurent said, "Excuse me, miss," and when she looked up, he showed her his badge and said, "I'm the Barron County sheriff, and you're under arrest. Put your hands on the trunk lid, please."

She sputtered, "What? What? What did I do?"

She tried to back away, but bumped into Lucas, who said, "Put your hands on the trunk lid, please."

She put her hands up on the trunk lid as the patrol car stopped directly behind her and the driver got out. Laurent quickly patted her down, and then the deputy cuffed her as a crowd started to congeal down around the squad car.

A woman called, "What'd she do?"

"She escaped from the hospital," Laurent said. "She's a nurse, she's got the Ebola virus. We're trying to keep her away from contact with other people. We don't think she's really a danger, so don't be worried. Well, not too worried."

The crowd thinned, and the cuffed woman said, "I do not, I do not—"

Lucas said, "They all say that," to the crowd, and to the woman, "Do what the doctor says. We're trying to help you."

One of the uniformed cops read her rights from a re-cital card—more mumbled than read, Lucas thought—and five seconds later, she was in the back of the patrol car, on her way out of the park. Lucas and Laurent fol-lowed, leaving the reserves behind to watch the park, and keep an eye on the woman's two clown-faced friends.

———

THE UNIFORMED COPS had been told not to talk to the woman; they wanted what they had to say to be a shock. They caught up with the patrol car halfway to town, and followed it in.

At the sheriff's office, a female clerk gave the woman a more thorough search, took a thin back-pocket wallet away from her, and a cell phone, and then the uniformed deputy locked her in the holding cell.

Lucas and Laurent walked over to Pat's to get sandwiches and soft drinks, sat at a picnic table outside on the sidewalk, ate, and took their time getting back to the woman. Lucas checked her wallet: it had seventy dollars in cash, a California driver's license for a Melody Walker, and a Visa and Macy's credit card for the same name.

Lucas called the driver's license information into the BCA and asked for a complete sheet on the woman. She'd been in the holding cell for more than half an hour before they turned on the video camera in the interview room, then went down to the holding cell.

She was frightened. When they opened the door, she was huddled in a corner, her hands in fists in front of her chest, her head slumped down. "I didn't do anything," she wailed. "What are you doing to me?"

That was an opening that Lucas had hoped for: she'd had her rights read to her, now the problem was to get her to ask questions and to talk.

"We're taking you to an interview room—it's just down the hall," Laurent said. They escorted her out of the cell and down to the interview room, and Lucas said, "Sit down." He pointed at a chair on the far side of a narrow table. She quickly sat down, while Lucas and Laurent loomed over her.

"You've been arrested on suspicion of murder on a Wisconsin warrant, Melody. That woman at the Hayward Gathering died. But you know that, because you helped kick her to death."

"I did not. I wasn't there, I didn't even know about it until yesterday," she blurted. "I was down by the bonfire, they had to come and get me."

Lucas looked at Laurent and spread his hands, a "There it is, and on tape" gesture. Laurent tipped his head and then nodded.

The woman said, "What?"

"When were you expecting Pilate to get here?" Lucas asked. "Or is he already here?"

"What do you know about Pilate?" she asked.

"Quite a bit. We know all about your little ritual out in the Black Hills, when you crucified Henry on that pine tree. We know about the dead drug dealer in Hayward, and we know about Skye. We believe you killed an actress out in Los Angeles. I might mention that both California and South Dakota have the death penalty—"

"I didn't have anything to do with any of that," she said. "Nothing. I never hurt nobody."

"How many people are traveling with Pilate, anyway?" Laurent asked.

She shrugged. "I don't know. Mmm, eight or nine

cars and the RV, I guess. Two people in every car, except for Jason, so . . . maybe nineteen people."

"Who actually killed Henry?" Lucas asked. "Who actually used the knife?"

Her eyes narrowed now, and she said, "Say, aren't I supposed to have a lawyer?"

Laurent nodded. "Absolutely. That's why we read your rights to you back at the park. All you have to do is ask."

"But there's a problem with that," Lucas said. He was walking an exceptionally narrow line—she'd asked whether she was supposed to have a lawyer, but hadn't actually asked for one, or demanded one. "I'm not trying to talk you out of getting a lawyer. In fact, I'm sure you're going to need one. The problem we're facing is, we've got a lot of you California killers running around out there—"

"I am *not* a killer!"

Lucas continued, ". . . and we have no time to fool around. Everyone we arrest is looking at the death penalty, except those who provide us with some substantive help. If you help us, you may avoid the death penalty. Normally, getting a lawyer wouldn't be a problem—and we'll get one for you right now, if you want—but lawyers take time. We don't have time. We have to find somebody to help us, and that's the person who gets the break. How much of a break, I don't know—but some break. Everybody else is going down. If we leave you with a lawyer, and find somebody else to help us before you get back to accept the offer—then the offer is no longer good."

"That's not fair," she said.

"Melody, do you think nailing Henry Fuller to a tree was fair?" Lucas asked. "Was it fair to kick Skye to death?"

"I had nothing to do with that," she said. "That was almost all the guys, and, well, a couple of the girls, but most of us girls, we could hardly stand to watch."

Lucas and Laurent looked at each other for another long moment, then Lucas said, "You know what? I think we should get her an attorney whether she wants one or not."

"We're on a pay-as-you-go basis with the Chippewa County defender up in Sault Ste. Marie," Laurent said. "He could be down here in a couple of hours, if I yelled at him. Unless he's in court, or something, that could take longer."

Lucas said, "Step outside for a minute," and when they were outside, and the door closed behind him, Lucas said to Laurent, "I don't like the way she's responding. There might be some kind of impairment issue here. Some kind of . . . psychological difficulty. I think you better get the lawyer on the road."

"Okay."

"Keep the video rolling, though. I'll go in there and keep her talking." When Laurent went to do that, Lucas stuck his head back in the interview room and asked, "Coke? Coffee? Water?"

"I'd like some water."

Lucas got a bottle of water from a vending machine, went back in and gave it to her. "We've got a lawyer coming now. You don't have to talk to us at all anymore, and in fact, I recommend that you don't. You never really did have to, though I told you the truth about getting a break for helping us."

"I don't want to go to jail," she said. "I never did nothing. To anybody."

"You were there."

"Not for that. Not for hurting people. That was all Pilate and Kristen and . . . and those guys. Not me."

LAURENT CAME BACK in the room. "He's on the way. He told me no more questions until he gets here."

"All right." Lucas looked at the woman and said, "Melody, umm . . . I think you'd be a lot happier in here than in the holding cell. It's kind of dark and cold in there. If we leave you in here, you won't try to run away or anything?"

"No, no, no, no . . ."

"We could probably get you some magazines," Laurent said, speaking for the camera. "The lawyer will be here in an hour or so and he has told us not to talk to you anymore, so we won't. If you need a bathroom or anything, knock on the door. Our clerk will hear you, and somebody will take you down to the restrooms."

THEY TOLD THE clerk to get the woman some magazines, then went back to Laurent's office.

"We got everything but an explicit confession," Laurent said. "Melody wasn't exactly a grim-faced Pilate loyalist, she was quick enough to unload on him . . ."

"Yeah, I think we got him, if we can find him," Lucas said. "I see two possible problems, though. I got the feeling that she's not all there, which is why I wanted her to have a lawyer—the lawyer's for our sake, not for hers. The other thing was, she wasn't specific enough. We got a good piece of it, but we need specifics, and if she's challenged on grounds of mental incompetence, and the decision goes against us, we're back to zero. We need to use her as a crowbar to get somebody else talking."

"Names and specific acts."

"Yeah. We need to pinpoint the actual guys who did the killings, and the people who inspired them to do it," Lucas said. "That means Pilate, if he didn't actually use a knife. The small fry, we need to keep them talking."

LAURENT CALLED THE deputies still at the Gathering. None of them had seen anybody who might be Pilate. The two men who'd been with Melody Walker had gone to look for her, after a while, and seemed puzzled by her absence. They'd walked down to the car to look around, but then had gone back to their blanket with a bunch of hot dogs and Dr Peppers and were still sitting there.

"You want to bust them?" Peters asked.

"Not yet, but you guys stay close to them," Lucas

said. "I would really like them to point us at Pilate. But be careful: keep in mind that they're nuts."

"We'll do that, but unless these guys are really, really stupid, their girlfriend's disappearance is going to start to worry them."

"I know: we're walking on a thin edge here," Lucas said. "We may change direction later in the day, so stay cool and keep watching."

When everybody at the park knew what they were doing, Lucas and Laurent spent a few minutes looking at Melody Walker's cell phone, and Lucas noted the numbers in her favorites list, but no names were associated with the favorites. Lucas called the numbers into the BCA duty officer, and asked that they all be pinged, with the results called back to him as soon as they came in.

"What next?"

"We need to get a response on those cell phone numbers, and we need to get back out to the park. If Pilate comes in, we want to be there."

13

RALEIGH AND LINDA crossed the UP like Columbus crossing the Ocean Sea, not knowing exactly where they were going, or what they'd find at the end, but dumbfounded by the lack of people: they were from L.A., and had never been in a place where you might find a square mile of space, or four or five, all to yourself.

Even the towns weren't really towns. Santa Monica was a *town*. Venice was a *town*. Marina Del Rey was a *town*. But the towns in the UP?

"Most of the goddamn buildings in Santa Monica got more people in them than that town," Raleigh said, looking back at the cluster of shops and houses around a convenience store, where they'd stopped for gas. He was right.

———

RALEIGH HAD HUNG around the Hayward Gathering, staying back in the crowd in his face paint, as instructed by Pilate. Linda was with him, a sad, heavy woman face-painted as a cat. During the Gathering, she wore a skintight black suit with a long cat's tail and black combat boots. Before she hooked up with the disciples, she'd been working retail at a Home Depot in Glendale, California, and hadn't been good at it. She'd never been able to remember what products were in which aisle.

She and Raleigh were in the crowd when Lucas and Letty found Skye and watched as the local cops poured in, with the big dark-haired plainclothes cop directing traffic. The dark-haired girl was the same one that Pilate had punched out. Raleigh could tell that she was hurting from the kicks in the ribs and she was already showing a massive welt under one eye.

He was at first puzzled by the big cop's relationship to the girl. He'd seemed angry when they found Skye, but controlled. His attitude toward the dark-haired girl was different: he was more upset by her beating than by Skye's death and he kept coming back to her, over and over. Raleigh had been watching them, and the other cops, for an hour, before he tripped off on it. Of course! She was the big cop's daughter. They looked alike, acted alike. They were close.

Interesting, he thought, but not critical. Pilate wanted the disciples to stay off their phones as much as they could, in case the cops had some way of tracking them, despite the phone shields, so he didn't bother to call in that night.

The next day, the local newspaper came out. Raleigh didn't read newspapers, but they were free around the Gathering, so he took a look, to see what the cops were saying. One thing they said was that a Minnesota cop named Lucas Davenport had been working with the Sawyer and Polk county sheriffs' offices, first on the rescue of Shirley (Skye) Bellows, and later on her murder.

"Our feeling is that she knew the man who killed Henry Mark Fuller in South Dakota, and that she might have approached him about the murder," Davenport had said. The story, and a photo, occupied the top half of the front page and the photo showed the big cop at the Gathering, with two deputies, and identified him as Davenport.

Below the story Raleigh found four police artist sketches of Pilate, Kristen, Bell, and himself: Pilate was listed as "Porter Pilate," the only time Raleigh had ever heard of Pilate having a first name. He, Kristen, and Bell were listed only by their single names. The image of Pilate was a good one: Raleigh thought he'd be able to pick him out, on the basis of the sketch alone. The sketches of the other three were not nearly as good, except that Kristen had those filed teeth, which would give her away to anyone who saw both the teeth and the drawing. As for himself and Bell, he doubted that anyone could pick them out.

Precisely at midnight, he took out his phone, shook it out of its sack—they all had sacks that supposedly blocked cell phone signals, so they couldn't be tracked—and turned his phone on and called Pilate, who came up immediately.

"Yeah?"

"They got one of those police drawings of you in the newspaper in Hayward," he said. "It's pretty good. If people see it, and you, they could pick you out."

"Shit. But that newspaper won't no way make it to the UP, right?"

"Probably not, but it's not the paper's drawings, it's the cops'. They might be spreading them around. You got to watch all the newspapers, in case you pop up somewhere else."

"Good information," Pilate said. "What else?"

"That chick you whacked just before we left, the one who got hauled away by the fat man. Turns out she's a cop's kid. At least, I think she is. They acted that way."

"Good. Happy to do it. What else?"

"That's about it. Anybody in trouble?" Raleigh asked.

"Not as far as I know," Pilate said. "They're all calling in right now. Talk to you later."

When Raleigh hung up, and had slipped the phone back in its sack, Linda asked, "Now what? We still camping out?"

"Nope. We're finding a motel. I'm gonna do you."

"Don't hurt me," she said.

"Gonna hurt you a little bit," he said. "That's what I do, huh?"

RALEIGH AND LINDA stayed for the whole Hayward Gathering. The Skye murder scene was still taped off on the last day of the Gathering, but there was only one sheriff's deputy keeping an eye on it. The cops were apparently done with it, and Davenport, the Minnesota cop, was no longer around.

Raleigh talked to Pilate most nights, at midnight, usually for no more than a few seconds—Pilate was getting paranoid. The four pictures printed in Hayward had also shown up in a paper in southern Wisconsin, where some of the disciples had gone to hide out. Pilate wouldn't say where he was.

Raleigh and Linda started out for the UP, with three days to go before the Sault Ste. Marie Gathering. They had money for food and gas, but not enough for a nightly motel. They did have a stash of weed, and just before leaving Wisconsin, managed to sell two ounces of low-grade AK-47 to a musky fisherman staying in a motel in Presque Isle.

"That only leaves us an ounce for ourselves," Linda whined.

"Gonna have to make do," Raleigh said. "Need the motels more'n we need the weed."

They needed the motels because Raleigh's sex life involved slapping Linda around, and then taking her orally or anally, which she hated. Which was why he did it. Or how he got the most pleasure out of it, when there was only one chick available, and nobody to watch. He didn't want her to enjoy herself. He wanted to *use* her, and for her to know that she was being used, like an appliance. She *was* an appliance.

"All you gotta do is toast the bread," he said. "You don't have to like it. That's what you're for. Shut the fuck up and get to work."

He was afraid to take that attitude in a park campground, where somebody might be watching or listening—he was not a man of the North Woods, but more of a city guy. Who was to know what might be back in all those trees?

Occasionally, at night, in a motel, after a particularly vigorous round of sex and assault, his eyes would pop open and he'd worry that Linda might wake up, while he was asleep, and stick a knife in his chest. If he got too worried, he'd wake her up and slap her around some more and maybe stick her again. 'Cause that was what he did.

They traveled like that, across Wisconsin, and then into the UP, and then to the Gathering, on its first full day.

He'd just parked, and gotten out of the car, when Davenport drifted by, paying no attention to him.

"There's that big cop from Minnesota," Linda said, from the passenger seat.

"Yeah. Gonna have something to tell Pilate tonight."

14

LUCAS SHOULDERED THROUGH the crowd, trying not to look like a cop, but couldn't help it. People glanced at him and gave way, sometimes with tiny smiles—*I know what you are.* They weren't hostile, but they were wary.

Lucas wasn't by nature particularly patient, except when he was working: there was a rhythm to surveillance, and when he was on the street full-time, he'd occasionally spent whole days and nights watching a person or a house or a business.

In addition to a psychological patience, he'd found the biggest assets in surveillance were an interest in faces, a decent novel, and a strong bladder. Not a big intellectual, he'd nevertheless spent an entire summer reading an English translation of Valentin Louis Georges Eugène Marcel Proust's *À la recherché du temps perdu* while knitting together the web of a major crack gang that spread over the Twin Cities. He couldn't read French, but the book had made him want to learn the language; he'd just never had time.

Now he ambled through the crowd, not in any particular hurry: he knew now that Pilate was coming, just a matter of time. The part-time deputies, Barnes, the Subway owner, and Bennett, the postmaster, were watching the two guys who'd been with Melody Walker.

Lucas spotted Randy, the fat man, still riding in the back of the John Deere Gator, still throwing out bottles of Faygo, and went that way. As he came up, the fat man shook his head. "Not a thing."

Lucas hadn't had much time to talk to him, but now he did: "What's up with you?" he asked. "What do you do for a living? You can't spend all your time passing out bottles of pop." He quickly amended that to "I mean, bottles of soda," remembering that he was now on the soda side of the soda/pop linguistic border.

Randy shook his head. "No, no. I manage a self-storage place down in Ann Arbor. Not much to do, you know. Keep the college kids from trying to live in the place, make sure nobody's running a meth lab. That's about it. 'Course, the pay's for shit. Sleep a lot. Play a little music."

"Yeah? What do you play?" Lucas asked.

"Guitar."

"Guitar? Tell you what: I owe you big for helping Letty. I'm serious. I owe you bigger than you know. How about I buy you a guitar? Something you don't have."

The fat man looked at him for a long moment, then said, "You're shittin' me."

"No. I'm not. You got a guitar that you want?"

"About fifty of them. You could get a Mexican version of a Gibson Les Paul for a few hundred bucks. Do that, I'd drive over to your house, wherever it is, and kiss you on the lips."

"That wouldn't be necessary," Lucas said, suppressing a shudder. He took a card out of his pocket and handed it to him. "Write your name and address on it, and the name of the guitar. I'll drop-ship it to you."

"How does a cop afford—"

"I have some money of my own," Lucas began. His phone rang and he said, "I gotta take this," and stepped away, into the privacy of a crowd that didn't care who he was talking to.

Laurent: "We have a problem. I talked to the sheriff over in Sawyer County about all those John Doe warrants and told him we had a name to fill in—Melody Walker. Ten minutes later I got a call from an assistant county prosecutor, whatever they call them over there. A punk. I told him we were offering breaks to the first people we picked up, if they weren't directly involved in the killings, because we need to know the names and other information. He said they won't recognize any kind of a deal we make with anybody."

"Goddamnit. What'd you tell him?"

"I told him our interview video might get accidentally erased because I don't know how to run the cameras so good, and then he'd have a known killer he'd have to let go, for lack of evidence, and everybody in Sawyer County would know it, because I'd tell everybody, and I'd tell everybody that it was his fault," Laurent said. "He said we'd better not do that, or he'd put all our asses in jail. I told him to go fuck himself, and he said, 'Hey, fuck you, too, you hick motherfucker.'"

"So as professional law-enforcement exchanges go, this wouldn't be in the top five," Lucas said. "Or even the top ten."

"No. He wound up telling me he'd get back to us after he talked to his boss," Laurent said. "Actually, he's going to get back to you, because I don't know the ins and outs of this cross-border stuff. I gave him your phone number."

"When's he calling back?" Lucas asked. "We gotta know what we can do."

"Didn't say. He sorta hung up on me."

"Okay. Listen, it's gonna be dark in a couple of hours," Lucas said. "We need to pick up those two guys, Melody's friends, if they don't, uh, you know, contact anyone from Pilate's group before dark."

"All right. I could call this Wisconsin asshole and give him a deadline, I suppose."

"Let's not annoy them. Let's wait an hour, and if they haven't called, then I'll call, and kiss a little lawyer ass."

"Okay. Better you than me."

"Yeah. I'm used to it," Lucas said.

He rang off and went back to Randy, who handed him back his card, with a name and address, and said, "One thing to keep in your mind: *Mexican*. If you order a straight-up made-in-USA Les Paul, you'll wind up filling your pants when you get the bill."

Lucas grinned and said, "That wouldn't be an entirely new experience for me. I almost did last week, with Letty."

The fat man nodded and said, "Say, you want a Faygo?"

"No, thanks. I had one last week."

LUCAS CRUISED FOR fifteen minutes, then took a call from Barnes, the Subway owner. "We got one male and one female subject approaching the two men under surveillance. They know each other. The two unsubs are both in Juggalo masks. Jim's watching from the other side."

"Call Laurent."

"Already did, he's moving up, but said to tell you he'll stay far enough back that they won't see him."

"Good. Call Frisell, Peters, and Bennett, tell them to get in a big outer circle so they can track the new people if they walk away."

"Do that," Barnes said, and he was gone.

Lucas made his way through the thickening crowd, thinking, *Unsubs*? Unknown subjects? Did everybody watch TV? Like the Minnesota deputy, with her *vics*? It wasn't dark yet, but the sun probably wasn't more than thirty degrees above the horizon, and the shadows were getting long. If they were going to move before dark, it'd have to be soon.

He saw Laurent in the crowd, who was as tall as Lucas, and so could look over the heads of most people. Lucas moved up to him and asked, "What do you think?"

"They definitely know each other, and pretty well. They walked up and the guys on the ground started talking with them, passed up a joint without being asked."

Lucas watched for a moment: the new ones included a heavy woman in a black catsuit, with a painted cat face, and a husky man in a black T-shirt and jeans, with a painted skull mask.

"Melody Walker said the guys did most of the killing. If these two people peel off from the first two, we should grab them. Separate them, brace the woman. If she's as willing to talk as Melody, we'll be a hell of a lot solider."

"All right. I'll call everybody and tell them what's up."

Lucas's phone rang again. He looked at it, and recognized the Hayward area code. "Your lawyer friend is calling back."

"Tell him to go fuck himself again," Laurent said.

LUCAS ANSWERED, IDENTIFYING himself, and a voice on the other end said, "Mark Hasselhoff, I'm the county attorney. I just talked to Rick—"

"I don't know Rick," Lucas said.

"He's the guy your sheriff talked to, and I told the young man that we might be better off to defer to the law enforcement agencies on the ground. We will recognize any reasonable bargains you make lesser offenders, although we'll have to leave it to a judge if there's a problem in deciding who qualifies."

"That's fine with me," Lucas said. "We've got one in custody, we're watching four more, and we believe all of

them were involved either actively or passively in the murder of the dope dealer and of Skye—Shirley Bellows—
there in Hayward."

"Good work, then. You'll have to tell me sometime
why a Minnesota guy was running things here, and now
over in Michigan," Hasselhoff said. "Anyway, I will call
you back in one minute and will leave a more official-
sounding approval of your actions on your voice mail, and
will do the same with Sheriff Laurent, if you would tell
him that."

"I will. And hey: thanks, Mark."

"I'll leave a message," Hasselhoff said.

LAURENT FINISHED HIS calls, and said, "We're
set," and Lucas told him about Hasselhoff. Laurent said,
"Hmm. Too cooperative. Makes me suspicious."

"Let's not look a gift—"

"They're moving," Laurent said.

Lucas had been looking at Laurent, and now he
turned back to the group on the blanket. The two people
dressed as Juggalos were moving away, straight through
the crowd toward the parking lot.

"Call your guys. If they're going to their car, we'll
take them there," Lucas said. "Tell Bennett and Barnes
to stay with the two guys on the blanket, everybody close
on their car, if that's where they're going, but stay back.
I'll make the first move."

Most of the cars were parked nose-in to a line of chalk,
like the stripe on a football field, or on a second line of

chalk fifteen yards behind the first one; a few were backed into the line. Lucas took the odds and cut behind the black-clad couple so that he'd be coming in from the driver's side of the car.

Laurent stayed out to his left, covering the passenger side. As they walked along, the couple were picking up speed, not quite to a jog, and were looking around, as if expecting to see someone they didn't want to see. It never occurred to Lucas that it might be him.

He could see the back of Frisell's head, well ahead of them, already at the line of cars. The teacher didn't stop, but kept going, never looked around. Good move. Peters was well out to one side, vectoring toward the car lot, where the couple would hit it. Sellers, the hardware store guy, was on the other side, closing in. They had the two targets surrounded.

Lucas began moving faster: he wanted to be close when they got to the car, wherever it was. As they came up to the parking area, they looked around, then zigged to the right. That left Laurent and Peters out of it, for the moment, and Sellers a bit too close. On the far side of the lot, Lucas saw Frisell on the other side of the second line of cars, looking back. He saw the couple make the turn, and matched it.

The two cut through the first line of cars to the second, and Lucas saw that they were heading toward a beat-up Subaru. He was going through the first line of cars, just as they got to it. They didn't unlock it, they simply split up, left and right, for the passenger side and driver's side doors, and popped the unlocked doors.

As the man turned to get in his seat, Lucas was clearing the first line of cars and the man saw him coming. Their eyes locked for a second and Lucas thought later that he may have thought, *Oh, shit.* He was both too close and not close enough: the red zone.

The man ducked down and a second later stood up again, Lucas now only three or four yards away, one hand on his gun, drawing it, and he heard Frisell shout, "Gun!" and the man's arm came up over the car door with a gun; he flinched at Frisell's shouted warning, but the hand kept coming up with the muzzle closing on Lucas when Lucas saw Frisell in the background with a pistol in his hand already leveled in line with both the gunman and Lucas, and Lucas thought later that he may have thought, again, *Oh, shit,* and dropped to the ground. The first of Frisell's bullets sliced overhead even as he hung in the air on the way down.

Most of it had to be reconstructed later, but Frisell fired seven shots: one of his bullets hit the outer edge of the lower lip of a twenty-eight-year-old cigarette salesman from Mt. Pleasant, and another went through the brim of a cowboy hat on a nineteen-year-old stock boy at an Abercrombie & Fitch at the Lakeside Mall in Sterling Heights. One went through the back of Raleigh's head, and came out just above his eye, another hit him in the back, ricocheted off his spine, exited under an arm, entered his triceps, exited again, and wound up a half inch into the car's dashboard. Where the other three went, nobody would ever know.

Lucas was sprawled on the ground with his arms

stretched in front of him, the .45 out too late but now ready to go, and the shooting was done. Laurent was off to one side screaming at the woman to put her hands in the air—she did—and Lucas got to his knees and then to his feet and ran toward the car and looked over the door. Raleigh had crumbled there, faceup.

The hole above his eye suggested that no ambulance would be needed; at least not for him. Frisell walked up, his .40 Smith pointed straight up in the air, looking past Lucas, and he said, "They kept telling me, 'Watch the background, watch the background.' I forgot, I just forgot."

Lucas looked back over his shoulder. The crowd was running in every possible direction, although most of them were running away from where Lucas was standing. In the middle of the field, a man was sitting on the ground and a woman was pushing what looked like a white T-shirt into his face.

Lucas said to Frisell, "Eject the round from the chamber—don't lose it—and give your gun and the round to Rome. I'll be right back."

He jogged across the field to where the man was sitting on the ground, pushed his way through the growing circle of Juggalos around him, squatted and said, "I'm a police officer."

"I think he's shot," the woman said. What Lucas had thought was a T-shirt was actually a roll of toilet paper.

Lucas said, "Let me see."

The man nodded, wordlessly, and took the roll away from his face.

"Not bad," Lucas said. "But you need some stitches.

We will get you there right now. Do you have somebody to ride with you, or follow us?"

"Me," the woman said. She was absolutely calm. "I'm with him. I knew something like this would happen. I told him before we came. I said, 'Andy, we'll get in trouble.' He said, 'No we won't, it's just a goof.' So, here we are, and sure enough, he gets shot . . ."

She was babbling. Lucas got on the phone and called Laurent, who said, "We got the girl. The guy's dead."

"I saw that," Lucas said. "We've got a guy here who might have been nicked by one of the shots. He'll need a ride up to Sault."

"I'll get a squad over there. One minute." He was gone.

Lucas said to the man and woman, "A cop car will be here in one minute. He'll ride you up to Sault Ste. Marie, and bring you back, if you don't need to stay overnight."

"What happened? Who was shooting?" the woman asked.

"You'll read about it," Lucas said.

HE JOGGED BACK toward the shooting scene, where a crowd had gathered in a circle around the dead man's car. As he ran, he saw a squad car headed for the wounded man. When Lucas came up, Laurent asked, "How bad?

"Guy was nicked in the lip," Lucas said. "If it had been a quarter inch the other way, it would have missed."

"Of course, if it had been a quarter inch the *other* way, he might have lost his jaw."

"Gee, you're just like Father Christmas," Lucas said. "Call Bennett and Barnes. I hope the hell they stayed with the other two, 'cause they're likely to take off."

While Laurent did that, Lucas glanced at the woman, who was now sitting on the front passenger seat of the car, and then walked over to Frisell, who tried to explain. "They kept telling us, 'Watch the background,' and I, shoot, I completely—"

"Man, you saved my life," Lucas said. "He was ten feet from me when you fired and I was late with my gun. He would have shot me for sure, might have killed me."

"He knew you," Frisell said.

"Yeah. I don't know why." Lucas looked at him closely. "You okay?"

"I'm fine," Frisell said.

"A lot of guys sort of lose their shit after a shooting."

Frisell shrugged: "Maybe I would, if I'd killed somebody innocent, or a bystander."

Sellers and Peters were there, and they both slapped Frisell on the back, and Sellers said, "Good shooting, dude."

"Okay. Frisell, keep an eye on the woman," Lucas said. "Get her out of the car, pat her down, sit her on the ground if you have to. I'd hate to have her pull another piece out from under the car seat. Sellers, Peters, keep the crowd off us."

They all did that, and Lucas took another quick look at the guy on the ground, and his gun—a chromed .38 revolver. That would have done the trick, Lucas thought, if he'd gotten a shot off.

Laurent came over and said, "Bennett and Barnes are on the job. They said the two guys are still there, they're standing up and looking over here, but they haven't left. Neither one has made a phone call."

"Gotta take them," Lucas said. "They'll find out soon enough. We don't want them warning Pilate."

"What should I do with Jerry's gun?"

"I don't know. Whatever department policy is."

Laurent showed a thin slice of a smile: "Now you're fuckin' with me."

THEY DRAPED THE dead man's body with a car cover that somebody had in a truck, and Laurent called a photographer from a local portrait studio to come out and take pictures of the scene. "It's not like we don't know what happened," he said.

"We still want lots of photos," Lucas said. "Especially of the gun and its relationship to the dead man's hand, and any other weapons you find. Bag anything like that. If you don't have bags, have a deputy go to a grocery store and buy some gallon Ziplocs. You want to document everything that tells our side of the story, that this guy was about to open fire into a crowd. We'll want some general crowd shots, too."

"But we know—" Laurent began.

"Because the guy with the lip is gonna sue your ass," Lucas said.

Laurent sighed: "Shoot. Man, if it's not one thing . . ."

"Let's go get the other two assholes," Lucas said.

"We'll haul them all downtown and do the interview room trick again."

"Maybe you better do that," Laurent said. "I better stick around here until this whole . . . body thing . . . is taken care of. I already called the funeral home."

"Okay," Lucas said. And, "Rome: the posse's done good. I'm proud to work with you all."

Laurent nodded: "Thank you. I'll tell them you said that." His phone rang and he answered and listened for a moment, then said, "Those two guys have picked up the blanket and they look like they're headed for Melody's car."

"Can't leave Frisell by himself . . . need witnesses that he didn't mess with the scene."

"He wouldn't—"

"I *know* that. You need witnesses for when it gets to court," Lucas said.

"Ah . . ." Laurent called the three men over, explained Lucas's suggestions, and Peters, the lawyer, said, "Smart. We'll keep Jerry away from the car."

Laurent said to Lucas, "So we're good here. I'll come back here while you go to town, but right now, I'm coming with you. Four-on-two."

They pushed through the crowd and a couple people asked what had happened, but they kept moving, and when they got to a thinner spot, started jogging, Laurent on the phone with Barnes, who said that the two men were almost at the car.

"We're coming," Laurent said. "Don't do anything until we get there."

Thirty yards out, Lucas saw the two men approaching the line of parked cars. One of them split off to the second car with California tags, while the other went to Melody Walker's car. Lucas said over his shoulder to Laurent, "I'll take the guy on the right. You guys get the other one."

Laurent nodded and they split up, and as Lucas came up to his man, he saw Laurent, Barnes, and Bennett surround theirs. Lucas's man saw them surrounding his friend, and he turned to run, nearly bumping into Lucas, who had his gun out and shouted, "Freeze. Freeze."

The man threw up his hands and screamed, "Whoa, whoa, whoa . . ."

A minute later, they were both cuffed. Lucas said to Barnes and Bennett, "Take them back to your trucks, both of you ride together, put them in the back. If they fuck with you, shoot them." His back was to the two men, as he faced Bennett and Barnes, and he winked. They nodded and Barnes said, "After what they did to that little girl, it'd be a pleasure."

One of the men said, "Wait, what girl?"

Laurent said to Bennett and Barnes, "I'll call Cronhauser, tell him we need to borrow his holding cell and interview room, and a guy to watch the doors. I'll tell him what happened, get you some help."

Lucas: "Who's Cronhauser?"

"Police chief. We got a co-op deal on lockups, when we get an overflow."

THEY WALKED WITH Bennett and Barnes to Bennett's SUV, got all four men loaded. Lucas said, "I'll catch you guys in town. Isolate them until I get there."

"What about Jerry?" Barnes asked. "Is he okay?"

"He says he's okay, but I'll take him along with me, get him away from the scene," Lucas said.

On the way back to the dead man's car, Lucas said, "Normally we'd leave this for a crime scene crew, but . . ."

"We can get a guy from Sault Ste. Marie," Laurent said. "The cops up there have a guy."

"Then get him started. Don't move the body until he gets here. Call whatever judge you use and get a search warrant for those two cars—Walker's and the other guy's. I want to pull the dead guy's wallet now, get him ID'd, take a look at his cell phone, if he has one. They were looking for Pilate. I hope he's not in the crowd, watching this, or he'll take off like a big-assed bird."

Back at the scene, Lucas checked the man's wallet, which identified him as Raleigh Waites, with an address in Reseda, California. Lucas didn't know where that was. Waites didn't have a cell phone in his pockets, but Lucas found one on the floor under the front seat, along with a misdemeanor amount of marijuana and a box of .38 shells.

The phone was wrapped in a stiff brown fabric bag with a Velcro snap. Lucas could feel a network of wires beneath the surface of the bag, but didn't know what that meant.

When he opened the phone, he found fourteen names in the directory, and a long list of recents. Lucas copied all the recents for the past three weeks—most were du-plicates, and most went to numbers in the directory. None of them went to a "Pilate," but one phone number went to a *P*. When he checked, he found that *P* had been called at midnight every day since Hayward, and at ran-dom times before that.

Pilate.

"I'll call this into my office, we'll ping him, figure out where he is," Lucas told Laurent.

"Good. I'll get on the mutual aid net and let every-body in the UP know what's going on. If we can find him, we should be able to grab him pretty quick."

SELLERS, PETERS, AND a uniformed deputy were still on crowd control. Laurent asked the woman her name, and she said, "Linda."

"Last name?"

"Petrelli."

Laurent read her rights to her, and cuffed her. Lucas peered at the woman's face: she showed no sign of tears or even fear. Her purse was sitting in the footwell of the car, and he dipped into it, found another wallet, and her driver's license. Linda Petrelli, as she said, with an ad-dress in Glendale, a town he *had* heard of.

He noted her name and address and the tag number on the car, and then he and Frisell escorted her through the crowd to Lucas's Benz, and put her in the backseat. Lucas asked, "You think you can drive?"

Frisell said, "Sure. Hey, I'm fine."

"You might not be as fine as you think you are."

"Well . . . how could you tell that? If I feel fine, and act fine . . ."

"All right, drive. I've got to make phone calls."

LUCAS HAD TO explain how the electronic transmission shift worked, which Frisell thought was weird, and they left the Gathering with the silent woman in the back. Lucas called the duty officer at the BCA and asked him to ping the phone numbers he'd collected. And, "Is Barb Watson there?"

"I think so. She hasn't checked out."

"Ring her for me—I don't have her number," Lucas said.

"One second. And listen, Sands wants to talk to you. He wants you to call him at his office. You want me to put you through?"

"No. If he wants to talk to me, he has my number," Lucas said.

"Lucas, he's really pissed," the duty officer said. "He asked me why we were paying for all this work for Wisconsin and now you're in Michigan . . ."

"So he can call me. Ping those numbers. And ring Barb."

Barb Watson was a technical specialist: when she answered her phone, Lucas described the brown bag he'd found around Raleigh Waites's phone. "You know what that is?"

"Yes, unfortunately. It's a kind of Faraday cage. It blocks the cell phone signals, both ways, in and out."

"Huh. Are they legal? Where do you get them?"

"Legal as far as I know. The Museum of Modern Art used to sell them."

"This isn't good," Lucas said.

WHEN LUCAS HUNG up, the woman in the back said, "Found out about Raleigh's phone bag, huh?"

Lucas half turned to look at her. "What'd you say?"

"He used to rape me all the time. He kidnapped me and he and the others used to rape me. Even the women." She spoke in a tone so flat, so uninflected, that Lucas thought she might be telling the truth.

"Where, uh, did he kidnap you?"

"Back in California. He kidnapped me from my job," Petrelli said.

"Doing what? Your job?"

"Worked at a Home Depot."

"Think anybody reported it? Should we call your folks?"

"Oh, probably not," Petrelli said. "The disciples made me go in and quit, and made me call my mom and tell her I was going to be traveling and not to call me."

"Huh."

"They been raping me for three years now," she said. "All the time, every night. Raleigh used to beat me up because that's what he got off on. They called me 'the designated rapee.'"

"All right," Lucas said. "We'll want you to make a statement when we get downtown here—"

"Butt, mouth, everything," she said.

"Okay, when we get downtown—"

She looked out the window at the trees. "It was awful," she said. She said it in a tone that she might use to order a sandwich.

THE TWO GUYS they'd picked up would be held at the city police station, while they took Petrelli to the sheriff's office, put her in the county clerk's office while they moved a protesting Melody Walker back in the holding cell. Then they moved Petrelli to the interview room, sat her down, turned on the cameras, and Lucas said, "We read your rights to you at the park. I'll do it again if you want."

"Nah. I just wanted to say that I was kidnapped and raped by all the disciples," she said. Then, "Just a minute." She stood up and pulled her cat tail off, dropped it on the interview table, and sat down again. "That's better."

"Let's go all the way back to the start," Lucas said. "Do you know if Pilate or the disciples murdered an actress named Kitty Place last year?"

"I wasn't there, but they told me about it," she said. She looked at Lucas for a moment, then at Frisell, back to Lucas: "Pilate and the guys all fucked her and then they cut her up and threw her in the ocean. But—she wasn't the start. Not even close. I think that's what they were going to do to me, when they were done with me."

"What was the start?" Lucas said.

"I wasn't there for it—but way back, I don't know . . .

maybe five years? They killed some guy by bashing his head with a rock. On a beach, near Malibu. They put him in the ocean, too. See, when they kill someone, they either put them in the ocean or they bury them up in the hills."

"How many have they done that to?" Frisell asked.

"Well, the second one they killed, one of the girls told me this, was a traveler guy, and he had this walking stick with a bird's head on it. Pilate kept it and every time they kill someone, he cuts a notch in it. There are like maybe . . . ten notches."

"Not really," Frisell said.

"Really." She nodded, and added, "I hate it when they kill somebody, because they get all excited and then they gang-rape me."

"Do you know where Pilate is now?"

"Well, he's around somewhere. But he's smart—he wasn't going to be the first person to show up at the Gathering. He sent his spies in, first. Raleigh was spying on you back at the other Gathering, he saw you and that girl that Pilate hit. Raleigh thinks she's your daughter. Wait: he *thought* she was your daughter. Guess he's not thinking anything, anymore."

Lucas felt the chill: he didn't want Letty and Pilate linked in any way. Didn't want Pilate or any of his disciples even *aware* of Letty. "But Pilate's around," Lucas prompted.

"Somewhere. Up here, I think. Raleigh was supposed to call him at midnight tonight and give him the all-clear."

"We arrested those two guys that you and Raleigh talked to, the guys on the blanket."

"Jase and Parker, yeah, they used to rape me all the time," she said. "Sometimes, both of them at once. They call it a double-team."

"Were they involved in the killings?"

She considered for a moment, then said, "Jase always was, Parker, maybe a couple of times, but he wasn't so much into it. I mean, he'd do it, but he wasn't really all hot for it. He was afraid we'd get caught—they'd get caught—and get sent to the electric chair."

Frisell: "You said this Pilate guy's got ten notches . . . How many were you there for?"

She stuck out her lip, considering again. "Maybe four? They were doing it a long time before they kidnapped me."

Lucas said, "Sit here for a minute. We'll be right back."

Petrelli said, "Hey, I'm helping you guys. What do I get out of it? I want something . . ."

"We'll talk to your lawyer about it," Lucas said. "He's on his way here."

He led Frisell out in the hall and Lucas said, "She's worse than Walker. There's something wrong with her."

"If she's been raped by everybody, for years . . ."

"Could be trauma," Lucas agreed. "After a while, your brain blows up. On the other hand, she could be trying to manipulate us—she knows the jig is up. Let's see if Walker's lawyer is here yet. If he's not, we could get her out—"

"I thought you said we weren't supposed to talk to her."

"We're not supposed to ask her any more *questions*—but we can talk to each other while she's around. If she blurts something out, I mean, we've told her not to talk to us anymore. On the video."

"What would we be talking about?" Frisell said.

THEY GOT WALKER out of the holding cell and took her to the back of the building to the vending machines where Lucas bought her a Diet Dr Pepper and a sack of Cheez-Its. He said to Frisell, "If Linda's telling the truth, we'll get everybody for rape, too. Not that we really need it."

"At least ten murders," Frisell said. "They really are going to get the needle. All of them. Ten. Fuckin'. Murders. Just unbelievable."

Walker said, "Linda? You got Linda?"

Lucas: "Yeah. Probably shouldn't tell you this, but one of your pals, what's his name . . . ?"

Frisell: "Raleigh?"

Walker said, "You got Raleigh and Linda?"

"Raleigh tried to shoot his way past us," Lucas said. "He was killed."

Her mouth dropped open: "You're lyin'."

"No. He was shot. Had a great big chrome revolver under the front seat of his Subaru, tried to pull it on us," Lucas said. "Now Linda's telling us the whole story: ten murders, at least. She's been kidnapped and raped—"

"Linda? Linda's the worst one," Walker said, gaping

at them over the Dr Pepper. "She wasn't raped: she'd fuck anything that moved. Any way they wanted it. She's the one, you know, that boy out in the Black Hills, she's the one who cut off his cock. She was dancing around with it, and he was still alive. If you look in her car, you might find it. She said she was going to make a leather weed pouch out of it."

They stared at her for a while, then Frisell said, "Oh, boy." And a few seconds later, to Lucas, "Where do these people come from? How do they get like this?"

"I don't know," Lucas said. "I told my daughter you'd hear all these urban legends, all these bullshit stories. I told her they never turned out to be true. Well, guess what?"

Frisell looked at Walker, then at Lucas and asked, "How do we know which one is lying? One of them must be."

"We got more people to question," Lucas said. "We better motor on over there."

THEY TOOK PETRELLI to the holding cell and locked her in, and put Walker in the interview room, locked up, and told the night deputy that the lawyer could talk to Walker, and probably Petrelli, but that he should talk to Lucas before he spoke to either of the women. "Tell him it's important to call me," Lucas said.

———

THE TWO MEN at the city lockup were named Jason Biggs and Parker Collins; the city had two holding cells, both as bleak as the tan-tiled cell at the sheriff's office, designed to fend off vomit and urine in the most efficient way possible. Biggs was in one cell, Collins in the other.

Barnes and Bennett, who transported them down from the park, said, "They're pretty hard-core. We tried to chat and Biggs told Collins to ask for a lawyer. They asked us for a lawyer. I told him that we didn't know anything about that, and you'd tell them, or Rome would."

Lucas asked Frisell, "You up for another conversation?"

"Sure."

A city officer asked if they wanted to use the interview room, and Lucas said, "Not yet." And to Barnes and Bennett, "You guys get their cell phones?"

"Yeah." Barnes nodded. "We bagged them."

"Look at all their recents and write them down. See if any of them list a *P* or a Pilate."

The city cop took them down to the first holding cell, where Biggs was locked up. They stepped inside, and Biggs, sitting on the tile bench, still wearing the vicious happy clown face, said, "You're not a lawyer."

"I'm a cop. You've got the right—"

"No shit. I want a lawyer. Now."

"Absolutely right," Frisell said from Lucas's shoulder. "Screw him. Why should we give him a break? We got everything we need from Linda and Melody. I'd stick the needle in this guy myself."

Biggs grinned at them through the red, white, and

black face paint: "Hey. I been bullshitted by better cops than you. I want the lawyer."

Lucas and Frisell backed out of the cell and the city cop locked the door behind them. Frisell said, "No Academy Award for that."

Collins was shakier. Frisell said, "Screw him. Why should we give him a break? We got everything we need from Melody and Linda. I'd stick the needle in this guy myself."

"What're you talking about?" Collins whined. "What'd those bitches tell you? They are the craziest bitches I ever seen."

Lucas said, "Ten dead, and *they're* crazy? You miserable piece of shit, I wish I'd shot you back in the park."

"I had nothin' to do with no killings. I was along for the ride, 'cause I knew some guys who could get us some dope along the way. I heard somebody say they killed this boy out in South Dakota and I took right off, I didn't want to hear about that shit."

"What about Neal Malin in Hayward? Was he your boy? One of your dope guys?"

Collins's eyes slid away. "I heard about that, too. They told me there was an accident. I wasn't there, but they said they was freebasin' or something and the RV exploded."

"What kind of freebasing gets your throat cut?" Lucas asked. "What kind of freebasing do you do with gasoline?"

"I don't know nothin' . . . I gotta have a lawyer. I can tell you about this, but I gotta have a lawyer first."

They backed out of the cell and Lucas told the others, "He might be the most reliable one. Let's keep him away from everyone else."

Bennett came up and gave Lucas a page ripped from a legal pad: "The phone numbers from their cell phones. The Collins guy had a 'Pilate.'"

"Excellent."

The city cop said, "We don't have facilities to keep people here. You gotta talk to Rome, tell him we need to start shifting people up to Sault Ste. Marie."

"I got that," Barnes said. "I'll talk to Rome, but we can probably borrow a bus from the school, or maybe get Amos Krall's van and haul them up in that."

They were still figuring out the logistics of it, when Lucas's phone rang and "Unknown" showed up in the caller field. "Yeah?"

"Lyle Ellis here—I'm the defender. I'm over at the sheriff's office. I was told you wanted to speak to me?"

"Yeah, Mr. Ellis. Listen, we've got two people there, where you are, and two more locked up at the city," Lucas said. "It would be good if you could rep them all, at least for the time being. Did the sheriff explain the problem to you?"

"Yes. As he sees it, anyway," Ellis said. "I understand you're from Minnesota, but I don't quite understand your status up here."

"We can talk about that later," Lucas said. "The two women being held at the sheriff's office tell us there are nineteen traveling killers, with maybe ten bodies behind them: think the Manson gang, but worse, with the leader still running around loose here in the UP. What I want to tell you is that you're dealing with people who in my opinion are probably insane. Literally insane and proven killers. You have to take care about your own safety. Do not get crosswise with them. In my opinion, you may want to take a cop in with you for the preliminary talk, and then, after they're transferred up to Sault Ste. Marie, talk to them privately only when you can have a bodyguard with you."

"You're not scaring me, Officer Davenport," Ellis said. "This ain't exactly my first rodeo."

"Maybe not your first, but it's different from anything else you've handled, because it's different from what *anybody* has handled, anywhere," Lucas said. "Nobody's dealt with this rodeo before. They're nuts. You need to protect yourself."

"All right. I'll think about what you've said."

"Mr. Ellis, I'll tell you what—you sound like a guy who's so sure of himself that he could get killed. Don't do that. There's one man who was *crucified* in South Dakota, before he was castrated and slashed to death, another who got his throat slit in Wisconsin, and a woman who was kicked to death."

"I'll try not to be stupid," Ellis said.

"Try real hard," Lucas said, and hung up.

Barnes said, "That must have been Lyle Ellis. He really *isn't* the sharpest knife in the dishwasher. I've known him for years. I'll . . . talk to him."

THEY LEFT BARNES and Bennett and the city cop to figure out a safe way to transfer the four disciples to Sault Ste. Marie—Barnes was arguing that the best way would be to chain up each one in the back of different SUVs, and drive them up separately. That would have all four of them in jail in three hours or so, and they wouldn't be able to communicate with each other. Lucas thought that was the best idea he'd heard so far, and said so.

While Barnes and Bennett handled that, Lucas and Frisell headed back out to the park. Frisell no longer had a weapon, but Lucas suggested that if he could handle it, having already been involved in a shooting, he could be useful walking around the park, keeping an eye on things.

"I don't want you to think I'm a cold-blooded killer," Frisell said. "But, look, Lucas—shooting that guy really doesn't bother me. Just doesn't. I got a kid hurt in a sophomore football game last year, and he tried to tough it out and didn't tell me, and got hurt worse. Cracked two vertebrae. That's been tearing me up for a year. I should have seen it. I should have known. He's still walking around in a girdle, almost a year later, and I kick myself in the ass every time I see him. But this Raleigh guy? Not a problem."

Lucas half laughed and said, "You and me both. I don't meet many people like us. I've been in some shootings, and they were all good, and the thing that bothered me most about them was all the fuckin' paperwork. On the other hand, I see cops who shoot somebody, perfectly good shooting, and they're never the same again. And it's real, they're not faking it."

"I believe that," Frisell said. "Not me, though. I didn't go there to shoot anyone. I feel about as bad as I would if a drunk driver crossed the road and crashed into me, and he died and I didn't. I mean, not very. And I'll tell you, Rome's the same way. And the other guys, too, I think."

"I hope it's really that way, that you don't wake up and find your ass has fallen off," Lucas said. Lucas called the new list of phone numbers into the BCA: "Ping them all. Let me know."

15

THE SCENE AT the park was Hayward all over again, a shifting mass of painted-face Juggalos and Juggalettes in a semicircle around the shooting scene, a couple of uniformed deputies keeping the crowd back. A fire pile was going up at one end of the field, while a band was doing a sound check at the bandstand at the other end.

Lucas and Frisell parked and walked over to the circle. Laurent spotted them, walked around some crime scene tape and came over and said, "Herb Jackson's down from Sault. Herb's their crime scene guy."

Lucas said, "Good," and told Laurent about the half-assed interrogations at the sheriff's office and the city jail. "It's really a matter of rounding them up, now. Only one guy's hanging tough, everybody else seems happy to deal."

"What about Lyle Ellis?" Laurent asked. "Did he call you?"

"Yeah, he's at your office now, should be interviewing the women."

HERB JACKSON, THE crime scene tech, was a little pissy about the way the scene had been handled before he got there, but that was typical, and didn't particularly bother Lucas: as far as he was concerned, covering the shooting scene was mostly a waste of time. There had been several witnesses to the shooting, and determining the exact location of each spent 9mm shell wouldn't make any difference one way or the other. But, that's what crime scene techs did, and he was usually happy enough to leave them to it. If nothing else, the county attorney could argue that the scene had been handled competently, when the county was sued by the guy who'd been shot in the lip.

On the other hand, he did have a priority. He said, "Herb, I need to talk to you over here."

As far from the crowd as possible: Lucas could see video cameras being pointed at them and some had zoom mikes. Laurent followed them over to the far side of the car, where Lucas quietly told them what Melody Walker had said about Linda Petrelli taking Henry Fuller's penis as a trophy. "If she's telling the truth, it could be in the car. Might not be obvious what it is . . . or it may be, I don't know. If you find it, treat it with care, because it's going to hang these assholes."

"Gosh darnit, I've never . . ." Jackson said. "I mean, I've seen some weird things . . ."

"Yeah. I know. Just be aware of what you're dealing with," Lucas said.

"Peters and Sellers are still out there, looking around," Laurent said. "Haven't seen any more plates from California."

"Herb needs to process the other two cars, the ones from Biggs and Collins," Lucas said. "Collins admits he's a dealer." To Jackson: "Take a close look for hidden panels and so on."

"I will. I did a class on that down in Lansing," Jackson said.

"What are you going to do?" Laurent asked Lucas.

"Hook up with Peters and Sellers, wander around the park. Raleigh Waites recognized me because Pilate left a spy behind at the shooting scene in Hayward, and he saw me working the murder scene down there. Pilate may have another one here . . . We have to be aware of that."

"Wish we could get our hands on that sonofabitch," Laurent said. "Teach him he doesn't bring this shit to the UP."

NOTHING HAPPENED. THEY didn't spot anybody.

Lucas, Laurent, Peters, Sellers, and Frisell walked every inch of the park, shouldering through the crowds, watching each other at the same time—looking for somebody tracking them. They saw nothing. An hour passed, and two. Lucas talked to the enormously fat man again, who'd seen nothing. The duty officer at the BCA called and said that the phones were being pinged through AT&T and Verizon, but they were seeing nothing at all.

"It's possible that they were warned and they've all got their phones sewn upside those special bags—or they pulled the batteries," Lucas told the duty officer. "Do this—get the phone companies to hammer on them from about eleven o'clock tonight until one in the morning. One of the women we picked up said Pilate might expect them to call around midnight. They might stay off the phones except for that window in the middle of the night."

"Gotcha. I'll pass the word along. Davy's got the night shift. I'll have him call either way, whether we get something or not."

LUCAS GAVE IT another hour and then told Laurent, "We should leave one guy here, to look at newcomers, but send everybody else home. They need to get to bed early tonight. If we ping Pilate at midnight, and locate him, we'll want to roll out and get on top of him. Get out to the site, wherever it is, throw a ring around it, and then hit him at first light."

"Just like deer hunting," Laurent said.

"Deer don't shoot back, usually."

"True. Okay, Peters has a court case tomorrow. I'll have him stay late, and send the rest of them home."

"I've got a question for you," Lucas said. "What if Pilate's not in Barron County?"

Laurent shrugged: "Up here, we have mutual aid agreements—all I have to do is call the sheriff's office in whatever county I'm going to, they'll say come on ahead, and I'm good. The budgets are so tight that nobody ever says no. If he's up here in the UP, I'm happy enough to go after him. This is all . . . pretty interesting. I think the guys would go, too. I'll ask."

"Good. Check with them. If he's deep in the woods somewhere, outside of Barron County, we might want help from the locals, too."

"I'll call around tonight, get set in advance," Laurent said. "Let me know as soon as you find out where they are."

"If they call me, you'll be the first to know," Lucas said. "Maybe it'll all go down easy."

"Raleigh Waites didn't go down easy. Neither did that Bony guy in Wisconsin."

"You really are Father Christmas," Lucas said. "You were supposed to say, 'Yeah, there'll be nothing to it.'"

"When I was in Iraq," Laurent said, "we had a standard answer for somebody who suggested that an op was going to be easy."

"Yeah?"

"Yeah: *Run!*"

LUCAS WENT BACK to the Holiday Inn, took a shower, laid out some clothes so he could get dressed in a hurry, called Weather, told her what was happening, talked to Letty for a while—she was hurting worse than she had the first day, but Weather said that was normal.

When he got off the phone, he turned off the light and tried to sleep. But it was too early, and he didn't. Instead, he lay in bed in the dark and thought about the possibilities, and when that got boring, called Del: "Is everything okay?"

"Well, yeah. I mean there aren't any emergencies going on. What are you up to?"

"Trying to sleep, but can't. Almost got shot today, don't tell Weather . . ."

He told Del about it, and Del said, "Jesus, you got lucky."

"Yeah, somewhat."

When he got off the call to Del, he turned the lights off again, couldn't sleep, got his iPad out, browsed the Internet for a while, eventually worked his way around to eleven-thirty, and two minutes later, got a call from the duty officer. "We got five hits on those phone numbers, right away. Two of them were in California, but three of them are up there in the UP. We got a hit on the Pilate phone number and two others. I got the GPS coordinates figured out. You got a map?"

"Let me call one up," Lucas said.

If the GPS locations were correct, the Pilate calls were coming out of a state park campground in the deep woods of Cray County, forty miles west and north of where Lucas was.

"Keep pinging them. We're on the way," Lucas said.

He was on his feet, pulling on his jeans. He called Laurent and said, "We're going to Cray County, talk to the locals there, wherever that is."

"Already did. I called all the sheriffs in the UP and we're good everywhere. We can pick up a couple of their deputies and maybe a couple more reserve deputies when we get there. The question is, do we want to go in there at one o'clock in the morning? We'd wind up chasing people through the woods in the dark."

Lucas thought about it, then said, "I guess not. I'm going, but let your guys sleep. It gets light what, at six o'clock? Forty miles? Get them up at four-thirty, get out of town before five-thirty."

"It's a straight shot over there. We go in a convoy, with lights, we can be there in less than an hour," Laurent said. "Peters is coming—he canceled his court date. Let me get you the names of the sheriff's deputies over there. You probably ought to check in with them. I'll call them and tell them you're coming."

LUCAS WAS ON the road a little after midnight, the names of the Cray County cops in his notebook and a hand-drawn map of the campground where Pilate was. There was nothing open in Jeanne d'Arc, not even the gas station, so he headed west. Twenty miles out, he spotted a combination sporting goods store–roadhouse–gas station that was still open, got a Diet Coke and a cheeseburger and fries to go, and got back on the road with a full tank of gas.

Lewis State Park was totally off the grid, on the far side of the county seat at Winter. Winter did have an open gas station/convenience store, and the clerk pointed him down the main street to the county courthouse. The annex in back, where the sheriff's office was, showed a light, but the door was locked and nobody answered when he knocked.

He had a phone number for the deputy on duty, called it, and the deputy picked up, said, "This is Carl."

"Carl, this is Lucas Davenport. I'm down at the sheriff's office."

"Hey. I'm out on road patrol, right at the far end of my run. You seen the store?"

"Yeah."

"They got good coffee, you could wait for me there," Carl said.

"I'm going to run out to Lewis Park, take a look at the situation."

"Okay. You're only about ten miles from there, so . . . if you just look around, and then head back, we'll probably just about meet up."

"Thanks. See you then."

TEN MILES OUT of Winter, he passed a highway sign marking the turnoff, but kept going, without slowing. At the first side road, which was a driveway, he pulled over, got out his phone: no service. He turned around and drove slowly past the entry road to the park. He could see nothing, not even a glimmer of light.

He drove back to Winter, working out exactly what he wanted to do. At Winter, Lucas tried his phone again, got one bar, called the BCA duty officer. "No more pings. Everything slowed down after midnight, and all of a sudden, they were gone. There's two phones up by Lake Superior and another one in the woods halfway between Winter and Lake Superior. I looked at a satellite view of the GPS location, but there's not a darn thing there."

When he got off the phone, Lucas tried his iPad, got one bar on that, too, but managed to slowly download a terrain map of Lewis State Park. The main feature, as with Overtown Park in Barron County, was a lake and a campground. Otherwise, the land around the lake was flat and probably swampy, since there wasn't much relief above the lake's water level. A Google satellite view showed a chunk of forest around the lake, and several expansive clear-cuts back from the entry road.

He was looking at the Google view when a Ford pickup bounced into the parking lot and an older man wearing a T-shirt, sweatpants, and gym shoes got out. Lucas stepped out to meet him, asking, "Carl?"

"Nope. I'm the sheriff, Phil Turner." He was a short man, thin, with a bristling white mustache and a thick chest and arms. They shook hands and Turner said, "Carl called me. I told him I'd probably be up until two. You'd be Davenport?"

"Yup."

"This guy still out at Lewis?"

"Don't know. Don't know full names, don't know most descriptions, don't know license plates, except they're most likely from California, but not for sure. They will be armed and they're willing to kill. Eager to kill."

"Well, shit."

"Yeah. Not a good situation," Lucas said.

"I called around for mutual aid, we'll have twenty deputies and reserve deputies from the surrounding counties here at five-thirty, including the guys from Barron County. How many people are we looking at?"

"I'm not sure. We think they started out with nineteen or twenty. We've taken down six of them, which would leave thirteen or fourteen, but they're not all at the park. We've got locations for at least three more cell phones, not at the park. If there are two people per cell phone, that would mean six people are out in the woods yet, so maybe . . . six or seven at the park? But we really don't know."

"Well, twenty deputies ought to be enough. Mostly got to be careful not to shoot each other. The lake's the best part of a mile off the highway, but there's some logging roads that come off the park road. There's one about two-thirds of the way in that leads back to a clearcut. We put the cars in there, block the road out, and walk in."

"Sounds like a plan," Lucas said. "Where are we hooking everybody up?"

"Right here. Don't have a motel, but I got a couch if you want to try to catch a couple hours of sleep."

"I'm okay," Lucas said. "How many of those logging roads come off the main park road?"

"Four or five, I guess," Turner said.

"I think I'll go back over there and park off the road. Watch for anybody going out."

Turner nodded. "Okay. I could send Carl over there with you, he's not doing anything anyway, except driving around. We could stick him in a driveway off the highway, you see California plates going out, you could tag the car until we got far enough from the park that we could run him down without waking anybody else up."

"Can Carl . . . I mean, is he . . ."

"Competent? Yeah, sure. He's okay. And he has an M14 we got from the feds with twenty-round magazines. He can punch holes in cars all day."

"I don't want any cops killed," Lucas said.

"Neither do I—but if these guys are as bad as you said they were, I don't want them driving away, either."

"All right. If you're good with Carl backing me up, I'm good with it, too," Lucas said.

CARL SHOWED UP a minute later and they decided that he'd park in a driveway a mile or so west of the park turnoff. After a few more words, they loaded up and headed back toward the park. Carl dropped off a mile out, did a two-point turn, and backed into the driveway.

Lucas continued on in the dark, found the lake turnoff, drove a hundred yards down the narrow gravel track, found a narrower dirt track going off to the left. He turned in, drove fifty feet down the track, checking it out in his headlights, then backed out to the main road, turned around, and backed into the side track. When he was thirty feet off, he moved the front seat back as far as it would go, killed his lights and engine, and settled in to wait.

He'd had a long day and let himself doze. He never went completely asleep, he thought, not deep enough that he wouldn't wake up if a car went by; but he wasn't disturbed until his iPhone alarm went off at five o'clock. His mouth tasted like a chicken had been roosting in it, and his back hurt. He took care of the mouth with a stick of gum, stepped out of the car to do a few toe touches, and called Carl. "Time to go in."

"I think. I was about to give you a call. Didn't see anything on my end."

"Meet you back at the sheriff's office."

TWELVE DEPUTIES FROM three counties were waiting for him at the sheriff's office in Winter. Then Turner, the sheriff, showed up, got out of the car, and said, "Roman and his guys are ten minutes out. They got six guys, two regular deputies and three reserves. One more reserve guy might be coming a little later, he had a kid got hurt last night late and had to take him to the emergency room in Sault Ste. Marie."

"Hope it's not bad."

"Nah. Might have a broken fibula in his leg, he was shooting baskets with some friends, got a little rough. Anyway, he walked around on it, but about the time he was supposed to go to bed, the pain got bad. They took him over to the doctor, who sent them up to Sault."

"All right: so we got twenty." Lucas looked over the crowd in the parking lot. There were patrol cars from three counties, and a varied collection of trucks and SUVs. All but two of the deputies were men, and about half were wearing uniforms, the rest a motley of camo, canvas, and denim. Subtract the uniforms, and they might have been setting up a deer drive.

Laurent and the Barron County crew arrived a few minutes later; Laurent came over and said, "Doug Sellers's kid broke his leg."

"I heard. I think we should be okay."

Laurent nodded: "Let's get the show on the road."

THEY GATHERED THE deputies around a pole light outside the sheriff's office and outlined the plan: go in, quietly, park about four hundred yards from the campground, with two of the cars blocking the road.

Once they were all parked, they'd go single file down the road until they got close enough to see the park: "It should be light enough to see by the time we get there," Lucas said, waving off to the east, where the night sky was beginning to lighten. "You guys with rifles, keep the muzzles up in the air. I don't want to see anybody pointing a muzzle at somebody else's back. Guys with sidearms, keep them holstered. When we get in there, we want to nail down every tent, car, RV, whatever. Nobody comes out. If somebody gets aggressive . . ."

They talked it out, and when everybody agreed that

they knew what would happen, a guy in camo pants and a CAT shirt suggested that they stop down at the store for snacks and coffee.

"Good idea," Turner said. "Load 'em up, boys. And girls. But don't stay in the store more'n a minute or two. We gotta roll."

One of the women had to pee and hurried into the sheriff's office, and then one of the men had to, and everybody else headed down to the store, where Lucas loaded up on Diet Coke and crunchy-style Cheetos. Five minutes later, Turner did a head count, and everybody was set, and they took off.

LUCAS HAD ONCE been a deer hunter, though he'd given it up about the time he married Weather—she didn't particularly object to the idea of shooting deer, and rather liked venison spaghetti and meatballs, but she'd read a paper that said that lead bullets, especially of the expanding variety, contaminated much of the meat with lead particles.

No lead particles in the diet of *her* children . . . But over the years, Lucas had spent the equivalent of three or four months sitting in deer stands or still hunting, and had learned that at dawn, it was too dark to safely shoot; but within fifteen minutes, you could read the small print in a newspaper, and could plainly see two or three hundred yards out.

That transition happened as the cop convoy rolled

down the road toward the lake. When they turned in, headlights were useful. By the time they all got parked, and got the exit road blocked, they were in full daylight.

Most of the members of the posse were carrying rifles, and most of the rifles were .223 black rifles. Carl had his M14, and another man carried a semiauto .30-06, both of which would be useful if they had to bust up an RV.

Laurent led the way out, followed by his reserve deputies, all of them in uniform now and all of them military veterans carrying black rifles. Lucas moved with them, with Carl and Turner following behind Lucas.

Everybody automatically shut up as they were walking along, strung out in a line with four or five yards between them; a few squirrels were chattering away in the woods, and a crow was complaining, but other than that, there was no sound but the crunch of their feet in gravel.

They detoured around a few wet spots in the trail and finally topped a low ridge and started down a gentle slope toward the end of the lake—they could see the curve of the shoreline, and as they got closer, Lucas could smell coffee.

A boat ramp was straight ahead of them, with three boats tied off to one side of the ramp. The road curved to the right, and as they walked down into the open, they saw a line of camping spaces along the lakeshore. Maybe half of them were occupied, mostly by pickups with campers. Three people, two men and a woman, were sitting around a fire on canvas camp stools at the first camping space, and they all stood up as the posse moved out of the woods with their guns. They called someone, and a second woman came down from a camper.

Lucas moved forward, caught up with Laurent, and told the guy behind him to "wait here, and pass the word to everyone to stop where they are." The column stopped, still mostly back along the trail, and Lucas and Laurent walked up to the campers. One of the men, tall with a white beard, asked, "What the heck's going on?"

Their trucks both had Michigan plates.

Lucas said, "We're looking for a bunch of people with California plates on their vehicles. Have you seen anybody . . . ?"

One of the women said, "I was walking back from the clear-cut yesterday before dark, I was up there picking blueberries, and I saw a car with a California license plate. Only one, there was a man and a woman inside."

"Where'd it go?"

She pointed down the line of camping spaces. "Down there somewhere. Everybody wants to get close to the ramp, but they were late in the day, and no boat, either, so I suppose they could be anywhere down there . . . but close to the end of the campers."

The car, she said, was several years old, and probably a Honda or a Nissan, "or one of those, not American," and dark blue or green. Because of the curve of the lake, Lucas couldn't see more than two or three campsites, but no one in the camping areas could see them, either. He waved for the rest of the deputies to come down, and they gathered behind the pickups.

"We'll go down as a group, not all together, but not

all strung out, either. Stay as close to the edge of the trees as you can, they won't see us coming until we're right there."

"How many are there?" Turner asked.

"Only saw one car, two people," Lucas said.

THEY STARTED OUT again, but bunched up closer now, rifle muzzles up in the air like lances. They passed nine more camping sites, each with a pickup or a van parked in it, then an empty camping space, another SUV, then, past two more empty camping spaces, a dark green car. Lucas pulled his gun, and he, Laurent, and Laurent's deputies crept toward it. California plates.

Behind the car, on the other side of a cold fire ring, they could see a blue tent, a self-supporting four-man version, with a rain fly. The front of the tent was zipped.

Lucas put a finger to his lips and Laurent nodded, and waved his deputies to a stop, and then Lucas and Laurent moved up to the car and peeked inside. It was empty. They moved on to the tent.

The problem with a tent was, you couldn't see into it and the occupants couldn't see out, but you could easily hear through the thin nylon fabric, and even more easily, shoot through it.

Laurent waved his deputies forward, to spots behind the car. Then he and Lucas eased up to the tent, not quite tiptoeing. From five feet away, they could hear a delicate snoring, like a woman's snoring, and when they were right outside it, the heavy breathing of a man.

Again, Lucas put a finger to his lips, Laurent nodded, and with his left hand, Lucas delicately grasped the zipper pull on the front flap of the tent and quietly pulled it down. He got it all the way down, then put two fingers through the flap and spread them, and peeked inside. Two people in sleeping bags, their feet toward the flap, on air mattresses, with packs at the back of the tent. There were two horizontal zippers at the bottom of the flap, and Lucas and Laurent slowly pulled them sideways, until the flap was fully open.

When they'd pulled the flaps all the way back, Lucas looked at Laurent, then clenched both fists and made a pulling motion—if they did it right, they could yank both sleepers right out of the tent, still cocooned in their bags.

Laurent smiled and nodded. The woman stirred and said a word, in her sleep, like she might be coming up. Lucas slipped his pistol back in its holster, jabbed a finger at the sleeping bags, and they both took hold of the ends of the bags, and Lucas said, "Now!"

They yanked the bags out of the tent and the woman began screaming and the man said, "What the fuck! What the fuck!"

Laurent shouted, "You're under arrest, don't move your hands! Don't move your hands!"

Both of them had been sleeping on their backs, and with their eyes open, were looking into the muzzles of four guns. Laurent said to Bennett, the post office guy, "Pull the zip down on that sleeping bag."

The woman was screaming, "What are you doing? What are you doing?"

Bennett pulled the zip down. The guy was wearing a T-shirt and Jockey shorts, and they pulled the zip on the woman, who was wearing a T-shirt and underpants, and then Turner, who'd looked into the tent, said, "We've got a gun here, and what looks like a bag of marijuana— yep, it is—and some telephones. Three telephones."

LUCAS ASKED THE man, who was still on his back, "Where's Pilate?"

"Don't know what the fuck you're talking about," but the woman said to the guy, "I told you. I told you. He punked you, you dummy. He did it on purpose to see what would happen."

The guy said, "Shut up!"

Lucas said to the woman, "How did he punk you? Is he right here? Where is he?"

The guy said again, "Shut up!"

But the woman started to cry, and Lucas said to the deputies, "Let's get the cuffs on them, get some pants on them, get them ID'd."

He pulled Turner aside and said, "As soon as they've got some shoes on, separate them. I want to talk to the woman without the guy getting on her case."

Turner nodded.

Lucas got the guy's wallet before the deputies helped him pull his pants on: Kelly Bland, of Los Angeles. The woman had a black tote with a silver sun-face on the side. Inside were a cheap Phoenix .22 automatic, a clasp wallet, a plastic bag with a wad of weed, and all the rest of the crap that women usually carry in totes. Her ID said that she was Alice McCarthy of Torrance, California.

When Bland and McCarthy had their shoes on, Turner's deputies hustled Bland to the other side of the car so that they could open the trunk. They did it smoothly, keeping Bland's attention, and by the time they had him there, asking about drugs and Pilate, Lucas, Laurent, Bennett, and Frisell had moved the woman down a path that led from the campsite to the water.

She was a tall, thin woman with protruding brown eyes, and fingernails that had been bitten to the quick. Bennett read her rights to her, and arrested her on marijuana charges, and then Lucas said, "I think you know the charges on the weed are a little bogus. You could go to jail on them, but what we really need to know about is Pilate. If you go to jail on Pilate, you'll never get out. Never. When this goes to court, you'll need all the help you can get, and we can give you some, if you start co-operating *right now*."

"I don't know where he is, but I'll cooperate," she said.

Lucas shook his head. "That's not good enough. You can't just say you'll cooperate, you've got to deliver something. What were all those phones for?"

"Pilate said Kelly would be our switchboard and everybody could call in to him and then he could tell everybody where to go, and then throw the phone away and nobody would ever catch us that way. The phones only cost like twenty dollars apiece. Pilate said that's the way all the drug dealers do it."

"Where's Pilate?" Laurent demanded. "You've got to know *something* about that."

"He's around here somewhere. We have some people at the Gathering who were supposed to call us last night at midnight, and they didn't, and Pilate was afraid to call them. But the rest of us talked at midnight, and we're gonna try calling the Gathering people at eight o'clock this morning. If they still don't answer, we're supposed to call Pilate and the rest of the people, and decide what to do. Like, Pilate's thinking that if something happened at the Gathering, we ought to scatter down into Michigan or back to Wisconsin, and then just keep going until we're back in California."

"What if you do get a call from the people at the Gathering?" Lucas asked.

"Well, if everything is okay, then we meet there today."

"How many more people are there? We know there were five at the Gathering yesterday, and you and Kelly make seven . . ."

"Maybe ten more," she said. "You knew about the people already at the Gathering?"

"Yes. They've been arrested," Lucas said. He didn't mention that one had been shot and killed. "How reliable would you say that Melody Walker and Linda Petrelli are? Can we trust what they say?"

She said, "Linda, maybe. But Melody's like one of Pilate's main women."

That struck Lucas as odd; backward from what he believed. They talked to her for another ten minutes, and then Frisell took a camera out of his backpack and made a video of her having her rights read to her, and then saying that she understood that she could have a lawyer but wanted to cooperate, and then they asked her all the questions over again.

When they were done, Laurent asked, "So we wait until eight o'clock? And then make up some bullshit story?"

"Let's see what Bland has to say, and then if he'll co-operate, we can probably nail Pilate down," Lucas said.

"If he won't, we could have Alice call him, tell him that Bland couldn't call for some reason, and have her talk to him."

"We could give it a try," Lucas said. He turned back to Alice: "Do you know which of the numbers is Pilate's?"

"Yes, sir . . . I can show you."

BLAND WOULDN'T EVEN speak to them, other than to say, "Lawyer."

Turner had him hauled into Winter to be locked in the town holding cell, and the whole posse tracked back into Winter to wait until eight o'clock. The out-of-county deputies agreed to hang around until they knew whether they'd be needed again, and Lucas called the BCA and told them to step up the pinging on all the phone numbers they had.

McCarthy identified the number of the phone Pilate was now carrying—the numbers listed as "Pilate" were for a phone he used in California as his main number, and didn't take on the trip, and the *P*, she said, was the phone he'd given to Kelly to use as a switchboard.

"He gave us this bullshit excuse, you know, about how everybody was used to calling that phone, so *we* should use it so there wouldn't be any confusion. He was setting us up to see what would happen."

At five minutes after eight o'clock exactly, prepped to give Pilate and the disciples a credible story, Alice made the first call, to disciples she said should be camping near Lake Superior. Lucas's ear was next to hers as a man answered.

"Where's Kelly?" the man asked.

"He's in this store, in Winter. We're getting gas. He was supposed to be back out by now. You know how unreliable he is. He must've gotten stuck at the checkout."

"Okay. Everything straight there?"

"Everything is with us, and the guys at the Gathering say everything's cool. If everything's cool with you, I'll call Pilate."

The man said, "Everything's clear here. We're with Chet, so you don't need to call him. See you at the Gathering."

She hung up and asked, "Was that okay?"

"That was fine," Lucas said. He cocked his head. "You're not fucking with us, are you?"

"What?" She shook her head. "I'm cooperating, I'm cooperating."

He peered at her, uncertain. Then, "Okay. Let's call Pilate."

She called and Pilate answered on the third ring: "Yeah."

"This is Alice. Jase just called, everything's good at the Gathering. And Richie says everything's good with those guys."

"Where's Kelly?" Pilate had a rusty-gate voice, a guy who'd smoked too much dope.

"We're in Winter, getting gas. He's stuck in the store, there's a line of people here, and after Richie called, I thought I'd better call right through to you. You know how unreliable Kelly is."

"All right," Pilate said. Pause. "See you at the Gathering, then."

He was gone.

BAD VIBE FROM the phone call. Alice looked up at Lucas, and it seemed to him that she was smothering a look of triumph. What had she done? Or maybe he was reading too much into her eyes . . .

LUCAS GOT A call from the BCA a minute later, from the tech support guy: the Lake Superior group was at Munising and Pilate was close to the town of Brownsville, twenty miles west of Winter, in Hale County. There were two Hale County deputies with them, and Lucas quickly found one and got him to call the sheriff. The deputy called the sheriff's cell, and handed his own to Lucas and said, "You're talking to Sheriff Hugh Butcher."

"Sheriff Butcher: we think they're right in your town, or close by, probably four to six people, two or three vehicles, one of them an RV," Lucas said. "The RV may have Wisconsin plates, the others, probably California. Don't approach them, they've all been armed, so far. Just try to track them. We're coming with the posse."

"Come ahead . . . we'll go looking."

MCCARTHY AND BLAND were left with Turner in Winter. The rest of the posse hustled back to their cars, led by Lucas. Frisell had ridden to Winter with Laurent and Lucas asked to borrow him for the ride to Brownsville: "I need to make a lot of phone calls and it'd be good if he could drive."

"Take him," Laurent said. "He doesn't have his gun, though, we thought it'd be better if he didn't, after yesterday. He's sort of along for the ride."

"That's fine. Listen, could you get me a number for wherever Melody Walker is up in the Sault jail? I need to talk to her, quick as I can."

"I'll get it as soon as we're moving, and call you."

A MINUTE LATER, they were on the highway headed west, a line of cop cars, pickups, and civilian SUVs led by Lucas and Frisell. Laurent called two minutes later and said, "I got that number for you in Sault. It goes to a mobile phone, they're walking it down to the cell where they're keeping Walker."

Lucas took the number down, and a minute later, was talking to a deputy in Sault Ste. Marie on the car's speakerphone. "We're just coming up to her cell," the deputy said. "Okay . . . Melody, Agent Davenport is calling you."

Walker came on: "This is me."

"If you were picked up by cops and they asked you to call Pilate directly . . . If I'd asked you to do that . . . would you have any way of warning Pilate that the cops had you?"

"Yes. You'd say that something was unreliable. That meant that everything you said on the phone call was unreliable and there was a cop with you."

"Thanks." Lucas rang off and groaned: "Sonofabitch."

Frisell: "What happened?"

"That goddamn Alice McCarthy warned off both groups—she told them that she was with a cop. I knew something was wrong, the way she was talking. I knew it, and I let her talk to Pilate anyway. Fuck me. Fuck me. Now they know we're coming."

"That's a bad thing," Frisell said. "Better to know it, though, than not to."

"Ah, man . . . I really screwed the pooch here. I really did."

16

PILATE WAS MOVING early, and at eight o'clock was parked behind the RV at the Crossroads Citgo gas station and convenience store. The Upper Peninsula had been a mystery to him. He'd traveled through barren areas of the Southwest, but nothing like this. In the Southwestern deserts, long stretches of absolutely nothing were punctuated by fairly large towns. In the UP, there were some long stretches of nothing—usually marked as state or national forests—but there were also farms and logging businesses, back roads apparently leading to something, logging equipment being moved around.

But the towns: there was nothing in them. He didn't really need anything they didn't have—there was usually a gas pump and convenience store. They just weirded him out.

Brownsville got a prominent dot on their paper map, but when they arrived, they found a scattering of houses, a few empty buildings, and maybe a dozen active businesses: the Citgo station; Tom's Skidoo Repair and Donuts, which also served coffee and weak soft drinks; Larabee Woodworking, which featured chainsaw sculptures of bears and fish, as well as a variety of cribbage boards; Pat's Diner and Quilt Shop, which had four booths and four tables and six stools along a bar, plus quilting supplies in a side room; a beer joint called Magic's, which was closed in the morning; and a large lot full of pine logs, but no sign of life.

There were a few more shops on the other side of the Citgo, but they hadn't bothered to go look. They'd passed a compact redbrick elementary school on the way in, and next to that, a matching, but even smaller, redbrick government and law enforcement center.

Kristen and Laine were pumping gas into the Pontiac and diesel into the RV when the call from Alice McCarthy came in: she said "unreliable," and Pilate said a few more words and rang off and said, "Shit. We got a big problem."

Kristen said, "We got more than one. The gas is *dribbling* out of this pump."

"Fuck the gas—we just got an 'unreliable' from Alice. The cops got her and they were making her call us."

He looked at the phone in his hand and said, "I got to get rid of this."

He was headed for a trash can when the phone rang again. Richie, who'd been north of them, up by the lake. Pilate answered, and blurted, "The cops might be listening to this."

"We were calling to warn you. We stopped for food

and drinks at this place, and got an 'unreliable,' from Alice, and were taking off, but my girlfriend bought this newspaper on the way out, and it says an unidentified California man was shot and killed at the Gathering in Sault Ste. Marie."

"What!"

"They're all over us, man. It's the California plates that are doing it," Richie said.

"You know that emergency place we talked about? To meet up?"

"Yeah."

"Go there. And throw away your phone."

"See you there."

Pilate hung up and said to Kristen and Laine, "Some California guy got shot by the cops at the Gathering. Had to be one of us."

"We got to get out of here," Kristen said. "We still need the gas. And you gotta go get Michelle and Bell."

Pilate looked around, got a paper towel out of the dispenser above the window-washing tub, put the towel on the ground and the phone on the towel, and stomped the phone to death. When he was satisfied that it would no longer work—and had separated the battery from the rest of the debris—he wrapped the pieces in the paper towel and threw it all in the trash can. "I'll get Bell."

Before he went to get him, he got his .45 out of the Pontiac and stuck it under his belt, and pulled out his T-shirt to cover it. Then he jogged across the street to the diner, where Michelle and Bell had ordered six cheeseburgers to go. The burgers were still cooking.

"Gotta go," Pilate said, when he came through the door.

"Couple more minutes, we oughta get some—"

"Gotta go!"

A heavyset woman with long yellow-gray hair was cooking the burgers, while trying to keep her cigarette ash out of the meat, and said around the cigarette butt, "They're not quite ready . . ."

Michelle was by the window, looking out, and said, "Oh, my God! Look at this."

A SHERIFF'S PATROL car had stopped in the middle of the street and two cops had gotten out. They were walking toward Kristen and Laine, who were still standing at the fuel pumps, looking at the cops coming toward them.

Bell turned to Pilate, who'd frozen in place, and then Bell pulled his revolver, an old .38, and said, "Let's do it."

Pilate said, "Wait!"

Bell said, "Bullshit, it all ends right here, if they take the cars away from us."

And in the next one second he was out the door with his gun, and then Pilate followed behind, pulling his .45, and Bell opened up with the .38 from forty feet, and then Pilate joined in, and the cops turned and tried to fire back but they went down in the street.

Neither of the cops was dead; Bell started toward them, the muzzle of his gun lowered to shoot down at them, to finish them.

At the gas station, Kristen had dropped to the concrete, afraid she'd be hit by wild shots, and Michelle and Pilate ran past the bodies in the street as Kristen got back up and yanked the nozzle out of the Pontiac's gas tank and then there was another shot, from out of nowhere, and Michelle went down and Pilate and Bell turned and saw the hamburger cook in the door of the diner, working the bolt on a rifle, and they simultaneously began firing at her and she ducked back inside the shop.

Then they were both out of ammo and Michelle was screaming in pain and Bell picked her up and carried her to the RV and threw her inside. Laine dropped the diesel nozzle on the ground but managed to get the cap back on the gas tank, and she and Bell piled into the RV, and they took off, the RV leading for the first fifty yards before Pilate's Firebird blew past it. As they passed the RV, another shot bounced off the angled back window of the Firebird, cracking the glass and ricocheting off to somewhere else.

A half minute later, they were out of town. Two miles down the road, Pilate looked back and saw the RV already a half mile behind. He slowed and told Kristen, "Get Bell on your phone."

She nodded and put the phone on speaker and punched in Bell's number, and he came up and said, "Michelle was hit in the back, she's pretty bad, we gotta get her to a hospital."

Pilate shook his head at Kristen and then said, loud enough for Bell to hear, "Let's get off somewhere up ahead and take a look."

Bell came back: "There's a pickup behind me, he's

staying way back but he's keeping up, and I think he followed me out of town. He might be tracking us."

They were coming up to a low hill, and Pilate said, "When you get over the hill and can't see him in the rearview, stop on the side of the road. We need to get the rifle out of the closet."

"Okay."

Pilate said to Kristen, "We're in deep shit, man, we're in deep shit."

They went over the top of the hill and pulled over into some weeds on the side of the road and the RV caught up with them and pulled in behind them, and Bell hopped out and ran around to the back and popped the door and Pilate vaulted inside and yanked open the closet door and pushed the clothes out of the way and got the black rifle and the big magazine and slammed it home and ran back outside.

He leaned against the side of the RV, and when the pickup came over the top of the hill he pulled the trigger but nothing happened, and for an instant he thought that the rifle was broken, and then remembered that he hadn't charged it, and he pulled back the charging handle and let it go and started firing, ripping through the full magazine.

The pickup shuddered to a stop and then began backing away, and Pilate kept firing until he ran out of ammo, and thought *Shit* again and ran back inside the RV and dug the second magazine out of the shoes on the floor of the closet, pulled out the first magazine, and jammed in the second as he ran back outside.

By the time he got there, the pickup had disappeared back over the hill, and he ran up the hill, and the pickup was now five hundred yards away. The driver had managed to turn it around and it was accelerating away.

Bell had lifted Michelle out of the RV's passenger seat and placed her on the ground at the side of the road. She was conscious and moaning, and there was a streak of pale pink blood by her mouth.

"If we leave her here, somebody'll see her . . . We could call somebody and tell them that she's here," Bell said.

Pilate turned away and then ran two fast steps to the RV and kicked the fender, once, twice, then whirled to Bell and screamed, "Why does this shit always happen? Why does this shit always happen to me?"

Michelle said, "I'm hurt really bad—"

Pilate lifted the rifle, and in an instant, shot her twice in the face. Laine and Kristen flinched away, and Pilate shouted at them, "Fuck her, she would have given us up. Sent us to the electric chair. I hate this fuckin' place! I hate this fuckin' place!"

They had to go. Before they left, they threw Michelle's body into a stand of cattails, then pushed it under and bent some cattails over it.

Had to go. Had to go.

They went. Once or twice, as they fled down the highway, Bell thought he caught the sparkle of glass in the rearview mirror, a windshield way back.

Nothing he could do about it.

17

FRISELL WAS HOLDING the Benz at a steady eighty-five on the narrow two-lane highway when the Hale County sheriff's car went screaming by at better than a hundred. Frisell put the right two wheels in the weeds, and blurted, "Jesus Christ," and then, "The guy in the passenger seat was waving at us. Something happened."

"Yeah, and it's something bad."

Lucas took out his phone and called Laurent, who was trailing a few cars back. "Something happened in Hale County," he said, when Laurent answered.

"I know. I've got Peters looking up the number for the law enforcement center . . . Hang on, he's getting it."

Lucas hung on, and a couple of minutes passed and then Laurent came back and said, "It's confusing, but there's been a shoot-out in Brownsville. The sheriff and a deputy were wounded bad. The shooters took off, but we're told there's a guy trailing him in his truck, and he's calling back on his phone. He says they just got off the main highway and are headed northwest toward the town of Mellon."

"Ah, shit, Pilate was there and they tried to take them," Lucas said.

"I think so."

"Where's Mellon?"

"Straight on through Brownsville for ten miles or so, then there's a branch highway headed northwest to Marquette. More of a back road than a highway, though it's paved and they can move right along. A couple miles on the other side of Mellon, there's a three-way intersection, an east-west road cuts across the one they're on. If they get to that intersection, finding them is going to get tougher, if we don't know which way they went."

"Gotta hurry," Lucas returned.

A minute later, he got another call from Laurent: "There's a state patrolman on his way to Mellon. If he gets there first, he can block the road at a bridge. There's only the highway, and if he jams them up, he should be able to hold them off. There were at least four of them, maybe five, but one of them may have been shot by a woman who owns the local café . . . and she was hit by return fire. That's what we're hearing. We don't know about the guy who's trailing them."

"Gotta go faster," Lucas said. "Gotta get there. How many highway patrolmen?"

"Only one, far as I know."

"Gotta go faster," Lucas said. "Call ahead to that

town, Mellon, is that right? Call them and tell them what's coming."

"I'll do that now," Laurent said.

Frisell leaned into the accelerator, crossed a hundred, and said, "Let me know when you get nervous."

"Not yet," Lucas said. He added, "I'm gonna reach past you."

He reached past Frisell to the dashboard and hit the switches for his flashers.

And they rolled, rapidly pulling away from the cars behind them.

THEY'D BEEN LEAVING Winter, twenty miles out of Brownsville, when the shooting started. They found out about it a minute or so later when the sheriff, who'd been shot, began screaming for help from his car, and the Hale County deputy's car passed Lucas and Frisell.

Fifteen miles, more or less. Frisell pushed the Benz to a hundred and ten and then chickened out, saying, "I don't think I can hold it much faster than this. Highway's too rough."

They got to Brownsville about nine minutes after the shooting, and fifteen seconds behind the deputies in the car that had passed them on the highway.

Both of the wounded men were still there in the street. It was a long run to the nearest hospital; the closest one was in Munising, where the phone pings had placed the second group of Pilate's disciples. Brownsville had no doctor, but there was a large-animal vet a couple of miles out and he'd been called to do first aid. He'd gotten there a minute before Lucas and Frisell.

THE SHERIFF WAS lying next to his car, at the end of a blood trail. He'd been shot in the middle of the street, and had crawled back to his car to call for help. Three townspeople were gathered around him and one of the deputies from the squad car was stuffing gauze packs into a wound on his side.

The sheriff had been hit in the side, the left hip and right calf, and was conscious. A deputy had been hit in the back, twice, high and low, and was unconscious, still breathing, still lying in the middle of the street in a pool of blood. The vet was working over him, trying to stop the bleeding.

Lucas looked at the sheriff and then called out to the circle of townspeople who were gathering around, "We need a door to use as a stretcher. We need a pickup and a mattress off a bed—and a box spring, if we can get it. We need it right now."

A group of the townspeople broke off, running for their houses, calling back and forth. A couple of them headed for a house that appeared to be abandoned. Lucas had gone to look at the downed deputy, when he heard a smashing sound. He turned and saw a heavy man in boots kicking a door off the empty house.

The vet looked up as Laurent came jogging over and

said, "Orville's gone if we don't get him to the hospital right quick. I'm losing his airway."

"We've got an airway kit in my car," Laurent said.

The vet said, "Get it! Quick!"

A woman was backing a super-duty pickup toward them, and somebody yelled, "We got the bed . . ."

The heavy guy was carrying a broken door toward them, and Lucas went that way, and shouted to four people struggling with a double-sized mattress and box spring, "Put the mattress in the pickup bed. Bring the door here."

Four of them carefully edged the sheriff onto the door. He moaned once, and muttered, "Hurts . . ." and they carried the door to the pickup and put the sheriff on the mattress.

A minute later they transferred the deputy onto the mattress next to the sheriff. The vet climbed into the truck with the woman deputy from Cray County, who was holding a plastic airway piece in the deputy's throat. The vet was now on the phone to an emergency room doc, and they took off, headed for Munising.

A WOMAN HAD also been wounded, somebody said, and Lucas went into the café to look at her. The woman was lying on the café floor, on her side, smoking a cigarette. She'd been hit on the edge of her hip. Unless she had a weak heart, she'd make it, Lucas thought, at least until lung cancer got to her. She'd lost some blood, but not a lot, and another woman was pressing a towel on the wound.

"We got to get her going," Lucas said.

"I'll take her in my car," the second woman said.

The woman on the floor said, around her cigarette, "What a pain in the ass . . ."

The second woman shook her head: "Margery—"

"What happened to the boys?" Margery asked.

"They're headed north," said a man who'd come through the door behind Lucas.

"How many were there?" Lucas asked the woman on the floor.

"Either four or five," the woman on the floor said. "I think there were two women pumping gas and two men and a woman in here, waiting for the cheeseburgers, which they never paid for."

"You don't have to be funny, Margery, for God's sakes," said the woman with the towel.

"I shot at them, but I was pretty shaky. I think I hit that one woman, even though I wasn't shooting at her, particularly. I saw Hugh and Orville go down and I grabbed my gun and let go."

As they were talking, a clerk from the filling station across the street ran up and said, "Ben says they shot up his truck, but he's okay. They kept going and he's still trailing them. He said they're definitely headed toward Mellon, but they're not going very fast because of the RV."

"We're going," Lucas said. He looked at Frisell and then asked one of the deputies, "You got an extra rifle?"

"In the trunk of the sheriff's car."

"We need it . . . And somebody get this lady to the hospital, quick as you can."

They got the rifle, another .223, and four magazines, and Lucas led the posse out of town again. He was driving this time while Frisell checked out the rifle.

"How far are we from Mellon?"

"Twenty, twenty-five miles, I guess," Frisell said.

"So . . . ten or twelve minutes."

"Only if you're driving a hundred and twenty." He looked up at the trees going by: "Oh, Jesus . . ."

"He's not here," Lucas said.

THREE MILES WEST of Mellon, a Michigan state cop named Richard Blinder was on the radio to a Hale County deputy about the shooting at Brownsville. "If they're coming my way, I can block the culvert at Mellon and hold them off for a while, depending on how many there are. I'll be there in two minutes, but for God's sakes, get me some help."

Two minutes later, running with flashers and siren, he hit the fifteen-foot-long bridge over a seasonal stream at Mellon, slewed the cruiser sideways, jogged it back and forth until he covered both lanes between the metal railings. The creek beneath the bridge had only a trickle of water at the bottom, and was mostly filled with wetland foliage.

The land was flat, and the road straight, and Blinder could see nothing coming at him. He got his rifle out of the trunk and jogged up the street to a convenience store/gas station. There were two cars parked at the station, three patrons and the clerk standing outside by the gas pumps. They saw him coming, turned toward him, and the clerk shouted, "They called us from Brownsville. We're holing up here and in the bar, and some people are getting guns and hiding out in their houses."

"All right, but it'd be better to get out in the woods. One way or another, this can't last long. They'll be here in five minutes."

Blinder ran back to his car and somebody came out of the bar and yelled, "Hey, Dick, you need somebody with you?"

"No, no, cover up. Barricade the doors. Get people safe."

THE TOWN OF Mellon had barely impinged on Pilate's consciousness. He was running hard in the Pontiac, leaving the RV behind. Had to get somewhere, far away, had to hide, had to find out what the cops knew and what they didn't. Mellon was nothing more than a pimple on the ass of the UP, and they'd picked it as an emergency rendezvous only because they could get gasoline there, and food, and they'd be close to a major intersection—or what passed for a major intersection. Back in L.A., it'd be called a bike path.

Kristen wasn't helping: "This whole fuckin' trip has been crazy," she shouted at him. "This was badly planned. Badly planned. Now we got every cop in the world chasing us. We'd have been better off if that bitch in Hayward had stabbed you a little. Get that sewn up, she's in jail, we get out of there. But no! You had—"

"Shut up, shut up, shut up. You want to get out? You want to hitchhike back? So shut the fuck up."

"I knew this was . . ." She paused, then said, "There's something up ahead. What is that?"

"That's that town . . ."

They could see a scattering of houses, and beyond that, a half dozen commercial buildings of some kind, with signs out front, and beyond that, more houses, and a car parked sideways across the street. As they got closer, they could see it was a cop car, blocking a narrow two-lane bridge: no way around it. No movie moves.

"OH, FUCK . . . IT'S a roadblock. Get the rifle, get the rifle. Load it up."

Pilate hadn't even planned to slow down for Mellon: he had plenty of gas, he'd just wanted to meet the boys at the intersection. They'd stashed the black rifle in the backseat, and Kristen turned in her seat, pulled the rifle out, and two long magazines, and said, "I don't shoot so good."

"You see that blue house down from the roadblock?"

"Yeah."

"I'm pulling in right there."

He'd slowed to forty miles an hour: they'd be at the roadblock in half a minute if they continued at the same speed. "Can't slow down too much, or they'll figure out what we're doing."

"What're we doing?"

"What you always wanted to do. We're gonna kill a fuckin' cop."

"I think we done that already."

They rolled on, not slowing, into the town, past a convenience store and gas station, a tire place/garage, a bar/café, a used-boat dealer, and a couple of low-rise commercial buildings, which appeared to be abandoned. They could see the cop on the far side of his car, holding up a hand, warning them to stop, a rifle on his hip, and two hundred feet away, Pilate swerved off the road, up a short gravel driveway and behind the blue house.

As soon as he was out of sight of the cop car, he jammed on the brakes, shifted into *Park*, grabbed the rifle, and ran to the corner of the house.

He peeked around the corner, and saw that the cop, a highway patrolman, had moved to the far back corner of his car and was aiming his rifle over the roof, right at Pilate. Pilate yanked his head back and ran around the house to the far side, peeked again. The cop was still looking at the other corner. Pilate couldn't see much of him, and the cop was yelling something that he couldn't make out.

He got up his guts, set his feet, and quickly poked the gun around the side of the building and fired three quick shots at the cop's head. The cop dropped, but Pilate had the sense that he hadn't hit him. He fired three more shots, this time under the car, hoping that ricochets might take out the other man.

No luck. He saw a quick flash of hat as the man went farther back, behind the car's tires.

The cop started shouting again, and then Kristen was behind him, shouting, "What should I do? What should I do?"

Pilate didn't know what she should do, but it didn't matter, because another car rolled up the highway, behind the cop. They could see the cop's hand as he waved the other car down. The car stopped, and a moment later, the passenger-side door popped open. Richie, who'd been up at the lake, and who'd come south to rendezvous with Pilate, got out with his rifle, poked it over the top of the door, and began firing at the cop. The cop made a stumbling run for the side of the bridge, trying to get into the creek or ravine beneath it, but was hit and knocked down as he got to the edge.

He went flat for a moment, dropping his rifle, then managed to pull himself up and throw himself over the edge of the bridge.

Pilate ran out from behind the house, toward the cop car, and Richie ran toward the bridge from his side. Standing back a bit from the bridge, they both looked into the space beneath it. It wasn't quite a creek, but not quite a ravine, either—more like a swale, currently occupied by a marsh. They could see where the cop had landed in the marsh weeds, a five-foot drop, and where he'd pulled himself under the bridge, but they couldn't see the cop.

"I think he's hurt, I hit him pretty hard," Richie

called. Then, in the best movie fashion, in which the speaker never got shot, he called, "Cover me."

He went out into the yard on the far side of the bridge, so he could better see under it, pointing his rifle at the bridge as he did it. He'd just squared up to the bridge, crouching a bit, when there was a single gunshot from beneath it, and Pilate saw the dirt spit up just in front of Richie's legs—the bullet must have gone right between them. Richie screamed something and ran back toward the bridge, where the cop couldn't see him.

Behind Richie, Ellen and Carrie had gotten out of the car. The women ran toward the bridge, then out on it. Ellen picked up the cop's rifle, and then Carrie stooped again and Pilate realized she'd gotten two or three more magazines.

Pilate shouted, "This way, this way . . ." and at the same time, fired a burst of three shots under the bridge, with no idea of where the cop might be. As he did it, Richie, Ellen, and Carrie ran across the bridge and around behind the house. Another car pulled up behind Richie's, and Coon and Chet got out.

Pilate yelled at them until they understood the situation, and Pilate and Richie fired two more bursts under the bridge while Coon ran up to the cop car. He stopped to look into it, and as he did, a bullet banged off the windshield. And then another, and Coon dropped behind the car as Chet, who hadn't stopped, dashed across the yard. A bullet whanged off an old clothesline post, not more than a foot from Chet's head as he passed the post.

Coon popped up and yelled, "I can't get out of here. They're shooting at me from the gas station."

Richie said, "Hang on," and he ran down to the corner of the blue house, then across an empty lot to a pink house, crawled to the front corner of it and started banging away at the filling station. The station's window glass went out with the fourth or fifth shot and Coon dashed across the open space to the blue house. Richie jogged back from the pink house and they huddled in the shelter of the blue house.

"We gotta get that cop and get him fast," Richie said. "We gotta move that car."

"No keys in it," Coon said, breathing hard, more from excitement than exercise. "That's why I stopped to look. He must've had them on him."

"Here's what we do—I mean you guys with the rifles," Kristen said. "One of you runs a way down that creek, and another one runs down the creek the other way, until you're far enough down that you can shoot under the bridge. That'll kill him or push him out in the open where we can kill him. Once we get him, we move his car off the bridge, bring the RV and the Firebird across, put the cop car back on the bridge, shoot up the gas tank, set it on fire, so nobody else can cross, and we take off."

"Works for me," Pilate said. His brain seemed stuffed with cotton; he was freaking out. Then, over Coon's shoulder, he saw the RV rumbling into town. "Here's Bell."

Bell hardly slowed coming through town and ran past them in the side yard of the blue house, and got out, wild-eyed. The RV had a half dozen bullet holes in it:

"It's like a fuckin' shooting gallery out there," he said. Laine got out of the passenger side, a streak of blood on her face. Bell looked back the way they'd come, and added, "That goddamn pickup's still back there. He followed us all the way down here."

Pilate went to look: the pickup was probably six hundred yards away, idling in the middle of the road.

"He's been tracking us the whole time."

"I'll get him," Bell said. "You guys hang here." He pulled a magazine out of his rifle and slammed another one into it. To Pilate he said: "This is it, man. This is the Fall. This is what we trained for. This is fuckin' *it*."

He ran behind the houses and commercial buildings along the main street. He'd gone two hundred yards and was jogging across an open space between two buildings, when a door popped open on a place called BAR and somebody fired a shot at him.

The shot missed, but he saw the door moving and fired back as he ran, ducking behind the next building. He went on, running hard, and at the last of the commercial buildings, risked running down the side of one of them, to look down the street. The pickup had backed away and was farther out of reach than it had been when they began.

"Shit." He jogged back toward Pilate and the rest of the group, sprinting through the open space where he'd been shot at.

"He's backing off—I can't get to him, but he's gotta be calling all the other cops from everywhere," he told Pilate.

"Too late," Kristen said. A black SUV was coming down the highway, flashers on the front bumper. "Here come some more of them."

Pilate looked around, wildly, trying to find a way out. He didn't want to hear that Fall bullshit.

Coon said, "Look—there's not that many of them. I say we fight it out here. We can take them. We get in these houses, we make them come to us. We're out in the fuckin' wilderness, they can't get help no more than we can."

Kristen said, "I knew we shouldn't have come. This was a bad idea right from the start."

"Shut the fuck up," Pilate said. "Let's do what Coon said. Let's take over some of these buildings and ambush the motherfuckers. Fight it out. We got a chance."

They all looked at him, his magic almost gone now.

"We do," he said. "We got a chance."

18

WAY UP AHEAD, Lucas could see the flashing lights of the state police car, and he said to Frisell, "Gonna have to pull up before we get there. We might have them trapped between us."

As the last words came out of his mouth, Laurent called from a trailing car. "Dick Blinder's calling us, he's been hit, shot, he's under the bridge. They're trying to blast him out. He says he's bleeding bad. There are two cars on the opposite side of the bridge, they're with Pilate. Dick thinks they left the cars and they're up in town with Pilate and the others. They've got rifles. Dick says if we can't get him out of that ditch, he won't make it."

Lucas took his foot off the gas. "Can you call him back?"

"Yeah, we got him on his shoulder set."

"Ask him if any of Pilate's people are in the ditch. If somebody's in the ditch with him, are they on the east side or the west?"

A moment later, Laurent came back. "He doesn't think anyone's in the ditch. He thinks they're all up in town."

Lucas couldn't see Laurent in his rearview mirror; Laurent was in his pickup, and didn't have flashers. Lucas asked, "Can you see me? Up ahead of you?"

"Yeah, but you're a way out, probably a mile or more."

"Okay, we'll wait for you. When you get close, we're gonna take off, and try to go around the town to the ditch. Follow along behind us. Tell Dick we're coming. And tell everybody else in the posse to take up positions on this side of town, block the road and wait, until we know what's going on."

"Got it."

"WHAT EXACTLY ARE we doing?" Frisell asked.

"Damned if I know. Gotta get closer before I can figure it out," Lucas said. "You ever been through here?"

"Sure. Once or twice a year, probably."

"Which side of the road has the most houses, and the least trees?"

"Oh, shit, I've never been far off the road . . . uh, God, I think the most houses would be on the left."

"If they're planning to shoot it out with us, or take hostages, they'll probably be along the main street,"

Lucas said. "I want to swing around them to the ditch. Once we're in the ditch, we'll have cover and we can get to Dick. What's his last name?"

"Blinder. Kind of an asshole, but I wouldn't wish him bad luck."

"Well, he's highway patrol, or state police, or whatever you call them up here. Being an asshole kinda comes with the territory." In the rearview mirror, Lucas could see Laurent coming fast.

"Get ready with that rifle. There's a canvas bag in the back, right behind your seat. It's a first aid kit. Get that out, and there's a hard box under the seat, right in front of the first aid kit. Get that, too."

Frisell popped his safety belt and Lucas started toward the town. Frisell came up with the first aid kit, and the hard box, and Lucas said, "The hard box is full of magazines for my .45. Give them to me. And buckle up."

Lucas put the magazines in his jacket pocket, and as Frisell buckled in, Lucas said, "Pucker up. Here we go."

"If I puckered up any harder . . ."

"What?"

"I can't think of anything funny."

"I know what you mean." Lucas took off as Laurent came up behind, and they rolled toward the town at forty miles an hour or so. At the edge of the built-up area, which sat in what amounted to a clearing in the forest, Lucas saw a long strip of vacant ground on the left, leading up to a concrete platform that might once have supported a gas station. Nothing remained of a building. Behind it was more open ground, and beyond that, a scattering of postwar houses.

"Going cross-country," he said. He slowed and turned into the empty concrete platform, then bounced across the crumbling curb at the back, and ricocheted and bounded and twisted over the rough, soggy ground behind it, his speed falling to ten miles an hour, eventually coming out on a gravel street that led through the scattered houses behind the business district.

He stayed on the road, glanced into the rearview mirror and saw Laurent was still with him. He accelerated, passed the first couple of houses, saw the ditch ahead of him, probably five or six hundred yards away. He could take the gravel tracks for most of the way, but there was a band of weeds and low shrubs along the line of the ditch.

They were moving faster now, passing the houses, bouncing through yards and back onto other tracks; they were a hundred yards out when there was a nasty crack from the backseat and Lucas felt a stinging burn on his neck, and Frisell blurted, "They're shooting at us, they took out a piece of the window."

"We're almost there, we're almost there—"

"You're bleeding, man."

"How bad?"

"Not too bad."

"Glass," Lucas said. He touched his neck and came away with blood on his fingers.

There was another crack from the back, but farther

back on the truck, and Frisell said, "Dumb shit isn't leading us enough."

He said it with such technical disapproval that Lucas
had to laugh, and then Frisell started, and they were
laughing when they crashed into the brush at the edge of
the ditch and were out and running. Laurent and one of
his uniformed deputies, Bernie Allen, were out of their
truck and running behind them, and they went down
into the ditch into ankle-deep water.

Crouching, they were out of sight from the town.
Laurent looked at Lucas's neck and said, "You got hit."

"Glass. Not too bad."

"All right," Laurent said. "I'll go first with the rifle.
Everybody behind me, five meters between you. If I get
hit, take out the shooter before you try to help me—no
point in anyone else getting shot. Jerry, follow me, we'll
put Lucas in the third spot, and Bernie, you cover our
back. Everybody got it?"

Lucas was about to suggest that he lead, but Laurent
was already spotting his move, and he started off down
the marsh, holding his black rifle at his shoulder, ready
to fire, and Lucas realized . . . *Laurent's done this before.*
So had Frisell. *He* was the tactical dummy in the group.

They were two hundred yards west of the bridge.
They'd covered a hundred of that when Laurent stopped
and put up a hand, then said, aloud, "We're getting
closer to the buildings, where somebody on the roof
could see us. Bernie, you cover the roofs. I'm going on to
the bridge. Lucas, you come behind me, but not until
you see me get there. Jerry and Bernie, come down one

at a time—we'll cover you from the bridge. We'll be moving fast now."

Everybody nodded, and Laurent took a breath and
ran toward the bridge, not bothering to crouch anymore.
Frisell and Allen half stood with their rifles, looking
at the rooflines of two nearby buildings, but nobody
showed, and fifteen seconds after he took off—it seemed
like forever—Laurent ducked under the bridge, and
Frisell said to Lucas, "Go."

Lucas went. He was carrying the first aid kit and ran
as hard as he could, but the creek bed was mucky and
he went knee-deep in the mud at one point—the muck
smelled like rotten eggs—and was breathing hard when
he struggled under the bridge.

He could see Blinder tucked up under the bridge deck,
right where the concrete abutments came down into the
bank. He was awake and had a gun in his hand, but in the
dim light, looked pale as a ghost: loss of blood, maybe,
or shock. He was wearing a jacket, but no shirt. Laurent
had ignored him and was half under the bridge, half out,
covering the roofs as Frisell came blundering down the
creek bed.

Lucas crawled over to Blinder, who said, "Glad to see
you, man. I'm hurting."

"Where are you hit?"

"Both legs and my butt," he said, in a voice that was
mostly a groan. "Ripped up my shirt and tried to plug
the holes, but I'm still bleeding. And I really fuckin'
hurt. Goddamn, I didn't know that gettin' shot hurt
this bad."

Lucas unzipped the first aid kit, found a bottle of morphine with an eyedropper top. "Gonna give you a squirt of this under your tongue. Don't swallow, just let it sit there for a minute. It'll kill the pain."

Blinder nodded.

As Lucas gave him the eyedropper of morphine, Frisell slid under the bridge, turned with his rifle, and joined Laurent in watching the rooftops. Lucas took a pair of scissors out of the first aid kit and began cutting away Blinder's pant legs. Laurent came over to help as Allen slid under the bridge; the wound in Blinder's butt was bleeding, but was basically a groove in a layer of fat. The through-and-through wounds in his legs were worse.

They threw the shirt-rag bandages away, replacing them with heavy gauze pads, binding them tight, and Frisell, who'd been watching them work, said, "We gotta get him out of here. That's a long run back and we won't have anyone to cover us."

Laurent said, "Well, we gotta do it. We need to get him up to Munising."

Lucas said, "Let's get him plugged up, then you can cover me. I'm going to run over to the cars on the other side of the bridge, see if there are any keys. If there are, we can take him out that way. It's only fifteen yards, instead of two hundred, and two of us could move him, while the other two cover."

Laurent nodded: "Yes."

Lucas asked Blinder, "How're you feeling?"

"That stuff in the bottle . . . starting to kick in." He looked sleepy.

"Good."

They finished bandaging him as well as they could, then Laurent took a call, listened for a moment, then said, "Good. Freeze it right there. We'll keep them from getting out on this side," and a few seconds later, "Ah, shit. Are you sure?"

He got off the phone and said, "They're saying the Brownsville deputy didn't make it."

They all sat for a moment, then Lucas said, "You guys cover the roofline and windows. I'm going for that car."

The three of them spread, two on the bank at one side of the bridge, one on the other side, and Laurent said, "We gotcha."

Lucas launched himself up the bank on the other side. The first of the two cars was fifteen or twenty yards away, the second, five yards beyond that. He ran hard, feeling the tension in his back where the bullet would hit, and dodged behind the first car . . . safe for the moment. He crawled to the door and looked at the ignition; no keys. He checked the front seat and the center console. Nothing.

He crawled back to the second car and realized, as he got close, that it was actually still running. The passenger-side door was closed but unlatched, and he pulled it open. An unfinished cheeseburger was sitting on the floor on the passenger side; he picked it up and threw it into the backseat.

Lucas slid inside, crawled into the driver's seat, got his legs beneath himself, trying to stay below the windshield level. There'd been no gunshots from the guys at the bridge, so he shifted the car into drive and steered it out around the first car, right down to the creek bank, where he stopped and put the car into *Park*.

The backseat would probably be too cramped for Blinder, so he pushed the passenger seat back as far as he could, then slipped out the driver's-side door and crawled over to the bank and down into the creek.

"Got the car right up above," he told the others. "We need to get him into the passenger seat, the backseat is too small."

Laurent said, "Excellent. Bernie, you and Lucas carry him up there. And Bernie, you're gonna have to take him up to Munising."

"Man, I hate to miss this . . ."

"Somebody's got to go and I'm saying it's you," Laurent said. "I need Lucas and you're less crazy than fuckin' Frisell. So: you're the guy."

Allen muttered, "Okay," and Laurent said, "You already done good, now you gotta run with him."

Lucas said, "The car's a piece of shit, and there's not much gas, so flag down the first car you see—first friendly car—and transfer over."

"Got it," Allen said.

Lucas and Allen joined hands, as in a hammock, and Frisell and Laurent helped put Blinder in the hammock, and went back to their guns. Lucas and Allen got to the edge of the bank, and Lucas asked, "Ready?"

"Ready."

The bank wasn't high—maybe five feet—but it was slippery and steep, and they were not moving fast as they dug their shoes into the bank and struggled up to the top. Once there, they hurried to the passenger side, and fit Blinder into the seat, and Allen ran around to the driver's side as Lucas buckled Blinder in.

Laurent fired two shots and shouted, "Second story, second window, left," and a bullet cracked off the bridge abutment and Laurent and Frisell opened up again with their rifles and Allen backed away in the car as Lucas slid down the bank into the creek bed.

When Frisell and Laurent stopped shooting, Lucas risked a peek over the top of the bank. Allen was a hundred yards away and still backing up, then a hundred and fifty, and he made a quick turn onto the shoulder, brought the car around, and drove off.

Lucas ducked back and said to the others, "He's gone."

"Okay," Laurent said. "Now we just gotta root these other motherfuckers out, without getting any more of us shot."

"THERE'RE NO COPS in Mellon, right?" Lucas asked.

Laurent shook his head.

"Would there be anyone who'd have everybody's phone number?" Lucas asked.

"Maybe, but I don't know who it would be."

"We need to find out what's going on with the people in town. Call up whoever you're talking to, in the posse, ask if anyone's got a good phone number."

Laurent got on the phone and Frisell, who was lying

on the town-side creek bank, said, "I saw somebody running, they went into that little pink house . . . looked like a local woman. Didn't look California."

"Just now?" Lucas asked.

"No, when we were shooting at the window up there . . . There's still somebody there, by the way. If he peeks around that windowsill one more time, he's gonna get a chest full of .223."

"If it was a local, and they were running into the pink house . . . that probably means there aren't any Pilates in there."

Laurent said, "They're making a call. They got two numbers, but it's a husband and wife, so they could be in the same place." He put the phone to his ear again, and Lucas and Frisell went back to scanning the town.

There were six visible commercial buildings in Mellon, all single-story except two, which had two stories. The buildings were weatherworn, a little dirty, with what looked like vinyl siding. They could only see the side of one of the two-story buildings, but had an angle on the other one: the front windows were blank, unadorned, and dirty—the building was empty, Lucas thought. The houses were either shingled or had vinyl siding and several of them were faded pastel colors in blue, green, yellow, and pink; all of them had garages.

Laurent was still on the phone and Lucas said to him, "Tell whoever's on the other end of the phone, to make sure that they've got the road blocked. Park those patrol cars across it. They'll have access to cars in there, and they might try to bust through the line. Can't get across this bridge."

Laurent did that, listened for a minute, then said, "They talked to a Mrs. Boden, who said she's in the gas station with the clerk, and none of the Pilates are in there, and they're both armed. She said there are more people in Ted's, that's the bar, and they're armed, too. She knows that some of the Pilates are in the Old Eagle Inn, which is that two-story place where they were shooting at us from the window."

"We already knew that," Frisell said.

Laurent continued, "There are a couple of artists living in the inn, she hasn't seen them, so the Pilates may have them. She doesn't think the artists have guns. There might be more Pilates on the other side of the street in the old hardware store. She thinks there might be some in the blue house by the creek."

Frisell said, "That's right there," and pointed to his left.

Lucas left Frisell and, walking in a deep crouch, crossed under the bridge and crawled up the bank where he could see the blue house. Laurent knelt beside him a few seconds later. The house stood by itself, in an open yard, with a garage around back, fifteen or twenty yards from the house.

"That looks tough," Laurent said.

Lucas said, "I think we sneak back to the trucks, then go farther back in the brush and circle around to the posse."

"What if they sneak across the creek into the woods?" Laurent asked.

"Sneak to where?" Frisell asked. "Nearest town is probably fifteen miles down that way. They'd die out there in the woods, and they couldn't walk on the road without being seen."

"They got keys for that car."

Lucas said, "Give me your rifle." And to Laurent, "Tell your guy in the posse that they're going to hear some gunfire and not to get excited about it."

As he did that, Lucas crawled up the bank, waited until Laurent said, "I told them," and Lucas fired a shot into each of the car's three wheels that he could see. That done, he slid back down the bank and handed the rifle to Frisell, and said, "They'll need some tires before they take the car anywhere."

"All right," Laurent said. "I'll go first. They can't see me from that window, but they probably could from the roof."

"Be best if they thought we were still here . . . probably be a good idea to crawl down there," Frisell said.

"That's a goddamn mud hole," Laurent said.

Lucas looked at him and said, "You already look like the fuckin' swamp monster. A little more mud won't make any difference."

Laurent said, "Goddamnit," and started off at a fast crawl. It took him a minute to get far enough down the creek to stand up, and wave Lucas over. Frisell came in a couple of minutes after Lucas, and they continued walking up the creek, past their vehicles, out of the settled area and into the woods.

Ten minutes later, they emerged on the other side of town, where the posse was dug in.

THE POSSE HAD strung a line of cars across the road and over the shoulder and into the trees on both sides. No way out that way.

Peters, the lawyer, wearing a bulletproof vest, had been organizing the cops. He waved Lucas, Laurent, and Frisell over behind a van, where he'd set up with a couple of deputies with radios.

"We've got more phone numbers, and we think we know where everybody is. We think there are eight or nine of them, five or six men and at least three women. Some of them have rifles—I guess you know that. There's a good possibility that they have a couple hostages at the inn. Hasn't been any shooting that wasn't either from you guys, or at you guys."

The Pilates were apparently holed up in structures that formed a rough triangle, and there were probably two or three people in each building. "We need to talk to them," one of the deputies said. "Be better to talk them out of there, than try to shoot them out."

Lucas nodded. "You're right about that. If we could get a phone number for those artists . . . the ones that might be at the inn . . . we could try ringing them."

Peters said, "Nobody knows the artists real well—

they've been there for three weeks, pretty much camping out. Nobody's lived in the inn for years. We know their names are Sandy and Larry Birch, but we don't know where they come from. Someplace around Detroit, maybe."

"Do they have a car?" Lucas asked.

"Don't know," Peters said.

"If we could get their tags . . . we could get everything else."

"That's like the whole story of this chase," Laurent said. "If we only had the tags."

The deputy said, "What about a white flag . . . ?"

"Better you than me," Lucas said. "They've already shot three cops in cold blood. I don't think they're gonna quit because we wave a hanky at them."

Peters said, "Before we do anything, I want to put a patch on your neck. You sort of sprung a leak there."

"Is this gonna hurt?" Lucas asked.

"I think so," Peters said.

19

THERE WERE NINE disciples, holed up in three different places, hooked up by their cell phones. They knew there were some townspeople in a couple of other buildings, because they'd traded gunfire with them.

"We ain't in California no more," Pilate said. "Every fuckin' body up here's got a gun. Even that old lady in the hamburger shop, shot Michelle."

Pilate, Kristen, Bell, and Laine were all on the second floor of the inn, while Coon, Richie, and Carrie were in an abandoned hardware store, and Chet and Ellen were in the blue house. Pilate was looking out a window that faced a line of cars near the entry to the town; Bell was looking straight down on the highway; Kristen was watching the back, and had shot at Lucas's SUV and Laurent's truck, scoring three hits on the trucks, none on the passengers.

Laine was watching the creek side. She said she thought all the cops had left the bridge, going back the way they'd come in—she'd seen flashes of movement, all going that way, three times, and nothing since. The fourth man had driven the wounded cop out.

Bell had fired a shot at the people taking the cop out, and had gotten a face full of plaster for his trouble, blown off the walls by a dozen rounds of incoming fire. He hadn't tried that again.

Pilate's group had two captives, and there was one captive in the blue house. When Pilate and his group had run up the stairs of the inn, they found the top floor to be completely open—there'd once been several rooms up there, but it appeared that the place had been stripped even of the walls, although a lot of two-by-four uprights were still in place. The outer walls were now hung with a dozen crazy abstract paintings done on four-foot-by-eight-foot plywood panels; the artists had been sitting on the floor, eating, when Pilate and the others stormed the stairs.

The artists were now sitting in a corner, a hippie-looking couple with long hair and dressed identically in jeans and T-shirts and running shoes; they'd both been crying for a while, but now they simply huddled on the floor and watched.

KRISTEN WAS RAGING: "This was done not right. This is all fucked up. We're gonna pay now . . ."

Laine was screaming at her: "Shut up, shut up, shut up, I didn't have anything to do with this."

Pilate asked Bell, "How far do you think it is to all those cop cars?"

Bell shrugged. "I don't know. Think about it in football fields. How many football fields is it?"

Pilate peeked out the window again. "Five, six?"

"Something like that."

"So how high above their heads do we shoot?"

"I don't know," Bell said. "A foot? You see anybody down there?"

"Yeah, sometimes."

"Let's knock some windows out."

THEY CRACKED WINDOWS on all four sides of the top floor, and then Bell stood back a bit, aiming through one of the windows, at the tops of the cars they could see out at the edge of town. "I'll clear the snot out of their noses," he said.

He emptied the magazine at the vehicles and then both ducked away from the windows, getting low on the floor. Laine stopped screaming at Kristen as they listened for incoming fire. The woman artist began crying again, and Bell said, "If this gets as bad as it looks, I might fuck her. I mean, why not? It could be my last chance forever."

"If it's your last chance, why not the golden pussy?" Pilate asked.

Laine, the golden pussy, said, "Fuck you guys."

"I'm gonna look out there again," Pilate said. He crawled to the window and peeked out: saw no movement at all.

"They're gonna try to sneak up on us," he said. "I'll tell you what, Kristen and I should go downstairs, in case they try to get in there somehow. You guys keep a lookout up here. They'll most likely come in from the back or the front, where they've got those trees and houses to hide behind. So you guys look out those ways, and Kristen and I'll keep a watch on the creek side and over toward the bar. If you see anything, yell."

Kristen wanted to argue: "I think we should all stay together."

Pilate said, "If they come in, they'll have to come in the first floor first. Once they get in there, it's all over for us. Somebody's got to be down there to meet them."

"We really fucked this up," she said. "We're gonna get killed for sure."

"Get your ass downstairs," Pilate snapped. And to Bell, "Keep watch. Yell the minute you see something. And don't go fuckin' around with that hippie. When we get out of here, you can do whatever you want with her. But right now, you best be looking out the windows."

Pilate went down the stairs ahead of Kristen, the rifle tracking possible targets ahead of him, like he'd seen people do in the movies. They could hear Bell and Laine arguing upstairs, and Pilate put a finger to his lips and said, quietly, "We gotta get the fuck out of here. They'll surround us, sooner or later, and then they'll kill us. We shot those cops back in Brownsville, they're not gonna let that go."

Kristen whispered back, "You mean . . . ditch everybody?"

"You want to die?"

"No."

"Then we got to get out of here, before they move in," Pilate said. "Knock the glass out of the windows on the creek side, and then I yell that we see something down the street, and we call up Chet and Ellen, and tell them the same thing, and then everybody who could see us would be looking the other way."

"I got it, I got it," Kristen said. "But we're about a million miles from anywhere."

"It'll take a while for them to roll over the town. If we get into the woods, we can stay back in the trees and run along the highway until we see a car coming, then we flag it down . . . and take it."

She nodded. She knew what "take it" meant. She thought about it for two seconds, then asked, "Why me? Why not the golden pussy?"

"You can get pussy anywhere—I need somebody willing to use a gun, and you're a better shot than Bell. You in?"

She nodded: "I'm in."

"Let's break out some windows," Pilate said.

20

THE POSSE HAD gathered in a Boy Scout–like circle, around Lucas and Laurent, and Lucas said, "We need to get three or four people back under that bridge. We've got them contained at the moment, but if they all ran out into the woods, it'd be a hell of a job to track them all— or even know if any got away."

Laurent said to Frisell, "Jerry, you've already been back there, so take Jim and . . . Any volunteers?"

A half dozen cops and reserve deputies raised their hands and Frisell pointed at two who were carrying black rifles and wearing vests, and said, "How about you two? We'd all have the same weapons, same ammo."

The two chosen men nodded, and Lucas said, "Okay. Another thing you guys have to do. One of you should get back in the trees and run along the road for a half mile or so, to stop traffic coming in." He turned to Laurent: "You ought to send somebody in uniform down the other way, too. Don't let anyone in who isn't a cop."

Laurent nodded. "We need to break into compass-point groups. We'll have Frisell on the north, but we need more groups in the woods, where they've got both cover and concealment, on the east, west, and south sides."

Lucas said, "Then you and I, and a couple of other guys, can try to sneak up to the inn. I think I see a way in. We'll need guys with vests: So who'll that be? Who has vests?"

They broke into the compass-point groups, including Frisell's. As they got ready to move out, Lucas said, "You all know how dangerous this is—some of us will be scrambling around in town. Don't shoot anyone if you're not sure of your target. There'll be townspeople and reserve deputies without uniforms, and we don't want to be killing each other. Be careful. Be careful."

The compass-point groups moved out, leaving behind the men who'd go into the town with Lucas and Frisell. They started by calling the woman who was holed up in the gas station, who said she'd call a guy in the bar and have him call Lucas directly. "I'd just give you his number, but he might not believe you. But I'll vouch for you, because you're with Walt, and I know Walt."

Walt was the guy who first called her.

Lucas hung up, stared at his phone, and a minute later, it lit up with an incoming call. "This is Ralph Setzer."

"What's your situation there?" Lucas asked.

"We got six people here, two shotguns, a rifle, and two handguns," Setzer said. "We've barricaded the doors. We got plenty of beer and brats, so we can hold out indefinitely."

"Glad to hear it," Lucas said. "Save one of the brats for me."

"We'll do that."

Behind him, Laurent laughed and said, "Gotta love those fuckin' hosers."

"We're gonna try to come in through the side," Lucas said. "If you'll push one of those windows open, we think we can get there without getting shot at."

"When are you going to do this?"

"Right away," Lucas said.

"C'mon ahead. We'll get the windows open for you. We'll put a chair out there, the windows are a little high."

"Next few minutes," Lucas said. His neck was bothering him: Peters had used tweezers to take a few pieces of automotive glass out of his skin, and said he didn't think that any had really penetrated. He'd covered the small cuts with Polysporin and a gauze pad, but now the wound was beginning to itch.

Nothing to do now but ignore it.

Lucas said to his group, "We can dodge along behind houses until we get a line that'll let us go directly to the bar. The big problem, of course, would be if one of Pilate's people is inside one of the houses. So we go in groups. Guys in uniforms will lead, so the locals don't freak out and shoot us—Rome will lead, then Peters, and I'll follow. The rest of you guys will stay back one house, under cover. Three of you should watch the windows we're exposed to. You see movement at the windows, fire a shot high over the window, through the wall. If they break out a window and you see a gun, then take them out. We don't want to kill anybody, but we don't want them killing us, either. Everybody got it?"

"Just like hopscotch, going in," Laurent said.

"The other two guys," Lucas said, "should be looking backwards. If one of Pilate's guys that we don't know about is in a house, and lays low until we go by, he could back-shoot us. So two of you should be looking at windows behind us."

When they were sure that everyone knew his assignment, Lucas and Laurent led the way out.

FRISELL AND THE three men with him walked in the woods past Lucas's SUV and Laurent's truck, and one of the cops saw the bullet holes in Lucas's SUV windows and whistled. "That would tend to tighten your testicles," he said.

"Tightened mine," Frisell said. "Since I'm the squad leader here, I'll make the call and say that I'm going down to the bridge and I want Jim to come with me, because we've worked together. One of you guys has to go straight across the creek and into the woods, and down the highway, and stop traffic. Any preferences?"

One of the deputies suggested that the other guy should do it, and the other guy shrugged and said, "Okay," and they left it at that.

Frisell went first, down the creek and under the bridge. Jim Bennett, the post office guy, was next, followed by the third deputy. The fourth guy crossed the creek, climbed the opposite bank, and disappeared into the trees.

They missed Pilate and Kristen by five minutes.

LAURENT, PETERS, AND Lucas led the way into town, crossing the open spaces in a hurry, huddling behind the houses they'd reached while they looked at the next one, searching for signs of life or guns. They saw no one, and after the last short sprint, climbed on a folding chair and through the window into the bar. The people inside had little information about who was where, but thought that most of the people in town were either in the bar or in the gas station. A few had holed up in their houses, doors locked. Most of them had guns and were willing to use them. The state cop had given them just enough warning to get organized a bit, but not completely synchronized.

"Somebody's in the blue house, we know that," the bartender said. He was a meaty guy with a mustard-stained white apron, with a shotgun in his hand and boxing scars under his eyes. "I mean, one of these crazies, or maybe two or three are in there. We know they're in the hardware store, because they were shooting at us after we shot at one of the crazies—he was out in the open and we know he was one of them. We missed him, though. We're pretty sure they're in the inn and we think they've got the artists. We don't think anyone warned the artists."

"We've been shot at from the inn, so we know they've got that for sure," Lucas said.

THERE WAS AN empty lot between the bar and the inn, with eight windows on the inn facing the bar and three in the bar facing the inn. All the inn windows had been broken out, but they could see no faces or movement behind the windows.

Lucas, Laurent, and Peters crouched behind the bar windows, looking across at the inn, and Lucas asked Laurent, "What do you think?"

"If we can take the high ground, we can get them out of the hardware store and the blue house—but if they get up on that roof, we've got a big problem."

Lucas nodded. "That's what I think. We got to get them out of there."

"You got a plan?"

"I do, but it's sorta horseshit."

LAURENT CALLED IN the deputies who'd been assigned to cover Lucas's group as they went for the bar. Once inside, he gave them their directions—they'd be covering the windows of the inn, both first and second floors, and the edge of the roof. While he was doing that,

Lucas called Frisell at the bridge, and when he'd told Frisell what he wanted, Frisell said, "We can do that. When do you want it?"

"Stay by the phone. When we're cocked and ready to go, I'll call you."

"We're all set here. Go anytime. Good luck."

Lucas, Laurent, and Peters went out the back door of the bar, and edged close to the corner nearest the inn. Peters said, "I'm the tiniest bit scared. Nothing to quit over, though."

"Think about what a great fuckin' story this'll make— we'll be living off this for years," Laurent said.

Lucas said, "Shut up," and called Frisell. He said, "Anytime you're ready. Aim for the ceilings."

Three seconds later, a barrage of gunfire hit the second floor on the other side of the inn, the three cops in the creek bed deliberately aiming at a sharp angle up through the windows, hoping the slugs would embed in the roof and not go ricocheting around inside the upper floor.

As soon as the shooting started, Lucas, Laurent, and Peters dashed for the corner of the inn, where they couldn't easily be seen by anyone inside. They crouched at the corner for a minute, until the gunfire stopped.

Behind them, in the hotel, they could see the rest of their group at the windows, ready to open fire if anyone showed at the windows of the inn. In the sudden silence after the spurt of gunfire, Lucas said, "I'm going to peek," and at that moment, a woman began screaming on the second floor and then a man began shouting: it didn't sound like terror, it sounded like an argument.

Lucas peeked through a broken ground-floor window, a quick half second. Saw nobody, dropped to his knees, and waited. No reaction. Looked again, this time a longer peek, then another, then he whispered to Laurent and Peters, "You're not going to believe this, but there's nobody in there. At all. It looks like it used to be a kitchen, and there's nobody in there."

"Can you get through the window?" Laurent asked.

"I could if we could get the window open." Though the glass had been broken out, the wooden crossbars that held the glass panes were still intact.

Laurent was the lightest of the three of them, so Peters made a stirrup with his hands and boosted Laurent high enough that he could reach the lock on the double-hung window, and turn it open. When that was done, he dropped back to the ground; the window had been painted shut, but with some careful pressure on the side bars, they were able to get it loose enough to lift.

Lucas went through the window first, with his pistol, which would be handier than a rifle in the close confines of the kitchen. The wooden floor squeaked underfoot, but he managed to tiptoe to the kitchen door and peek out into the lobby. Nobody there—nothing but a vacant spot where a check-in desk used to be, a pile of what looked like discarded curtains, and stairs going up to the second floor. The whole place smelled of mold and wood rot; a bird's nest was stuck on a corner beam, with a little pile of black-and-white-speckled droppings on the floor beneath it.

Lucas motioned to Laurent, still outside the window,

and he pushed himself through, followed by Peters. They opened the kitchen door and stepped out into the lobby: nobody there. The windows on both sides of the building had been broken, as though somebody had been stationed there, but had gone somewhere else.

There had been two restrooms down a hall that led to a back door. The doors had been scavenged off the restrooms, and they stood open to the hall. Lucas took off his shoes and tiptoed down the hall, checked the two, found them empty—somebody had taken out all the fixtures, including the lights and paper-towel dispensers. The remains of a condom dispenser still hung from a wall in the men's room, but it had been smashed open and now looked like a toaster that had been hit by a train.

Lucas tiptoed back down the hallway, and called the other two men together. They could still hear a man and a woman, apparently arguing, and a third woman crying, and Lucas whispered, "Sounds like things are tough up there. I need you guys to get on both sides of the stairs, hiding below banisters. If you see a guy with a gun, shoot him."

"Where'll you be?" Laurent asked.

"I'm going to *slide* up the stairs," Lucas said. "I did it once before. If they stay busy up there, I should be able to take them. You gotta take care of me, because if that guy's got a gun, and I believe he does, and if he walks up to the top of the stairs and looks down at me, I'm gonna be SOL."

"This does not sound entirely sane," Peters said.

Lucas grinned at him. "Well, what can I tell you? We need to get them out of there. And that crying woman up there . . . something's going on."

Laurent nodded, and said, "Show us where you want us."

LUCAS SET THEM up at the bottom of the stairs, but off to the sides, where they would be mostly hidden against a quick glance. Lucas would also be hidden, from anyone back away from the stairs. If anyone walked to the stairs and looked down, he'd be right there.

"Ready?" he whispered to Laurent and Peters.

They both nodded.

Lucas duckwalked to the bottom of the stairs, then stretched up the risers, his .45 pointing up the stairs. After listening for a few seconds, he pushed himself up another step, and then another.

A man was shouting, "That cocksucker ran off on us, is what he did. You always knew he put himself first. You always knew that, but he was always 'outlaw this, the Fall coming that,' and so you thought, well, maybe he's the real thing. But he never was. He was just another asshole. If I could find that cunt, I'd cut his fuckin' heart out."

"What're we gonna do, Bell?" a woman asked.

"I'll tell you the second thing I'm gonna do. I'm gonna wait until one of those cops sticks his head out from under that bridge again and I'm gonna shoot him in the fuckin' head. But first, I'm gonna skull-fuck that hippie. They're gonna kill me, but I'm gonna fuck her first."

A woman began crying again; Lucas was on the ninth step of fourteen when he heard running steps coming toward the stairs. He quickly slipped back two and then a woman was there with a rifle in her hands, looking right down at him, and there was a bang from below, from Laurent or Peters, and the woman went down, and Lucas scrambled up the steps and saw the man gaping at the woman on the floor, and the man was swinging his rifle around and Lucas fired at him and missed and the rifle was almost around on him and Lucas fired again and this time hit the man in the throat, about a foot higher than he'd been aiming, and as the man began to slip down, shot him again, almost as a reflex, and the man twisted and went flat.

The woman who'd been crying was sitting in the corner with a man and now began screaming hysterically. Lucas climbed the last couple of stairs, aware that Laurent was coming up behind him, and Lucas shouted, "Are there any more? Are there any more?"

The man shouted, "No. There were, but they went downstairs."

Lucas moved up to the woman who'd been shot, kicked the rifle away from her. Laurent had shot her in the chest, just where it joined her shoulder. She was groaning and bleeding heavily, her eyes flat with shock, but Lucas thought she'd make it if they could stop the bleeding and get her to a hospital.

Laurent was thinking the same thing, and said, "We gotta stop the blood. What about the guy?"

Lucas was striding across the floor and looked down at Bell, shook his head. "He's dead." To the man and the woman in the corner, he asked, "Are you hurt? Bleeding?"

The man said, "No, no."

Lucas popped the magazine on his .45, and slapped another one in. Peters was at the top of the stairs with a first aid kit, and was packing the entry and exit wounds in the woman, and called to Laurent, "Rome, run downstairs and get a couple of guys to come over from the bar. We got to take her out the same way we came in."

Laurent ran downstairs and Lucas could hear him shouting. Lucas walked over to the woman, whose eyes had gone dim with shock. He asked, "Where's Pilate?"

She moaned again, but she'd heard him, and she said, "He ran away. We think he ran away with Kristen. He tricked us."

"Goddamnit."

HE WALKED TO the front of the building and looked down at the blue house, across the street, and not far from the creek. He went back to the woman and asked, "Are you talking to the other people on a phone?"

She nodded. "Bell has it." She looked at his body and the spreading pool of blood that seeped out from beneath it. "Had it."

"Do the people in the blue house have hostages?"

"They didn't say they do. Am I gonna die?"

"Yeah, but not today," Lucas said. Then he felt mean for saying it, and added, "We'll get you to a hospital quick as we can. You should be okay. What's your name?"

She said, "Laine."

Peters said, "The guys are coming in, they're bringing a blanket, they'll take her out in a hammock."

Lucas went to the dead man, found a phone in his jacket pocket, looked at the recents, called up the latest one and tapped *Call.*

A woman answered instantly. "What?"

"I'm a cop. We shot Bell and Laine and we've taken over the inn building. Pilate ran away with Kristen."

"You fuck. You fuck." But fear was riding through her voice.

Lucas said, "If you're in the blue house, you've got one minute to walk out the back side with your hands in the air. We've got marksmen under that bridge. They're gonna start hosing down the house from there and we'll start from up here. So, you quit, or we kill you. Your choice."

The woman said, "I gotta talk to Chet."

"You got one minute," Lucas said. "And tell him hello from Pap, in Minnesota."

He called Frisell and said, "We want you guys to do the same thing to the blue house as you did to the inn, in two minutes. Or a couple people may come out the back with their hands in the air. If they do, walk them into the creek bed and arrest them. Be careful about hidden guns . . ."

"Got it," Frisell said. "Two minutes, if they don't come out. You got the inn? We heard some shooting."

"Yeah, we got it."

BEHIND HIM, TWO of the deputies who'd covered their advance into town came up the stairs, carrying a quilt. Peters began helping move the wounded woman onto the quilt, while Laurent came over and stood by the front window next to Lucas. Lucas said, "Peek, don't stand there gawking like a dumbass."

"Sorry," Laurent said. "Wish I had a cigarette."

"Nasty habit," Lucas said.

"I know. That's why I stopped twenty years ago."

The phone in Lucas's hand rang, and the woman said, "I'm coming out the back, right now, my hands are over my head."

Lucas asked, "What about the guy with you?"

"I don't think he's coming," she said.

AT THAT MOMENT, a man walked out the front door of the blue house with a rifle, with the attitude of a man who deeply, seriously didn't give a shit, even about himself. He raised the rifle and began shooting at the window where they were standing, and Lucas and Laurent lurched back into the room and went to the floor as bullets winged off the windowsill and buried themselves in the ceiling.

———

THE SHOOTING STOPPED for just a moment, and Laurent low-crawled to the window, peeked as Lucas shouted, "No, no!" and Laurent said, "Fuck him," and stood up and shot the man, who had just jammed another magazine in his rifle. The man fell down in the street, and Lucas came over and looked down and said, "Nice shot, I guess."

In the silence after the shooting, they could hear Frisell shouting at the woman: "Hands all the way up. All the way up," and they saw the woman walking with raised hands through the weeds toward the creek.

There were two more recently dialed numbers on the phone, and Lucas punched the first of the two. No answer, and no ring. He tried the third number, and a man answered. "You in the hardware store?"

"Yeah. This a cop?"

"Yes. Pilate ran away, Bell is dead, Laine is shot, but might make it if we can get her to a hospital, and Chet's shot in the street. You should be able to see him. We don't know if he's dead or not. As long as you're in the hardware store, we can't help him. If you quit now, we might be able to save his life," Lucas said.

Behind him, Laurent said, "I don't think so."

Lucas held up his finger to quiet him—honesty was not always the best policy—and the man said, "Hold on." Lucas waited, then a woman came on and asked, "How do we know that Pilate really ran away?"

"Well, you could call him."

"He said not to call him unless it was an emergency," the woman said.

Lucas rolled his eyes at Laurent, and then said, "Chet might be bleeding to death in the street. We're about to shoot that hardware store so full of holes that it'll look like a fuckin' colander. Excuse the language. We've got fifty cops out here with machine guns. You want to call Pilate first, that's fine, because I'd say, all things considered, that you have an emergency."

After a few seconds, she said, "Okay."

Lucas could hear a man talking in the background, and then she said, "We're coming out the front, don't let anybody shoot us."

"Wait three minutes, then come out. We've got to calm some people down, after you shot those cops up in Brownsville."

"Brownsville. We didn't go through Brownsville. We were up at the beach."

"Okay, but give us three minutes. How many of you are there?"

"Two. Two of us. Just me and Richie. We'll come out when you say so. Don't shoot us."

LAURENT CALLED THE cops at the compass points, told them to hold off firing at the disciples when they showed themselves in the street. Lucas called the bartender, and the people holed up in the gas station, and told them not to shoot. Then Lucas and Laurent went down to the ground floor and stood by a window where they could see the front of the hardware store.

Peters and the deputies had rolled the wounded

woman in the quilt, and Lucas told them to wait to see what happened: if the people in the hardware store surrendered, they wouldn't have to try to wrestle her through a window.

When everybody was set, Lucas called the woman back, and when she answered, said, "Come on out."

Ten seconds later, the front door of the hardware store opened and a tall natural-blond woman poked her head out. They knew she was a real blonde because she was naked. She stepped out into the street followed by a man, who was a natural brunette and just as naked. They stepped out to the edge of the street with their hands raised.

"What the hell is that all about?" Laurent asked.

Lucas stepped outside, his .45 leveled at the two naked disciples, and said, "It's an L.A. thing. If you surrender naked, it makes it harder for the cops to say they thought you were going for your gun."

"Well, I guess that's true," Laurent said. "Although the guy appears to be in possession of a .22."

LUCAS AND LAURENT kept their guns on the disciples and two of the deputies nervously approached them, handcuffs dangling from their hands. Peters and the other three deputies came out the front door, carrying the wounded woman in the quilt.

Laurent moved to his left so he wouldn't be shooting at the deputies if the naked people produced guns, from the legendary back-cheek holsters. As the deputies got close, Lucas saw movement in the hardware store window and screamed, "Watch it, watch it," and the deputies flinched and then a spray of shots blew through the hardware store window and the deputies went down.

Lucas didn't know if the deputies had dropped to make smaller targets, or had been hit, but Laurent had gone to full-auto on his rifle and was blowing up the front of the store and Lucas ran across the street toward the side of the hardware store, scared to death, peeked in a side window and saw a man squatting next to a pile of firewood that had been stacked in the middle of the floor, the man's hands covering his head as glass and splinters rained down on him from Laurent's return fire. The man had a black rifle in one hand. He saw Lucas at the last minute and Lucas emptied his .45 at the man, who stood up and did a little death dance and then fell back.

Lucas dropped the magazine and stepped back to the front of the store and saw four people down in the street: both deputies and the two naked people, all of them dappled with bloodstains. Laurent was walking toward them and Lucas shouted, "We gotta clear the store."

Laurent shouted back, "Okay," and Peters, who'd dropped his corner of the quilt that held the wounded woman, jogged up and asked, "Who's going first?"

Laurent said, "I will. I got the big gun. Barney, you cover the window. If you see anything, open up. Lucas, get back around to the side and see if there's anybody in front of me when I go in."

Lucas went back around to the side, peeked through the window again, and yelled, "Go!"

Laurent gave the building a preliminary squirt, three rounds through the front door, and splinters and dust flew off the door, and then he was at the door, kicking it open. Nothing moved. He stepped inside, and Lucas was aware of people shouting in the street, but nothing moved in the store.

They cleared it in one minute. Their technique was bad, dangerous, hurried; but then, they were in a hurry.

When they were ninety-nine percent sure there were no hidden disciples inside, Laurent called one of the un-injured deputies to stand inside the door, ready to shoot at anything that suddenly appeared from nowhere, and then he, Lucas, and Peters went back to the street.

The two naked people were dead, hit multiple times from multiple angles, by both the deputies who'd been carrying the quilt and the civilians in the bar. The deputies had been shot in the legs. One was showing arterial bleeding from one leg, and Peters put a pressure bandage on the wound and tied it down with a wrapping of nylon rope, and then put lighter pressure on the wound in the other leg, and they loaded him into a truck. Almost as an afterthought, they loaded the wounded woman, Laine, in the same truck, and the driver took off for the hospital in Munising.

The other deputy wasn't showing as much blood, but had a broken leg. They handled him as delicately as they could, putting him in the backseat of a station wagon, and the driver took off.

The two artists had come out of the inn and the woman was taking photographs with a small Panasonic camera, focusing on the dead naked disciples. Lucas felt like smacking her in the mouth, but didn't. Instead, he shouted, "Get out of there, get out of there; you're messing with a crime scene."

She stepped back but didn't stop shooting.

"We've got to go house by house," Laurent said. He looked around and people were beginning to drift into the street. Frisell and two other deputies were coming toward them, with the woman they'd taken prisoner at the creek. Laurent told Frisell and Peters to organize a search party.

"There are at least two people missing," Lucas said. "Pilate and his girlfriend. They may be holed up or they may have taken off. The guy in the inn thought they ran for it. But: we gotta take it slow and easy."

THEY TOOK AN hour working through the town and found no more disciples. Nor had they seen any sign of Pilate or his girlfriend.

Early in the search, Lucas and Laurent had gone into the hardware store to check the man who'd opened fire on them in the street. Lucas had hit him seven times, including one wound in the head and three in the chest, any one of which would have killed him.

As they looked down at him, Lucas said to Laurent, "We've got to find Pilate. If we don't, the killing isn't over. They go to a house, somewhere, shoot the people and take their car and we won't even know what to look for, until somebody finds the bodies."

"They had to go out the back," Laurent said. "I'll get everybody looking down that way. They can't have gotten too far."

"I don't know," Lucas said. "They might already have hijacked a car."

They went back outside and Laurent looked at the three dead disciples in the street—the man from the blue house and the two naked people. "This was a right straight war. They're gonna make movies about this one."

"Maybe. But Pilate won't be playing himself," Lucas said. "Not with one dead deputy and two wounded."

A deputy was hurrying toward them. "Got another body. Old lady in the blue house. They shot her and stuffed her in a closet."

Laurent groaned. "Had to be one more, didn't there? My God, these people . . . these people . . ."

21

WORD OF THE shoot-out in Mellon leaked to the
media almost immediately—Lucas suspected the artists—
and when it did, rental car agencies in Sault Ste. Marie
and Marquette ran out of cars in ten minutes.

Lucas told Laurent, "You gotta warn everyone to be
careful about what they say. You'll get a hundred professional assholes landing on you. It'd be best if you did
most of the talking, and your reserve guys, because
they'll not only be the ones the media want to talk to,
but they're all pretty smart. Don't let any bullshitters get
in front of a camera or you'll pay for it later."

"They'll want to talk to you," Laurent said.

"Not so much and I'm going back home," Lucas
said. "This is a Michigan deal. There's three dead in
Wisconsin, eight or nine dead in Michigan, more dead
in South Dakota and California, so far, and none dead

in Minnesota. Guess where I'm from? I'm just here helping out . . ."

"You gotta stay at least until the state cops get here, because, uh, if I remember right, you shot two of those dead people yourself," Laurent said. "As long as you're waiting, you might as well help us chase down Pilate."

"Not much I can do to find Pilate—he's out in the wind now," Lucas said. "You're right about making the statement, though. I'll stay for that."

PILATE AND KRISTEN had gone out the window on the lower level of the inn, had run to the creek, then up the creek until they were deep in the trees. Pilate turned up the far bank and Kristen hissed, "Where're you going?"

"Down the highway."

"Listen—you're going the wrong way. They're gonna eventually figure out that we ran for it, and they're gonna expect that we ran away from the town. What we gotta do is, we gotta run *around* the town, and go out the other way."

Pilate said, "You might be right . . . I was *thinking* about doing that."

"Then let's go. We got no time. Every cop in the world's gonna be jammin' in here."

They ran halfway around the town—three hundred yards, all back in the woods—when Kristen, who was leading the way, froze and held up a finger. Human voices. Kristen jerked a finger to the left, and they moved deeper into the woods, as quietly as they could.

Another hundred yards around, they reached a tree that had fallen, but was caught three-fourths of the way down in the crotch of another tree. Pilate climbed up on the trunk, tested it for stability, then climbed as high as he could on the slanting trunk. When he'd gone as far as he could, he peered back to where they'd heard the voices.

A minute later, he climbed back down and said to Kristen, "Bunch of guys with guns. They're looking at the town. They're surrounding it."

"We gotta keep moving."

FIFTEEN MINUTES OUT, they saw a uniformed cop with a car parked across the highway, turning around a car that had wanted to drive through. They walked for another half an hour, a mile at most, slow going in the woods. They heard several random shots from town, then a long sustained burst of gunfire. Kristen looked back and said, "That didn't sound good."

"We gotta get out to the road and grab a car," Pilate said. "You gotta do it. You run on one side, you see a car coming, you flag it down. When the guy rolls the window down to see what the problem is, you shoot him."

She nodded. "I can do that."

"Then let's get closer to the road, where you can move out when a car comes."

The first car came from behind them, followed quickly by another moving fast. Pilate said, "Not them. They gotta be cops."

Ten minutes on, a pickup came down the road toward

them and Kristen broke out of the trees and ran toward it, waving frantically. The truck slowed. A big guy sat behind the wheel, the only person inside. He stopped, rolled down the window, and asked, "Are they still fightin' in—"

Kristen pulled the gun from her back waistband and *BANG!*

Kristen shot him in the head from three feet and the man fell back onto the center console.

Pilate was there, ran around the nose of the truck, yanked the door open and shouted, "Help me drag him, help me drag him out."

Kristen ran around and together they dragged him through the roadside ditch and behind some brush, then ran back to the truck. They turned, and headed back the way they'd come that morning, moving fast, now.

Kristen was driving and Pilate climbed into the back of the double cab, where he found a toolbox and a tire. He pushed the tire up on the seat, with the toolbox, and said, "Listen, they won't be as worried about a woman driving alone. If we come up to a roadblock that we can't beat, I'm gonna lay on the floor back here and pull the toolbox and tire on top of me. You be polite and talk us through."

"Fat chance," she said.

"Yeah, well, keep the gun under your leg. If it's one cop, take him, but shoot either high or low. With all this shooting, he'll be wearing a vest, so you got to go over it or get under it."

"They'll kill us," Kristen said.

"They'll kill us no matter what," Pilate said. "Right now, we at least got a chance."

They made it down to Engadine in twenty-five minutes, and an hour later, were coming up to St. Ignace, where the Mackinac Bridge came up from Lower Michigan on I-75.

"Once we get across that fuckin' bridge, we're free," Pilate said, his first show of enthusiasm since he'd kicked Skye to death. "Once we get out of shitkicker heaven, they ain't gonna find us. We got a thousand roads we can take back to L.A."

"You think they won't know about us in L.A.?"

"Shut up and learn something. My wholesaler brings the dope up from Mexico. He goes back and forth all the time. He can get us down to Mexico."

"What would we do there?"

"Shit, I don't know," Pilate said. "We could figure out something. We'll still have our guns—"

Kristen said, "There's a gas station. We need gas . . . and what the hell is that?"

Straight ahead, a couple hundred yards beyond a truck stop, they were looking at the back end of what looked like an L.A. traffic jam.

"I don't like it," Pilate blurted. "Pull into the pumps. Pump some gas and ask somebody what's going on."

Kristen pulled in and pumped gas while Pilate lay below window level in the truck. He could hear her talking to somebody and then he heard nothing for five minutes. When she got back in the cab with a sack full of junk food and a six-pack of Budweiser and another of Coke, Pilate asked, "What?"

She muttered, "Stay down and don't talk."

She pulled back on the highway, and Pilate sat up and looked back. "What was that?"

"The cops have blocked the bridge. They're shaking down every car coming out of the UP." She looked at him: "So what's the plan now?"

He thought about it, then said, "First, we need a different car."

22

THE MEDIA CAME in like a bad rain, barely preceded by the Michigan State Police, who took over the town and began organizing a countywide house-by-house search for Pilate and Kristen.

The surviving disciples couldn't or wouldn't provide a last name for either one of them. "That's not something we did—we all had one name," said Laine Archer, of Eugene, Oregon, when she talked to the state cops at the hospital in Munising, before being taken into surgery to repair her shoulder. She was sure Pilate and Kristen were on foot: they'd snuck out of the lower floor of the inn just a few minutes after they'd gone to their assigned spots in the triangle of buildings.

When the state police began arriving, Laurent took Lucas aside and said, "Look, when you make your statement, they're gonna want to know how all this happened—why it didn't happen some other place. And maybe they'll be looking for somebody to blame."

"I can handle that," Lucas said.

"Why would you want to get tangled up in it?" Laurent asked. "We tell them that you came here to provide us information about a group of roaming killers, and to identify Pilate and his crew—but that I was running the show. Nothing wrong with any of that. That I made the decision to take them out, right here. That we believed that they were about to kill the two artists, and I'm sure the artists will back us up on that. If we do it that way, they won't have anybody to hang. One local cop is dead, three more are shot, all of them were shot without warning or mercy. We give them a choice: they can either celebrate what we did or take Pilate's side in a media war. I don't think they'll choose door number two."

"You're a smart guy," Lucas said. "We'll do it your way."

And that's what they did. As state cops raced from one house to another, in a circle thirty miles across, a captain named Ferguson took Lucas aside for a statement, and Lucas followed Laurent's proposed story. When they were done with him, they told him to hang around for a while, they were having the interview transcribed and he'd have to sign it.

Laurent had been given the same treatment, as was everyone else who'd been involved in actual shooting, including three civilians from the bar who'd opened up on the naked disciples after the deputies were shot.

The lady artist's camera and memory card were confiscated, over her protests. The state cops told her that she'd probably get them back, sooner or later.

AFTER THE INTERVIEW, Lucas was out in the street when two TV cameramen came jogging up, led by good-looking women with microphones: "Officer Davenport . . . could you give us a comment, your version—"

"I better leave that to the Michigan state police. I understand that they're planning a press conference."

He saw Laurent and Frisell watching and he waved them over and said to the reporters, "Here are two of the main men in the whole operation. What they did, taking out this gang . . . it was right on the edge of unbelievable. I've never seen anything quite like it, to tell you the truth. Everybody in Michigan should be proud about what they did up here today."

The reporters got a more extensive commentary out of Laurent and Frisell, and then Laurent called Barney Peters over, and Lucas told the story of Peters doing first aid on the wounded.

Late that afternoon, a woman named Constance Frey called to say that her husband, Louis Frey, had heard about the shoot-out in Mellon, and despite her protests, had gotten his gun and jumped in his truck to help out. He had not come home, and was not answering his cell phone.

During his debriefing, Lucas had mentioned that they'd tracked some of the disciples with cell phones. A state police officer approached Lucas, and asked if Lucas could ping Louis Frey's cell phone to see where he was. "We could do it ourselves, but since you're already set up to do it . . ."

Lucas did and was told that the cell phone was a mile or so south of town, right on the road. When they went to look, they couldn't find Frey. They began calling his phone, as they walked along the road, and eventually heard it ringing from behind some brush across the roadside ditch.

He'd been shot once in the head, but for some reason, was still alive, though he couldn't move and he couldn't talk. They loaded him into a police car and sent him to the hospital in Munising.

One of the state cops told Lucas, "I know you were doing the right thing by chasing these assholes down, but I wish you'd done it in some other state."

Lucas thought, *Fuck it*, declined a ride back to town and walked back by himself.

HALFWAY BACK, HE took a phone call from Jenkins. "I'm standing here with Shrake and Julie Katz and her cadaver dog." Lucas had lost track of who was doing what with the Merion case: it seemed like he'd last talked to Jenkins or Shrake about a hundred years earlier.

"At Merion's cabin?"

"Across the road from his cabin. The fuckin' dog indicated . . . is that what they call it? Indicated? Yeah, anyway, he indicated, and we're looking at the end of one of those banister things. I don't see any blood, but the dog says it's there. We've stopped digging, we're getting the crime scene crew out there."

"Good doggy," Lucas said. "Listen: my buddy Park Raines is going to claim that you guys planted it. It won't work, because if there's blood, we'll get DNA from it, and if Merion handled it, we could have his DNA, too. But Park's gonna say that you planted it. So don't touch anything."

"We haven't touched anything."

"Good. Call the sheriff's department and ask them to send a couple of deputies to stand guard, so you won't be involved anymore," Lucas said.

"What about you?"

"What do you mean?" Lucas asked.

"You oughta be here for this, when the news gets out," Jenkins said. "You know, for the glory."

"Yeah, whatever," Lucas said. "Get the ball rolling. For Christ's sakes, don't contaminate anything . . . Hey, Jenkins: you got him. You fuckin' got him."

Made him happy, and he picked up the pace. Called Weather with the news, and told her, "I can't get back tonight. I'll be back tomorrow."

"You don't have to hurry—don't try to drive back at a hundred miles an hour."

WHEN LUCAS GOT back to Mellon, Peters and Frisell were sitting on a bench outside the convenience store eating ice cream cones. It was a hot day and Frisell said, "You better get one if you want one. This place doesn't usually have a herd of reporters and cops hanging around, and they're going fast."

"Everything's going fast," Peters added.

Lucas got the last Diet Coke and the second-to-last cone, and came back out, and Frisell and Peters moved over so he'd have a place to sit. Frisell looked down the street, to where state crime scene people were making measurements and calculating angles and taking photographs.

"I think Clooney will probably play me in the movie," he said. Frisell looked at Peters and Lucas. "How about you guys?" Peters said, "Tom Cruise." Lucas thought for a moment and said, "Scarlett Johansson."

Frisell said, "Really? Is there something you haven't told us?"

"No, no. It's just that I'm sure she'd need first-person coaching through the part, some in-depth consultation," Lucas said.

"Probably," Peters said, catching a drip that was running down the side of his cone. To Frisell he said, "I'm changing mine to Angelina Jolie."

AT THE HOLIDAY Inn that night, Lucas had just gotten out of the shower, when Weather called and said, "Is there any way to see Channel Three up there?"

"I don't know how," he said. "Why?"

"Because you're in a couple of big stories," she said. "We just saw the promo for them . . . Hang on, Letty wants to talk to you."

Letty came on and said, "Dad . . ."

"You still hurting?"

"Yeah, but never mind. Can you get online?"

"I got Wi-Fi in the room," he said.

"Then you can watch Channel Three online. You gotta hurry."

LUCAS WAS RIGHT at the top of the news, in a way.

First was the story out of Michigan, video from the reporters who'd talked to Lucas, Laurent, Frisell, and Peters that afternoon, about the fight in Mellon, which was being headlined as High Noon in the UP.

The second item was a press conference called by the BCA, to announce that further important evidence had been discovered in the Ben Merion murder case, in the shape of a bloody club found near Merion's Cross Lake cabin.

Henry Sands made the announcement, attributing the find to "hardworking BCA detectives" without mentioning names but his own, and to BCA laboratory personnel who would be processing the evidence through the St. Paul laboratory.

"We won't know the DNA results for some days, but I have been told that there is a substantial evidentiary sample available to us."

He talked for a while, with the TV people calling out, "Director Sands . . . Director Sands . . . Director Sands . . ."

23

PILATE AND KRISTEN worked their way north to Prospect Avenue, got on I-75 and headed for Sault Ste. Marie, away from the blockaded bridge. They drove around town, and found what they were looking for on Tenth Avenue West, an area of older homes, probably from the post–World War II era, small houses on large lots.

They spent some time cruising the whole area, then did it again, and then a third time, until Pilate pointed and said, "There. Right there."

A white-haired woman was pulling her Taurus station wagon into a detached two-car garage. There were no lights in the house and Pilate said, "She either lives alone or her old man ain't home yet."

The old lady dropped the garage door and limped into the house, carrying a bag of groceries. They waited until she was inside, parked the truck in the street, and walked up to the door and knocked.

The old lady came to the door and asked, "Can I help you?"

Pilate said, "Yeah, you can."

He'd already checked the screen door to make sure that it was unlatched. Now he yanked it open, put his hand in the old lady's face, and hurled her back against the entry wall, where her head rebounded with a wet smack. Kristen came in behind Pilate and shut the door while Pilate kicked the old lady in the head three or four times. When Pilate was pretty sure she was dead, the two of them checked out the house.

Everything suggested that the old lady lived alone, including a single plate and a cup and saucer sitting in the kitchen sink. They dragged the old woman to the basement stairs and threw her down, then went outside to move the vehicles. The second slot in the garage was half full of crap—boxes of family photographs, thirty-year-old skis, corroding bicycles. They managed to clear enough space to fit the truck inside, and pulled the doors down.

Back inside, they checked the grocery bag—potatoes, grapes, milk, cereal. They found a couple of chicken pot pies in the refrigerator, and half of a quart bottle of bourbon in the cupboard.

"Everything we need," Pilate said. "We could hole up here for a couple days, if we have to."

BUT THEY COULDN'T, really. The UP was getting organized.

They caught the six o'clock news and found out what had happened in Mellon—and that they were national celebrities. The cops had dug up a driver's license for Kristen Jones—Pilate said, "Jones? Jones?"—and had excellent identikit images of Pilate.

"While we're waiting to get out of here, we gotta change the way we look," he said.

"You could shave your beard," Kristen said. "Though I'd miss your little beard braids."

"My beard? I'm gonna cut it *all* off—beard, hair, everything. Shave my head. You could get one of those lesbo haircuts like Ellen had."

"Wonder what she's told the cops." They'd seen pictures of Ellen in handcuffs, being led into a police station.

"Probably everything," Pilate said. "I never trusted that bitch."

THEY ATE, TALKING about the fight in Mellon, the last things they'd seen, then went into the bathroom to cut their hair. Pilate looked at himself in the mirror and said, "You know, I can't cut it all off. I won't feel like myself. How about a soul patch?"

THE OLD LADY had a wall of photos of herself and a man who must have been her husband, showing them through the years, with four children, and then a bunch of grandchildren. One of the photos showed the old lady, many years younger, giving the man a haircut with an electric clipper as he sat on a wooden chair in a bathroom, with a towel around his neck. They dug through the bathroom drawers and a linen closet and, sure enough, found the clippers.

The clippers were crude and Pilate kept flinching when the clipper-head yanked at his hair, but they got it done, and finished the job, both his face and scalp, with a throwaway lady's razor.

When she was finished, Pilate looked at himself in the bathroom mirror and said, "I hate this. I look about twenty fuckin' years older."

"That's a *good* thing," Kristen said. "I'll tell you something else: your head looks about half as big as it used to and your nose looks twice as big. You don't look nothin' like that drawing."

Pilate cut Kristen's hair, taking his time, looking at the way her hair lay across her head, and when he finished, Kristen turned this way and that, looking in the mirror, and then said, "You know, maybe you should have been a hairdresser. Looks pretty good. Makes me look like a boy."

THEY WATCHED THE news on satellite TV, and it was a scream-fest. They caught CNN first, Wolf Blitzer, and then a local station out of Traverse City.

Both CNN and the local station had video shot minutes after the shooting ended. The video had been shot by the woman artist, who said she'd been held captive and had been threatened with rape by the disciples.

She had apparently sold her video to every TV station in sight, and complained that the Michigan state cops had confiscated her original memory card and camera. She'd seen that coming, though, and had saved the video to her laptop before the cops got to her.

One of the videos showed a tall thin cop firing a rifle out the window, while another one, with a pistol, huddled on the floor, watched. Before he pulled the trigger, they heard the thin cop say, quite clearly, "Fuck him," and after he fired, the other cop walked to the window and looked out, and then said, almost conversationally, "Nice shot, I guess."

The camera then tracked down across the floor where a group of men surrounded a body on the floor, and then to another man who lay in a pool of blood. Kristen was sitting on the couch, eating a pot pie, and said, "Bell. Bell and Laine."

Pilate said, "Motherfuckers. That could be us."

Toward the end of the newscast, the anchorman asked people throughout the UP to check on their neighbors, but to do so carefully: "Don't just walk up to a house, but watch to see if your neighbors follow their usual routine. If something seems different, call the police and report your suspicions."

"We gotta get out of here before daylight," Pilate said. "Maybe . . . I don't know. Get as far away as we can in one day in the old lady's car, then . . . take a bus? Or grab another car."

They hadn't had any decent sleep for a long time, it seemed, and they crawled into the old lady's double bed after watching the news. At five o'clock in the morning, they ate cereal and milk, then rummaged through the old lady's closets and found hats and jackets that no Californian would ever wear. They also took the thirty dollars in the old lady's purse, along with her driver's license and Visa card.

When Kristen put on a wide-brimmed straw hat with a white bow, she looked in the mirror and said, "I'm a fuckin' church lady."

"Church lady is good," Pilate said.

Kristen said, "If you had a ring in your ear, you'd look like Mr. Clean."

They gassed the car up at a station on the edge of town, where a sleepy clerk told Kristen that the I-75 bridge was still blocked.

With that option gone, they headed west, on the far north side of the peninsula, toward Duluth, Minnesota, eight hours away.

They found a road atlas in the car, which Pilate read as Kristen drove.

"We'll be in Duluth before three o'clock. Can't go back to Pap's because they either caught Chet or killed him, and they'll be onto Pap's by now."

A while later, he said, "If we go south to Minneapolis, we'll be good. Stay there overnight, next day, drive to

Kansas City, dump the car where they won't find it right away . . ."

"Walmart parking lot."

"Catch a bus and we're good," Pilate said.

Another while later, he added, "That big fuckin' cop and his nosy kid are from down there. That's something to think about."

24

LUCAS SAID GOOD-BYE to the posse the next day at Pat's, the sandwich shop across the street from Laurent's office, shaking hands, slapping backs, reliving the shootout at Mellon, speculating on the location of Pilate and Kristen. The mood was frenetic, half excitement and half regret, still mixed with anger about the cops who'd been shot. Four of the five of them were still alive, but one had lost a leg.

Everybody agreed that the fugitives certainly had Louis Frey's truck and were hiding somewhere.

"Best case, they're hiding in the woods. Worst case, they stuck it in somebody's garage where nobody'll find it for a while, killed the owners, and holed up," Lucas said. "This thing isn't over until you've nailed them down."

Laurent said, "We'll get them. We will. By the way, you know when you guys were sitting on a bench, eating those ice cream cones and talking about who'd be playing you in the movies? Guess who I got a call from this morning? It's some producer out in L.A. and he's talking about options and so on."

Lucas said, "See you on the red carpet."

IN THE END, Lucas got out of town a little before noon, drove too fast going home, and would have pulled into his driveway right at eight o'clock if a couple of TV trucks hadn't been blocking it.

He parked in the street behind the last TV truck and a pretty blond woman hopped out and he said, "Oh, shit."

Jennifer Carey and he had a relationship that went back a couple of decades. More than that: Lucas was the father of Carey's first daughter, who was now in high school. Carey had married another man long ago, who had more or less adopted Lucas's daughter, not counting private school fees and college tuition, all of which was fine with Lucas.

But Carey still had the mojo on him. She couldn't read him as well as Weather could, but was still better than fifty-fifty on when he was lying. She was walking straight at him with a microphone thrust out at his face, and a trailing cameraman.

Another woman popped out of the lead truck, Annie McGowan, who was now anchoring at Channel 11. She rarely was on the street with a cameraman, but she was now, because she also had an edge on Lucas. Lucas did have one advantage: the two women were not friends and a catfight was possible. Then he could arrest them both for assault, send them down to the Ramsey County jail, and go to dinner.

He got out of the car, fists on his hips, saw Letty jogging across the lawn. She came up and slapped hands with Carey. Letty had interned at Carey's TV station for three years, as a high school student, under Carey's watchful eye. Letty nodded at McGowan and asked Lucas, "Where's Pilate?"

"I don't know," Lucas said, as the microphones came up. "The two best possibilities are that he's out in the woods somewhere in the UP, or that he made it across the Mackinac Bridge before we got the roadblocks up and is hiding out in Detroit."

"Do you think he'll surrender when he's caught?" Carey asked.

"Depends on how it happens. He'll run as far as he can. If he's cornered and doesn't have any options, he'll quit. Fundamentally, he's a coward. When we caught up to them in Michigan, he organized his disciples for a fight, then when the fight started, he snuck out the back door and ran. Abandoned his so-called friends. Some of them were actually dying for him and he was sneaking away into the woods."

McGowan held up three fingers and asked, "Do you think he'll surrender when he's caught?" and then counted the fingers down one-two-three, which would allow her editors to cut her question in, before Lucas's response. When she'd built in a little space for her editors, she turned to Letty, with her enormous black eye, and asked, "Do you agree with your father? When you tried to save your friend, this Pilate beat you up."

"That's all he's good at," Letty said. "Beating up women. He kicked my friend Skye to death, over in Wisconsin, and the guy they crucified in South Dakota was just a nice, gentle boy. Pilate is an enormous . . . I can't say it on TV, but he is one. A vicious one."

Carey held up three fingers and asked Letty, "Do you agree with your father? Pilate attacked you . . ." then counted down one-two-three.

Lucas answered a few more questions, and declined to answer some that he thought might be legally sensitive.

"I can't actually answer all your questions, because I'm being deposed tomorrow at the BCA. We'll send copies to all the departments involved in the case. Copies of the depositions should be available through the BCA, whenever the authorities . . . think they should be."

He let the women get a couple of reverse shots over his shoulder, showing their faces in close-up, asking the questions they'd already asked, and then he called it off. "I gotta go say hello to my wife and get something decent to eat. I haven't had anything all day."

When the cameras and microphones were off, McGowan said, "I can see your handiwork in that witch Daisy Jones getting the Honey Potts interview."

"Jeez, Annie, try to be a little more understanding of an enterprising colleague," Lucas said.

"I was a little annoyed myself," Carey said. "You really set that up?"

"I was out of town when she did that interview," Lucas said. "My hands are clean."

"How about your cell phone?" Carey asked. "Is that clean, too?"

"Jennifer . . ." Lucas began. Then, "Listen, you guys have been here, when I wasn't, and you hang around the courthouse. What are people saying about the Merion case?"

"I've heard that your old basketball buddy Park Raines started sniffing around for a deal about five minutes after that baluster came out of the ground," McGowan said.

Carey said, "I gotta say, he's one eminently fuckable attorney. In my opinion."

"You're right," said Letty.

Lucas: "Hey! Not in front of the old man."

"And he's even better than he looks," McGowan said, with a moment of silence following. Then, to Lucas, "Anyway, the baluster sealed the deal. I've even heard that Martin Bobson might take the case away from his boy prosecutor and give it to somebody more serious."

Carey: "Somebody must have briefed you on what balusters are."

"Fuck you," McGowan said.

"Why would you fight with each other?" Lucas asked. "It's Daisy's tire treads that are running across both your chests."

They both said, at the same time, "Fuck you."

Letty said brightly, "Everybody's feeling scrappy tonight, huh?"

———

THE TV TRUCKS left, and Lucas pulled the SUV into the garage and dropped the door.

Weather was inside reading *Microsurgery Letters*, and said, "I hope you won't get in trouble for talking to those people."

Lucas kissed her on the forehead and said, "You know, I don't care anymore. About getting in trouble with anybody."

Weather looked at him: "You're okay?"

She meant the depression problem. "I'm feeling pretty cheerful," Lucas said. "I was working with a police force that was stripped down to almost nothing, and in some ways, it seems to work better than anything we've got in the Twin Cities. People in the UP know they have to take care of themselves, because nobody else will. So they do."

"All right, if you say so," she said. "I reserve the right to smirk when it all goes wrong."

25

PILATE AND KRISTEN, nervous as cats all the way across the Upper Peninsula and then Wisconsin, relaxed a notch as they crossed a bay off Lake Superior on Highway 53 and rolled into Duluth, Minnesota, past long lines of boxcars. They were two states away from the manhunt and that much safer.

Pilate was driving and merged onto I-35 north and got off at Michigan Avenue. Kristen, looking out the window at the town, said, "There's a used clothes store around here. I can smell it. We need some different clothes. We look too L.A. Like, not from here."

"What we really need to do is see a news program, find out what's going on," Pilate said. "See if they found the old lady. If they find her, and we don't know it and we're driving this car, we're toast."

They drove around for a while, but didn't find a used

clothes store. As they were about to give up, Kristen pointed to two oddly dressed women in funny hats waiting to cross the street, and said, "Stop there—we'll ask them."

The women were Catholic nuns, and one said, "Why, yes. There's a place about six blocks that way, called Round It Goes. It's on the right, next to the bookstore. You can't miss it."

Being nuns, they didn't say that it was an adult bookstore, but Round It Goes was right next to it. Fifteen minutes into the store, they found a blue suit that fit Pilate, with a light blue dress shirt and a striped necktie. His own shoes were acceptable, if a little too pointy.

Kristen found a short-sleeved brown dress that dropped an inch below her knees, and brown shoes with low, wide heels. She checked herself in the mirror and said, "I look like one of those nuns."

"Which is about as far away from us as you could get," Pilate said. "Nuns ain't pretty, but nuns is good."

On a rack next to the door, Pilate found a white straw hat with a narrow brim, put it on, and asked Kristen, "What do you think?"

She considered the hat, then said, "You look like somebody I know."

He dropped his voice: "But not Pilate."

"No, not Pilate."

THE TOTAL BILL came to thirty-six dollars, and they went to look for a TV. After two miscues—sports bars—

they found a dark and nearly empty bar downtown, put on their sunglasses, went in, got beers served in a booth in the back, where they could see the second-string television. There was a ballgame on, but neither the bartender nor the other two patrons was looking at it, and Pilate asked the bartender if they could change stations to CNN or something like that.

"Sure." He used a remote to change stations, then said to Pilate, "You remind me of someone. Are you a musician?"

"Play a little ukulele," Pilate joked, as he headed back to the booth.

They didn't have to order a second beer. CNN was in full disaster mode, with at least three reporters wandering around the UP. They seemed to be as astonished by the place as Pilate and the disciples had been.

At one point, Wolf Blitzer said, "One of the key actors in this North Woods clash, agent Lucas Davenport of Minnesota's Bureau of Criminal Apprehension, has been out of touch all day, as he drives back to Minnesota. We're hoping to have an interview with him this evening. In the meantime, the search continues for the ringleaders of the Los Angeles murder and drug gang who . . ."

The identikit picture of Pilate came up, along with the photo of Kristen. The old lady hadn't been found. After the summary, Blitzer tolled out the dead. Pilate was transfixed as a reporter read the roll: the disciples had essentially been wiped out, save for a few who were jumped by the cops at the Sault Ste. Marie Gathering, one who survived the Mellon shoot-out untouched, and one who was wounded at Mellon.

CNN had all their full names, most of which Pilate never knew.

"I'm amazed Laine was shot. If I'd thought any of them would have given up, it would have been her," Kristen said.

"She's still got time to fuck us," Pilate said.

Kristen leaned forward and whispered, "The bartender keeps looking down here at us. I think we're ringing a bell with him. Maybe from the pictures?"

Pilate leaned toward her: "Wonder if he's called a cop?"

"I haven't seen him on the phone," she said.

"Let's go. We've heard enough. Get out of here, get a motel down in the Twin Cities. We can watch the news tonight."

She nodded and they pushed out of the booth. As they passed the bartender, he smiled broadly, snapped his fingers, and pointed at Pilate. "I got it. The ukulele tipped me off. Leon Redbone, right?"

Kristen kept walking, but Pilate put his finger to his lips and said, "Don't tell."

Then he was out the door. On the sidewalk, Kristen was biting into her arm so hard, that later, she found a little row of bruises where her pointed teeth cut into the skin.

"Shut up," Pilate said.

She tried to talk, but nothing came out but a low gurgling laugh, until finally she gasped, "Leon . . . Redbone. Where's your fuckin' banjo, Leon?" She bit into her arm again as they walked back to the car.

That night, in a motel on the airport strip in south Minneapolis, they watched the interview with Davenport and his daughter, on Channel Three.

"That motherfucker," Pilate said. *Coward? Only fights women? Ran out on his friends?* "He's smearing me, he's ruining my whole fucking reputation."

Kristen said, "Keep your voice down, for Christ's sakes. They can hear you three rooms down. And what difference does it make? You can never be you again . . . ever."

"Fuckin' coward? Fuckin' coward?"

"Keep your voice down." She'd seen him like this, when he'd pick up an insult and turn it into a cataclysm. That's how they wound up killing Kitty Place: because another woman had insulted Pilate.

Late that night, three o'clock, Kristen woke up and heard Pilate rattling something. She turned her head and opened her eyes. He was pointing his .45 at the darkened television. He said, aloud, "Coward?" Pulled the trigger and the hammer fell with a metallic smack and he racked the slide again.

LETTY CAME DOWN the stairs wearing dark slacks, low heels, and a dark blue silk blouse: dressed up to talk to the cops. Lucas looked at her and thought that she'd never work undercover as a cop, unless it was a very classy assignment. With her dark hair, she gave off a little too much of a private school vibe. Of course, if she focused on economics at Stanford, she could be a real undercover weapon if she investigated economic crime, where the criminals wore five-thousand-dollar suits.

She looked at Lucas and said, "You look like a rich cop." Lucas was wearing a navy blue suit, English loafers, and a very pale blue shirt made in France.

"Why not a banker?"

"Bankers don't have noses that are crooked from being broken or scars like yours. But cops do. I mean . . . look at Jenkins. Or Shrake."

"Please," Lucas said. And, "You ready to go?"

"We need to stop at a Caribou for some iced coffee."

"Not a problem."

THE DAY WAS perfect: low eighties, bluebird sky, the slightest touch of a breeze. If the Minnesota August lasted all year, nobody would live anywhere else. That hadn't always been true, he told Letty, as they went out to the Porsche. There had been the whole era of the infamous St. Paul Smell, but that was gone now. Forever, he hoped, because it *had* been nasty.

They made it to the BCA in twenty-five minutes, with a stop at Caribou Coffee so that Letty could get a Cold Press iced coffee and a Diet Coke and scone for Lucas, and they dropped the top on the car and took their time.

Sands was waiting in an adjoining office, talking to an agent, but jumped up the instant he saw Lucas and Letty. "Lucas, we gotta talk." He looked at Letty, recognized her, and said, "Your daughter can wait in your office."

THE MINUTE THEY got in his office, Sands turned around and poked a finger at Lucas, raised his voice and said, "What the hell have you been doing out there? You had responsibilities here, and instead, you go tearing around the countryside, *not even in Minnesota*, you get five cops shot and one of them killed."

"Don't shout at me, Henry," Lucas said. He said it calmly enough, but Henry took a quick step backward.

"You don't fuckin' threaten me, Davenport. I've had enough of this shit, your goddamn gang operating however they want, that fuckin' Flowers pisses off a state senator, who's *still* calling me—"

"I didn't threaten you, Henry. In fact, I'm in the process of reevaluating my position at the BCA. I don't think I'm up high enough in the food chain to avoid the bullshit. I'm gonna talk to the governor about moving me up another step or two, so I can do some actual investigation, instead of sending my men out to blow moronic state senators."

Sands put up both hands, said, "Okay. Okay. You talk to whoever you want. But the first thing you do is, you figure out how you're going to pay for this little excursion to Michigan. What are you gonna do when we get sued by some—"

"I'll pay for it," Lucas said. "If we get sued and lose, I'll pay for it. I'll pay for my own mileage, my own hotels, won't put in for any overtime. Henry, we wiped out a gang that butchered at least ten innocent people, and quite possibly more, including a crucifixion. You want me to go on television and tell people that Henry Sands disallowed my travel expenses for killing off a gang that slashed an actress to death and crucified a young boy from Texas? You want to be famous, I think I can manage it," Lucas said.

"You're threatening me again," Sands said.

"I'd never threaten you," Lucas said. "If I got to that point, I'd just bust your fuckin' nose. In the meantime . . ." Lucas gave him the finger. "Fuck you."

"Hey! Hey!"

Sands's voice cut off when Lucas pulled the door shut.

LUCAS AND LETTY gave their statements about the Wisconsin part of the investigation, sticking close to the statement they'd given the Sawyer County Sheriff's Department. Lucas expanded into the conflict in the Upper Peninsula. Everybody called them depositions, but they weren't really, because there was no swearing in, or an opposition attorney to monitor them. Real depositions would come later, if somebody decided to sue. Given the viciousness of Pilate and the disciples, Lucas thought that successful suits would be thin on the ground.

The statements took an hour and a half, then they shook hands all around, and Lucas and Letty stopped at Lucas's office on the way out. Del was sitting there, reading a hippie newspaper, and when he saw them coming, he shook his head.

"I understand you got harsh with Henry."

"I let it out a little," Lucas agreed. "Why?"

"There's a hot rumor going around that he's going to bring you up on a bunch of charges, try to get you fired, or at least, suspended for, you know, months. Demoted, probably."

Lucas smiled and said, "Well, as some great philosopher should have once said, *it is what it is*. Don't worry about it, Del. Though you might want to keep your head down: avoid as much of the stink as possible."

"Lucas, the whole group is talking about ways to back you up. We're all with you—"

"Easy, man, I got this," Lucas said.

Lucas got his briefcase and he and Letty headed out of the building. Crossing the parking lot, Letty said, "Del's a good friend."

"Yes, he is. So are Flowers and Jenkins and Shrake and Elle and Catrin and a half dozen other people. Some of them aren't really friends, but they're okay, like Shaffer—I didn't like him, but he did a good job, and he didn't like me, but he knew I held my end up, so we were fine with each other. Other people, like Sands, they're a drag on the system. They're our biggest problem: there are too many bureaucrats and all they worry about is sucking on the neck of whoever's paying them. Just the way it goes."

Two minutes later, they were out on Maryland Avenue, headed for I-35, neither one of them saying much, comfortable with not talking.

Letty was driving.

———

PILATE SAID, "THERE they are."

He was parked on Phalen Boulevard, looking slightly down into the BCA parking lot.

Kristen whimpered, "Let's get out of here. Pilate, they'll kill us."

"Shut up. They're not gonna kill us. We'll get them away from here, out in the open, and *BOOM!*"

"Yeah, *BOOM!*"

Davenport and his daughter had gotten out of the slick-looking Porsche, and, leaving the top down, went inside the building.

"He said on TV he was just going to make a statement. Couldn't take long. You're driving, I got the gun," Pilate said. "If we get down a quiet street where we could pull up beside them . . . All we need is five seconds to get away from the scene, and we're gone."

"This is so fuckin' crazy. They're going to kill us."

"You think I'm a fuckin' coward? You think I'm a fuckin' coward, don't you?"

It went on like that, back and forth, with growing silences between outbursts, and they waited, and waited some more, and it was almost two hours before Davenport and his kid came out of the building and got back in the Porsche, the girl in the driver's seat.

"We look for a quiet block," Pilate said. "They'll be moving slow on the city streets, right out in the open in that little car."

LETTY TOOK THEM out to I-35 and back toward home, easing onto I-94, then speeding up, slashing through the traffic. Lucas said nothing, because she'd learned from him, and he was enjoying the ride. They got off at Cretin and she took the left at the top of the ramp, got caught by a red light at Marshall.

Letty asked, "Do you think I'm paranoid?"

"You mean, like you're starting to think I might cut off your Amex?"

She looked at him with cool, serious eyes. "No. Would you believe me if I said I think we're being followed, by two people in an old car?"

Lucas smiled and said, "Yeah, I'd believe you." He looked straight ahead, then glanced into the right wing mirror. "Which one is it?"

"That old red car, like a station wagon. It's about six cars back in the left lane. I kind of noticed it when we were coming out of the parking lot. I thought I saw somebody inside, but they like ducked. When we were going down Maryland, I saw them turning behind us. Then we got to I-35, and they got behind us there, too, but stayed back, and they followed us to I-94. When I sped up, they did, too—but they still stayed back. Now they're still behind us."

"Goddamnit, it could be them," Lucas said. "I've been shooting off my mouth on TV about what assholes they are, and they're crazy. I even told them where we'd be today, when I talked to Jennifer and Annie last night. They couldn't get out of the UP going south, so if they did get out, going west . . . they could be here."

"Now what?" Letty asked.

"Let me think," Lucas said.

A MINUTE LATER, he said, "Okay, here's the deal. Don't let them catch us. Keep going straight south, all the way to Ford Parkway, then hook over to Cleveland, go all the way down to Highway 5, then over to the Mall of America."

"Why the mall?"

"Because it's full of cops," Lucas said. "And the Bloomington chief is a friend of mine and he can have things set up by the time we get there. And it's a logical destination."

LUCAS GOT THROUGH to the chief on the chief's personal cell phone, explained the situation. "Here's what I want to do. You know when you get off 494 onto Cedar, then you slide over and go up and then down that ramp that curves over in front of Nordstrom's?"

"Yeah. Lindau Lane."

"That's it. With all those roads going through there, Lindau is like a concrete chute. If there's shooting, it shouldn't be a problem. We won't kill any bystanders. If you have a couple cars down around the bend, where it turns by Nordstrom's, he won't be able to see them until he's right at the roadblock. And there's no way out of the chute."

"I get the concept," the chief said. "We'll put a couple of unmarked cars north of 494, and they'll fall in behind them, so when he comes around the corner, we'll have him boxed."

"Gonna need some guys who are willing to shoot," Lucas said. "If these assholes think they're gonna die, they'll try to take us with them."

"Keep your phone open: I'll be calling you," the chief said.

Letty said to Lucas, "Still back four or five cars."

"Try not to clip a light and leave them behind."

"WHERE IN THE hell are they going?" Pilate asked.

"Don't know. I almost lost her on the freeway. She drives like she's in L.A., and this piece of shit drives like it's still back in Michigan," Kristen said.

They got down to Highway 5, followed Lucas and Letty past the airport where it merged with I-494, and then Pilate saw a sign for the mall. "They're going to that Mall of America. Man, that's great. We follow them right to their parking space, slow down, I nail the guy, and we go. So many cars out there, so many people, so much noise, we'll be lost in five seconds."

"Ah . . . I don't know, man, I don't know."

Then they could see the mall south of the highway. Pilate said, "Doesn't look that big. The malls in L.A. are twice as big."

LUCAS SAID, "EASY now."

"I really love this shit," Letty said.

"Letty, goddamnit . . ."

"Well?"

"Okay, okay."

"There's the off-ramp," she said.

IT ALMOST WORKED.

The red Taurus—Lucas had picked it out in the wing mirror—followed them right off I-494 and then down and up again on the Lindau Lane chute. Lucas saw two boring unmarked sedans jostle through traffic and get in behind the Taurus. Cop cars. The Taurus kept coming.

Lucas said, "We've got them boxed. Speed up, fast now, hit it and stay right."

Letty dropped two gears and floored it and the Porsche virtually leapt down the chute.

"Don't scrape the fenders! Jesus, don't scrape the fuckin' fenders."

The car's soft fat tires were squealing their hearts out when Letty went around the curve to the left, and ahead saw four squad cars on the ramp, with a small gap on the right side, big enough for her to get through. She'd gained two hundred yards on the Taurus, and it was now out of sight behind the curve. Letty didn't slow down as they approached the gap and a couple of Bloomington cops on foot, who had apparently expected her to *ease* through it, jumped back.

Lucas said, "Jesus, Jesus," as the concrete wall flew past a foot from his nose. Through the gap, Letty hit the brakes, hard. Lucas surged forward in his safety belt, and when they were stopped, he looked at her and opened his mouth but nothing came out, and she smiled and said, "Not a scratch."

He popped his safety belt and jumped out. "Stay down."

As soon as Letty had gone through the gap, one of the waiting Bloomington cop cars moved into it.

That's when the glitch developed.

THE PORSCHE SUDDENLY leapt away from them. Kristen screamed, "What is . . . What are they doing, did they see us?"

"I don't know, I don't—"

Kristen had accelerated, in a futile attempt to keep up, and when she came around the turn, she had barely enough time to stop before hitting the cop cars that were blocking the road. An ugly yellow car was right on her tail, and she yelled, "Cops behind us."

As they screeched to a stop, the car fishtailed a little, and Pilate popped the door and disappeared. Where did he go? She didn't know. She got out of the car and held up her hands, heard cops shouting at her, and she stood still, but twisted her neck around looking for Pilate. He had vanished.

Then she saw Davenport running away from her, down the ramp, a gun in his hand, and a few cops trailing, running hard.

PILATE KNEW IT was over: the cops were going to kill him. Before the car had even stopped, he was out, and he took three steps to the concrete railing and looked down. Fifteen feet? He slipped over the railing, hung for a minute, then let go, landing on the grass below.

Something popped and pain surged through one foot, and he felt like his asshole had kept going when his body stopped. He ran under the ramp for a few seconds, but couldn't stay there, and he darted across a narrow street, between two oncoming cars and into a bunch of small trees and headed for Nordstrom's door.

He kept thinking, *Gonna make it, gonna make it, gonna make it . . .*

He was wearing the blue suit, with the .45 in his pocket, and he took the gun out as he ran. He'd jacked a shell into the chamber when they were tracking Davenport. He came up to Nordstrom's, expecting to be hit between the shoulder blades at any minute, realized that the cops couldn't shoot because of the crowd ahead of him: crowds were his friends, now. Off to his left, he got a glimpse of somebody coming after him, and realized that Davenport was only a hundred feet away.

Pilate blew into Nordstrom's at a dead run, past a big bearded guy in a Green Bay jersey, knocked a kid down, then another one, like bowling pins, almost went down himself, and somebody yelled, "Hey," and he went straight on ahead, clothes, shoes, purses, and cosmetics. He could see the exit to the mall proper, and he glanced back, and Davenport had closed the gap. He didn't have time to turn and shoot, so he lifted the gun straight up and fired into the ceiling.

Shoppers shrieked and scattered in all directions, which helped a little, but not enough. He risked another look back and Davenport was even closer, and he had a gun.

Then he was out of the store, looking for any kind of help he could get.

WHEN PILATE FIRED into the ceiling and the crowd exploded into the aisles, Lucas was probably only fifty feet behind. He couldn't shoot because of all the people milling around him, and in the shooting lanes behind Pilate. Even if he hit Pilate in the middle of the back, the slug could go on through and clip a bystander.

Pilate went straight out the store exit into the mall, then bent to the right around the escalators. Lucas went wider right, to make sure he wouldn't be ambushed.

He wasn't. Pilate had gone straight ahead and vaulted the counter at the Caribou Coffee, where he had a heavy young woman by her blond hair, his pistol aimed more or less at her face.

Lucas came around the escalator and Pilate screamed, "Get away from me! I want a—"

Lucas never found out what he wanted. A getaway car? An airplane to North Korea? A spaceship?

He never found out because the young woman picked up the large soy macchiato that she'd been steaming, and flipped it over her shoulder into Pilate's eyes.

Pilate screamed and pulled away from her and in that sliver of opportunity, Lucas shot him through the bridge of his nose.

Then the screaming *really* got started.

26

LUCAS'S PREVIOUS EXPERIENCE with the media was dwarfed by the response the cops got on the mall shooting, partly because one of the local TV stations initially referred to the shooting as an "apparent terrorist attack." Later, they pulled back to apparent "domestic terrorism attack" and finally to "a shooting."

An extremely attractive PR woman for Nordstrom's dashed around from one media group to the next, chanting, "The shooting was in the mall. It was not in Nordstrom's. The shooting was in the mall, it was not . . ."

The shooting, of course, became known as the Nordstrom Shoot-Out.

The egg laid by Henry Sands dwarfed all previous eggs by an order of magnitude. "A shoot-out at Nordstrom's? And it was planned?"

Informed of Sands's reaction, the Bloomington chief,

who thought the matter had been handled rather well, given the freakishly successful parachute jump by Pilate, said, "I think Director Sands should check his head." That was enough of a non sequitur that somebody at the press conference inevitably asked, "Why?" The chief said, "Because right now, it's where the sun don't shine."

The chief pointed out that one crazed killer was captured alive and another was killed after a courageous action by a brave, quick-thinking coffee clerk, and no bystanders were hurt. Who was Sands to denigrate that, from an office in St. Paul?

Caribou Coffee gave the clerk a one-hundred-dollar gift card. When word got out, they upped it to a thousand.

The shooting took place a little after noon, and Lucas and Letty pulled into their driveway at six o'clock. Weather came to the door and stood on the porch with her arms crossed. "Hmm," Letty said.

"Reamed" was the appropriate description of what happened next, Lucas and Letty agreed later.

When the reaming slowed, Weather gave Lucas a letter from the BCA, delivered by special messenger. Inside, Lucas found a letter saying that the Bureau of Criminal Apprehension was considering the bringing of disciplinary charges against Lucas and his attendance was required at a meeting the following Tuesday at 10 a.m. The letter said that it would be "appropriate" for Lucas to seek legal counsel. It was signed by Sands.

"What are you going to do?" Weather asked him.

"Don't know."

THE NEXT MORNING, Lucas drove a few blocks across the neighborhood to Willie's American Guitars, and after a long consultation, wrote a check for a little more than ten thousand dollars for a vintage Les Paul guitar. It wasn't the most expensive one, but neither was it the cheapest. He at first quailed at the price, but then thought, the Faygo-throwing fat guy may have saved Letty's life. He had the store ship the guitar, which they would do as soon as the check cleared.

Laurent called on a cell phone, on speaker, with the rest of the reserve deputies standing around, and asked him for a blow-by-blow description of the Nordstrom shooting. Lucas gave it to them, and Frisell said, "Man . . . I wish I'd been there."

"We all do," Laurent said.

LUCAS GAVE LAURENT the license plate numbers on the red Taurus and the Sault Ste. Marie police tracked it to the old lady's house. They found her at the bottom of the stairs.

When Laurent called Lucas back to tell him, he said, "The only thing about the whole fight that really mystifies me is those two naked people. Why the hell did they do that?"

"I don't know," Lucas said. "Maybe they thought they could be decoys and that Coon guy would take out all of us. But really, I don't know. Remember, they were crazy."

"Still bothers me," Laurent said. "Another thing. The congressman from up here says he's retiring so there'll be an open seat next year. A Democratic Party guy got in touch, wondering if I might be interested. The funny thing is, a guy from the Republican Party got in touch with Peters . . ."

"I got no advice on that, but I'll be interested in what you decide," Lucas said. "I'm not sure you're enough of an asshole."

"Maybe I could learn it," Laurent said.

"I don't know. Sometimes I think it's a skill you're born with. Or not."

LAURENT CALLED AGAIN late that afternoon to say that Laine, in consultation with her state-appointed attorneys, had told the state cops about the murder of Michelle. Her body was located the next morning by a state road crew.

THE GOVERNOR'S CHIEF weasel called and said, "Hold for the governor."

Lucas held and Elmer Henderson came on. "There's a rumor going around that Henry's going to try to fire your ass. Conduct unbecoming a BCA agent, insubordination, blah, blah, blah."

"Well, I've been advised to seek legal counsel," Lucas said.

"You want me to fire him instead?" Henderson asked. "He could resign on Monday."

Lucas thought for a moment, then said, "I appreciate the thought and the agency would be better off, but don't do that. Everybody would know what happened, and when you start running for the vice presidency, the Republicans will look for every single thing they can get on you. An accusation of blatant meddling wouldn't help."

"We could crush that in a couple of minutes," Henderson said.

"You might not have a couple of minutes to spare, when the 'Henderson Hoagie' thing gets out there."

"What! What! Lucas, where did you hear that phrase?"

"Governor, every sentient being in Minnesota's heard it. They admire you for it. Whether it'll play in, say, Colorado or Oregon, I don't know."

Lucas heard Henderson ask the weasel, "Is that true? That everybody in Minnesota knows?"

The weasel said, "Yes."

The "Henderson Hoagie" referred to the governor's fondness for three- and four-ways with nubile young Seven Sisters coeds while he was a student at Harvard. Supposedly, ketchup was involved.

Henderson came back. "Well . . . whatever happens with Sands, come talk to me afterwards."

AT THE END of the week, an FBI friend called to tell Lucas that the feds had been through both the fingerprint and DNA databanks and had found no matches at all for Pilate. He'd had two driver's licenses in his wallet, both from California, one for a Robert D. Johnson and another for a William S. Smith. Both were apparently obtained by fraud. Nobody had any idea who he really was. And a cop from North Dakota called and said he'd encountered the Pilate group at a restaurant, and had taken down the license plate numbers of every one of their cars. By the time he found out that somebody might have needed them, the fight was over.

On Sunday morning, at breakfast, Weather asked him for the fifth or sixth time, "You know what you're gonna do?"

Lucas nodded. "Yeah."

"I got a box in the garage," she said.

"How'd you know I'd need a box?"

THAT AFTERNOON, HE climbed the steps to the BCA. Not many people were around, but an agent leaving the building stopped on the stairs, looked at him with the box, and said, "Don't do it, man."

Lucas shook his hand and said, "Thanks for the thought."

He'd been in his particular office for seven years, but he had never been much for stuffing it with personal items. He started packing what was there, and a couple more investigators came to the office door, the female agent carrying another box. She said, "Let us help you with that."

"Okay."

They cleaned the place out in fifteen minutes, then Lucas got a piece of official stationery, wrote: "Dear Henry. I quit. On a personal note, go fuck yourself."

He put his ID inside the envelope, wrote Sands's name on the outside, and slid it under Sands's office door.

The male agent said, "Succinct. Succinct is always good in inter-office communications."

The agents walked out to his Porsche with the two boxes and the female agent said, "I'll never forget the night up in the swamp . . ." And she went on for a while, about a dark night with Lucas and his gang of agents when she killed a man. Lucas peeled off his sport coat and his shoulder holster, dropped the coat and gun on the passenger seat. The woman agent finally ran down, they all shook hands, and Lucas got out of there before things turned maudlin. He'd still have to call Del, Jenkins, Shrake, Flowers, and a few others. He'd do that in the evening.

When he got home, he ran the garage door up and Letty came through from the kitchen. Watched him get out of the car, and asked, "You're retired now? You're gonna go sit in a goddamn rowboat for the next thirty years?"

"Don't know what I'm gonna do," he said.

"You gotta do something."

He grinned at his worried blue-eyed child. "I'll find something. And I promise you this: it won't involve a goddamn rowboat."

"Good," she said. She picked up the .45 off the passenger seat. "Then you're gonna need this."

Lucas took the gun.

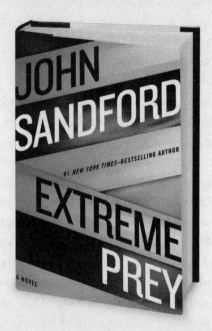